1049 Club

.

1049 Club

Kim Pritekel

P.D. Publishing, Inc.
Clayton, North Carolina

ISBN-13: 978-1-933720-72-2

9 8 7 6 5 4 3 2 1

Cover design by Linda Callaghan
Edited by: Day Petersen / Lara Zielinsky

Published by:

P.D. Publishing, Inc.
P.O. Box 70
Clayton, NC 27528

http://www.pdpublishing.com

To those who continue to dream and reach: never stop.

Also, to the one who "just is".

Chapter 1

Inching through First Class at the front of the airplane, Denny DeRisio nearly choked on her mouthful of Coke when she realized who she was passing. Almost thrown off by the baseball cap and dark glasses, she stole a second look. The silver watch clinched it. In every dust cover picture she'd ever seen of author Rachel Holt, the beautiful young blonde had been wearing it; and there it was, on her left wrist, glinting slightly in the sunlight shining in through the oval window. It didn't seem as if anyone else had made the connection yet, as no one was paying Holt any special attention. It helped that Denny had just been reading *People* magazine in the John F. Kennedy International airport terminal while waiting for her flight to board. There had been a small blurb in the Passages section, mentioning that the author's twenty-seventh birthday was coming up.

Hearing someone behind her clear their throat impatiently, Denny moved on to her own seat, 5C. "Happy birthday, Rachel," she murmured with a little chuckle, sighing as she buckled herself in. It would be a long flight, but she was looking forward to it, heading to Italy for two weeks to visit her father's family. She hadn't seen them in almost five years, and she missed her cousins.

Denny rested her head back against the seat, listening to the sounds around her — people softly murmuring "Excuse me" and "Sorry about that" as they, too, got settled. She looked forward to removing her contacts; her eyes felt dry and irritated. Her blue eyes opened as she heard a soft, "I need to get through."

"Oh, sorry." She sat up, tucking her long legs in as a young woman, about sixteen, carefully passed to the other aisle seat in the middle section of the 767. Denny smiled over at her then started to relax again.

"Oops, one more."

Looking to the aisle, Denny saw an older version of the teenager and once again tucked in her legs. The woman passed by and settled in the middle seat and Denny was finally able to get comfortable. She loved to fly, which was a good thing because this was going to be one long flight.

Her mind roaming to the successful author seated not twenty feet from her, Denny glanced up toward First Class. When Rachel Holt's first novel, *Conspiracy,* had hit the racks three years earlier, it had taken off like a rocket. The twenty-four year-old had been launched into the world spotlight, winning numerous awards and much acclaim. She was young, beautiful, and painfully elusive — an enticing mix for a knowledge hungry fan base. She had been hunted ruthlessly, her green eyes having graced just about every magazine cover, whether Rachel was aware of it or not. She had only agreed to sit for one interview, and that was with the daily talk show hostess, Maureen Conifer. Regardless of how private and shy the petite blonde was, her readers never seemed to get enough of her books. Sitting pretty with four novels on the shelves, Rachel Holt's place in contemporary author stardom was secure.

Denny grinned at her thoughts as she brought out the paperback she'd bought at Borders that very morning on the way to the airport. It was Rachel Holt's latest in trade paperback, *Willing To Conquer*. Typically not one for history, or thrillers, the coffee shop owner was drawn nonetheless. The books were extremely well written and enthralled her from the turn of the first page. The emotions ran deep and intense, and the detailed accounts of each time period were astounding. After finishing *Coattails and Pomp*, Denny's curiosity was aroused to the extent that she began researching the Victorian era.

Now that the author was present in person, even though she was behind dark glasses and her short, blonde hair was tucked under a baseball cap, Denny turned her novel over, opening the back cover to the black and white photo. Rachel Holt looked off into the distance, the light shining in her eyes, making them almost translucent. She wore a simple light-colored button-up, though it could only be seen from just under the collar and up. The sweater was open, probably unbuttoned two or three down, giving the author an air of casual ease. There was no information below the picture, other than: Rachel Holt lives in the northwestern United States.

"That's a good one."

Denny looked to her right at the woman beside her who was glancing at the book in her hands.

"Finished it two days ago."

"I hope I like it. Picked it up on my way in today." Denny turned the book back over and rested it in her lap.

"Have you read her others?"

"Sure have." For a moment Denny considered whether she should tell the obvious Holt fan the author sat just on the other side of the First Class bathrooms. Deciding against it, she sighed deeply, content to be on her way as the plane slowly began to back away from the gate, ready to taxi.

From time to time Denny glanced up from her reading, half-heartedly listening to the instructions from the flight attendant: in case of an emergency, do this, don't do that; if you don't feel you can perform tasks at the emergency exits; so on and so forth. She turned her attention back to the novel in hand, losing herself in the life of a young slave during the time of Alexander the Great.

Mia Vinzetti and her mother, Gloria, were headed to Milan, where Gloria had grown up with her grandparents, Paolo and Lizbeth. Having smoked for fifty-six years, Paolo had recently been diagnosed with lung cancer. His prognosis was grim, and while Mia was out of school for the summer, Gloria wanted to go to Italy to be with him.

The sixteen-year-old glanced over at her mother briefly, noting she was already neck deep in one of her romance novels. Mia was excited about the trip, never having been to her mother's homeland before. Lately they had been fighting constantly, and Mia hoped the trip could help ease some of the tension between them. She was going to be graduating high school the following summer, and didn't want to go off to college in California, on the other side of the country, with them fighting. Mrs. Marcum, Mia's counselor at school, had assured her that the family bickering was typical of her age group, but Mia knew she harbored a lot of resentment toward her mother for often not being there: missing school performances or awards ceremonies. Mia knew it was childish clinging since her father had disappeared from her life before she was even born. Never marrying, Gloria had raised her alone, often working two, sometimes three, jobs just to keep them afloat in their small Brooklyn apartment. Gloria was doing the best she could but, still, things were difficult.

When Mia was able to push her anger aside, she greatly admired her mother, though she'd never told her so. Gloria's parents were killed when she was a girl, and so she'd been swept off to Milan, where she'd had a wonderful childhood courtesy of her grandparents. As a young woman, she'd been swept back to the United States by Mia's father, a Navy man.

Life had been tough for the two Vinzetti women, but all in all, they'd done pretty darn well together. Mia loved her mother deeply. She just wished Gloria had more time for her. Yet at the same time, she wished her mother would just leave her the hell alone. The girl pushed her long, dark hair back off her shoulder as she grinned at her own ambivalence.

As the pilot announced the plane had reached cruising altitude, Mia sat back and closed her eyes. She hated to fly.

Dean Ratliff hated to fly. He hated travel of any sort, mostly because he hated to do anything remotely new or different. Will, his partner of thirteen years, basically had told him if they didn't do something this summer, take some sort of a vacation, he was going by himself. Will tried to say Dean was controlling, but Dean felt Will was simply sick and tired of sitting home every year, surrounded by every electronic gadget known to man, expensive French furniture, and Dean's beloved dogs, but seeing nothing, doing nothing, going nowhere. Dean absolutely did *not* understand what was wrong with staying home, surrounded by every electronic gadget know to man, expensive French furniture, and his beloved dogs.

Dean had reluctantly agreed to this trip, and then Will had to work! They were to meet up in Milan. Dean sighed heavily, resting his head against the cool window.

Holding on tightly to the armrest on either side of his seat, Michael Dupree was not surprised to hear his wife chuckle. Glancing down at her, he just barely saw her shaking her head in mirth at his actions.

"Y'all think this is funny, don'cha?" he asked, halfway chuckling himself.

Melissa Dupree looked up at him. "Honestly? Why, yes. I do."

Michael grinned, leaning down to quickly press a kiss on the lips of his wife. "I love you, baby," he said softly, so glad he had been able to make this trip happen for her. They'd been married twenty years. Thursday was their anniversary. He knew Melissa had always wanted to see Italy and all its historic treasures. From their house in Beaumont, Texas, she'd only ever been able to see them on the History Channel or via books from the library. When he'd come home from work, having picked up their airline tickets and itinerary from his brother's house where he'd been hiding everything, he thought Melissa was going to break down and start crying right when he gave it all to her, along with a single red rose.

Michael was surprised when his little woman not only started crying, but nearly bowled over his 6'4", 235 pound frame. That night they'd made the sweetest love. Remembering that, he reluctantly let go of one of the armrests and put his arm around her slight shoulders.

Melissa laid her head against her husband's linebacker-like shoulder. "I love you, Mike. Thank you for this."

Michael Dupree considered himself the luckiest man in the Lone Star state. He'd been a young buck of eighteen, lost and doing nothing but causing trouble and raising hell when he met a lovely young redhead who put him in his place, throwing an entire mug of beer in his face when he got out of line. He'd never let her out of his sight since that night. Melissa had put up with a lot from him over the years; three kids and a mortgage later, the big mechanic couldn't be happier. He hoped he'd finally made his petite wife happy and proud, too.

Michael knew he should just sit back and relax. They'd be on the plane for a long, long time.

"Man, she looked a bit worried, didn't she?" Dr. Pam Sloan commented to her boyfriend, Austin. The veterinarian watched as the blonde flight attendant hurried through First Class and disappeared inside the cockpit, the narrow door closing after her with finality.

In the seat behind the vet, Rachel Holt also noted the flight attendant's harried behavior. She leaned into the aisle to see if she could discover any additional information, but the flight attendant was gone. Taking a deep breath, Rachel tried to return her thoughts to her laptop, her fingers tapping away on the keys. Her attention was captured once again when the cockpit door opened and the flight attendant made her way back down the aisle, her face *too* expressionless for Rachel's liking. She followed the woman's progress back into Coach, briefly meeting the bright blue eyes of another passenger before turning back to her writing.

Denny DeRisio caught Rachel Holt's gaze for just a moment, feeling a slight thrill a famous person knew she existed, if even just for a moment, then the blonde turned away. Denny's euphoria was short-lived as she felt a tap on her arm. She turned to the woman next to her, who'd introduced herself as Gloria Vinzetti.

"Do you think something's wrong?" Gloria asked, her short, dark hair falling into her eyes.

Denny shrugged and shook her head. "I don't know, but I doubt it."

"Well, that flight attendant sure acted like she had a fire lit under her butt."

Denny smiled. "I'm sure everything is fine." She went back to her book, vaguely aware of mother and daughter speaking quietly to each other. Hearing louder murmuring around her, Denny looked up from the book again to see whether her fellow passengers knew something she didn't. She caught the eye of others who were all doing the same.

"Miss?" An older man further back in the plane stopped the flight attendant as she made her way back up the aisle from where she'd been speaking with the gathered flight attendants. "Is there a problem, miss?"

The hostess smiled and patted the man's shoulder. "Everything's fine, sir." But she hurried on.

Michael Dupree snorted as he woke himself up, opening droopy eyes as something stirred him. Melissa was sound asleep, her head cradled on his shoulder. The big Texan looked around to figure out what had awakened him. Reaching to the window on his right, he pushed up the flimsy shade and saw glittering blue waves not very distant beneath him.

"Shouldn't we be flying a bit higher?" the man in the seat in front of him asked, looking at Michael from between the seat and the curved wall of the plane.

The Texan shook his head, still looking outside. "I don't know. Ya'd think."

Head tilted, Dean Ratliff perused the airline brochure, reading the small list of onboard alcohol that could be ordered for five dollars a drink. "Perfect," he muttered, stuffing the brochure back into the seat pocket in front of him. He craned his neck until he spotted a flight attendant talking to an older man, not seven rows behind him. He flagged her down as she headed back toward the front of the plane. "Excuse me, I'd like to order a drink. When are you going to be coming by with the refreshment cart? I mean, you guys still *do* that, right? Lord knows you've stopped most of the other services."

The blonde smiled, but it didn't reach her eyes. "We'll be getting to that shortly, sir. We ask for your patience."

"Hey! I want my drink, damn it!" Dean called out to her retreating back. He met the gaze of his seatmate. "I intend to write a letter to the airline when I get home. She was rude." Sighing unhappily, Dean crossed his arms over his chest, looking around to find another *helpful* flight attendant, maybe that little blonde cutie with the trimmed goatee he'd seen just before take off.

"All right, John, I've talked to all of the attendants. What do you want us to do now?" the flight attendant asked, wringing her hands. She felt sick.

The pilot sighed heavily, feeling sweat gathering under his armpits. "I've taken her as low as I dare," he explained. Everyone in the cockpit was well aware that individual waves were now visible in the ocean below. "We have no choice. Prepare the passengers. Don't tell them what's happened, just advise them to follow precautionary procedures."

Nervously pulling at the buttoned collar of her uniform shirt, the blonde nodded stoically, but tears were burning behind her eyes and her heart was pounding in her chest. She left the cockpit, walked over to the First Class cubby and picked up the onboard phone.

Denny heard three soft dings, then saw a redheaded flight attendant hurrying to the area in front of their seats. Denny, Gloria, and Mia sat in the emergency row, so they were near the wall with the flight attendant's jump seat, where she sat during take off, as well as her phone. The pretty young woman put the phone to her ear, turning away from the prying eyes of her passengers. She whispered into the mouthpiece, her body rigid.

Denny and Gloria shared a pointed look and a very bad feeling gripped Denny. Something was wrong. Images of 9/11 flashed through her mind, and she prayed it wasn't anything like that. She tried to console herself with the knowledge that they were over an ocean, which was of no use to a terrorist.

The flight attendant hung up the phone, took a deep breath then turned to face questioning blue eyes. She forced a faint smile.

"Something's wrong, isn't it?" Denny asked, her voice quiet. The flight attendant mouthed the word *yes*, but her voice cracked so no sound came out. Denny swallowed hard, nodding in understanding. The public address system crackled to life and suddenly a tinny voice was announcing emergency procedures while the redhead helped passengers successfully don inflatable life vests and find pillows for possible impact.

Rachel Holt's fingers shook badly as she tried for the third time to get the rubber lift vest around her head, the orange/red plastic sliding into place. She noticed the woman across the aisle having trouble with hers, so she reached across as far as the seat belt would allow and helped as best she could. As she sat back, she met the gaze of the woman sitting in front of her, brow creased with terror, which Rachel had no doubt mirrored her own expression.

The plane lurched forward, and everyone screamed in surprise and fear. Pam Sloan watched as a small, rubber ball rolled down the center aisle toward the cockpit.

"Thomas!" Mandy Ryan grabbed her son by the arm. He was crying as his ball disappeared down the aisle.

Dean Ratliff rolled his eyes. *Stupid kid. Sit down!* He turned his attention from the young mother and the small boy still crying about his stupid ball, and instead focused on a large man sitting by the window, a small woman nearly sitting in his lap. He was apparently trying to whisper words of comfort into her ear, but they came out as some sort of macabre murmuring.

All around him, Dean heard sniffles and cries, and saw panicked faces on his fellow passengers. He himself was grabbing onto the armrest with claw-like fingers, his stomach lurching with every sporadic movement of the plane. He glanced up as the public address system squawked to life.

Denny listened as the captain almost shouted a slew of instructions to his captive passengers. He apparently no longer cared about trying to keep his charges calm; there was no time for that. Her intent blue eyes landed on the two women sitting in her row, mother and daughter crying and holding on to one another for dear life.

Denny closed her eyes. *What I wouldn't give to have Hannah here right now, holding me, telling me everything will be okay.* Suddenly remembering something from Flight 93, she snatched her cell phone and powered it on. The cheery chirp as it came to life seemed like a sick mockery. One signal bar.

"Fuck," she hissed, as she pressed the number one, then send. The phone's ring was sporadic.

"Den...ney?...ought you were...air?"

"Hannah! Hannah, oh God, thank God." Denny could feel her tears spring to life. "Honey, I love you! Something's gone wrong!"

"...at? I can't under...ou. Wha..."

"I love you! Always know that."

Dead. The connection went dead. She didn't have much time to think about it as her stomach fell about thirteen stories. She fought the urge to throw up as the plane lurched again, everyone screaming as the plane tilted dangerously, a man screaming as he flew out of his seat because he had unbuckled himself. His cries were cut short as he slammed into the wall mere feet from Denny's head. She yelped in surprise, unable to take her eyes off the fresh red splotch on the oatmeal colored plastic.

Rachel Holt heard an awful thud behind her, but didn't dare to look. She was too busy trying not to cry as the seatbelt dug into her midsection. She reached out desperately to the seat in front of her. *Damn First Class!* The seat ahead of hers was too far away to gain any real purchase. Just when she was about to unbuckle the belt in order to try and take a breath, the plane lurched back, slamming everyone back into their seats. From somewhere in front of her came the unmistakable sounds of someone vomiting, followed by the equally unmistakable smell, making everyone grimace.

Gloria Vinzetti clutched her rosary, eyes squeezed tightly shut as she chanted the Lord's Prayer over and over, her mouth moving soundlessly. She could feel her daughter's hold tighten on her arm as the plane righted itself. The hot, coppery smell of blood scented the air.

Mia clung to her mother, knowing Gloria was praying enough for both of them. She didn't dare look around, terrified of what she might see. She'd already heard frantic murmurings about fire erupting from one of the engines, and black smoke was following the plane's descent into the ocean.

I don't want to die like this! Mia's mind screamed over and over, thinking of the things she'd never done and never would do. Her quiet tears were overshadowed by those of the woman sitting with her husband, several seats back.

"I'm so sorry, Mel, so sorry," Michael Dupree whispered over and over to his wife as they clung to each other. "God, I'm so sorry." If only he hadn't surprised her with this damn trip, they'd be at home watching their new dish television.

Denny wished she could shut out the horrible screaming of the plane as it cut through the whipping air, the plane once more tilting nose-down. She could feel the plastic covering on the armrest beginning to give way beneath her iron grip. Regardless, there was no way she was releasing it. The plane righted itself again, then Denny was jostled like never before. There was a loud bang as something hit them from underneath, and the sound of screeching metal seemed to last forever. When it stopped, there was a horrible rushing sound.

Oh, Jesus...

There was a second jolt, with a louder bang coming from much closer beneath them. Suddenly there was an amazing amount of light bleeding through the cabin, followed by a deafening scream, like the day itself was wailing its anger, pain, and regret.

"They're gone!" came a yell close by, then Denny realized she'd said it. Fingers of ice clenched at her lungs, stealing the very air from them.

The scream was replaced by a whistle that made Rachel Holt's ears ring. Her eyes squeezed tightly shut as she opened her mouth in a soundless scream, her voice stolen along with her breath. Somehow, from the back of her mind, all the instructions she'd heard millions of times before during take off came back to her. Rachel reached under her seat and pulled the tabs she felt there. She was nearly knocked out of her seat as the plane skipped across the water for a third pass, a bit more of the tail section flying out into the water. Rachel was jerked to her left, smacking her head on something hard, her stomach flipping end over end along with the world, light shining in bright and intense, along with the pain.

Under other circumstances, Dean would have thought it amusing as he watched a pair of eyeglasses suspended in air, the hair of the lady across from him standing on end, like it had a life of its own, his own loose polo shirt ballooning up around his neck. Just for that one perfect instant, everything was weightless and at peace.

Pam Sloan screamed as Austin's seatbelt gave way and he slammed up against the ceiling of the plane, then flew out of sight. She did not see him get sucked out of the missing tail section.

Rachel Holt's eyes grew big as saucers as the cockpit door bulged then broke free in one terrifying second, the heavy, metal door flying through the cabin, taking the head of an unsuspecting flight attendant with it. Rachel had no time to process this before a flood of water followed, instantly filling the airplane, the immense pressure pinning the author in her seat.

Denny groped frantically for the seat release, her blue eyes squinting against the cold salt water, trying desperately not to take a much needed breath, her natural instincts shutting everything down, her fingers working spasmodically. She was thrown forward as the plane began to sink headfirst into the blackening depths. Panic filled her anew as she realized what was happening. Her fingers went back to her seat, working relentlessly to pull the floating device of the cushion free. *Damn it! Why the fuck didn't I pay attention to those instructions?*

Oh, God! Oh, Jesus! Hang on, baby! Hang on! Michael Dupree thrashed wildly as he unbuckled Melissa, her limp body beginning to float up from the seat. The Texan could see where she'd been hit in the head with something as the two halves of the plane had separated. His lungs burning for air, Michael knew he had to get them out of there, and he had to get them out now. With the superhuman strength of the desperate, Michael kicked with everything in him, trying to get them to the surface. He ignored the intense pain in his right arm and shoulder, barely even feeling it. He did feel himself kicking something hard, but he didn't care. Nothing mattered but getting Melissa to the surface.

Blinded by the sudden sunlight, attorney Dean Ratliff blinked several times, gasping and appreciating air like he never had before. In that single moment, pushing through the water's surface, he thought that just maybe everything would be okay. Then reality struck. He thrashed around in the water, nearly freaking out altogether when he came face to face with a woman who was very much dead, her big, brown eyes staring sightlessly at him. Shivering in disgust and fear, Dean turned away, only to be confronted by a bloody mass of flesh.

"Oh God," he whimpered, blindly pushing through the water, trying to get away from both of the dead, the memory of the woman's eyes boring into his very soul. Something else bumped him, but Dean couldn't look to see what it was. He didn't want to see that dead woman following him. Not even looking to see where he was swimming to, Dean muttered to himself, a slight scream escaping his lips now and then as he saw something that traumatized him further. Before he knew it, he was alone — no bodies, no plane parts, nothing.

Eyes huge, Dean swirled about to look all around him. He was completely alone.

"Aww, fuck."

With a sputter, Michael Dupree emerged from the cold depths, clutching Melissa to his chest, doing his damnedest to hold her head above water. Her head wound began to bleed anew, the red turning pink as it mixed with the water in which they bobbed.

"Hold on, baby," he gasped, looking around them, trying to get his bearings. "Gonna be okay, Mel. Gonna be okay." Michael saw a piece of the wing floating not far away, the metal glinting in the harsh overhead sun. "Almost there, baby. Almost."

The mechanic tried his best to not let the gore around him distract him. He had a singular mission to get himself and Melissa out of the water. Growing up in the Gulf, Michael knew all too well the dangers they faced, like sitting ducks in a world foreign to them.

"Okay," he panted, the exertion and injuries he'd sustained sapping his energy. "Up ya go, baby doll." With a grunt, Michael heaved

Melissa's form onto the makeshift raft, then levered his own body up to lie next to her, flopping down on his back, wincing as his arm and shoulder injuries made themselves known again.

Blinking slowly, then squinting against the harsh glare, the teen in the raft next to Dr. Pam Sloan groaned softly. As she opened her eyes, the girl lurched, throwing up into the water.

"Hold tight, honey. You took quite a hit to your head."

The girl groaned again.

"What happened?" She turned over onto her back. She sucked in a frantic breath, looking around. "My mom. Where's my mom?" She met concerned brown eyes.

"We'll deal with that later. Let me see your head." Pam pushed the girl's long, wet hair out of her face and focused on the deep gash above her left eyebrow. She looked around but found nothing useful. She looked down at herself, ripped off a long piece of her shirt and wadded it up. "Hold this to your head, honey. We need to get the bleeding stopped."

Pam leaned back, taking several breaths as she waited for the intense adrenaline rush to subside. She needed her wits about her to get her and the girl out of their situation. As it was, things didn't look too promising. Bits and pieces of luggage and debris floated around them, along with the bodies of those who had drowned or been thrown from the wreckage. In every direction, there was only water as far as the eye could see.

"I think there's someone over there," the teen said, her voice soft.

Pam's gaze followed where the girl was looking. In the water, barely hanging on to a large wooden suitcase, was a slumped figure appearing to be losing their grip.

"I'll be right back." Pam slid into the water and quickly swam over to the small blonde. "I've got you," she whispered, taking the woman into her arms. "Paddle with your feet," she instructed, feeling the woman's feeble attempts to help. At the raft, which was the emergency ramp that had inflated on impact, the teen helped both women out of the water.

Rachel coughed, her stomach hurting with each movement. Finally she was able to lay back in the raft and catch her breath. It took everything she had to pull in a full lungful of air without crying out. She could feel her heart pounding as her mind tried to reconcile where she should be with where she was. Finally her green eyes opened and took in her surroundings.

"Thank you," she managed, pushing herself up so she was sitting against the hard edge of the ramp. She looked at her fellow passengers, a terrified and bleeding teen girl, and an older woman, maybe in her fifties, contemplating the cut on the girl's head. That woman nodded, glancing briefly over to Rachel as she brushed wet hair out of her eyes.

"Crazy day, huh?"

"Yeah." Rachel ran her hands through her hair, pushing it out of her face and tucking it behind her ears. She prayed her stomach would hold out; the thought of throwing up made her stomach hurt more. She stared up at the sky, bright blue with a few floating bits of cotton. It was a beautiful day, and it felt as though they were being mocked. Only the lapping waves broke the silence.

"Where do you think we are?" the older woman asked, her voice almost shrill in the stillness of the day.

Rachel shook her head, her voice shaky as she responded. "I don't have any clue." Rachel could feel her shock slowly oozing into mortal fear. She curled up against the side of the ramp, her arms wrapping around her folded legs, forehead resting on her knees. *We're dead.*

A cheek twitched as a tiny sand crab scurried across the sand and then through wet strands of black hair. Long fingers clawed into the hard-packed shore, then released.

Chapter 2

Gripped by fear unlike anything she had ever experienced, Hannah Donnelly pressed the phone to her ear, even though she knew the signal had long since been lost. That had been the weirdest phone call she'd ever received, and she didn't fully understand it. Hell, she could barely understand Denny. The only thing she'd gotten out of it all was Denny loved her.

The cordless phone slid from her ear and was tossed to the couch beside her, her brain numb. As though electricity jolted through her, Hannah was on her feet, scrambling for the remote control, hurriedly flipping through the channels to see if there was any news. She had the feeling something had gone terribly, terribly wrong. When there was nothing on television, she grabbed the phone book and began looking up airlines.

"Conrad! Get back in here and finish your dinner." Meredith Adams sighed heavily. It was going to be a long couple of weeks with her precocious twelve year-old grandson. "Conrad! Get—" She froze when her husband of forty-two years plowed into the kitchen, frantically pulling open drawers in the kitchen desk. "Walter, what are you doing? You're making a mess."

Walter, breathing hard, looked around the kitchen, praying what he was looking for would suddenly stand up and reveal itself. Running a hand through salt and pepper hair, he finally met his wife's eyes, the anger now slowly melting into fear.

"Where's Melissa and Mike's flight information?" he asked, his heart pounding.

"Why?"

"Damn it, woman, where is it!"

The atypical roar of her husband's voice startled the plump woman into action. She hurried over to the phone cubby where she kept all phone numbers, addresses, and incoming bills. Tugging out the folded computer printout, she handed it to him. Walter took it, fingers trembling as he tried to unfold the paper.

"Walter!" Meredith cried as she rushed to her fallen husband.

"What am I?"

Brad Schuester looked up at his boss, who despite his dress shirt was standing with arms straight up over his head, hands clasped, his body tilted to the right.

"Uhhh, crazy?"

"No! The leaning tower of Pisa!" the blond man exclaimed, slapping Brad playfully on the shoulder.

His assistant shook his head with a slight chuckle. "You're wanting to rub this in more and more, aren't you, Will?"

"Absolutely." The architect grinned. He clapped his hands and grabbed his suit jacket from where he'd tossed it onto a nearby chair. "I'm out of here, Brad. Have a good couple of weeks with Whitley; I'll bring you back something good."

"You better!" Brad called after his boss, chuckling at Will's enthusiasm.

Will Ash whistled happily as he left the firm he worked for in downtown Manhattan. He would head back to the home he shared with his partner, Dean, shower and change, then he'd be off. He couldn't wait to see Dean in Milan the following night. Will grinned, thinking of the new toy he'd picked up, hoping Dean would play along and not throw a fit as he usually did with something new. He *also* hoped the airport people wouldn't think he had a snake packed in his bags.

Chuckling at the thought, Will hailed a taxi, juggling his briefcase while he grabbed the cell phone out of his inside jacket pocket, the vibration making his left nipple tingle.

"Hello?" he said into the tiny mouthpiece as he climbed into the backseat of the waiting Yellow Cab.

"Will?"

"Naomi? Hey, sweetie. How are you?" Will sat back against the smelly bench seat, crossing one finely pressed pant leg over the other. He could hear that something was terribly wrong from the tremor in Dean's sister's voice. "What's the matter?"

"Will, have you been watching the television at all?"

"No. I'm just leaving the office. What's wrong?" He was beginning to feel the first trickle of worry, and couldn't help but look up into the sky. Just about every New Yorker did that at the first sign of trouble these days. Expecting to see the worst, he was surprised to see a bright, sunny day above the steel monsters around him.

"It's Dean. Will, I think his plane is missing."

"What!" Will sat bolt upright, his blood going cold, and the cabby glanced at him in the rearview mirror. Will quickly prattled off the address to the cabby, then returned to his call. "What do you mean his flight is missing? What's the flight number?"

"Flight 1049."

Matt Frazier looked up at the sound of footsteps approaching his desk. "Did you find her?" Hope was evident in his voice. As his friend and fellow homicide detective nodded, Matt sighed, sitting back in his chair. He loosened his tie as he waited for the details.

"She hopped a plane, headed to Milan, Italy." Burt Langley took a seat across from his younger cohort.

"Italy?" Matt was stunned. Reading his partner's eyes, he saw nothing but genuine sorrow. "Shit."

"What happened, Matt?" Burt watched closely, knowing there was something he wasn't being told.

Matt sighed, running a hand through dark hair, making it stand on end. It was time to come clean. It might help to ease his conscience. "I got caught."

Sausage fingers rubbing his rounded chin, Burt studied Matt. "Doing what?"

Hazel eyes flicked to meet piercing blue. "With Diana." Matt's eyes dropped, unable to meet the stare of the man he'd always respected, and from whom he wanted respect.

Burt chuckled. "Got caught with your fingers in the honey pot, huh, kid?"

"This isn't funny, Burt! My wife left the country."

"Yeah, she did. Might want to think about that." Burt groaned softly as he pushed up on his meaty thighs. He tossed a pinwheel mint onto Matt's desk. "Have a mint, kid. Be happy."

Matt glared after the older man, nearly drowning in his own self pity. "Shit."

He pushed away from his desk, switched off the computer and shrugged into his jacket. Gathering his keys in his hand, he grabbed the mint as an afterthought.

The house was quiet and dark, as it had been for the past four days. Feeling Rachel's absence acutely, Matt realized just how badly he'd fucked up. He unbuckled his shoulder holster and secured his weapon before stripping off his jacket and shirt and flinging the unknotted tie into a corner, where it landed with the tie he'd worn the night before.

Matt flipped through the mail that had fallen to the floor through the mail slot beside the door. *Nothing interesting, nothing from Rachel.* Why had she gone to Italy? As far as he knew, she knew no one there, had no reason to go there. Tapping his fingers on the arm of the chair where he'd flopped, Matt glanced at the DVD player's green clock numbers. It was seven-fifteen in Oregon; that meant it was after ten in New York. He wondered whether Rachel's editor and best friend, Reenie, would know anything.

"Hello?" said the smoky female voice on the other end of the line.

"Reenie, this is Matt. Have you heard from Rachel?" The detective wasn't sure whether or not he should put his cards on the table, whether he should tell the editor he knew exactly where his wife had run.

"As a matter of fact, I have."

Nothing more was forthcoming, and from the cold tone of Reenie's voice, Matt knew the ace he thought he had up his sleeve was, in fact, his house of cards falling all around him. He would find no allies here. Deciding to play it straight, Matt sighed. "I fucked up, Reenie. Okay? I messed things up. I need to talk to Rachel."

After a long pause during which Matt's heart thudded loudly in his ears. "You can't talk to her right now, Matt. She's not available."

"I know she's on her way to Italy. What time did she leave? What flight?" Matt sat forward in his chair, ready to pop up and write down any information Reenie would give him.

"It shouldn't surprise me that a cop can find out where his wife is at all times, but for some reason, it does. Look, Matt, give her some time away from you. She's hurt right now and needs to go off on her own and lick her wounds."

"In Italy?" Matt was incredulous. "Who the hell does she know in Italy, for Christ's sake?" He ran a hand through his hair, feeling his anger building but knowing he'd have to restrain it.

"She went to start researching her next novel, Matt. She was planning this trip anyway, just took it sooner rather than later."

"Please give me her information and itinerary, Reenie. I'm her husband and I have a right to know." He was tired and resigned.

"And Rachel has the right to do her own thing and she deserves her privacy. I think you walked all over your *rights* the moment you fucked another woman in Rachel's bed."

Matt grimaced, knowing the woman was right but not about to let her tell him what his rights were, or were not, in his own marriage. "Who the hell do you think you are, Reenie? Give me my wife's information!"

"No. If Rachel didn't give it to you herself, then she obviously doesn't want you to have it."

"Bitch!" Matt slammed down the phone, the force dinging the handset in the quiet room. "Fuck!" The couple's cat ran into the spare bedroom at the crash that followed.

"I do not understand. My granddaughter and great granddaughter are to be on this flight, no?" Paolo Vinzetti tapped the piece of paper he'd presented to the ticket clerk at Milan Malpensa Airport. "Where is the flight?"

"As I've said, sir, I can give you more information once we have it," the clerk said, tired of repeating the same information to the old man. The situation was stressful enough without this old geezer down her throat. Without ceremony, she turned her back on the him and disappeared around a corner.

Shoulders slumped and shaking his head, Paolo slowly walked over to join his wife, Lizbeth, who waited patiently for him. "Nothing."

About to sit, the old man with the full mustache saw a young man with short, well-styled dark hair hurrying over to him. The man was dressed in a suit with the airline logo on the lapel.

"Signore, wait, please."

Paolo looked at the man, Lizbeth joining him at his side.

"I am Franco Lilitaly. I work for US Airlines here in Milano. I'd like to talk to you."

Paolo nodded, glad to be getting some information on the whereabouts of his Gloria and Mia. He and his wife were led to a room with a big conference table surrounded by chairs. Lizbeth felt her heart beginning to flutter. *What was all this about?*

The door was securely closed before Franco Lilitaly spoke again. Sitting opposite the elderly couple, he swallowed, fingers fidgeting as they laced together. He knew he couldn't put it off any longer.

"We have gotten some very bad news: the flight your loved ones were on has been lost."

Paolo's thick eyebrows drew together. "Lost?" He couldn't understand.

The man nodded. "Yes. Lost at sea. They are searching now. We have not abandoned hope that passengers will be found alive, but we have to acknowledge that lives likely have been lost." He looked into the two sets of eyes that stared woodenly at him. His heart broke as the woman crumpled and grabbed her husband's arm. "I am so, so very sorry."

A lone figure sat out on her front porch, staring up into the night sky. As she watched the stars twinkle down at her, she wondered if one of those was her mother's smile. Though she and her mother had problems in the past, she loved and respected her mother's dedication to her practice as a veterinarian — the best in town. It bothered her, however, that they'd never be able to reconcile their issues.

Chapter 3

Something tickling. Itching. *Stop!*

Blue eyes opened on a very up close and personal view of something pink and ugly. Gasping, Denny pushed to her knees, the small crowd of crabs scattering and burying themselves in the sand.

"Oh, fuck," she moaned. Hands grasped her head, which was pounding like a twenty piece marching band. Even her neck throbbed, vibrating with the pain. Taking several deep breaths, she blinked her eyes open again. Sand. All around her, sand. Behind her, the pound of the surf added to the fury in her head.

"Where the hell am I?" she whispered, rising on shaky legs.

She was drenched, her clothing sticking to her like a second skin, made even stickier by the salt water of... *What body of water is this, anyway?* She did her best to push her long hair out of her face, jumping with a small scream as another of those damn crabs fell to the sand at her feet and almost instantaneously disappeared into a hiding hole. "Little bastards."

Looking out to sea, Denny saw nothing but the water, with the single exception of a piece of something bobbing in a shallow pool a short distance away. She wondered if that was what she had floated in on. She remembered swimming, trying to pull herself out of the sinking plane, grabbing onto anything that would hold her weight. Finally, out in the bright, sunny day, she'd found... She shook her head. *What had it been?* Squinting, as she had lost her contacts in the ocean, she studied the white piece of something and realized it was part of the wall or floor of the airplane.

Airplane!

"Jesus!"

Denny shielded her eyes and stared out into sea. *Where did the wreck go?* It was almost as if she had been dumped onto the sand from the skies above. She smirked at the realization that was basically what had happened. *I need to figure out where the hell I am.* She needed to find some civilization, and prayed it was friendly.

"Kick, kick, kick, kick..." Dean had been repeating the mantra for what seemed like hours. Something told him that if he followed the waves, he'd end up drifting to land. Maybe he'd heard that on one of Will's Discovery Channel shows. Regardless, he was following the vaguely remembered advice, but he had just about reached the limits of his endurance. It was hot, and he was beyond thirsty. He was surrounded by endless gallons of water, and yet it was good for nothing better than taking a piss in. The irony wasn't lost on him.

Dean had initially paddled back toward the wreckage and snagged himself a choice piece of floating debris. The guy who had been buckled to it was dead anyway. Holding on to the seat cushions for dear life, he lay across them on his stomach, only his feet in the water, and those he lifted from time to time whenever thoughts of sharks popped into mind. *Damn Will for watching that damn Shark Week on Discovery.*

He tried to focus on the mental image of his partner, thinking of the thick hair on Will's chest that he loved to run his fingers through. He thought of Will's smile and wit. Dean couldn't help but smile at that. The night they had met had been amazing, and totally unexpected.

Dean was a second year law student when he was invited to a kegger. Ordinarily he wouldn't have been caught dead at such a raucous gathering, but a gorgeous little piece of frat boy tail changed his mind. He spent all night following Ken around, until he saw the tall, dark drink of water standing in a corner, charming Maria Kasdan. Gazing over Maria's head, Will's piercing eyes captured Dean's, and didn't let go.

That night, and into the wee hours of the morning, they anointed every surface in Will's tiny apartment with their love making. Dean had class just two hours after he finally had his last orgasm, nearly having another in Ethics as he thought of his lover the previous night. Having already enjoyed the chase and the capture, Dean had no intentions of being with Will again, until he ran into the young architect at a deli a week later. They'd spent the entire rest of the day talking and the night having more mind-blowing sex. Thirteen years later, Will was the one bright spot in Dean's life. He loved him completely.

And now he'd likely never see his lover again. His feet faltered in their rhythmic paddling as he broke down. *I can't die out here all alone.* "Kick, kick, kick..."

Rachel didn't want to seem like a bitch, but she was getting tired of hearing the girl cry. Yes, she understood she'd lost her mother, but they'd all lost something, maybe just not a beloved person.

"Mia," she finally said, her head pounding from dehydration, "you're going to make yourself sick, crying out all of your moisture." She cracked open an eye to see the teenager sniffling and looking back at her. Rachel tried to give her an understanding smile, then closed her eyes again.

Her head rested against the padded sides of the ramp turned raft. She couldn't help but find the irony in the fact that she'd lost far more on dry land than she had in the middle of the ocean somewhere. She didn't even know for certain *which* ocean, though it was likely the Atlantic. The sun beat down on them and her skin was already burning. She wasn't sure how long they'd been adrift; her watch had stopped at exactly 2:30. She considered tossing the ruined timepiece into the ocean, but decided against it. Maybe she'd be able to get it fixed when she returned to Oregon.

Dr. Pam Sloan was grateful the blonde had said something about Mia's crying. Pam was thinking of her own daughter back home. Tracy was little more than ten years older than Mia. *What is she doing right now? Is she tending to the horses? Sitting on her front porch, as she did every night? Is Tracy star-gazing? Daydreaming?*

Pam's smile was bittersweet, and she felt the sting of tears behind her closed lids, which she didn't let fall. She had to survive this and return to Tracy, and to her grandson, Luke. She was so damn proud of him, only six and already able to ride, just like his mother. Tracy had mounted a horse before she could manage a set of stairs on her own two legs.

She glanced at their silent companion, all curled up at the other end of their raft. A young woman, in her twenties, perhaps. Her short blonde hair was dry now, the strands plastered to the woman's head with dried sea salt. Pam couldn't help but wonder if the woman had a mother out there somewhere, who was wondering where her daughter was. Maybe she even had children of her own.

"Do you think they know we're gone yet?" Dr. Sloan asked, her voice soft. Green eyes met her gaze.

"I thought about that, too." Rachel shook her head. "I don't know. I imagine they do. By the position of the sun, it's got to be late afternoon." All three occupants of the raft looked up. The sun was clearly on the other side of the sky from where it had been when their ordeal had begun.

"I'm so thirsty," Mia said, her voice a mere murmur.

Pam and Rachel looked at her, each feeling the parching of her own throat and neither able to do anything to assuage it.

The metal had become hot. Michael splashed water over the smooth surface of the piece of wing part to try and cool it down. He sprinkled water over his forehead again, wincing as the salt stung his sunburned skin.

Sighing heavily, he patted his wife's leg. "Hot day, honey. Too hot." He glanced at her; she hadn't moved in...he couldn't remember how long. She lay on her side, her back to him. "Mel?" As he carefully moved over to her, the wing bobbed, making him uneasy. "Honey?" He laid a hand on her shoulder, gently tugging her onto her back. Melissa's head fell to the side, eyes heavily hooded, sightless. Michael gasped at the dried blood smear on her head. "Baby?" He held a hand in front of her nose and mouth but felt no breath. "Melissa?"

The panic he'd been trying to subdue hit Michael full force. He touched Melissa's face; it was cold.

"Oh, God! No, no, baby, no." He gathered his wife up into his arms, and felt she was becoming stiff. He'd never cried in his life; the sting and wetness felt foreign and strange, but unstoppable. "Oh, Mel," he cried, rocking her against his chest. He thought of their children staying with Melissa's parents until they returned. *Oh, guys. I'm so sorry!*

Blue eyes squinted shut as Denny spat out the bit of water she'd tasted. *Salt water. Damn it!* Struggling to her feet, she looked around the small copse of trees and tropical flowers that lay just beyond the beach. There was a natural pond no more than fifteen yards in from the ocean. Denny had hoped that maybe it was fresh rainwater. No such luck.

Getting to her feet, she glanced at the shoreline to take one last bearing, then headed into the thick and prickly foliage. Before she had gone five feet, Denny knew she'd be lost in no time at all. Looking around dumbly, knowing damn well there was nothing useful anywhere in sight, the brunette fingered the edge of her t-shirt, which was almost dry, but stiff from the salt water. Chewing on her lip, she glanced back to the beach, hoping to see anything, any source of water she might have missed on her first examination. Looking back over her shoulder into the deep, green shadows of the dense jungle, she knew she had no choice. Dehydration was already upon her, her throat dry and scratchy, the skin of her face and arms burned badly from the prolonged exposure to the sun. She needed to find water and some sort of shelter quick.

She grunted as she tried to tear the hem of the shirt, hunger and dehydration making her sluggish and weak. She never ate before flying, and now that ritual was biting her in the ass. Finally the cotton ripped. Denny carefully tied the first strip around a branch closest to the beach, then with a sigh of resignation, headed deeper into the jungle. She hated tight spaces, so she ignored the flora closing in all around her and tried to just focus on the problem at hand — staying alive.

Rachel groaned softly, trying to turn to her side, but the sting came again. *Pee, pee, pee. Gotta pee!* Her green eyes opened and the author looked around her. The darkness was so complete, she couldn't tell where the sky ended and the sea began. Glancing up, Rachel wondered if it was heavy cloud cover that kept the stars from being visible. Funny how earlier in the day, floating aimlessly in an erstwhile slide, she'd thought about the stars, thinking that they'd probably be magnificent out here in the middle of nowhere.

She smiled at her own slight disappointment. When she was a child, her sisters, all three of them, would lay out on the grass in the backyard, gazing up at the stars. They inevitably fell into their game. Veronica, the oldest, would pick an area of the sky. Daisy would pick the grouping, and Danielle would say what she thought it looked like. Three pairs of eyes would look to the youngest, waiting for Rachel to weave a tale of the stars, maybe make up some ancient god, or just some crazy explanation of why a giant rabbit made of stars was gracing their night sky.

Before she realized it, Rachel had a full blown grin on her face. She could hear Daisy, her sister closest in age and friendship, running inside.

"Momma! Momma! Rachel said a snake slithered up a tree and into the sky! Is it true?"

Maybe Daisy was watching her from the very sky she studied. Maybe she'd be joining her sister up there, she and Daisy looking down on the other two.

Rachel had learned the hard and very painful way just how short life could be. One day she got a call from a distraught Daisy about the test result from her gynecologist. The next, Daisy lay dying in Rachel's spare bedroom. It was a year and a half now that she'd been gone.

As the moon peeked out, only a teasing look from behind heavy clouds, tears glistened on sunburned cheeks. Rachel shivered as some rolled down into her ear; she didn't bother to wipe them away. No one was awake to see them. She hadn't been able to write a single word in the six months she'd cared for her sister, paid for all of her treatment. Every day, Rachel sat with Daisy, talking with her, crying with her, holding her and praying like she'd never prayed before. Danielle and Veronica came as often as they could; their parents were long gone. The four Holt girls were all that was left of the family, and they stuck together.

That last night, something was terribly wrong, Rachel felt it. It was the one night Matt didn't argue with her about sleeping in Daisy's room rather than in their own bed.

The blonde tossed and turned on the day bed that had been brought in next to Daisy's bed, finally waking up, the echo of a nightmare still fresh. Sitting up, she looked over at her sister, fear and dread gripping her heart.

"Daisy?" When there was no response, Rachel got out of bed, her bare feet sinking into the thick carpeting, just installed three months before Daisy's arrival. "Daisy?" Rachel carefully placed a knee on the mattress, crawling over to the stick-thin body that lay at the center of

the big bed. Daisy lay on her back, head rolled to the left, facing away from Rachel.

Rachel could still feel that coldness; there was nothing else like it in the world. It was that feeling of fake, rubbery skin, almost hard to the touch. The tears came faster now, Rachel's grief at losing her beloved sister suddenly segueing into sorrow at the very real possibility of her own imminent death. *Will it be weeks? Days? Hours?*

Deciding this vein of thought was not going to help anything, Rachel pushed herself up into a sitting position, swiping at her eyes and sniffling quietly. She could barely make out the shadowy forms of Pam and Mia huddled at the other end of the raft. All three of them were dehydrated and hungry. They had tried to sleep away their hunger pangs and discomfort for the majority of the evening and into the night. Rachel wondered about the time, then remembered why she'd woken in the first place.

"Shit," she muttered, trying to decide what to do. She could jump over the side for a couple minutes, do her thing then climb back in. *What if I lose my grip and fall? Neither Pam nor Mia would know.* She could hang her butt off the side of the raft and pee all over herself. *Scrap that idea.* She was contemplating just peeing in her pants when something caught her eye.

The raft rocked gently as she moved, turning to face behind her. The moon was still playing peek-a-boo, and in a moment of illumination, something caught her eye. No matter how much she squinted, it was just out of her visual grasp. Then, almost as if a beacon from above, lightning split the sky.

"Land!" She nearly fell off the raft in her excitement, turning to her raft-mates. "Pam! Mia! Wake up! Land!" The blonde turned back, making sure it wasn't simply a mirage from an emotionally overwhelmed mind. It was still there. She could feel her tears start anew as relief washed over her.

The raft rocked violently as a jubilant Pam crossed to the end of the raft and knelt next to the blonde. "Oh, sweet Jesus," Pam whispered, her arm wrapping around Rachel's shoulders.

Sandy colored eyebrows drew together, then flinched, and his nose wrinkled at a new smell in the air. Dean raised his head, crying out at the painful crack from his back, a consequence of lying in the same position for hours on end. When he realized what was different, he nearly fell off his tiny life raft while trying to turn over, and his back cracked again. No matter.

"Rain!" He raised his face to the sky, opening his mouth and squeezing his eyes shut as the sweet water fell upon him. He stuck his tongue out, desperately trapping every drop he could. Realizing that wasn't working all that well, he cupped his hands, lapping at the small pool that gathered there. He wanted to cry in relief, his throat finally opening, his chilled body responding to the stimulation.

Once Dean had drunk his fill, he looked around, wondering if some land mass had also miraculously appeared. No such luck. His relief at having water was short-lived as he realized just how hungry he was. *What I wouldn't do for a giant platter of lobster.* His mouth watered at the thought.

Lying down again, which allowed him to feel much steadier, Dean stared up into the sky, barely able to keep his eyes open as the drops fell. Lightning made the sky glow every few moments, and Dean felt like he was stuck on the Millennium Falcon in that *Star Wars* movie, moving at light speed, or warp speed, or whatever the sexy Han Solo called it. It was like that with snow, too. He remembered driving at night and turning the headlights on bright, watching as the snow pelted the lights and windshield, just like the rain, at warp speed.

Dean had never felt so alone, yet he was surrounded by God's creations. How could something be so beautiful, yet so incredibly unforgiving? How many ships had gone down in these very waters? How many people had died where he lay? Would he be one of them? Would anyone back home, other than Will, care? Would anyone from his law firm come to mourn his passing, crying at an empty casket, as no doubt his body would never be found?

Dean felt anger course through him at the unfairness of it all. He hadn't even *wanted* this damn trip! Why was he being punished? What, was it the pilot's time to go, or what? How had he, one man, survived that awful crash? And basically without a scratch. Dean wasn't bleeding anywhere, wasn't hurting anywhere, other than his back and stomach from hunger pangs. He'd released his bladder several hours ago. Was he meant to survive this ordeal, turn into Tom Hanks and talk to a volleyball? Except in his case, it would be goddamn seat cushions!

Maybe if he survived he could have a TV movie made about him or something. How cool would that be? Maybe Collin Ferrell could play him. Dean grinned at that idea.

A life together — three kids, a nice home, and happiness. Gone. All gone in the blink of an eye. Michael stared up at the falling rain, the cool wetness easing the sting of his sunburned flesh and ravishing thirst. But even the rain couldn't ease his torn soul or broken heart. He could feel the solid form in his arms, the coolness of Melissa's skin, could still smell the shampoo she'd used that morning.

Not sure what was rain and what was tears, Michael held tighter to the only woman he'd ever loved. He smiled, thinking of the bright-eyed woman his Mel had been. The way she wouldn't let him get away with *any*thing. She'd give him that look that made him stop whatever he was doing, guilt immediately filling every fiber of his being. Why had she stayed with him through the years? She had put up with his drunken tirades, losing jobs, and years of fighting. Never did she falter in her love for him. Finally one day he'd woken up and realized that all his searching, all his bastardly escapades were for naught; everything he could want or need had been by his side the whole time. He'd left his beer untouched on the bar, dropped a few bills, and hurried home to make love to his wife.

Michael smiled, thinking of his three kids: Alan, Jennifer, and Conrad. What a handful they all were, and yet every day Melissa handled them with grace. What were they going to do without their mother?

"I'm sorry, guys," he told the rain.

"Pull it, come on!" Pam ordered with a groan, using her full body weight to try and tug the raft onto shore, flanked by Mia and Rachel. Finally the three women managed to get the heavy inflatable slide out of the water and then all three collapsed on the hard-packed sand.

Rachel had never in her life been so glad to touch land and she grabbed fistfuls of sand in delight. Taking deep breaths, she allowed herself to be helped to her feet then nearly lost her footing again as she was pulled into a monster hug with Pam and Mia joining in on the excitement of survival.

As the blonde ran off into the bushes, Mia ran her hands through her hair, pushing it out of her face.

"Help me, Mia," Pam said, tugging on the raft. "We need to get this flipped. We're going to need shelter from the rain."

"Shouldn't we let it gather water?" the girl asked, glancing around the tiny beach on which they'd landed.

"I think right now we need shelter more." Pam glanced up as a streak of lightning split the sky and thunder growled through the heavy clouds. "We've got to get dry."

Rachel had never been so relieved to pee in her life. That discomfort taken care of, she shivered as she realized her skin was cold, and beyond wet. *I doubt I could be any wetter if I were standing at the bottom of a swimming pool.*

Hurrying back to the beach, she grabbed a side of the heavy raft to help Mia and Pam turn it over. It finally flopped over, propped up on some thick foliage.

"Get underneath it!" Pam instructed, yelling to be heard over the thunder and the rain coming down in a deluge. The three women huddled together, watching their new world from the relatively dry safety of their fort.

Mia was once again in Pam's motherly embrace, feeling numb. Her body and mind were in shock, unable to handle the fact she'd just survived a devastating plane crash, lost her mother, and was now stranded on some piece of rock with two strangers, and was most likely going to die. These facts somersaulted around in her brain as Mia shivered violently and wished she'd gone down with her mother.

Pam felt the young girl trembling and studied her with a drawn brow. She was worried about young Mia. This catastrophe was a lot for anyone to handle, and even more so for a teenager who had so many other things to cope with during that time in their life. She was afraid the girl was in shock, and knew she had to keep a careful eye on her. She looked over at the blonde, meeting her eyes for a moment, shaking her head to signify her worry.

Rachel's gaze left Pam's and moved to Mia. She knew the girl was devastated, and could relate, knowing exactly how she felt. Reaching out a cold, trembling hand, Rachel took Mia's in her own and met the girl's brief gaze. She smiled when she felt a slight return squeeze from Mia's hand.

As the women watched, to their astonishment, as quickly as the rain had started, it stopped, trickling to a few drops before ceasing altogether, until only the sounds of water dripping from the plants filled the night. With the pounding of the rain now quieted, they heard another sound in the distance.

"What is that?" Rachel said, straining to hear. "A beat. Like a..." she listened again, "like a drum."

"Oh God," Pam muttered, eyes wide as she tried to take it all in. "Have we landed on Easter Island, or something?"

Rachel said nothing, only tried to listen. "Maybe someone lives here."

"Maybe they have food," Mia said quietly, peeking out from under the overturned slide.

"Maybe *we'd* be the food," Rachel supplied, her overactive imagination already whirling. Part of her wanted to explore, another part of her terrified at what she might find.

"Damn it, bastard," Denny growled, turning the coconut around, again, to see if she had made *any* progress. With another growl deep in her throat, she turned back to the rock and continued to pound the stubborn shell against the sharp edge. Suddenly, after another half dozen poundings, she squealed in delight as liquid burst from the small crack. "Yes!"

She raised the coconut to her mouth, swallowing down the cloudy water-like milk, almost moaning in pleasure. The rain water had been wonderful, but her stomach was revolting, craving sustenance. The milk drained, Denny proceeded to break the shell apart, piece by stubborn piece, until she was able to scrape the pure white coconut from the inside, greedily sucking it from her fingertips.

As she ate, Denny looked out from her shelter in the thick foliage, where she had managed to stay dry during the deluge. The storm was trickling down to nothing more than a simple rainstorm. For the first time since she had discovered there was trouble on the flight, Denny felt halfway good. She was relieved to be safe and out of the water, and to have found some sort of food, even if it was minimal. Tomorrow, in the light of day, she'd explore the island and see what else she could find. If she were really lucky, there would actually be civilization, but she had serious doubts about that. For tonight, she'd stay in the little niche she'd found and try to get some sleep.

Dean was wakened abruptly when a huge wave toppled him into the ocean. Air bubbles and a smothered cry erupted to the surface. He sank further down until his ruined Gucci shoes came into contact with something hard. Instinctively, he pushed off the bottom and shot back to the surface, gasping and clawing blindly for the seat cushions. They were gone.

Bobbing in the water as the sun began to break the horizon, Dean tried to gather his wits about him and figure out he was going to do. The flimsy life preserver from the airplane was already deflating, and he couldn't tread water forever. Suddenly something occurred to him. Ducking his head back under water, he realized he did in fact see something solid. Shooting back down, his feet hit the surface maybe seven feet down. Breaking through the water again, Dean looked around him, swishing in the water. He couldn't believe what he saw.

With a cry of triumph, he began to frantically swim toward land, maybe a hundred yards away. *I can do this! I have to do this.* He was exhausted, hungry, and in desperate need of dry clothing, but it didn't matter. *Land!* The muscles in his arms and legs burned as badly as his lungs, but Dean pushed all of the misery to the back of his brain, doing his best to not think about it. Once he hit solid ground, something other than just a reef, he could collapse and let his body rest.

His legs finally gave out and he fell first to his knees, and then to all fours. Dean's breathing was dangerously rough as he crawled up onto shore. Shoulders heaving with sobs of relief, Dean leaned down and pressed his face into the wet, cold sand, then looked up into the sky, just beginning to paint color across the horizon. He was not a religious man, but this seemed like a blessing if ever he'd seen one. "Thank you," he whispered. "Oh, thank you, God."

"Amazing, isn't it?"

Dean screamed at hearing the voice of another person. He sprang to his feet, stumbling back as a wave crashed onto shore, taking him with it. He splashed in the receding water, spitting out a mouthful of salt water. The woman walked over to him, a smirk gracing her lips. She held out a hand to him and he eyed her, stunned and even more relieved, as he took the help and regained his feet. "God *is* a woman."

"Are you okay?" Denny asked, amused by just how big around the man's eyes were. He nodded dumbly. "Were you on the plane?" Again he nodded. "Me, too. Welcome to Paradise." She opened her arms, indicating the island, still shielded in the blue light of predawn.

Dean was suddenly overwhelmed again, relieved not only to have found land, but also another living person. He grabbed the woman with the long, dark hair and crushed her to him, feeling her stiffen in surprise then wrap her own arms around his back. He couldn't control his tears, though he felt like a fool crying in this strange woman's arms. To her credit, she said nothing, just held him and let him cry it all out.

Denny wasn't entirely surprised by the man's reaction. Her own emotions had gotten the better of her more than once since she'd found herself lying on the beach. In truth, she was beyond glad to have him there. Two heads were better than one, and maybe they could combine their skills and knowledge to figure out a way to get home.

"I'm sorry," he said after a while, stepping back from the brunette. "I was just so damn glad to see another person."

"It's okay. I understand." Denny kept a hand on his shoulder in silent understanding as he wiped his face clean of tears, leaving smears of wet sand in their place. She smiled, bringing a hand up to gently swipe at the sticky grains. "I'm Denny."

"Dean." Smiling in gratitude, the new arrival was able to make out some of the woman's features, but only just. He could tell her hair was dark and her eyes light. Judging by the splotchy light and dark on the woman's face, her skin was no doubt as sunburned as his own. "How long have you been here?" he asked, noting that both her hair and clothing were dry.

"I'm not sure. I think I woke up some time late afternoon, over on the beach." She pointed to the spot where she'd awakened. Dean glanced over his shoulder in the general direction of where she pointed, further down the beach. "Come on, Dean." Turning, Denny led the way back to her shelter. She'd heard something which had woken her, and she'd run to the beach in hopes of finding a search boat or plane. Instead she'd found Dean, trying to make his way to land. The extreme disappointment had nearly brought her to tears, but she was glad to be able to help a fellow survivor.

Dean followed, gasping as a branch of some sort of plant smacked him in the face when it slipped from his grasp. Glaring at the offending foliage, he shoved it aside, trying to keep up with his guide as she led him deeper into the jungle. He noted bits of material tied to branches; they looked like torn shreds of cloth.

"Are you hungry, Dean?" Denny asked, folding her body down to her bed of leaves. She could no longer see his face, but heard an eager "yes" that made her smile. "It's not much, but it's something." She handed him one of the precious baby bananas she'd managed to find when she realized the coconut wasn't going to be nearly enough. The fruit was tiny, but it was better than nothing.

Dean snatched the banana from the woman's hand, almost growling like a rabid dog as he tore through the skin. Humming in delight at the slightly bitter taste, he chewed thoroughly between bites, nearly turning it completely to mush before swallowing, wanting to prolong every bit of the tiny banana.

Denny understood all too well. She handed the man a leaf filled with rain water. Muttering his gratitude around the last bite of banana, Dean took the leaf, careful to keep it cupped as he drained the fresh, clean liquid it held. Still hungry but feeling immensely better, Dean leaned back against a thick cushion of foliage, the first smile of the day on his lips. "Thank you."

"You're welcome."

Rachel groaned softly as she turned over, something in her back pinching, causing her to wake with a start and a soft cry. Green eyes opened and she looked around, blinking as the light of a new day slowly crept in under the edge of the overturned raft. Pam and Mia were sound asleep, but Rachel decided it was time to get up, stretch, and explore. She couldn't help thinking about the same time yesterday, early morning sometime. She had been at Reenie's tiny apartment, lying on her couch and trying to decide what to do. Torn between staying for another few nights with her friend or going home, Rachel had decided to do neither.

Crawling out from under their shelter, the blonde looked up into the sky, still dark blue, but the edges of the world were on fire, the light leaping up into the clouds to paint them orange and pink. It was truly beautiful. Rachel stood at the water's edge, committing the sight to memory so she could reproduce it in a novel somewhere. If she got the chance.

Rachel was amazed at how much the scenery had changed overnight. They had landed on a tiny beach, shrouded by rocky cliffs on either side, waves crashing against them. White foam flew up into the air, backed by lush greenery so thick it looked as if it would take a hatchet to make any headway getting through it. No matter, Rachel knew she had to try. If they were going to survive and get home, she'd have to see what they were up against, and what resources they had to draw from.

Taking a deep breath, Rachel shoved her hands into the back pockets of her jeans, wishing she hadn't lost her baseball cap in the ocean. It would be nice not having to worry about things crawling in her hair. She climbed up the small hill that led to the jungle, slowly picking her way through the first layer of growth, eyes looking every which way, unsure about what type of wildlife might roam in these trees and vines. She also tried to stay mindful of dangerous spiders, bugs, and snakes.

Taking it slow, Rachel couldn't help but marvel at her surroundings. She'd lived in Oregon her whole life, surrounded by the wooded beauty of it. She'd traveled all around the world in the past five years, researching her novels and exploring all there was to see in each place — France, Israel, Rome, and Greece, even Japan. In each country, she was awed all over again, and this place, regardless of the circumstances, was no different. Startling and inspiring colors jumped out at her. *What I wouldn't give to sit up against a tree with my laptop and capture all this on paper.*

Rachel found it amusing, and slightly disturbing, that even though she was in a dire situation, which could possibly prove to be fatal, she couldn't help thinking with her pen instead of her head.

Chuckling, Rachel didn't see the figure until she'd nearly run her over. Gasping in shock, a hand going to her rapidly beating heart, she looked up and met equally startled blue eyes.

Chapter 4

"Frazier here," the detective said, latex-clad fingers holding a bullet casing up to his eye.

"Matt, Captain Washington needs you back at the precinct ASAP," said Regina Mason, front desk clerk.

Matt lost interest in the casing for a moment. "Did she say why?"

"Nope. Just told me to give you the message."

"Okay. I can be there in about half an hour."

"Okey doke. I'll let her know."

"Thanks, Reggie." Matt snapped his phone closed and slipped it into the holster clipped to his belt. "Hey, Burt," he called out to his partner, who was talking to a member of the coroner's office. "I need to head back to the office right away. I'll be back as soon as I can."

Matt trotted across the street to his car, buckling himself in before merging the sedan into traffic. In a way he was grateful for the reprieve, no matter how brief. His mind was not on his job at the moment, and the victim lying dead on the sidewalk deserved better than that. He hadn't heard from his wife in five days, and though he wasn't worried about her, he *was* worried about his marriage. She hadn't called him, even if for nothing more than to yell and scream at him. How he wished she'd do that, but he knew better. Rachel was an introvert; she lived inside her own head and emotions. He'd often wished she'd let him in, but she never would. Though he wasn't about to blame his infidelity on her, he wondered if maybe the distance she insisted on keeping from the rest of the world, even her own husband, hadn't helped things either.

Hating the taste of stale cigarettes, Matt popped a stick of gum into his mouth as he pushed through the front doors of the police department. He waved and called out a greeting to the ladies working in the office, then headed back into the maze of the inner workings of Madison PD, Madison, Oregon.

"Come in," Captain Peggy Washington called out, phone receiver in her hand. Her fingers were poised over the keypad to punch in her home number. She needed to make sure her son had picked up his little sister from soccer practice. She glanced up as her office door was pushed open, Detective Matt Frazier popping his head around the corner. "Oh, Matt. Come in." Peggy set the receiver back in its cradle. Her son could wait.

"What's up, Cap?" Matt asked, plopping down in one of the two chairs in front of her metal desk. He flung an ankle over his knee, jiggling his dangling foot, a nervous habit he'd always had, though he was aware it drove Rachel crazy.

Peggy sighed heavily, leaning forward with her elbows on her desk blotter. She looked the detective in the eye. She'd known Matt Frazier since his first day at the Academy, where she'd taught a self-defense class. He was a good guy, and she hated to be the one to tell him the news, but the Chief had insisted, knowing Frazier liked and respected her.

"I've got some bad news for you, Matt," Washington began softly, the mother of four in her coming out.

"Okay." Matt's heart began to pound and his brain whirred, trying to review everything he'd done in the last six months.

"You had Burt Langley gather some information on your wife, about her whereabouts—"

"Oh, Cap, I didn't think—"

Peggy Washington held up a hand to silence him. "Matt, the plane your wife was on went down somewhere in the Atlantic."

Matt stared at his boss, blinking several times as the words slowly penetrated his brain. A coldness rushed through him, making him shiver.

"What?"

"I'm so sorry." Peggy met his gaze and held it, trying to make sure he was okay. Matt nodded, but his jaw muscles were working overtime. "I think it's best you take some time off."

"No. Uh," Matt pushed up from the chair. "I need to get back—"

"Detective, I am ordering you to go home, at least until Monday. Okay?"

"All right." Matt left the office, his stomach roiling.

The house had seemed dark and empty before, but now, now it just felt...dead. Matt ran a hand through his hair, his eyes burning with unshed emotion. He still felt sick, chewing three pieces of gum on the way home to get the taste of regurgitated meatball sandwich out of his mouth.

Tossing his keys and wallet on the breakfast bar, he walked on shaky legs to the living room, noting the answering machine blinked with eight messages. He didn't have the heart to listen to them; he didn't want to talk to anyone. Besides, none of them would be from Rachel.

Matt fell into the La-Z-Boy chair in front of the TV, head in his hands, shoulders heaving as his grief and regret hit him between the eyes. *She can't be dead. She can't!* Somewhere through his grief, he heard the phone ring, the answering machine picking up on the third ring.

"Hi, you've reached Rachel and Matt. Please leave a message. Bye." Rachel's voice pierced his heart.

"Matt, this is Reenie again. It's imperative that you call me right away." Matt could hear the emotion, the editor's voice thick and nasal. She'd obviously been crying. "Please call me today."

The dead air was heavy and filled with expectation. Matt didn't want to talk to her. *Why didn't she tell me Rachel's flight number, damn it! How could she have kept that from me?* Matt's tears returned. He knew he was being unfair; none of this was Reenie's fault. It was all his. Raising his face to the ceiling, he squeezed his eyes shut, crying out his grief to the night.

Naomi rested her cheek against the top of Will's head, where it rested just under her chin. He had his arm slung over her stomach as her fingers ran through his hair. Together they watched the newscast of the crash, now on every channel. It was amazing, unheard of. The plane had crashed in the middle of the ocean, yet three people had been rescued, one half-dead, the other two badly injured, but alive.

"That's incredible," Naomi whispered, eyes riveted to the footage. She felt her brother-in-law's nod, followed by a sniffle. None of the three people was Dean. The camera showed the three arriving in New York, a crowd mobbing them, then flickered to individual reunions. An older couple enveloped a woman with short, black hair, the trio crying. The older man was then on camera speaking in Italian, his words translated closed caption-style at the bottom of the screen:

"I'm so grateful to get my granddaughter back. I'm just greatly saddened by the loss of our great-granddaughter."

Another woman was being wheeled in a wheelchair by a man, who was smiles from ear to ear. Two young children flanked the wheelchair.

"It's a miracle!" the man said, voice cracking. *"I couldn't believe it when the phone rang and it was Candice on the other end."*

An NTSB official appeared on screen. *"The investigation has already begun, the rescue mission sadly turning to a recovery mission. Divers are trying to locate the black box."*

Naomi and Will turned the TV off as the newscaster began to explain what the black box was and how it worked. Will stared off into space, fantasizing, not for the first time, that one of the survivors had been Dean, and he had been on the other end of that phone call.

"Want to hear something strange?" he said at length, voice soft, wistful.

"Hmm?" Naomi brushed hair away from Will's boyish features. *If you had been straight...*

"Somehow I feel like I'd know if Dean were dead. I know that sounds crazy, and totally full of fantasy, but..."

"You don't feel that he is?"

Will was quiet for a moment, mulling it over and over in his head. Finally he shook his head. "No. No doubt it's just wishful thinking, but somehow I don't feel it. I'm sure it's just because it hasn't hit me yet."

"You guys do have an amazing connection, Will." Naomi thought about her brother and the man she'd been comforting for two days now. Dean's partner was beyond distraught, and no doubt felt Dean's loss more acutely than anyone. Since the first day Dean had brought Will home to meet everyone, Naomi had seen the specialness of the men's relationship and bond. It truly was something to behold. Though Naomi had no doubt Dean was gone, she also had no doubt Will could still feel him. *Hell, maybe her brother was around them right now, and that was why Will's feeling was so strong.*

The reunion was an emotional one — not a reunion of friends, but a gathering of strangers reuniting with humanity, though Denny was almost beside herself to see Mia step out from under the overturned slide. She hugged the girl tight, not having to ask about the teenager's mother. Mia's tears told her all she needed to know.

"I can't believe there are so many of us," Dean said, eyeing everyone, his methodical mind already forming thoughts and impressions of each of the women stranded with him. "Where were you guys all sitting?" He looked from one to another, finally settling back on Denny.

"Up in 5C. Mia and I were right behind First Class," the brunette explained softly.

Rachel was listening, arms crossed over her chest. She realized that she remembered seeing this woman on the plane, though briefly. She also felt as if she'd noticed her in the terminal.

"I was in First Class," Pam said, leaning against a rock face.

"Me too," Rachel said softly.

"Well, I was back about halfway, not quite to the wing."

"Good thing," Denny said, pushing some wind blown strands behind her ear. "Any further back and you would have been gone."

Dean nodded. "I know. We were all lucky."

Pam looked away, remembering her boyfriend sitting next to her one minute then gone the next, sucked out as the cabin depressurized from the in-rushing air, along with many other passengers. The air was heavy with bad memories and grief. Mia began to sob softly.

"So!" Needing to change the subject and mood, Dean clapped his hands together. "Where is everyone from?"

"Buffalo," Pam said, munching on a banana Denny had provided.

Denny nodded. "Me too."

"Brooklyn," Mia almost whispered.

"My partner and I have a loft in Manhattan," Dean supplied.

Rachel smirked. "Guess I'm the only non-New Yorker here." All eyes were on her; she felt shy in the face of their attention. "Oregon."

"You were far from home," Dean said, eyebrow raised. Rachel looked away and he noted her suppressed emotion. *I think there's a story there.*

"How is everyone holding up? Injuries? I'm not a doctor, but I may be the closest thing we have." Pam looked around, noting a variety of bumps and bruises on everyone except Dean. She'd also noted the way the beautiful brunette seemed to hold her arm against her body. The veterinarian walked over to her. "Let me get a look at your arm, Denny."

"Oh, we have our very own mother hen on the island," Dean said, indicating Pam with a flamboyant flourish.

Rachel glanced at him, then turned to watch Pam and Denny, Pam murmuring assessing questions, Denny's responses soft. She wondered if Pam had some medical training; she seemed to know what she was doing. The next thing she knew, the older woman led the brunette around behind a wall of foliage.

Denny sucked in a breath at the white hot pain that shot through her arm as she tried to pull her sleeve off around it. With Pam's help, she removed her shirt.

Pam studied the arm and shoulder, grazing gentle fingers over the discolored flesh. "Denny, I think this is dislocated," Pam said, glancing up into the brunette's glacial eyes. "I really need to put it back in place."

Denny swallowed hard, but nodded. *It can't hurt anymore than it already does.*

"Okay, honey, here we go." Pam stepped up close to Denny's side, wrapped one hand around Denny's forearm and used the other to steady the shoulder of the injured arm.

Birds squawked and flew out of the trees as a cry echoed over the island, startling both animal and human occupants. Three sets of eyes stared into the thick foliage. They glanced at each other, then back into the brush. Rachel shivered at the pain that cry carried. At the same time, she realized there were birds on the island, which meant eggs for eating. She hoped they would come back.

Pam whispered words of apology as Denny took a shaky breath and got herself together. She barely took in the explanation that Pam was going to make a sling for her arm. Denny leaned against a thick grouping of undergrowth as Pam went to find some vines.

Denny felt the pain slowly washing over her in lapping waves. She closed her eyes, taking in lungfuls of the freshest air she'd ever breathed, strongly scented with the salt and wildlife of the sea. She felt queasy, but she couldn't afford to lose any of the food she'd already taken in, so she just stayed put, holding her arm in the exact same position Pam had put it, keeping it close to her side, her left hand holding tight to her elbow.

"Is she okay?" Mia asked as Pam emerged from the foliage, eyes already scanning the beach.

"Yeah. Had to do a closed reduction on her shoulder," the vet explained absently. Unlikely as it was in a post 9/11 world, where nothing sharper than a comb's tooth was allowed on board, she called out, "Does anyone have a knife?" glancing over to where Rachel and Dean stood, both looking at her.

"In my checked luggage," Dean said helpfully. Pam glared, then stared at him. "What? It was a joke." He watched as she approached him, noting the look in her eye and taking a step back from her.

"Give me that," she said, pointing.

The man looked down in confusion. Pam reached for his thick Armani belt, unbuckling it. He covered her hands with his, trying to push her away. "Hey!" He hadn't had a woman try to undress him since Mary Taylor when they were seventeen. Oh, what a disaster *that* had been. "Did you hit your head or something?"

"I need your belt!"

"*What!*" Dean was pissed, slapping at Pam's hands and stumbling backward in his haste to get away from her. "This is a two hundred dollar Armani!"

"Yeah, well now it's a two hundred dollar sling."

"I don't think so!" He looked at her, incredulous. She expected him to give up his belt for a frigging *sling*? *No way!* "Keep your damn hands off me, woman."

Thoroughly angered by the prima dona's selfishness, Pam stalked after him, grabbing his shirt in her fist. "Listen to me, and listen good, Dean," she said within inches of his face, eyes hard. "We're stuck here, all of us, and we have *got* to cooperate with each other. Do you understand me?"

"Guys!" They both turned to see Denny standing a few feet away still holding her arm. "This isn't worth fighting over. Pam, we can find something else, vines or my shirt or something. Don't beat the guy up over it."

Rachel stared at the brunette, noting she was now dressed only in her jeans and a bra. Her shoulder looked ugly — bruised and badly swollen. Dried blood had caked to a bad gouge on her upper arm, near her shoulder. Looking down at her own attire, guilt swept over her. "Here." Walking over to Pam, Rachel held out her hand, her own brown leather belt dangling from it.

The older woman looked down at it, then smiled up into amused green eyes. "Thank you, Rachel." Glaring over her shoulder at Dean, she took the offering then walked over to Denny.

"Thank you," Denny said through gritted teeth as Pam tethered her arm to her body. Rachel gazed at her and nodded, and Denny was taken aback by the color of the author's eyes. The magazine pictures hadn't done her justice. Denny's eyes never left her as Rachel turned and went over to sit on a boulder looking out over the ocean.

Dean glared at the erstwhile doctor, his gaze traveling over the wrinkled, ruined shirt she wore, which clung to her slightly plump frame. He took in the rough, calloused hands as they made sure the belt was cinched tight around the brunette's injured arm, and he snorted derisively. "Bitch," he muttered. Arms crossed over his chest, he walked in the opposite direction from Rachel.

Oh boy. Denny watched the scene unfolding before her. They'd all been together for a whopping fifteen minutes and already conflicts were occurring. This wouldn't do. Glancing up, she met Pam's gaze. "You know, we're all pretty messed up here, Pam," she began softly. "I think we need to have some patience with each other."

The veterinarian met Denny's striking blue eyes again, then blew out a breath, returning her gaze to the task at hand. "He needs to learn that we all need to work together to get through this," she said, her voice soft, yet firm.

Denny remained silent; she had said all she felt needed to be conveyed. There was no sense beating a dead horse.

Pam looked at her handiwork. The arm and shoulder had been stabilized against the brunette's body. "How does that feel?"

"It hurts like a bitch, to be quite honest, but it'll do." Denny took several deep breaths, trying to rid her head of the cotton in which it seemed to be wrapped. She wondered if she wouldn't have been better just to leave her arm as it had been. At least she'd gotten used to the pain.

"Where are we going to sleep tonight?" Mia asked from behind Pam. Both women looked at her. "It was so cold last night." Dark eyes looked from one to the other.

"Good question, kid," Denny muttered. She'd only been able to get sporadic sleep the night before, shivering as the island cooled down tremendously from the hot, humid heat of the day. "That breeze off the ocean can be brutal."

"Everybody gather 'round!" Pam called out, clapping her hands.

Mia glanced at Denny, who shrugged her one good shoulder, then winced at the movement.

Pam waited until she had everyone's attention. Meeting everyone's eyes, even the still angry Dean, she barked out orders. "Dean, gather wood so we can make a fire. Rachel, start gathering food, and Denny, help her by making some sort of container to keep it all in. Mia, you and I are going to start gathering materials to make some sort of shelter."

Everyone was just staring at her, so Pam clapped her hands again. "Let's go!"

Rachel looked at the older woman with a clear expression of disbelief.

Dean voiced the thoughts clear from Rachel's expression. "Excuse me, but I'm not your kid, and you'd do well to remember that."

Denny watched as if she was following a volley at a tennis match, a feeling that she needed to intervene creeping over her. Voices were beginning to rise, disturbing more birds. "All right!" she cried, stepping between Pam and Dean, who had stepped closer to one another. "Let's stop this before you two scare away our dinner." She looked from one to the other. "Dean, would you please gather some wood? We're all going to freeze tonight if we can't make a fire. I'd do it myself but..." Denny glanced down at her injured arm. Dean glared one last time at Pam, then turned kinder eyes to Denny and nodded. "Thanks, man. I really appreciate it." Looking into Dean's eyes, she thought she might very well be recognizing a kindred spirit. Dean seemed to feel it, too. He gave her a small smile, then turned and disappeared into the foliage. "And be careful!" Denny called after him.

Denny watched Rachel's anger turned to amused surprise as Dean hurried off to do Denny's bidding. Pam, too, had softened her stance, but only a little. The older woman, so obviously used to being in charge, was no doubt seething as that control was whipped right out from underneath her. Pam headed off though, taking Mia with her, leaving Denny alone with Rachel on the beach.

"That was pretty slick," Rachel said lightly and smiled.

Denny smiled, almost shyly, as she made her way over to Rachel. "Yeah, well it won't do us any good if everyone's fighting and angry. This isn't an episode of *Survivor*."

Rachel nodded. "You did good."

"Thanks." Denny felt her stomach knotting, feeling strange that she was standing there talking with a New York Times best-selling author. "Listen, um, I didn't want to say anything in front of the others, but," she toed her shoe into the sand, "I think you're an amazing talent." Shy blue eyes rose to meet twinkling green.

"Thank you, Denny. I appreciate that." Rachel's smile was soft. She looked with concern at the injured arm. "Are you going to be able to do this? If you need to just sit down..."

"No. I'll be okay. I've got another one." Denny wiggled the fingers of her left hand and flapped her arm like a bird. The blonde chuckled, making her smile. "Come on. Let's get dinner and make an island-style fridge."

Michael grunted, instinctively reaching out, trying to keep his hold. His eyes ached. The lids were badly sunburned and the eyes beneath, as dry as sandpaper. Again he grasped the edge of his raft with a death grip. Looking around, he realized they'd managed to catch a nasty bunch of waves. Hearing a scuffling sound, the Texan glanced to his right.

"Mel!" Michael flung himself over to where his wife's body had slid down the slope of the metal and was quickly disappearing beneath the surface of the unforgiving water. "No!" He groped for her, desperate to try and catch his wife's hand, part of her shirt, *something*. She was gone. Slamming a large fist into the metal, Michael cried out like a wounded animal. As he stared down into the inky depths, he thought of following after her. After all, what did he have without her?

"Daddy!" The squeal split the day in two, short legs galloping across the front lawn, the roar of the little boy's father following close behind.

"I'll get you!"

The boy squealed again, his grin a mile wide. He screamed like his big sister as large hands caught him under the arms and whipped him up into the sky before he landed on his father's shoulders and could see the world from a whole new height.

"Daddy? Can you help me?"

Large fingers did their level best to help a fifteen year-old girl braid her hair, both father and daughter laughing at his fumbled attempts.

"Hey, Dad, check out the way this motor revs! Listen to that..." Grinning like a fool, the young man of twenty-one pushed down on the gas pedal of his newly rebuilt Trans Am.

Michael blinked at his own reflection, seeing the faces of his three children instead of his own heartbroken expression. At that instant he knew he had to live, had to go on. He was all they had left.

Rachel looked up into the dauntingly tall tree, thinking of her noticeably *not* tall stature. Licking dry lips, she heaved herself up, trying to find something to hold onto, her heart pounding as she tried to forget about her fear of heights. She couldn't allow herself to look down and see the progress she'd already made; she'd lose her courage completely then.

"You okay up there?" came the call from far below.

"Yep!" she called back, stopping herself from looking down. "Just peachy," she muttered, heart rising to her throat as she slipped slightly and grabbed onto a vine wrapped around the thin trunk of the palm. Eyes closed, she held on for dear life as she tried to get her balance and her courage back. Opening her eyes, she called, "Look out below!" and took out the stick she had tucked into her pants. She used it to shove at a clump of coconuts, grunting slightly as she tried to hit them harder. Finally three of them came loose and fell into the foliage below.

Denny stepped out of the way of the falling bombs. *It wouldn't do to survive a plane crash in the middle of the ocean only to die from getting smacked in the head with coconuts.* They had a small pile already, coconuts they'd gathered from the ground, where Denny had found them the night before. She was using her shirt as a makeshift sack to carry them.

Rachel growled at the last coconut, which was being far too stubborn for an inanimate object. Nearly falling from the tree herself, she grabbed onto the vine, breathing heavily. Blinking sweat out of her eyes, she glanced out over the trees around her to the ocean beyond. Blinking again, she tried to focus in on something she saw out there in the water, something... *Shiny?*

"Oh my God," she whispered, heart beginning to pound. She narrowed her eyes, squinting against the distance to try and make out what it was. The sunlight glinted off of it. *A boat? Could it be a boat?*

"What's wrong?" Denny asked, watching the blonde.

"I see something," Rachel called down, raising an arm and pointing.

"What?"

"I don't know. Can't tell. It's...it looks like metal."

Denny felt her own heart beat begin to race, the faintest bit of hope trickling through her. She caught the final coconut as it fell, though Rachel hadn't touched it again. Her amusement was cut short as the blonde scurried down the tree.

Landing with a soft grunt, she turned to Denny briefly before running through the trees toward the water. "Come on, follow me," she called back.

Both were out of breath when they broke out of the trees and onto the beach. Denny joined Rachel at the water's edge, where she stood, hand raised to shield her eyes from the fierce sun, trying to focus in on whatever she had seen from her perch in the palm.

"Does that look like a boat to you?" Rachel whispered, almost afraid to breathe the possibility.

"I don't know." Denny would have done anything for binoculars. Something in her gut told her disappointment was coming their way.

"What's going on?" Dean asked, running up to the two women. He saw the blonde extend an arm, pointing. Following her finger, face scrunching up as he looked into the bright sun-lit water, he saw something glinting, bobbing in the water. "What is that?"

"We don't know," Rachel said.

Clinging to his newfound reason to fight to survive, Michael looked around, trying to figure out exactly *how* he was going to survive. As if something answered his prayers, he saw...something.

He rose to his hands and knees, squinting. *No way.* "Oh my God," he whispered. Realizing what he saw wasn't a trick of the mind, Michael began to paddle, making little progress, other than starting to drift to the left. "Shit."

Dean's heart fell as he realized it wasn't a savior that was approaching, just a bit of what looked to be debris, more likely than not, from the wreckage. Angrily waving it off, he turned and stormed back across the beach to where he had begun piling wood.

Denny and Rachel stayed put, both feeling the letdown of their own disappointment. Rachel felt the sting of unshed tears, which she quickly swallowed down. About to turn away, she stopped and stepped forward, the water barely teasing the toes of her shoes. "Wait," she muttered. "There's someone out there."

"What? Are you sure?" Denny tried to focus, but was half-blind from losing her contacts, so her distance vision was for the birds.

"Yeah. There's someone on that piece of metal!"

Michael slid his body around until his legs were in the water up to mid-thigh. Holding on as best he could, he used what little energy the adrenaline provided and began to kick. The wing finally was on its way toward the land that lay before him taunting him. Lowering his head, Michael put all he had into it, pounding into the water, feeling the refreshing spray rain down on him. Soon he was panting heavily, but it didn't matter; he had to make it.

"Look! They're coming this way!" Rachel exclaimed, racing down the beach toward the area where the drifter was heading. Denny followed closely behind, the blonde's cries having garnered attention from Pam and Mia. Even Dean was interested again. The five survivors waited on the shore, watching.

Breathing hard, feeling his legs cramping and his body giving out, Michael, looked up, nearly breaking into tears when he spotted a figure on the beach, arms waving high above their head. A new wave of energy filling him, the paddler kicked on.

Rachel could now clearly see it was a man, the churning of water behind him indicating he was kicking to power his makeshift raft toward them. The kicking stopped from time to time, the man collapsing on his metal "boat", then he'd start again. Remembering how shallow the reef made the water closer to the shore, Rachel hurried out into the water, feeling the cool saltiness splashing her skin and tasting it on her lips. She could hear the others following.

"I can't do this," Michael panted. No matter how great his desire to touch land, how great his need for food and water, he just couldn't force himself to kick even once more. The Texan looked up in despair, and then he did cry — at the sight of five people hurrying toward him, water up to their waists, then shoulders, and finally they were swimming.

"We've got you," a woman's voice said.

Michael's vision was blurry and he was unable to make out her features, only that she had light colored hair. He felt hands on his legs, then movement as his craft was pushed ashore. Sturdy hands under his arms and around his waist helped him to his feet and Michael wobbled onto the solid sandy bottom, his legs giving out when he was still in knee-deep water. Crying in relief and frustration, he collapsed, but his angels wouldn't allow him to give up.

"Come on, man, almost there," another woman's voice said. Gathering the last remnants of energy, Michael made it to shaky legs, half walking, half dragged, to the sandy shore, where he collapsed once more, panting heavily.

"Drink this."

Something was put before him, *cupped leaves maybe?* Whatever it was, it was filled with water. Michael nearly dumped it in his haste to drink. Gulping down the cool sweetness, it slid down his parched throat and brought the dying flesh back to life.

"Here."

Michael looked up and saw a man holding out what looked to be a tiny banana. Not caring what it was, he grabbed the offering, frantically trying to peel it, almost sobbing when his fingers wouldn't work.

"Hey, hey, slow down."

Looking toward the speaker to his right, he saw a woman with long, dark hair squatting next to him. She took the banana from him, peeled it, and handed him the stubby fruit. Her smile was like the sunlight through the clouds to Michael's broken heart and body. He couldn't even manage a "thank you" as he took the fruit from her, eating it in two large bites.

"More?" he croaked.

Denny nodded. "Yeah, but wait big fella. Take it slow."

"Are you an angel?" he asked, staring into the bluest eyes he'd ever seen. They twinkled with the owner's smile.

"No. Just a survivor, like you. All of us are." Denny indicated those who stood around the large Texan. He looked at each of them, really seeing everyone for the first time since he'd landed. He realized he actually recognized a couple of them.

"How long have you all been here? How long has it been?" He turned back to the woman who still knelt beside him.

"I've been here since the day it happened, two days ago. Have you been drifting all this time?"

Michael nodded. "Yeah. Me and my wife."

Denny stared at him.

Eyes dropping, he answered her unasked question. "She uh, she didn't make it." Michael was tired of crying like some sissy girl, so he swallowed it down. Now that he was safe, had some water and a tiny bit of food, he needed to concentrate on getting back home to his kids — the rest could wait.

"I'm really sorry."

Rachel stood with her arms crossed over her chest, watching the interaction between Denny and the newest member of their club. She listened to the easy way the brunette talked to him, and the way he responded to her. It looked like the man was close to tears, and he was certainly exhausted. Rachel couldn't help but smile as Denny pulled the newcomer into a tight hug then released him, a hand still on his back as she talked quietly to him, their words barely discernible.

"It's going to be okay," Denny murmured, smiling at Michael. "We're all going to get home."

Michael nodded, absorbing the warmth and compassion like a mother's embrace.

"In fact, when Rachel over there spotted you, we were all trying to get organized. Come on, let me introduce you to the clan." Denny stood, holding a hand down for Michael. Once on his feet, he leaned on her until he got his balance then turned to face the others. "What is your name?" Denny asked.

"Michael Dupree," the Texan said, shaking Denny's offered hand.

"I'm Denny, that's Rachel over there, Pam, Dean, and Mia."

Michael nodded. "Good to know y'all. I can't thank you enough for your kindness." He looked at each and every face, mentally tallying those survivors he was with, trying to figure them out from their stance, facial expression, or just the way they looked. The blonde looked to be a quiet sort, her body language closing her off from everyone else, her eyes watchful, taking everything in. The brunette with the blue eyes, her eyes were open, accepting, and extremely expressive. He sensed a genuine presence there. The older woman Denny had called Pam studied him with open candor, sizing him up, looking him over. Her face was hard, with lines born of a hard life and hard work. She didn't trust easily. The young girl, standing not too far from Pam, looked like a deer caught in very bright headlights. The girl didn't look as though she knew where she was or why she was there. Then there was the guy standing over by Rachel. His clothes and stance said more than his words could. Though ruined, it was obvious his duds were fine and expensive. His chin was raised ever so slightly, giving him an air of superiority, whether imagined or real. One arm was crossed over his stomach, the elbow of his other arm resting upon it, a finger absently rubbing against his lips.

"Well, why don't you relax here, Michael Dupree, and the rest of us are going to get back to trying to get some food and shelter, okay?" Denny slapped the man on the back lightly then walked back over toward Rachel. They both disappeared back into the foliage.

The light came in through the fluttering curtains of white lace. Dark eyes blinked several times, trying to hold back a new onslaught of tears. She hadn't been successful yet, but maybe this time. A soft knock sounded at the closed bedroom door.

"Entrato, Nonna."

The door slowly opened with a slight squeak, then closed just as softly. "How are you, my child?" Lizbeth Vinzetti set down the tray of tea with lemon she'd brought. She sat on the edge of the narrow bed, placing a worn but soft hand on a cotton-clad shoulder. She looked at her granddaughter's back, shoulders hunched and head tucked slightly. The light shining in through the window made the black hair lying against the pillow shine.

"I feel dead inside," Gloria said, feeling the tickle of a tear running down the side of her nose and slipping down across her lips.

"My dear, dear quello piccolo."

More tears squeezing out, Gloria's eyes slid closed as her grandmother's fingers ran through the short hair at the back of her head. Lizbeth could see Gloria was falling apart, and she leaned over, hugging the younger woman's slender shoulders to her plump bosom. She whispered comforting words to her distraught granddaughter, her own pain pushed aside to ease Gloria's. She and Paolo had flown to New York when they'd gotten word of the amazing rescue of the three survivors from Flight 1049. It was unheard of, and the rescue had made news all over the world. They had been with their granddaughter at her Brooklyn apartment for three days, watching as doctors came and went, along with well-wishers and mourners. Gloria refused to see any of them except the doctors, and even that had been a fight. The tiny apartment was littered with flowers and cards, the fridge filled to capacity with mainly uneaten offerings of condolence and support.

"Why did this happen, Nonna? Have I not lost enough in my life?" Gloria's words were whispered and shaky. "I have to lose my parents, now my daughter? Papa is sick and will soon leave me, too."

Fresh sobs wracked the woman's body, her grandmother holding on tighter, knowing there was nothing she could say, no explanation that would make any sense of the insanity and unfairness of the situation. Gloria just needed to know she was loved; for as long as that love lasted, it was there.

"You have to trust that she's in a good place, my Gloria. She is now with my Carmina," Lizbeth whispered, thinking back to her own daughter, knowing full well the depth of Gloria's pain. "We will get through this. Maybe you come back to Milano, yes?"

Gloria sighed. She had no idea about anything anymore. She didn't know if she could leave the apartment; all of Mia's things were still tucked neatly into her bedroom across the hall, the bedroom where Gloria's grandparents were staying.

"I don't know, Nonna. I just don't know."

It was dark. And cold. Mia stared out over the ocean, the moon-light glittering across its waves. Under different circumstances, it would be beautiful. She stared out over the water, knowing her mother was under the surface somewhere, without even a grave marker, or a grave for the teenager to visit. But as long as she was on the island, she'd be able to visit the death dealing ocean every day.

The sixteen year-old brought her legs up, wrapping her arms around them, resting her chin on her knees. Glancing up into the pitch black sky, Mia was amazed. Living in the busy, bustling city, she never got to see such an incredible night sky, so completely velvet, colors true and in amazing contrast — black sky, silvery, twinkling stars. Someday she'd like to put that sky on her bedroom ceiling and be able to look up into the purity of it every night.

It was amusing — six people, and none of them could figure out how to get a fire started. The rain hadn't helped things. Any wood Dean gathered was still too wet to burn, and all of their efforts, mainly those of Pam and the new guy, Michael, had resulted in nothing but a lot of foul-smelling smoke. Ultimately they'd all gathered under the shelter Pam and Mia had managed to make, crude at best, and more of a lean-to than great shelter. The shared body heat had helped them stay a bit warmer, for sure, but everyone was still squeamish with each other, all virtual strangers, and tried to keep a polite distance. It was amusing to the girl, and yet sad. Even in a desperate situation, propriety won out over good sense. She wondered how long that would last.

Everyone seemed nice, and that was good. Mia hoped they all could get along until they somehow managed to get off the island. That inevitability brought her thoughts to her new life without her mother. Where would she go? She had no family in America. She figured she could go live with her great-grandparents, but she had no desire to leave New York, and besides, her great-grandfather was terminally ill, and no doubt her great-grandmother would follow soon after. Then what?

"You okay?"

Mia glanced over her shoulder to see Rachel standing just behind her, her blonde hair turned silver in the moonlight. The teenager nodded and turned back to the water. Suddenly she realized she didn't want to be alone, and patted the sand next to her. She felt the woman sit.

"Beautiful," Rachel commented softly. *Yet another scene to commit to memory.* She glanced at the girl. The look in the dark eyes said it all, but Rachel thought it might help Mia to talk. "Want to talk about it?"

Mia shrugged. "I'm just so sad. I know it may sound naïve, but I never thought I'd have to live without my mom. I guess maybe I thought she'd be around forever. Stupid, I know."

"It's not stupid, Mia," Rachel said gently. The warm gaze of the teenager met her own. She thought Mia would be stunning one day. Her dark eyes were almond-shaped and gave her an exotic appearance. Her dark hair was long, thick, and soft to the touch. "I lost my sister and best friend a year and a half ago. To this day I still think of ways I could have let her know how much I loved her. Things I should have done, if only I'd known we had such little time."

"Exactly! I shouldn't have fought with her so often." Mia looked out to sea. "Maybe this is my pun—"

"Don't!" Rachel felt anger flare to life that this sweet, young girl would dare take this tragedy on as her own doing. "Don't say that, don't even *think* that." She turned so she fully faced the teen, her knees almost touching the girl's side. "Mia," she said, her tone gentle, a hand resting on Mia's shoulder, "what happened was a terrible, terrible accident and we may never fully know why it happened. But it was just that — an accident. Your mom's, well, what happened to your mom was just part of that accident. I don't mean to make light of your pain, because I know firsthand just how real it is, but Michael lost his wife, and Pam lost her boyfriend. Those people died because of something larger than all of us, beyond anyone's understanding and comprehension."

Mia turned to look into intense green eyes turned gray in the darkness. "Do you really think so?"

"I know so, sweetie." The blonde smiled, squeezing Mia's shoulder.

Mia smiled slightly, looking down at her hands, which now fidgeted atop her knees. Rachel was so nice and beautiful. Her and Denny both. Mia felt shy and uncertain around them, both just enough older than her to make her feel really young. The feeling quickly faded as another admission escaped her lips. "I feel like I should have died with her, Rachel. Maybe I still should."

Rachel wasn't surprised by Mia's words; she herself had felt the same way after Daisy was diagnosed, then died. She kept her voice even yet firm. "Do you think your mom would want that for you?"

Not even having to think about it, Mia shook her head. She could almost hear her mom's voice encouraging her to continue. She knew in her heart Gloria would want nothing more than for Mia to make the best of her situation until she could make it better. After all, that's what her mom always said she was doing back home in Brooklyn.

"Make your mom proud, Mia. Do justice to the lovely young woman she's raised." When Rachel saw she had the shy gaze of the teen, she smiled. "Okay?" Gently playing with a strand of the dark hair, Rachel waited for a response. Finally Mia nodded, a small smile tugging at her lips. Without warning, Rachel found herself with a bundle of teen hugging her enthusiastically.

"Thanks, Rachel," Mia whispered against Rachel's shoulder.

Chapter 5

Like a goddamn tennis match! Blue eyes followed the pacing complainant back and forth, back and forth. Finally Byron Timmons had enough. "What else can I do for you, Mr. Ash?"

"What do you mean, what *else*? You haven't done a damn thing for me *yet*."

"Mr. Ash—"

"Do something!" Will planted his hands on the police sergeant's desk, leaning on his arms as he stared the officer down. "What are you going to do?"

"Mr. Ash, we've *done* everything that we can. It's not in our hands. You need to speak with the Coast Guard, the airline—"

"I've done those things!" Will pushed off the desk, running his hands through his hair, frustration making him nearly burst out of his skin and throttle the unhelpful officer.

Timmons sighed heavily. "Look, Mr. Ash, I feel for you, I really do—"

"Do you?" Will turned on him, noting the gold band on the officer's left ring finger. "If your wife went down in a plane crash, Sergeant Timmons, and you were left behind, would you not want to do everything you possibly could to find her?"

Byron sighed. "Look, Will, I understand what you're going through—"

"No, you don't! How dare you say you have the first damn clue what I'm going through? My partner is out there somewhere, all alone."

Will felt like screaming in his frustration; he knew there wasn't a damn thing the cop behind the desk was going to do for him. Snatching his suit jacket from where he'd laid it over the chair in front of the desk, he turned to leave.

"Mr. Ash..."

Will turned. Byron Timmons was scribbling on a piece of paper. He stood and extended his hand to the architect. Eyes narrowed in suspicious curiosity, Will snatched the paper from Byron's hand, glancing down at a name and phone number. He looked at the officer with a raised eyebrow.

"We grew up together. She'll give you a deal." Byron looked the tall man in the eye, giving him the best smile he could under the circumstances.

"Thank you," Will said, unsure what this Garrison person did exactly.

As if his mind was read, Timmons said, "Garrison owns Davies' Hangar. She flies mostly cargo trips, but she can help you out. Tell her I sent you."

"I'm very grateful. Thank you, Sergeant." Will extended a hand and the cop took it in his warm one. They shared a brief bonding moment, one human being trying to help another, then it was gone. Will gathered his jacket and tucked the paper into his pocket, then walked out of the police station with as much dignity as he could muster.

It had been two weeks since the crash; two weeks since he'd spoken with Dean; two weeks since he'd seen, or kissed him, or told him he loved him, at least to his face. Every morning on awakening and every night before sleep, Will hugged Dean's pillow against his chest, the Egyptian cotton, 400 count, still smelling slightly like the smaller man — his shampoo, the scent of his skin and cologne. Will had even suffered through the disapproving looks from their housekeeper when he refused to allow the sheets to be changed or washed.

Will's boss had tried to make him take time off, but he couldn't do it. He needed to work, needed to keep busy. Naomi was helping him to put together a memorial for Dean, something for their friends and scattered bits of family. Naomi didn't share Will's insistence that Dean was alive, but she supported him nonetheless. She had been wonderful, and more than a rock for him, which was amazing considering she'd lost her only brother. Hell, Dean was her only sibling. The service would be Saturday afternoon, followed by a small, catered get-together at Will and Dean's loft.

Stepping out into the hot day, Will took in the sounds and smells of the city his man loved so much. Dean would step out onto their balcony, hands crossed at the wrist as they dangled from the wrought iron rail, looking down over the streets and people. The softest smile would grace his full lips as he people-watched.

Will was filled with a lot of guilt. He had put Dean on that plane, a trip his partner never would have taken of his own volition. If Will hadn't been so damned pushy about getting out of the city for a while, about seeing something new, something different...

Taking a deep breath, Will hailed a taxi and pushed those thoughts from his mind. He knew they would only serve to hurt him. He hurt enough; he didn't need any more.

He was glad that Jane and Peter Ratliff were actually involving themselves somewhat in the goings on of clearing up Dean's life. The attorney's parents had been to the loft the previous weekend, helping Will go through Dean's things. Jane had insisted on having something that had belonged to her little boy, and Will had agreed, allowing her to take any one thing she wanted. It had nearly broken his heart when she'd chosen Dean's college class ring. Dean had been very old fashioned when they were dating, and had given that large, chunky ring to Will to wear, a symbol of how serious he was about their relationship. It wasn't until the two men had exchanged rings four years ago that Will had stopped wearing it. But there was no way he could deny Dean's mother the memory she had chosen.

"Has he said anything yet?"

Jennifer Dupree shook her head, strawberry blonde bangs falling into her eyes and tickling her freckled nose. She sat on the metal folding chair, knees together, skirt covering her legs just so, just like her mamma taught her. Meredith Adams sighed heavily, glancing over at her youngest grandchild, who stood by the tree, away from everyone else. His suit fit well but his shoulders were slumped, light-colored eyebrows drawn. She'd always fancied that Conrad Dupree looked kind of like Prince Harry of England, just much less wealthy.

"We've got to do something." Meredith turned her attention to the two matching white coffins, empty except for the one thing each of the kids had picked to put inside to commemorate their parents. Their grandmother had no idea what had been chosen, and it wasn't her business to know; that was private between the children and their mother and father.

Meredith worried about the children. She knew how angry Conrad was, though at twelve years old, he had no idea where to put that anger, just knew that he felt it and that it was because his mamma and daddy were dead. They were all angry, angry at the good Lord, at the pilot, and at the grass at their feet. None of it made any more sense than the other, but it was there all the same. Walter almost hadn't made it through the ordeal of the past two and a half weeks. Meredith shivered at the memory of that night, when Walter had fallen down nearly dead on their kitchen floor, his heart unable to withstand the grief that had stricken him in the moment he realized his little girl was dead.

Trying to keep the family together was the only thing keeping Meredith sane. What Walter and the kids didn't know was that during her nightly baths, the grandmother of six cried herself nearly dry, the tears splashing in the hot water. If she didn't have to run after those kids all day, school being out for summer and all, she would have fallen apart long ago. A mother shouldn't have to arrange her own daughter's funeral. It just wasn't right.

The preacher began to speak. Jennifer rested her head against her grandmother's shoulder. Meredith could hear her oldest grandson, Alan, crying softly behind her. Walter sat next to the boy, the two men holding each other up. Meredith wouldn't allow the tears to fall — she had to remain the glue, if only for a few hours more, until she could take her nightly bath.

Reenie's eyes welled with tears as one of the dearest friends she'd ever had walked over to her, bright, beautiful blue eyes so kind and filled with compassion.

"Hey," Beth said softly, pulling the smaller woman into her warm embrace. "I'm so sorry, Reenie, so terribly sorry." She held her friend for a long time, letting her cry. Beth hadn't known Rachel Holt personally; she'd only met her briefly a couple of years ago. But Reenie saw in the compassionate gaze that Beth could recall all the times Reenie had talked about Rachel — about her unhappy marriage, about Rachel's immense talent, and about how Reenie had been after the author to move to New York for years. Beth had made Reenie's place her first stop when she'd hit the city in town for a stint on Broadway.

"I just can't believe she's gone," Reenie said, her tears slowing. She truly had no idea she could produce so many. It seemed all she'd done for the thirteen days since she'd heard about Rachel's plane going down was cry. Pulling away from Beth, Reenie led them over to the couch, where they sat close together, knees touching. Blue eyes gave her their full attention as Reenie shook her head in bewilderment. "She had such an amazing future, Beth. I've never seen someone with so much inside of them that was just waiting to get out and make the world a better place."

"You really cared a lot about her," Beth said softly.

"Yes. She was my best friend."

A new waterfall began and Beth took Reenie in her arms. "Loss is not easy, Reenie," she whispered, "no matter what form it takes. But I promise it gets easier. Soon you'll be thinking about all the good times you had together, smiling to yourself as you drive down the street, thinking about something crazy Rachel said or did." There was a faraway look and a gentle smile in Beth's eyes. "Your heart will mend, my friend. I promise. Even so, Rachel will always occupy a special place inside you."

"It's such a waste, Beth. God, such a waste." Reenie's tears dried up again, for the moment, her head resting against Beth's strong shoulder. "I never saw this coming."

"We never do. People don't realize that, in the blink of an eye," Beth snapped her fingers, "it can all be gone. Rachel knew how much you cared for her, Reen. She stayed here before she left, right?" Beth felt her friend's nod. "No doubt you two had the time of your lives."

Reenie chuckled, remembering the craziness she and Rachel had shared the night before the fateful flight. They bought several bottles of wine and got completely schnockered as they bashed every man they'd ever known. More than once Reenie had wondered what if. What if things had been different? What if she could have turned her deep affection for Rachel into something physical? Maybe then the author wouldn't have jumped on a plane to run from her husband.

"We always have so much fun together. Had." Reenie's face crumpled again, Beth holding her tighter, rocking her and cooing softly.

Beth was curled up on Reenie's couch, flipping through the channels of late night television. Due to the lateness of her evenings on stage, Beth had become a night owl. Reenie had finally fallen asleep three hours ago.

As the knocking sounded at the front door, Beth uncurled her body and crossed the dimly lit loft. She peeked through the peephole and saw a warped version of a man standing in the hallway. "Who is it?" she called out, having no intention of letting a strange man into her friend's apartment at one-thirty in the morning.

"Matt Frazier," the visitor answered, running a hand through his hair, strands wet from the pouring rain outside. He didn't recognize the voice on the other side of the door, so he added, "Rachel's husband."

Beth quickly unlocked the numerous locks on Reenie's door, finally pulling it open to view the man before her. His brown hair was plastered to his head and hanging in his eyes. The suit he wore was wrinkled, and he looked like he'd slept in it for two days.

Matt looked at the gorgeous woman standing in the doorway, stunned into silence for a moment before he remembered why he was there. "Uh, hi. I don't think we've met." He extended his hand and Beth automatically grasped it.

"Hi, Matt. I'm Beth Sayers, a friend of Reenie's."

Matt nodded, looking over her shoulder. "Is she here?"

"Yes, but she's asleep. She's had a rough night." From the dark circles under Matt Frazier's eyes and several days growth of beard, Beth surmised he hadn't had a red letter day, either.

"She knew I was coming. We talked on the phone."

"She didn't mention it, but come on in. Get dry and warm up. Want some coffee?" Beth led him into the apartment, flicking the light on in the kitchen as she entered. She heard Matt's affirmative response behind her, and set about getting the coffee maker perking. Reclosing the bag of fresh coffee, Beth placed it in the cabinet then turned and leaned back against the counter. "I'm so sorry about Rachel, Mr. Frazier. I only met her once, but I know how much she meant to Reenie. I can't imagine how hard this must be for you."

His smile was sad. "Thank you. I appreciate that. I have to say," he ran a hand through his already disheveled hair, "this has been the most difficult thing I've ever had to deal with. Reenie and I are going to be meeting with Rachel's publisher tomorrow to finalize a few things."

Beth nodded in understanding. "You're not from the city, are you?"

"No. We live in Oregon." Beth watched as Matt cringed. *Guilty about something*, she thought.

"Beautiful state. I lived there for a year or so in my early twenties." Beth crossed her arms over her chest, head tilted slightly as she studied him.

"Do you live in New York, then?" Matt peeled his wet jacket from his shoulders and folded it over the back of a kitchen chair.

"Nope. Right now I'm in Arizona. Reenie lets me stay here when I have a show in the city," she explained. Reaching behind her, she grabbed two coffee mugs and set them on the counter.

"A show?"

"Broadway or off-Broadway, depending. Sometimes I do summer stock." Beth shrugged. "Just depends on what I feel like doing."

"Wow. An actress, or singer, or dancer...?"

Beth chuckled. "I'm certainly not a singer, and I don't exactly have two left feet. I'm an actress."

He nodded approvingly. "That's great. How do you know Reenie? Are you a writer, too?"

"Oh, God no! I can barely write a decent letter let alone a masterpiece like I hear Rachel has written." Beth tried to maintain her smile as Matt's eyes darkened with pain. "Reenie and I met during the days when Reenie was a talent scout for a local agency; we've been good friends ever since."

"Matt."

They both turned to see Reenie entering from the dining room. Without a word, Rachel's husband walked over to the shorter woman and took her in a warm embrace.

Beth felt like she was encroaching on a very private moment and decided it was her cue to exit stage left.

Chapter 6

Dark blonde eyebrows drew together as green eyes studied the ring of rocks and sticks before her. She smelled smoke, but could not see any sign of fire. Leaning down, Rachel tucked a strand of hair behind her ears, squinting at the small stack of carefully arranged twigs. *Come on, you bastard.* It was her eighth attempt at starting a fire, trying every configuration she could think of. Never in her life had she felt so stupid or inept.

"Shit," she muttered, wracking her brain to set up a ninth try when she saw something fluttering. "Fire! I have fire!" The blonde moved a stick aside and saw a tiny flame licking its way over another twig. "Yesssss!" Rachel watched in utter fascination. It was almost like she'd never seen flame before, so exciting it was to see it for the first time since the plane crash.

At Rachel's cry, Dean ran from the jungle where he'd been gathering food. "What happened?" he panted.

"I got it started." She grinned at him then turned her full attention back to the budding flame.

Dean fell to his knees beside her. "If only I could add a little of *my* flame to give it a boost," he joked, drawing a chuckle from the blonde. "I never thought I'd be so thrilled to hear someone yell fire."

"Me, either." Together they watched in silence as the flame chewed up the kindling, with Rachel slowly adding more as the fire's hunger grew.

"It's beautiful, Rachel."

"Thanks."

"Here, have some nuts for your troubles." She accepted the small handful, freshly picked, and chewed contentedly. Dean leaned back on his elbows, stretching long legs out in front of him and crossing his ankles. He looked up into the seamless blue sky, eyes closing at the radiant sun that shone down on them. "I wonder what Will is doing right now," he said, voice soft.

Rachel glanced over at him, tossing another nut into her mouth. "Who's Will?"

"My partner." Dean's sigh was heavy and sad. "It kills me — what he must be going through right now, thinking I'm dead."

"I'm really sorry, Dean. I know how much you must miss him."

"Like my own breath."

Rachel studied Dean's profile, the growth on his chin and upper lip giving a more rugged, handsome look to the baby-faced man who had crawled up onto shore. "How long have you been together?" As she listened to Dean's story about him and Will, she felt wistful. She couldn't imagine still speaking so highly of a person after being with them for more than ten years. What was that kind of love like? She and Matt had only been together for four years all totaled, and she had little respect left for her husband.

"What does he do?"

Dean smiled up at the sky, eyes still closed. "He's the best damn architect in Manhattan."

Rachel also smiled, then she snorted. "I hope you don't mind the questions. Asking them is my favorite pastime."

Dean cracked an eye open and glanced over at his beach-mate. He looked at her profile — the delicate features, soft, full lips. Rachel truly was a beautiful woman. Yes, she was beautiful, but it was more than that. She was...cute? Dean wasn't sure that was the word either. She had a gentleness about her, despite being aloof. He hadn't quite gotten a handle on her over the week they'd shared on the island. Usually he was good at reading people, nailing down what made them tick. Not this one; the petite blonde was an enigma. Her awareness and curiosity made it easy to see the intelligence behind her green eyes, and her mind was *always* turning, but she never revealed what she was thinking. She'd be a great poker player. Or attorney.

"Are you a reporter or a shrink?" he asked warily.

The blonde chuckled, shaking her head. "Neither. Just a curious person."

"Okay. But turn about... It will come, so beware." He raised an eyebrow and Rachel nodded in acknowledgement.

As they sat in companionable silence, Rachel thought about the man sitting next to her — opinionated, selfish, somewhat childish at times, and definitely flamboyant. She knew Pam wasn't fond of him, and Mia didn't quite know what to make of him. Michael, who was slowly recovering from his physical ordeal as well as the loss of his wife, Melissa, avoided him. No doubt Michael sensed something different about the gay man; the tall Texan was a man's man — deep voice, gruff, and crude — everything Dean wasn't. Even so, on more than one occasion Rachel had noticed Dean checking out Michael's ass in his tight Wranglers. If Michael ever caught him, no doubt there'd be hell for Dean to pay. They were a motley crew, everyone, including herself, trying to find their place among the dysfunctional family.

A natural loner, Rachel was finding it difficult to find the solitude she so craved. Every hour of the day there was something to be accomplished to contribute to their survival. She certainly had a new appreciation for her life back home. If she was hungry, she opened the fridge or kitchen cabinets. If there was nothing there that appealed to her, she jumped into her car and headed to the nearest Burger King or grocery store. If she had to go to the bathroom, she'd tug her pants down, do her thing, and clean up. Life was simple: one, two, three. When she was tired or cold, she simply curled up in her soft bed, covered by an even softer comforter.

Last night she had lain on the hard ground, a layer of palm fronds for a mattress, the cold air coming off the ocean caressing and chilling her flesh. She had curled up onto her side, bringing her knees as close to her chest as she could, feeling like she was about to be born again. The other sleeping bodies around her had all been so tempting, their body heat a beacon to her, but she just couldn't bring herself to give in to her desire for warmth. By nature Rachel wasn't a touchy, feely kind of person. She accepted hugs from friends, and in fact loved physical affection, but something inside her — irrational fear of rejection, perhaps — wouldn't allow her to initiate physical contact, unless the other person was under duress or had managed to penetrate into Rachel's tiny inner circle of trust. It was childish and crazy, she knew, but true all the same. So, rather than sharing body heat with virtual strangers, she had tried to curl up even tighter and sleep.

Rachel was suffused with guilt. Over the past week, she'd watched her fellow castaways go through a myriad of emotions: anger, grief, profound sadness, and frustration, just to name a few. She watched as they fought with one another or went off by themselves, crying when they thought no one was looking. Meanwhile she found herself looking forward to each day, wondering what new adventures and circumstances it would bring. She was actively filing away every sight, every sound and scent, which would sometime be taken out and dusted off for future story fodder. *Did that make me a horrible person?* While acknowledging the tragedy of those who had lost their lives, and the pain of those family members who were being torn apart back home, she didn't regret their situation.

Her thoughts strayed to her husband. What was Matt thinking of all this? Was he relieved? Now he could have his mistress, a woman whose identity Rachel did not know. All she knew was the woman had rather large breasts and apparently thought a lightning bolt shaved into her pubic hair was fun for the whole family. *Was Matt even sad?* Rachel couldn't allow herself to think about Reenie, who she knew would be devastated. Her dark-haired friend was the one person in the world, next to Daisy, who the blonde trusted with her every emotion.

Sighing, Rachel stared into the growing flames.

Whipping her head back, Denny felt the long, wet strands slap against her mostly naked back. That first day, her shirt had been ruined and torn as they'd used it for a food container. She wasn't keen on walking around in her jeans and bra, but it did keep her cooler in all truth. She just pretended the slight belly she had didn't exist.

Reaching behind her, the brunette grabbed the thick rope of her wet hair, squeezing out the excess water, gasping as the cold stream slid down her back and into the waistband of her panties. Looking around to be certain she was still alone, Denny slid the panties down her legs and set them to dry on a rock next to the small, freshwater pond set at the back of the island. It was surrounded by high rock walls and moss covered ledges. An incredible waterfall served nicely for a shower, even if they had no soap. They'd had another drenching rain the night before, so the waterfall was running strong. As the hours passed, it would peter out until the next rain.

Denny had spent the past couple of days exploring as much of the island as she could. She figured it was anywhere from three to five miles across and comprised mostly of dense foliage. There were three separate beaches, though two were smaller, and the one where Rachel, Mia, and Pam had landed was very rocky. Denny had found her bathing spot the day before — secluded, beautiful, and the only freshwater waterfall on the island. It wasn't long before guilt made her share the spot with Pam and Mia, who had been making their own assessment of the island.

The water in the pool was cold, run-off from the waterfall, reaching to just below Denny's naked breasts which had become a giant road map of goosebumps converging on painfully erect nipples. A shiver passed through her as she dunked her entire body, spitting water as she rubbed it out of her eyes. She used some torn material from her shirt, trying to wash off the sweat from her pits, under her breasts, and between her legs. Denny had a phobia about exuding body odor, so being stranded was also a test of her patience and tolerance. She was doing her best, washing the best she could daily, in the pond, and in the ocean before that, but she still felt sticky and gross. She wasn't a particularly vain person about her body, but she *was* vain about her hair — thick and glorious, and clean! It was almost an obsession for her. It was nearly killing her to not be able to wash or brush it. Hannah always teased her about it.

Hannah.

Denny continued the mindless task of rinsing off, her skin quickly getting used to the chill of the water. The air was still hot, though she was in almost total shade supplied by the surrounding trees. Her mind veered to her partner, the woman who had been haunting her dreams. If she closed her eyes for even a moment, Hannah's dark eyes came to mind, twinkling mischievously as they always did, even if the brunette was being as good as gold. That had been one of the things that had made Denny fall in love with her in the first place.

At twenty-five, Denny was the manager of Mile, a popular coffee hot spot in downtown Buffalo, learning the tricks of the trade from her boss and friend, the owner, Joni Sanchez. Twenty years older than

Denny, Joni was feisty and knew every trick to running a successful business, and she taught them all to her protégé. Joni knew, someday, Denny would have her own place. And she'd been right.

On Denny's twenty-sixth birthday, she went to the bank and opened discussions about taking out a business loan. She'd always had a good head for business, but had no experience and no formal education. Nor did she have any collateral. That made financial dealings nearly impossible. Eventually she'd managed to convince someone to take a chance on her dream, and financing was obtained. She retained a local realtor specialized in commercial properties, and suddenly she was in business.

The old shoe store began to take shape as a coffee shop, its bare, brick walls and twenty-foot ceilings cleaned and painted. Used equipment was purchased and put into place, and a mixed bag of tables and chairs were tastefully arranged. She had already started hiring, the would-be baristas mopping, cleaning, lifting, grunting, and sweating along with their boss to get DeRisio's ready in time for the projected opening.

It was the day before opening and Denny had done all of her hiring, but had forgotten to take down the Help Wanted sign. The bells above the door jingled as a woman stepped through and looked around.

"We open tomorrow," Denny said, glancing up from where she was trying to fix the bean grinder.

"I want to apply for a job," the woman said, stepping up to the counter and leaning over it slightly.

Denny looked at her briefly before realizing her hand was stuck in the motor. "Shit," she whispered, trying to be cool as she yanked on her hand. "I'm fully staffed," she grunted, cursing.

"Do you need help?" the woman asked, slightly amused.

"Nope. Got everything perfectly under control."

"So I see."

The woman snickered and Denny glared at her over her shoulder. "You must not want a job very badly, laughing at the person who would be your boss." Though Denny was joking with the attractive woman with the dark hair and flirty eyes, the look of remorse on the woman's face was just too good to resist teasing her.

"Look, I just got out of a really bad marriage and I desperately need a job. I'm available for any shift, any day, doing whatever you want done. Just please give me a chance."

Denny stopped what she was doing, stood up straight, hand still caught in the machine, and looked into the woman's dark eyes. The desperation was there, but so was a natural fire.

"What's your name?"

"Hannah."

"You help me get unstuck, and I'll think about it."

Older than the rest of the crew at twenty-eight, Hannah was a wonderful employee, helpful and smart. She and Denny hit it off immediately and began to spend a lot of time together. Hannah was one of the only full-time people at DeRisio's because she wasn't in school and was available for any shift. Denny began to count on her, and eventually promoted her to manager. It only took six months before Denny realized she'd fallen in love with her employee, but she'd had no clue Hannah was in love with her. One night, while they were cleaning up after a busy night when a local band playing in the corner had brought in a large crowd, things between them had broken wide open and the back room had seen more flesh than any room in a public place should. The next day Hannah told Denny she wanted more than that one night together, but couldn't date the boss, and so she was giving her two weeks notice.

Denny climbed onto a rock in a rare sunny spot in the canopy of trees to allow herself to dry and warm as she stared up into the cloudless sky. *What is Hannah doing? Is she okay? Is her Aunt Moira there for her?*

She brought her hand up, wiping at an escaping tear. The amusing thing was, Hannah would love the island. The dark-eyed woman loved the ocean and relished any time in the sun and surf. They'd vacationed on the island of Kauai in Hawaii on their sixth anniversary, and Denny nearly had to drag Hannah to the airport, her dark eyes filled with tears at leaving paradise. Now, ironically, it was Denny who was stranded in paradise. Fate sure had a sick sense of humor.

Denny heard something and quickly grabbed her jeans, holding them in front of her naked body as a blonde head emerged from the dense foliage.

"Oh! Sorry." Rachel was about to scurry away when she heard a soft invitation.

"It's okay. Go on in; the water's great." Denny grinned, lying back down, though she kept herself covered.

The blonde entered the small refuge. "Are you sure? I can come back later."

"Not mine to hoard. Help yourself." Denny closed her eyes as she rested her head back on her arm, trying to give Rachel some privacy. "Do you want me to go?" she added.

"No. I'm not going to run you out, Denny. You were here first."

The brunette was unable to stifle her grin. "That reminds me of my older brother and me when we were kids. I called it first!" Denny heard Rachel chuckle, and then there was the telltale rustle of clothing being removed. "Man, we used to fight over the front seat."

"I call shotgun!" they both exclaimed in unison.

Denny's eyes opened and she saw Rachel grinning up at her from the pool. "Exactly!" Denny sat up, drawing her legs up to cover her breasts, but making sure her jeans were placed just so over other parts further south. "Do you have any siblings?"

Rachel nodded, dipping her head and smoothing her hair back out of her face. "Sisters. I am the youngest of four."

"All girls?" Denny rolled her eyes at the blonde's nod. "Oh man. Your poor parents."

"Nah. We weren't all that bad. Hell, I was every parent's wet dream." Rachel chuckled, an evil twinkle in her green eyes. "I did no wrong — no smoking, no drinking, no sex; in fact I was a total prude. It was pretty sad."

"Really? Quite the good girl, huh?"

"*Too* good. I was extremely self-righteous." Rachel laughed, lowering herself until the water was up to her shoulders, enjoying the coolness on her skin. "It was pretty bad."

Denny smiled, lying back on her rock in the sun. "I was evil. My father has a head full of gray hair, and I think I gave him every one. I finally got a clue in my early twenties. Or more likely, I was of age and on my own, so acting out wasn't as fun anymore." They both laughed at that, then a companionable silence enveloped them. After allowing Rachel some time to perform her ablutions, Denny put voice to a question rolling around in her head for over a week.

"What do you think happened?"

Rachel didn't have to ask Denny what she meant. She climbed out of the cool water, allowing it to fall from her flesh in sprinkled waves. Tugging on her underwear and bra, Rachel climbed onto a rock similar to Denny's. Finally she answered. "I've wondered about that, too. I think it must have been engine failure or something like that."

"Does that happen in this day and age?" Denny glanced over at Rachel, trying not to notice the woman's beautiful body, basically naked as her wet underwear was virtually see-through.

"I don't know." Rachel shook her head slightly, staring up into the sky.

Denny interrupted the melancholy thoughts clear on Rachel's face. "I hate the nightmares I have now. It's like they chase me, you know?" She glanced over to meet Rachel's gaze and saw the blonde's nod.

When Rachel spoke, her voice was soft, filled with compassionate understanding. "I do understand." She looked into Denny's eyes.

"So, does anyone else realize who you are?" Denny cracked a grin, which the blonde returned, though it was incredibly shy. Rachel looked back to the sky, presenting her profile to the brunette.

"I don't think so. I haven't said anything and I don't intend to." She glanced quickly at Denny, conveying all she needed to with a flash of her green eyes. Denny chuckled again, nodding her understanding.

"Oh, by the way," Rachel said absently, closing her eyes as she soaked in the day, "I got a fire started."

Goddamn, what I wouldn't do for my Stetson. Michael stood on the rock, feet spread wide as he studied the shallow pool of seawater below. He clenched his hands, feeling the slight edge of his fingernails biting into the rough palms of his large hands and then he stretched his fingers again. The sun beat down on his head, his scalp burning, and the rays on the glittering water were almost blinding as he had been staring into them for the past hour. He let out a war cry as he pounced on a long, silver fish that swam into the pool as the tide came back in and filled the small water pit.

"Shit!" he exclaimed as the squirming fish got away from him. Again. With a heavy sigh, he took his place again, stance wide and ready.

"Do you realize just how much easier that would be if you had a spear?" Dean asked from where he lounged on the beach.

"When you can do better, you let me know," the Texan said between clenched teeth, never taking his eyes off the pool as he waited for the tide to come in again.

"Jesus, Michael!" Dean exclaimed. "You've been at this for an hour, like some sort of Neanderthal or something. You're never going to catch anything that way."

Michael had heard just enough out of the lazy bastard's mouth. He whirled on the man, hands clenched into fists. He was pissed enough at not being able to catch anything, and the little fruit sitting on his flaming ass was doing absolutely *nothing!* "Listen here, you little queer, keep your fuckin' mouth shut or I'll shut it for ya!"

"What did you call me?" Dean got to his feet.

"I ain't got no use for fairies, so stay clear, boy." Michael's growl made his intent clear. He over-topped Dean by a good five inches, and used that to good effect, squaring his wide shoulders. The paler man was small beside the linebacker-sized mechanic.

"Give it your best shot, Bubba."

"You little bastard!"

"Hey! Stop it!" Pam ran down the beach and threw herself between the two men, a hand on each of their chests. Michael fought the urge to throw the vet aside and go after his target. She looked from one to the other. "What the hell is the matter with you guys? Jesus! The redneck and the queer." She laughed wryly. "It sounds like a bad sitcom."

Michael took a step back and Pam's hand dropped away from him. He took several deep breaths, muscles in his jaw bulging with the effort of restraint. Dean brushed himself off, also taking a slight step back from the older woman, his eyes never leaving the Texan.

"Now, either you boys kiss and make up, or stay on opposite sides of the island. I'm sick of pulling you two apart." Michael glared at her words. "It's a form of speech, Michael! For crying out loud!"

He said nothing, just turned and walked back to his fishing hole, hands clenching and unclenching at his sides, muttering about fairies and fruit flies.

Dean held his chin higher, his pride in tatters, but he wasn't about to let that son of a bitch know that. "Thank you, Pam," he said softly, then turned and disappeared into the foliage, memories of too many locker room encounters and beatings flowing through his mind.

Mia grunted lightly as she stretched her body out as far as possible, trying, trying, trying... "Gotcha!" She reeled in her prize, nearly losing her balance and falling ass over appetite off the rock ledge on which she was perched so precariously. Dragging herself and the heavy suitcase back to safe ground, Mia panted with exertion. She set the large, heavy Samsonite alongside another bag that had drifted to shore, making sure there were no more in sight.

Licking her lips, the teen plopped down on her butt and crossed her legs under herself. The first bag, which looked to be most likely a carry-on, was the type with a roller board, though three of the four plastic wheels were missing and the fourth wheel was cracked. The handle was broken off and jagged. The girl tugged it toward her, grunting; it was waterlogged and heavy. She looked for any sort of identification. Not that it mattered, but she wanted to be able to send up a thanks in her prayers that night.

The zipper was intact, but its teeth were jammed. Mia tugged at it, the slippery metal persistently slipping out from between her fingers. She managed to open a small space, but no further. Leaning down, her dark eyes peered into the shadowy depths of the bag, and saw nothing. She looked around her and spotted a low twig on a nearby tree. Hurrying over to it, she plucked it off and sat back down in front of the bag, jamming the stick into the small opening and using it for leverage.

It took nearly ten minutes for Mia to get the bag unzipped, but finally the zipper teeth gave and the she flipped the top open, excited about what she might find. Inside she found layers of soggy clothing. It had been two weeks, and all of them were shedding clothing day by day, or cutting up what they had. The heat made pants impractical, and shirts and undergarments were getting unbearable, even after soaking and rinsing them. The clothing in this suitcase, that of a stranger, would mean the world to the castaways.

Mia removed the first layer, unwadding it and stretching it out. A t-shirt. A very *large* t-shirt. Setting it aside, the girl brought out the next treasure — a large pair of men's briefs, followed by what would have been socks, but were now soaked, stretched blobs of material. The bottom of the bag was lined with wet magazines, no longer recognizable, the pages sticking together, images and writing one big black smudge. She set those aside, unsure whether or not they could be used for anything. Perhaps kindling, once they dried. She moved aside a few more articles of clothing, and some items that were no longer identifiable, and then her eyes went wide. Tucked in an inside pocket was a cache of chocolate, still wrapped, which for some reason had been put into Ziploc baggies, and so had been kept safe and dry.

"Eureka," she whispered, holding the chocolate up for inspection. They'd been eating what they could, coconuts and the tiny bananas, and fish when Michael could catch one. Mia had already begun to drop weight, and she could see the results of the limited fare in her companions' faces, too. The girl realized the treasure she held in her hands, and frantically tore into the baggie, ripping it in her haste. The smell of chocolate rose to her nose, and her dark eyes closed as a soft moan escaped her lips.

Mia found it ironic, since she'd never been one for chocolate or sweets, but never in her life had anything tasted so good. She stuffed a square into her mouth, eyes squeezing shut as it melted against her tongue, taste exploding in her mouth. She eyed the rest of the big bar, but knew she couldn't eat it all. A place with no toilet paper wasn't one where she wanted to get sick.

Reluctantly setting the chocolate aside, Mia turned back to the bag. Checking the other zippered pockets, she was astonished to find a razor and... Eyes wide, Mia realized she was looking at another Ziploc baggie with the greatest treasure of all.

"Soap!"

Mia was tearing down the beach, waving something in her hands. Dean and Denny looked over at the girl from where they worked on their giant S.O.S. bonfire stack.

"What the hell is she yelling about?" Dean asked, seeing the brunette shake her head as she stood from where she'd been kneeling, rearranging the wood.

"Look!" Mia was waving something enthusiastically over her head and nearly fell over Dean in her excitement. He steadied her, now as curious as all get out. "Look!" she said again, showing them the baggie.

"Oh," Dean sighed, falling to his knees. It was almost as if someone had just shown him the most beautiful piece of art. His hands flew to his mouth, eyes unable to leave the precious object the girl held in her palm. He leaned in, closing his eyes as he inhaled the scent of Irish Spring, a soap which he didn't even like, but at that moment it was the most fabulous thing in the world.

For her part, Denny had visions of clean hair. She shook the thoughts out to get a clear head. "Where did you find this?" she asked Mia, stepping closer to the girl, eyes never leaving the bar of soap.

"Some luggage drifted to shore, over there." She pointed toward the smallest and rockiest of the three beaches.

"You're shitting me!" Denny stared as Mia shook her head. "Show me."

"While you're gone..." Dean snatched the soap from Mia's hand, greed written all over his handsome face.

"I'll hold onto that," Denny growled, snatching the soap back. She knew full well they'd never see the soap again if Dean got hold of it. He followed behind grudgingly as Mia led the small parade up the rock face to her spot where the two pieces of luggage still sat, awaiting exploration.

Denny fell to her knees, looking through the pile of clothing Mia had already removed from the smaller bag. No longer seeing it as clothing, she was deciding what could be done with the material. Where they were, other than the proverbial fig leaf, clothing wasn't much of a necessity. In the past week the rest of the crew had started to follow her lead, dispensing with various articles of clothing, walking around in only the bare essentials. The men were bare chested and the women in their bras or undershirts. Only Rachel kept her pants. Denny hated wearing only her underwear, and figured the large shirt would make a great sarong.

"Hey, look!" Dean exclaimed from his spot beside the larger of the two bags. He held up a very realistic cyberskin dildo, waving it proudly over his head.

Denny nearly fell over backwards in surprise, then was overtaken by belly laughter, which did make her fall over when she saw the look on Mia's face. The girl's innocent naiveté revealed itself as she first looked confused, then perplexed, then curious, then turned an amazing shade of red as realization dawned on her. Dean joined in the laughter as the girl hurried down the rocks, deeply embarrassed.

Rachel's eyes were narrowed, a slight wrinkle forming in her brow. When Rachel cursed softly, Pam glanced, watching her fingers for a moment before turning back to her own project.

"How are you getting the weave so tight?" Rachel finally asked.

Pam reached over and took Rachel's piece from her. "Watch."

As Rachel paid close attention again, Pam's nimble fingers wove the long, strong blades of wild grass together, the hold tight in neat little green squares. *Okay, I can do this.* She took the bit back from the doctor, studying the intricate weave, ready to give it another try.

"No. Rachel, it won't keep anything out if it's not tight enough."
Pam was getting exasperated with the blonde. *Why isn't she getting it?
It isn't that hard.*

"Damn. I can't get this!" Clearly Rachel's own patience was
running thin. "I'm not stupid," she muttered, "I got an 'A' in Home
Economics."

Pam chuckled, feeling some of her own tension disperse with
Rachel's rising frustration. She looked up to see Denny heading their
way, a finger held to her lips. The coffee shop owner snuck up behind
Rachel, a piece of chocolate held between her fingers. She leaned over
Rachel, bringing the treat close to her nose, but out of her sight.

Rachel's brow furrowed at the smell, and she looked over at Pam,
seeing a snicker on the older woman's face. Looking back over her own
shoulder, Rachel saw Denny standing behind her with a grin on her
face, the chocolate square extended.

Rachel flew to her knees, facing Denny and snatching the
chocolate away. "Where did this come from?" she asked, popping it into
her mouth, eyes closing in pleasure.

"Mia found luggage. Come on, ladies. We've got a nice little
treasure trove."

Rachel was on her feet in an instant — anything to get away from
weaving the roof! She followed Denny to the beach, where Dean and
Mia were looking over a display of what looked to be garage sale items.

"Does anyone know where Michael is?"

"Who cares," Dean muttered, fingering a pair of shorts he had his
eye on.

"I'll find him," Pam offered, heading into the brush.

Rachel plopped down into the sand, leaning back on her hands,
legs crossed at the ankles. She had wondered if anything would wash
up, and was surprised it had taken so long. She studied those around
her, noting their varied reactions to Mia's tremendous find. She
glanced over at Denny, the brunette pulling her long hair back away
from her neck and back. She looked hot, her cheeks flushed.

As green eyes scanned back over the items laid out before them,
something caught her eye. Rachel slowly sat up, then got to her knees,
crawling over to one of the bags. The burst of laughter was so quick, it
startled Denny, who had been lost in her own world.

Using a sock as a glove, Rachel grabbed the dildo, holding it up to
study it more closely. She eyed the attorney and her green eyes began to
twinkle. "Dean, you really should put your toy away. After all, we *do*
have minors here." The red flush on Dean's face was priceless, as was
Denny's bark of laughter.

With the quick rebuttal that was the bread and butter of every
attorney, Dean tossed back, "I don't know, blondie, it looks more your
size than mine."

Denny was astounded, a perma-grin on her face as her eyes went from one to the other.

"Hmm, I dunno," Rachel flicked the end of the dong, amused as it bounced back, setting off a new round of laughter. "I'm not sure if it's man enough for me."

"What's going on?" Pam asked, stepping out of the jungle with Michael in tow.

Rachel, feeling rather feisty for some reason, held up the toy. "Dean has been enthralling us with tales of the sword."

Dean gasped, flying across the pile of stuff between him and Rachel, snatching the dildo out of the blonde's hands. "I have *not!*"

"Fuckin' queers," Michael muttered, walking over to stand between Mia and Rachel. When someone cleared their throat, he turned and he found himself toe to toe with Denny.

"Excuse me?"

He looked into her angry gaze, surprised and confused. His mouth opened then closed, then opened again. The brunette cut him off before he could say anything.

"I don't appreciate that, Michael."

"What? I was talking about Dean—"

"Yeah, well I'm a *queer*, too, so keep your mouth shut. Okay?" She stared up at him, unflinching, waiting for his response. His eyes widened, surprise and shame filling them. "We all have to live here together, so how about if we stop with the name calling?"

Duly chastised, the Texan's head fell. No, he didn't like fairies, but he did like Denny and respected her. He wasn't going to apologize for his views, so instead he gave the brunette a submissive nod and turned and walked away, sitting off by himself.

Rachel had watched the entire thing, which had taken place less than three feet from her. She had been shocked at Michael's behavior, as well as Denny's revelation.

Everyone was quiet, the air tense. No one was entirely sure what to do. The mirth from earlier was certainly gone. Dean merely sat silent, watching, waiting, almost holding his breath. He met Denny's gaze, a small smile of kinship curving his lips. She didn't return it, but nodded in acknowledgement.

"Okay," Pam said, clapping her hands together to clear the air. "What have we here?" She began to pick through the items from the suitcase.

Denny sat back, watching as everyone talked over what to do with the most important items — soap, razor, brush, as well as three toothbrushes and a single tube of Crest. The way everyone's eyes lit up at these items, the brunette knew the allotment of these cherished toiletries could be difficult. Desperate situations were cause for desperate acts, and though everyone seemed to get along for the most part, those items were gold on the island and would disappear.

Pam seemed to be reading Denny's mind. "Who gets to be in charge of all this stuff?" She looked from one person to the next, everyone meeting her gaze then that of their neighbor.

"I suggest a vote," Rachel said softly, once again leaning casually back on her hands.

"Agreed." Pam nodded. "Rachel, who's your vote?"

The blonde chewed on her bottom lip for a moment, thinking about her choice. She had a name echoing in the back of her head, but looked at each individual person first, to make sure she didn't want to change her mind. Finally her gaze settled on the coffee shop owner. "I vote for Denny. She's proven trustworthy and she gets along with everyone here."

"I second that," Mia quietly chimed in.

"I think it should be me," Dean said. "I think the women would use it up, since they have longer hair. They have a motive to hold onto it."

"Thanks, Dean." Rachel tossed the dildo at him, nearly hitting him in the head with it.

"Michael?" Pam asked, turning to the Texan, who was playing with the sand at his feet.

He glanced up, meeting her gaze. "I'm fine with it being Denny. I don't want ya'll barkin' at my door for soap."

Shocked, Denny looked at each of them, not sure if she wanted the responsibility.

"Okay. Denny it is."

Too late. All eyes on her, the brunette nodded reluctantly. "Okay."

Later, Denny sat up on one of the many rock ledges, looking over the ocean as she dried. She'd taken a bath with soap for the first time in two weeks, and had brushed her teeth. She was a happy camper. For the most part. She knew it was silly to let Michael's comments get to her, but she couldn't help it. She'd heard about his and Dean's near fight the week before, but just let it go. This time she'd heard Michael's bigotry, and had seen the disdain in his eyes. She liked the Texan, even respected him, yet he obviously didn't feel the same.

"Tube of toothpaste for your thoughts," Rachel said softly, moving to sit beside the brunette.

Denny glanced over at her and gave her a smile before looking back out to sea. "My thoughts aren't worth an entire tube. Maybe a squeeze."

"Are you okay?" Rachel asked.

"It's pretty stupid, really. Not sure it's worth talking about."

"If it's upsetting you, then it's worth talking about."

"What Michael said..."

"Bothered you?" Denny nodded. "I'm sorry. I had no idea you were gay. I think everyone knew about Dean, but..."

"What? They didn't realize I was a big, bad butch?" Denny smiled at Rachel's shy grin. The blonde shook her head and turned away. "Yeah, I don't exactly telegraph it, do I? Not now, anyway. You should have seen me when I was younger — spiked hair, torn clothes, the whole thing. Boots." She chuckled at the girl she used to be — the true rebel without a clue.

"Do you hear that kind of stuff a lot? Disparaging remarks and names?"

"Not to me personally anymore. But I hear them, and it hurts." Denny was silent for a moment, deciding whether she wanted to go any further. Rachel's quiet acceptance won her over, and she decided to talk it out fully. "When I was in my late teens, I dated a guy I went to school with. When I was out with him, kissing him, whatever, I had my best friend in mind. I'd see her face, pretend it was her I was kissing, all that. Hell, sometimes I think it was the only thing that got me through the make-out sessions. I used to keep a diary, wrote about her all the time." Denny's voice fell to almost a whisper. "I was so in love with her."

Rachel listened, glancing at the brunette from time to time, taking it all in.

"Then one day my brother was snooping and read what I'd written in my diary. And I quote, 'I really, really, REALLY want to have sex with Casey.' He told my parents, and my dad beat me with a belt and kicked me out."

"Oh, Denny," Rachel breathed.

"I was in my room trying to recover when he walked in, a roll of trash bags in his hand. He slammed them down on my dresser top and simply said 'get out.'" Denny's eyes filled at the memory. It had been a long time ago, but her heart had never healed. She blinked several times, trying to make the physical manifestation of her hurt go away. Rachel said nothing, but placed her warm palm against the warmer skin of Denny's back, rubbing soft circles. "He used to call me 'queer' all the time."

"What about your mother?"

"She let him do it, all of it. After he told me to get out, I marched into the kitchen where they were — him at the breakfast bar, her at the counter — her back was toward me as she kept making coffee. I just ignored him, and I told her that if she let him do this, she'd never hear from me or see me again. She didn't say anything." Denny swiped at a tear that had fallen. "Not a damn word. I turned around, headed right back to my room, and started packing."

"Where did you go?"

"I escaped to a friend's house for the weekend, then moved in with my grandmother until graduation. After that, I got my own place and moved on."

The smile with which Denny graced Rachel was big and bright, and full of shit. Denny knew the blonde could see right through it, yet Rachel reached out. "Come here."

Denny allowed herself to be enveloped in a warm hug, the feel of Rachel's skin against her own a balm to her sad, lonely soul. The situation was getting to her. At first it had almost been like an adventure, a vacation from reality. Now, as time was going by, it was dawning on her it was no vacation she could just check out of and take a flight home. She was truly stuck, stranded. She couldn't return to her life, return to Hannah, her shop, none of it.

Rachel rested her head against Denny's shoulder, surprised she'd taken such initiative. Even so, she had to admit, though the hug was intended to comfort Denny, Rachel found it comforting as well. She felt lost in so many ways. Her life back home had been in a state of upheaval. Even if she returned to Oregon tomorrow, what would she return to? She couldn't return to her marriage and pretend everything was okay. Rachel had the feeling no matter what she went back to, no matter what state her personal life was in, after this experience, she'd never be the same. She was a changed woman on so many levels.

They sat for a long time, watching the sun go down and absorbing the simple pleasure of human comfort, affection, and mutual understanding.

Chapter 7

Hannah Donnelly sighed as she opened the strongbox that had been hidden on the top shelf of the closet in the master bedroom. With shaking hands, she inserted the key into the tiny lock and turned it with a small pop. The lid was heavy, and squeaked slightly on its hinges. Inside she saw some bank papers, the velvet box in which she kept her grandmother's ring, and the very edge of some currency. Slowly pushing the bank papers aside, Hannah saw the money come into view. Her hand went to her mouth as she remembered so well what it was for.

"Here, we'll put the big bills in here," Denny had explained, taking the four one hundred dollar bills from Hannah and tossing them inside the strongbox. She grinned at her partner. "That way we won't be tempted, and can save."

Hannah slowly lowered herself to the bed, eyes never leaving the money. She reached inside the strongbox, taking the bills out and holding them in her palm. They had just counted them three weeks ago — seven hundred and fifty dollars.

"See? There's our souvenir money!"

Hannah remembered how the baby blues had twinkled at Denny's declaration. It was for their annual trip to Disney World, a place to which they were both addicted. They had each started taking at least fifty dollars from every paycheck so they wouldn't have to pay for the trip on their credit card, as they had just about gotten it paid off.

Crumpling the money in her fist, Hannah brought her hands to her face, the tears flowing again. She had been looking for Denny's insurance papers, and instead found yet another piece of her partner, something else to remind her of her loss. She was haunted by the all too brief phone call — grateful for it, and yet hearing Denny's panicked voice in her head again and again.

"Han..a! ...annah, ...d, thank God. Hon...y, ...ove ...ou! Something...wrong."

"What? I can't understand you." Hannah felt her stomach twist as it was gripped in fear. *"What?"*

Then strangely, clear as day, "I love you! Always know that."

And then the line went dead.

Sniffling and wiping her eyes with her sleeve, Hannah set the money aside and turned back to the strongbox, pursuing her original objective. Grabbing a handful of papers, she thumbed through them, having to read the forms sometimes two or three times as her concentration was shot. Finally finding what she sought, Hannah tugged the folded forms out of their envelope and shook them open, smoothing out the creases. As she read the legal talk and terms, Hannah felt her stomach roil. No amount of money meant anything. All she wanted was to have Denny back.

"Damn you, Denny!" she cried, throwing the forms off the bed and then sending the strongbox to follow them. Rage radiated through every cell and made her tremble. She was angry at Denny, angry at the cousins in Milan who asked her to visit, angry at the pilot, and angry at God.

Will glanced down at the directions again, looking for the number of the exit that would take him to Warwick, Massachusetts. He found it, flicked the turn signal on the rented car, and made his way through the sleepy coastal town. He checked out the small, quaint houses and easy life of a Saturday afternoon.

Davies' Hangar was supposed to be just up ahead, and as Will took a left on Carlton Place, he saw a sign for it, and also saw a low flying airplane buzz overhead. He followed it as it crossed the general area, then took a sharp right toward the runway, undoubtedly about to land. Pulling up beside an old pick up truck, Will turned off the engine.

As Will stepped into the cool, air conditioned front office of the hangar, he was greeted by a redheaded woman with stylish glasses. "Good morning. Can I help you?" she said cheerfully.

"Will Ash. I have an appointment with Garrison Davies."

"Ash, Ash," the woman muttered, clicking her computer mouse a few times and then absently pushing her glasses further up onto her nose.

"Hey, Penny, is my ten o'clock here yet?" a woman's voice asked, heading over to the coffee machine near the redhead's desk. The blonde woman, dressed casually in old, worn jeans and a t-shirt, poured herself a cup, nearly burning her mouth on her first careful sip when she saw the good looking man speaking with her secretary.

"Yeah, that's him," said the redhead, smirking at the rolled green eyes of her employer and long-time friend. She decided to keep her usual flirting to a minimum with the suit standing in front of her.

"Will Ash," he said, taking the few steps to the pilot, hand held out.

"Garrison Davies. Care for some coffee, Mr. Ash?"

"Uh, no, thank you."

"Okey doke. Follow me."

Will followed the petite woman down a long, narrow hall, solid wall to the right, large windows looking out into an all cement hangar to the left. A couple of small planes were in the large space, and a few men hurried around, barking orders and laughing at each other.

"After you." Garrison smiled at her guest, waiting for him to enter the small office that had been her father's before he'd died ten years earlier. Will straightened his tie and jacket before sitting stiffly in the avocado green metal and vinyl chair, crossing one ankle over his other knee. "So," Garrison flopped down in the squeaky chair behind the desk, her focus on the man across from her, "what can I do for you?"

"As I explained on the phone, my partner Dean was on Flight 1049, the one that went down a month ago. Airline and NTSB officials won't give me much to work with, other than that it went down somewhere in the Atlantic. The plane experienced a systems failure, which in turn caused the plane to turn woefully off course from its filed flight plan."

Garrison nodded, sitting back in her chair and rocking slightly. She remembered hearing the story about the plane that had taken off from BUF. She had used the airport several times over the years in her cargo business and knew it well.

"The Coast Guard and every other official agency have done what they could, but I want more."

"What kind of 'more'?"

"There were three survivors, Miss Davies—"

"Garrison."

"...and I believe there were others."

"Why do you believe that?" The pilot sipped from her coffee, absently brushing a few strands of golden hair out of her eyes.

"Well—"

"Garrison?"

Both looked at the door and the teenage girl that stood in the doorway. Her blonde, curly hair fell into her eyes — big, blue eyes — looking from Garrison to her visitor.

"Oh, I'm sorry!"

"It's okay. What's up, Parker?"

"Can I go? Did you talk to Keller?"

"We did talk about it, and you can, but you *will* be home by ten!" Garrison held up a single finger to emphasize her edict. The girl, no older than fifteen, squealed, launching herself at the seated pilot for a tight hug, then with an apologetic smile to Will, she bounded back out of the room. "Sorry. My daughter." Will raised an eyebrow indicating his disbelief that Garrison was old enough to have a daughter that age. "Long story." The pilot grinned, waving it off. "Continue."

His throat suddenly dry, Will swallowed, now wishing he had accepted the offer of coffee. He knew what he was about to tell the pilot was crazy, he didn't actually understand it himself, but he refused to let his nervousness show. Sounding confident and believing every word he said, Will met Garrison's frank gaze. "My gut tells me Dean is still alive. I can't explain it, but I can't accept the lame answers I've been given."

Garrison Davies studied the man for some time, gauging his sincerity. What she saw in his eyes was an intelligent man who knew what he was asking. She thought about it for a moment, thinking — *what if it were Keller out there, lost at sea?* And with their business, that *could* happen. Would she ever give up looking for her, or for Parker? *Not on your life.*

"All right, Will. I'll try and help you."

For the first time during their meeting, Will Ash's composure slipped and his hands came up to rub his face, deep shuddering breaths hidden behind them. Finally his hands landed in his lap, and he smiled. "Thank you, Garrison. Thank you."

"Here."

Reenie accepted the cup of coffee and, as she raised it to her lips, she smelled the touch of bourbon Beth had put in it. The tall actress sat down, immediately curling her legs up under her. She took a small drink from her own mug, wincing as the hot liquid burned her mouth. Cursing under her breath, Beth set her mug aside, turning to face Reenie.

"How did your meeting go?"

Reenie sighed, blowing over the black surface of her drink. "It went okay. Rachel's lawyer wants to see Matt and me next week. Time Warner is going to continue to publish any of her work that is still under contractual agreement, including reissuing some of her older novels. You know, cash in on this whole thing. Typical." Reenie sighed again, running a hand through her short hair, making it stick up in random places.

Beth snickered as she reached over and smoothed some of it back into place. "Is her lawyer here?"

Reenie shook her head as she swallowed. "No. I'll be heading to Oregon." She was silent for a moment and then looked over at her friend studying the toe of her colorful sock. "Beth?"

"Hmm?"

"I'm sorry I missed your opening night the other day. I read the reviews. They said that Pippa kicked some serious ass on that stage." She smiled at Beth's shy acceptance of the congratulations.

"It's a fun role. I wish you could have been there, but don't worry about it. I know you've got a lot going on right now." She smiled at the woman sitting next to her. "Don't sweat it, 'kay?"

Reenie smiled at the absolution. "Okay." Taking a deep breath, she pushed herself up from the couch. "I'm going to bed." She leaned over and placed a gentle kiss on Beth's cheek, then brushed her fingers across it with a soft smile. "'Night."

"Good night, Reen. Sleep well."

Reenie disappeared behind the closed door of her bedroom. Setting her coffee mug on the dresser, Reenie stepped out of her clothes, leaving them where they lay on the floor, before grabbing the mug again and climbing into the huge bed. She reached over to turn off the bedside lamp, but thought better of it. She knew her mind was still far too awake to allow her to sleep, even with the bourbon that warmed her. Her mind was racing, events and thoughts from the past weeks swirling.

Matt had gone home two days ago, and Reenie couldn't help but want to cry at the memory of his face, the look in his eyes. That first night he'd shown up, they'd talked late into the night. He had admitted his weakness, as well as his confusion where Rachel was concerned. He didn't understand why she had shut him out so completely, never allowing him to truly see inside her. He shyly admitted that even when they made love, Rachel's thoughts had seemed to be miles away.

"I have no excuse for what I did, Reenie, but I've given it a lot of thought, and as crazy and pathetic as it sounds, I think I really just needed attention."

At first Reenie had wanted to scoff at his words, throw accusations at him, but in fairness, the logical side of her mind knew he was right. Reenie knew Rachel well, and though she loved her friend very much, she didn't always understand her. Hell, sometimes Reenie felt Rachel shut *her* out. Though she would never condone what Matt had done, she and Matt had come to an understanding that night, something they hadn't been able to do in the years they'd known each other.

Reenie's thoughts settled back on Rachel. Her tears had dried up over the weeks, but she still felt the loss acutely. Rachel didn't get to New York to see her as often as they both would have liked, and Reenie knew her own schedule was beyond ridiculous, so the chances of her getting to Oregon to visit were slim to none. Still, they had swapped daily emails and called each other every couple of days, if only to talk for a few minutes.

With Rachel missing, Reenie had to stop herself more than once from picking up the phone and dialing the numbers more familiar to her than her own. One time she actually *had* picked up the phone, dissolving in a puddle of tears when she realized her folly. In that moment she wanted to hate Matt, to blame him for Rachel's death, but then she'd taken a deep breath and grudgingly admitted to herself Rachel had been planning the trip to Milan anyway. The situation with Matt had just sped up the process.

"Damn you, Rachel."

Chapter 8

The hut, if it could be called that, was tiny, barely large enough for the four women to stretch out. They'd woven together enough fronds to create a sturdy skin which wrapped around the trunks of six trees in a near-perfect hexagon, thus creating the walls. Rachel and Pam wove the thatched roof together, each proudly examining their creation every chance they got. The roof, along with the foliage overhead, helped to keep them dry, but it still got cold at night. Each man had his own tiny hut, radically different from that of the women in both style and practicality.

Denny was alone at the moment, giving her the opportunity to take out her stolen prize. As the designated keeper of the soap, she knew she had nevertheless abused her position by hoarding something else, even though it was for a good cause. She hoped she'd done the right thing.

Glancing quickly out the tent-like flap, she ensured that she was still alone and then crawled to the corner of the hut, digging quickly, like a dog, with the dirt flying backwards between her spread legs. She uncovered a stiff edge, and carefully tugged until it was completely free of its hiding place. A smaller object followed. Denny looked at it, turning it in her fingers then licking the tip and pressing it across her palm.

"Yes!" she whispered as it made a mark. She gathered her treasures and crawled out of the flap into the humid evening. She needed to talk to Rachel, and knew just where to find her.

Rachel lay on the rock ledge overlooking the ocean, her favorite spot. It wasn't far from the waterfall, and she liked to dry on the ledge after bathing. Bathing. That was an exercise in patience. The bar of soap Mia had found in the baggage nearly a month ago was gone. Everyone was trying not to throw tantrums when they had to go back to just rinsing off. Rachel swore she had smelled a rather minty Dean the other day, and wondered if he'd decided to use his allotted toothpaste ration for deodorant instead.

Smiling at the visual that engendered, green eyes closed, absorbing the smells and humidity around her. Up on that ledge, by herself, Rachel found peace, which amazingly enough, was difficult to find in paradise. Most often, she just felt lost. Every day was a struggle, mostly an emotional one. Everyone felt the weight of time running out. It was a small island, and the resources they had located were limited. They had no medical supplies, and even Pam's years as a vet couldn't bring about magical cures. *What if one of them became seriously ill? Or hurt?*

Rachel tried to stave off these thoughts; they added a heavier weight to her heart, and she had no outlet. That, for her, was the most difficult thing to face. Back home, she dealt with anything and everything because she had her writing. She'd vent her frustrations or joys in her work. She had always seen her incredibly fertile imagination as a blessing and a gift, but now it was becoming a curse. Now, her inventive mind was stifled. She created constantly in her mind, always weaving ideas and visuals together, but now they were just crowding together and causing an impassable information jam that sometimes made her want to cry. Characters and circumstances-to-be-written woke her up in the middle of the night, each vying for attention and their place in her conscious mind.

Frustration was causing Rachel to become withdrawn and angry. It was almost like constipation of the imagination — a swarm of ideas, but absolutely no way to get them out. She was even getting desperate enough to turn into a sort of bard, muttering to herself as she walked through the jungle, whacking at the foliage with the hatchet they'd made from the random golf club in a piece of washed up luggage. Sometimes she was tempted to tell her tales during the quiet time the six spent together almost every night, a fire made in their permanent fire ring at the center of the beach, not far from the pyramid of logs ready to be lit for an emergency beacon. Somehow, Rachel couldn't bring herself to do that, to open that part of her to them. Sure, millions of readers had read her thoughts, ideas, and imaginings, but they were the nameless, faceless millions.

Rachel Holt's air of cool aloofness, her hallmark to those in her industry, was actually a façade protecting a shy, vulnerable woman. She injured easily, and so took refuge behind the closed doors of privacy and silence.

The blonde was drawn from her thoughts when she heard movement in the foliage below and the slithering of pebbles down the side of the rock ledge. Pushing up on an elbow, Rachel looked over the side, seeing the top of a dark head as Denny climbed up to her.

She liked Denny; the woman always had an easy smile for everyone. She also made Rachel feel comfortable. Not many people could do that. Rachel smiled, scooting to make room as Denny sat beside her.

"Hi," Denny said.

"Hey." Rachel nodded out toward the setting sun. "Beautiful, huh?"

"It really is."

"What's everyone up to?" Rachel asked, glancing over at her companion.

"Uh, lemme see." Denny sighed. "Dean and Mia were eating seconds of the fish Michael *finally* caught." They both sniggered at that. "And Pam, not sure. Michael was out swimming last I saw." She glanced at Rachel's profile. "You okay?"

"Yeah. Fine. Just needed some 'me' time."

"Oh, shit. Want me to—"

"No." Rachel met her gaze briefly then looked away. "No. You're fine."

"Well, good, 'cause I brought you something."

Based on something from a page in her own life, Denny had a gut instinct about Rachel's increasing self-imposed isolation. One of her employees, Amy Tella, was an artist, and always carried a sketchpad around with her. More than once Denny had busted her for drawing in the back room of DeRisio's. Amy had told her if she couldn't create, she couldn't breathe. Denny wagered Rachel was the same way.

Almost giddy at giving her offerings to Rachel, Denny smiled broadly. "Don't tell anyone, but I've been taking advantage of the powers vested in me." She chuckled at Rachel's look of confusion. Without another word, she produced the two pens she'd found in one of the suitcases, and the pages of the ruined magazine, which she'd left to bleach in the sun for a week. Now, pages stiff and a yellowish-white, they were a crude tablet, but would work.

Rachel's eyes fell to Denny's hands. Green eyes grew huge when she realized what the gift was. "Denny!" she breathed, a hand going to her mouth. Her gaze flickered to pleased blue eyes. "You hid this from the others?" she said, half in awe, half in suspicion.

"What are they going to do with it, write letters to stick in bottles? Come on, Rachel. We don't have any bottles." She winked then was nearly bowled off the rock ledge by the enthusiastic embrace of the grateful author. Denny hugged Rachel back, pleased her gift had been so well received.

When Rachel pulled away, she tried to smile through her tears. Clear to Denny, the author was deeply touched. "I think this is the most wonderful gift anyone has ever given me." She looked down at the pens — one black, one red — and the stiff, parchment-like paper in her other hand.

"I assumed, I mean, I know you're a writer, and haven't been able to write, and..."

"That wasn't a bad assumption, Denny. Ironically enough, before you climbed up here, I was thinking about just how antsy I was getting. Hell, I was about ready to start writing in the sand."

Denny chuckled at the image. "Forget the S.O.S. then. You just write us a novel on the beach and an overhead plane will spot it."

"Yeah, then with our luck, they'd get so into trying to figure out what it says, they'd crash, too." They both sobered at the thought then smiled guiltily. "That was bad." But the bit of wry humor gave Rachel the chance to get her emotions under control. "You know, it's funny —

since we've been here, my emotions have been all over the map. Either I'm hugely moody and just this side of tears, or I feel numb."

"I know what you mean." Denny pulled her knees up and wrapped her arms around them. "At first I thought it was because I was so close to my period." She grinned at Rachel's shocked expression. "What? Haven't you noticed that you can always tell which one of us is on the rag?"

The blonde grinned, her eyes twinkling. "Because the lucky party hides out in the jungle for at least three days, and suddenly the larger leaves start disappearing by the bushel?"

"That would be why. I will never, *ever* complain about a tampon again."

"Amen to that."

They were quiet for a moment before Denny spoke up. "Rachel?"

"Mm?"

"Do you think we'll ever get back?"

Rachel saw the troubled expression in Denny's eyes and wished she could soothe it away, but instead, she shook her head slowly. "I don't know, Denny. I just don't know."

They were silent for a long time, each woman lost in thought. At one point Rachel thought Denny had fallen asleep, but then her smooth, low voice cut the silence.

"What will you write about? Do you have a story idea?"

"Always." Rachel grinned. "Seriously," she insisted, at Denny's look of doubt. "Even when I'm working on a particular novel, I'm always fighting with myself to keep other ideas tamped down and out of the way."

"Do you write those ideas down? Like to use at some other time?"

"Nah." The author tapped her head. "It's all in here. My emotions drive me, and my emotions and moods, which are seriously intertwined, change from moment to moment. Drives my husband crazy."

"No doubt. How long you been married?"

"Four years."

Denny noticed the change in the blonde's voice, but said nothing about it. "I once saw a picture of you two in a magazine. Handsome guy."

"Yeah, he is."

Denny was surprised at the flat tone of Rachel's voice. If they were talking about Hannah right now, she'd be lit up like a Christmas tree. She waited for Rachel to elaborate, but nothing more was said for a few moments.

"What about you, Denny? Are you married...or at least the equivalent?" Rachel straightened her legs and laid back on the ledge, one knee bent, the other leg outstretched. She rested the paper and pen beside her and folded her hands behind her head.

"Yeah." Denny's grin was huge, nearly splitting her face, but it quickly faded and she turned sad. "Hannah. We've been together eight years last April."

"That's a long time. You still really love her." It was a statement.

Denny copied the author's position and when at last she nodded, a soft smile played around her lips. "Yes, I do. She's amazing. I love her so much." She sighed. "I miss her terribly."

Denny's wistful voice made Rachel reflective as they both stared up at the emerging stars. "What do you think she's doing right now?"

"Well, depends on what time it is back home. I'd guess it's somewhere around, let's see, end of summer, so here it's probably pushing nine-thirty. Back home, let's say it was the same time, Hannah has just fed Rascal and is now curling up on the couch to watch the news." Denny smiled at the image of her very predictable partner in her mind's eye.

"I miss the news. Used to watch religiously. And I miss hamburgers."

"Hamburgers?"

"Yeah. Kind of random, huh? I had their taste in my mouth the other day and couldn't shake it. The meat," Rachel's eyes slid shut in imagined pleasure, "would be a nice, juicy patty, and loaded with the works — lettuce, tomato, onions, pickles, globs of ketchup and mayonnaise." She smacked her lips.

"You're not a nice person, Rachel." Denny chuckled. "You know what I miss most?"

"What?"

"Applesauce."

Rachel was incredulous. "Applesauce! Of all the wonderful things out there to eat, you miss *applesauce*?"

Denny grinned and nodded. "With cinnamon. Mm, mm, mmmm. I eat it with everything. Steak, gotta have my applesauce. Cereal, gotta have my applesauce."

"You'd make a great character in one of my books," Rachel said with a laugh. "Nice and quirky."

"Thanks. I think."

"How does..." With furrowed brow, Michael turned the object this way and that, raising it above his head to look beneath it, seeing the flat, wide bottom. He turned it over, pinky raised as he tried to make himself touch it with his fingertips. Grabbing hold of the base with the other hand, he waggled it, amused as the phallus sprang from side to side, dense and heavy, even though it was quite flexible. He couldn't help but glance down at his own denim-clad crotch, comparisons on his mind.

"Want lessons on how to use that?" Pam laughed out loud as the big Texan yelped, nearly throwing the dildo over his shoulder in his haste to hide it.

"Well, I was just curious, wonderin'... Aw hell." He slammed the rubber penis down on the ground next to the fire ring and cooking area. They had been using it as a cooking utensil for pummeling leaves and berries to a pulp and, tonight, when cleaning the fish, beating the poor, dead, sea creature with it to get as many scales off as possible.

"Great night, isn't it?" Pam asked, letting the poor guy off the hook. Even as a veterinarian, she knew that color of red wasn't healthy for anyone.

"Real nice. Gonna cool down good though," he said absently, staring up into the night sky, the roar of the ocean close. "When we was kids, we used to go swimmin' all the time down home in the Gulf."

"So you grew up in Texas?" Pam made herself comfortable on the sand, leaning back on her elbows.

"Yes, ma'am." Michael's Texas-sized grin showed how much he loved his state.

"I was down in Austin once and, I have to say, I've never seen state pride like Texans'. I even saw a bag of chips shaped like the damn state!"

Michael chuckled, whistling between his teeth. "Don't I know it. You're either born in Texas, or you're born somewheres else."

Pam chuckled, shaking her head. "Pretty damn sad."

"Oh, come on now. I hear you Yankees are the same way about your New York." Michael glanced at the older woman, a slight grin on his whisker-grizzled face. He couldn't help but think of the irony that Melissa had always liked a man with facial hair. *Why hadn't I just grown a beard for her?*

"This is true." Pam nodded in agreement.

They sat in companionable silence, Michael staring at the ocean, thinking of his wife, while Pam stared up into the night sky, thinking about another woman.

"I wonder what my daughter is doing right now," she said absently, her voice unusually soft for the typically loud, brash New Yorker. "I sure as hell hope she's okay."

"How old is she?"

"Grown. Has her own place, her own life."

Michael nodded in understanding. "My oldest boy, Alan, will be twenty-two this year. Can't believe it."

"Goes fast."

"It sure does." Michael sighed heavily, swallowing his emotion. "Can't believe my kids think they lost both their mom and dad."

Pam could feel the Texan's profound sadness. She reached over, covering his large hand with her own, giving him an understanding smile. "You'll get back to them, Michael. You have to believe that."

"I'm trying."

"Pull! Come on, damnit, pull!" Pam yelled with a grunt, eyes squeezing shut as she dug her heels in, hands burning with the exertion.

"Almost there...ack!" Michael growled, putting his shoulder and arm muscles into his pulling, feeling the strain under the sweat-drenched skin. He could feel Dean behind him, the attorney's soft hands trying to achieve better positioning, which nearly made him lose the leverage he'd already gained.

Denny locked her jaw in deep concentration, ignoring the tearing of the skin on her middle finger from the rough vine. She nearly went ass over appetite as the men gave a mighty yank. She tried not to cry out as their actions put even more strain on her right shoulder, which still ached when it got cold.

"No, no! Come on, women!" Pam howled, nearly screaming her encouragement.

"Come on, ladies!" Mia clapped wildly from the sidelines, watching Michael and Dean strain against the trio of Denny, Rachel, and Pam. "You're almost there! Almost got it!"

Pam was relieved to feel some give in the vine. She glanced across the large chasm filled with water and met Michael's gaze, both sets of eyes filled with a fire to win. The Texan gritted his teeth, head rearing back as he put everything he had into it, every muscle in his body flexing.

Rachel almost wanted to giggle at the absurdity of what they were doing — five grown adults, tugging and pulling on a rope made of thick vine, trying to yank the other team into the pit of water they'd created. Her concentration narrowed back to the contest as she felt some serious give, and could feel their team's anchor, Denny, right behind her, close enough to hear her grunt. Elation filled Rachel as they pulled the men over toward their side. Michael fell into the water, and the sudden release of tension on the vine created a domino effect that got them all.

Denny yelled out as she fell over backwards, Rachel falling on top of her, followed by Pam. "Oomph!" she exclaimed, feeling the softness of the blonde's body. She could hear Rachel laughing hysterically and couldn't help but follow suit, despite the fact she was barely able to breathe, let alone laugh.

Rachel felt arms encircle her waist, and the softness of Denny beneath her. Pam crawled off the top of the pile then Rachel tried to move off Denny but was laughing too hard. She fell down again, eliciting a grunt from the brunette beneath her. Finally able to get turned around, she looked down into twinkling blue eyes, which stood out even more against the red flush of Denny's cheeks.

Denny felt her heart begin to flutter and her stomach clenched at the feel of Rachel's breasts barely grazing against her own before the author pulled herself to her knees, then Pam helped her to her feet. Denny lay stunned, body suffused with heat and sudden need, which instantly brought images of Hannah to her mind and made her feel guilty for something she hadn't done. Finally she took the hand Rachel extended to her, allowing herself to be pulled to her own feet, though her balance was still a bit unsteady.

"You okay there?" Rachel chuckled, a hand on the brunette's waist to steady her. At Denny's nod, she gave her a quick squeeze then headed off to celebrate with the other two women by throwing barbs at the losers.

Denny stood stock still, gripped by an unfamiliar feeling for a moment and trying to shake it off. She had been without Hannah's touch for — she mentally thought about her calendar markings on the tree that she had started the day she woke up on the island — nearly one hundred and twenty three days. *Four months without a woman's touch. No, without* Hannah's *touch.* She ran shaking hands through her hair then joined the revelers.

"...easy when it's three against one!" Dean was saying, though he was grinning from ear to ear, despite still having sand plastered to the side of his sweat-slicked face.

"Oh, quit your whining." Pam laughed, slapping him on the shoulder. "You guys lost fair and square."

Michael grumbled, but nodded in concession.

"So, what do we get for dinner?" Rachel asked, eyes bright with victory. When Michael and Dean began to grouse, she cut them off. "Hey, hey, hey! That was the deal, boys. Whoever lost has to catch dinner." She pointed to the inflated slide they used as a raft to go into deeper waters to fish. "Out!"

Denny stood off by herself, mind reeling from the heat still traveling through her body. When she glanced at Rachel, the heat level soared, her body responding to the months of deprivation. Turning away, she headed into the thick jungle, Dean's knowing look lost to her back.

Taking several deep breaths, Denny tried to still her rapidly beating heart. She gathered up her long hair, taking the heavy load off the back of her neck to cool down. Guilt was her companion as she made her way toward the waterfall, slipping behind it to the small alcove which had become her hiding place when she needed to be alone.

Sitting heavily on the cool stone floor, she rested her head back against the wall and looked into the spray of water cascading not ten feet in front of her, the world beyond distorted and dulled. She blew out a long breath, trying to clear her mind of feelings and sensations, bringing Hannah's face before her eyes — her body, her voice, the smell of her dark hair, anything. It worked, and she calmed, convincing herself there was no reason to feel guilty. Rachel was a beautiful woman, no one could deny that, and the only one around who would interest Denny if they were back home, let alone stranded with two other women — one sixteen, the other a mother hen to them all.

"It's only natural," she explained to herself softly. "You did nothing wrong, only had a visceral reaction." She blew out a breath, feeling like her body was totally under control and she could return to the group.

"Anybody seen the food masher?" Pam called out as the men grunted, pushing the slide out to sea then climbing aboard.

Michael didn't like the idea of spending time alone with the flaming Dean in the middle of the ocean, but bit his tongue, knowing he had to honor his commitment to the gals back on shore who were counting on them.

The two men remained silent, neither wanting to be on a fishing expedition with the other, but knowing they had no choice. To make it as bearable as possible, they kept their mouths shut. Dean glanced at Michael, noting his vacant stare out into the expanse of water as they rowed the raft further into open sea, being careful not to get too far from land.

"This should do," Michael said, bringing up the oar made from heavy tree branches with vine wrapped around the end to create a large mass for displacing the water. Dean also brought up his oar, situating it to the side of the raft and then removing his shoes. He knew he looked like a dork with jeans ripped off to the mid-thigh, no shirt, and Gucci loafers. Modesty and fashion sense had long since gone by the wayside. All the same, he wasn't going to ruin his loafers beyond what they already were.

"You going or am I?" he asked, meeting the Texan's gaze.

Michael leaned over the side of the boat, staring into the depths, imagining all the fish swimming just beneath the surface. "I'll go." He met Dean's gaze levelly. "Think you can pull me back in?"

"Aye, aye, captain." With a salute and small smile, Dean watched the large man slide over the side of the boat and quickly disappear into the ocean, leaving nothing but waves and bubbles where he had just been.

Michael waited for his eyes to adjust to the salt water, blinking rapidly, and everything began to clear. It was so peaceful down there, quiet and dark, yet a whole world began to come into view, a world filled with alien plant life and creatures. It was like floating on another planet. Darting to his left, a huge, colorful fish came into his world, but

Michael turned away, knowing from his youth that it was a bad fish, not for eating. As a kid, they used to call them cyanide fish, because they could knock out a grown man with just a bit of the poison stashed in their bodies.

He kicked powerful legs and arms, moving further into the depths to see what his options were before he needed to surface for air. Just before he headed up, he saw a huge school of fish, big fat ones.

Dean saw the glittery outline of Michael as he rose toward the surface, breaking through with a gasp. The Texan hung on to the edge of the raft with one hand while brushing his hair out of his eyes with the other.

"Found 'em." He panted for a moment as he got his bearings again and filled his lungs. "Huge groupin' down there. Be ready."

"Okay." Dean watched the big man take an even bigger breath then he was gone again. Dean sat back in the raft, looking up into the sky where clouds were gathering.

Matt Frazier felt his stomach lurch as the plane hit more turbulence; his eyes closed as he white knuckled the armrest of his seat. All he could do was swallow and try and keep his breakfast down. The weather in Portland had turned bad as the plane was taxiing out, forcing them to stop and de-ice the wings. Again.

It was the second time he'd flown to New York since Rachel's death and now he hated to fly. He snorted. *New York.* It made him think of Reenie. Which then made him think of the drive they made to Eugene three months earlier to see Rachel's lawyer and the resulting betrayal he had felt upon hearing the terms of Rachel's will. Now she was gone, and all he could feel about that was grief, and guilt. Still, the reading of the will had been a shock.

Matt stared out the window at the white nothingness of clouds. After Rachel's sister had died, it had scared her so badly she had made a living will, in which everything except the house had been left to Rachel's remaining sisters and Reenie, save for a small percentage of her royalties, which would be Matt's. When they'd visited Rachel's publisher, the publisher signed those royalties over to Matt, as her husband and most immediate beneficiary.

Did she really hate me that much? And that was before I started seeing Diane.

Matt was hurt that the bulk of Rachel's assets had been willed to others, and not because he wanted her money. He wanted to understand why she had done it. He wanted his wife back so he could talk with her, try and understand her. He wanted another chance for her to let him in, let him understand her mind. Given her bequests, apparently she had not pictured them still being together when she died, however many years down the road that might have been. Or at the very least, she thought more of her sisters and friend than of him.

Life can sure be ironic. Like flying to a memorial for people who perished in a flight that ended in disaster.

Matt started as the captain's voice over the intercom let the passengers know they were getting ready to land. *Thank God!* He closed his eyes again as his stomach reacted to the changes in pressure as the plane banked to the right and then began to lose altitude and aligned with the runway. It wouldn't be long before he was somewhere he hadn't wanted to be.

A month earlier, Matt had gotten a call from a man named Stanley Wells, who was organizing a memorial for all those who had not made it home from Flight 1049. Matt hadn't wanted to go, unsure whether he could handle it emotionally, but Reenie had talked him into it, telling him maybe he would feel better if he could talk to some of the family members of those who had died with Rachel. Eventually, if reluctantly, he'd given in to her persuasions.

"Hi, Matt." Reenie pulled the disheveled man into a quick but firm embrace, and then offered to help with the large carry-on he'd brought. She glanced over at him a few times as he gave her clipped responses to her questions about his trip.

Reenie knew Matt was angry with her, but there was no help for it. She understood his hurt. She'd spent the past several weeks trying to figure out why Rachel had bequeathed her belongings as she had. She knew the author could be headstrong, but that turn of events was completely unlike her. As far as Reenie knew, at the time of Daisy's death, nearly two years ago now, Rachel was still committed to her marriage and trying to make it work, though there were problems. In truth, the disclosure of the amount of money she herself was to receive, once the paperwork was processed, had made her feel sick. She didn't want Rachel's money, and had decided to make other plans for its use. But she hadn't revealed that to Matt.

"So, are you ready for this?" she asked, slamming the trunk of her car closed after Matt tossed his bag inside. She glanced at him over the top of the car before they both climbed inside.

"I suppose." Matt sighed, running a hand through his hair, making it even messier than it had been.

Reenie was surprised by his appearance. Usually the good looking man was well groomed and well kempt — clothes neat and clean, face shaved, and body showered. Dark eyes traveling over his stained, wrinkled shirt as she stopped at a red traffic light, she finally asked, "What's happened to you, Matt?"

His tormented and tired eyes met her gaze, fingers absently pushing a random dark strand of sweaty hair out of them. "What's that supposed to mean?" he asked, nearly barking the words.

"It means you look like shit," Reenie said, once again getting the car moving.

"Thank you. I needed that." He looked out the window, mildly amused as he watched people walking along the sidewalk, jackets bundled tightly around them against the fierce autumn wind and cold. Halloween was a week away, and traditionally that was when the bad weather really set in.

"Well Jesus Christ, Matt! You look like you slept in your clothes for three days, and haven't taken a shower in nearly as long." She eyed him again. "What the hell? Why are you letting yourself go? It's not doing Rachel any—"

"Don't you dare fucking talk to me about Rachel or what she wants, *wanted*, thought, liked or didn't like. You don't fucking know!"

Reenie started, shocked at his outburst. She'd never heard him raise his voice before, and its booming anger filled the confines of the car. She could feel his pain, hear it in his voice. She was struck dumb for the rest of the drive to her place, where she parked in the underground garage and then preceded him to her door.

Matt stomped inside, feeing no remorse for his outburst. He had been stewing over the slap in the face from Rachel's will for months, unable to vent to the woman he most wanted to.

"Look, Matt," Reenie said, laying her coat over the arm of a chair, "if this is about the money—"

"I don't give a flying fuck about the money, Reenie!" He threw his bag to the floor and turned on her. "She didn't believe in me, in *us*, enough to think we'd be together when she died. So, if you think this is about money—"

"Believe in you? *Believe* in you!" Reenie fired back, her own pent up feelings surfacing. "Was she supposed to believe in you while you were out fucking another woman? Is that the trust you're talking about?"

Matt's guilt boiled into irrepressible anger. "What the hell do you know about that!" he roared, taking a menacing step over toward Reenie. "You don't know anything! Maybe if Rachel hadn't been so goddamned cold and distant—"

"Maybe she has her reasons to be cold toward you, did you ever think of that? Maybe if you had been more understanding, tried to get to the bottom of her distance; maybe if you had taken the time—"

"Stop it! Both of you!"

Reenie and Matt froze, turning toward the voice coming from behind them. Beth stood in the doorway of the guest bedroom, blue eyes flashing. Seeing she had their attention, Beth stepped into the room, her gaze hard and accusing.

"Do you think this is going to bring her back? Is this going to change what's happened? No! You both need to deal with the fact that

Rachel is gone, and nothing she did while she was alive matters — not the money, the will, fights, none of it." She sliced the air with her hand for emphasis. Softening her voice, she walked over to Matt. "Look, I don't really know you all that well." She placed a gentling hand on his arm and saw the anger start to leave his body. "You will never know why Rachel did what she did, what was behind her decisions, but ultimately they were *her* decisions. I know it hurts you and you are entitled to that hurt, but attacking Reenie about things in the past isn't the way to deal with it."

"But—"

"Shh." Beth placed a finger on his lips then turned to her friend. "What are you doing, Reenie? Your anger at Matt, whatever the reason, won't help you feel any better." She looked from one to the other. "You guys are displacing your anger at Fate onto each other, and it's not right and it's not fair. Neither of you deserve this." She looked from hazel eyes to dark brown, until finally Matt looked away, mumbling something about taking a shower.

Reenie plopped down hard on the couch, running a hand through her short, dark hair. "That went well," she muttered, glancing toward the hall down which Matt had disappeared.

Beth sat next to her, still a bit shaky from her outburst. She hated being angry, having dealt with far too much anger in her younger years. Back in those days, the theater had been the only thing to tame her, and... Well, she wasn't going to go there. The past didn't matter anymore, nor did the people who had filled it.

"You guys have got to stop fighting and blaming each other, Reenie. It only makes things worse," she said at length.

The other woman nodded dumbly. "I know. I just can't help it. I'm so goddamned angry with her, you know? Why does it still hurt so badly?"

"Because life is marching on. The year is moving by quickly and we're almost into the holiday season. After Halloween, it's Thanksgiving then Christmas." Beth looked down at her fidgeting hands for a moment, then met Reenie's searching gaze. "I remember when my dad left the family. Granted, he didn't die, but it sure felt like a death to a twelve year-old. It was summer time, and I felt lost and alone, left with just my mother, who I couldn't stand. I felt abandoned, and can't even begin to describe to you the anger I felt. Still do, I guess." She smiled, though the attempt was thin and sad.

"How long has it been? Do you see him much now?"

"He walked out of my life fourteen years ago, and no, I don't see him all that much. He has a new family with kids who are teenagers. I see him maybe once a year."

"And your mom?"

Beth shook her head. "No. She's still back in Colorado, no doubt drinking herself to death."

"At least you can still see him, Beth, even if it is once a year."

"But you have the luxury of knowing that Rachel didn't leave you on purpose, Reen. I'm not comparing apples and oranges here, 'cause your pain and Matt's pain are as real to you two as mine is to me. Know that your friend loved you and would still be here if she could, eager to talk to you every day, or whatever. And as for Matt," the actress glanced over her shoulder toward the bathroom, making sure he wasn't making an appearance, "he's letting his guilt over cheating eat him alive. I think he feels he pushed her toward getting on that plane, and therefore, by extension, it's somehow his fault."

"It is—"

"Rachel was a grown woman, Reenie. She boarded that plane of her own volition."

Reenie knew full well Beth was right, but was having a hard time admitting it to her heart. She needed something, some*one* to blame for Rachel's death, and Matt was the perfect choice. She sighed heavily.

The mirror above Gloria Vinzetti's dresser was oval and shadowed with age; it had belonged to her grandmother when she was a girl. Waste not, want not. She couldn't see it being thrown out. Looking at herself as she adjusted the collar of her black dress, Gloria sighed heavily at the familiar color. She hadn't allowed herself to wear anything else in the past months. The dark circles under her eyes made a better accessory than her pearls.

As ready as she would ever be, Gloria slipped into her jacket and grabbed her keys and purse. Never in her life had she dreaded something so badly. Well, that wasn't quite true — Mia's funeral had been the hardest day of her life — but this was a close second. She didn't want to be reminded of the tragedy anymore; she was tired of it. As it was, her beloved Rachel Holt's name and face were still plastered over the TV screen and magazine and newspaper covers. She had been astonished to find out her favorite author had been on the flight with them. At every bookstore in Brooklyn, Rachel's books were flying off the shelves, as avid fans mourned Rachel's death.

Traffic was bad, as usual, but that was okay. The holdup was delaying the inevitable, and Gloria just didn't know if her stomach could handle attending the memorial. Her Nonna and Papa had flown home more than a month ago, Paolo Vinzetti needing to get home to see his doctors. Gloria had been tempted to go with them, leave everything in America; she had nothing left to stay for. But Lizbeth had talked her out of it. Gloria's life was in Brooklyn, the place she'd raised her daughter, seen her grow from an adorable little girl to a bright, beautiful young woman. Truth be told, Gloria knew she couldn't leave.

She felt her daughter still with her in the apartment, and just couldn't let that go. She had a feeling Mia's spirit wouldn't be with her in Milan.

When Gloria arrived, the convention center was already packed, filled with the families of the two hundred and sixty-three people on Flight 1049 who had died in its crash. Banners which hung on the walls welcomed and directed guests. A number of people were already roaming about the huge ballroom, drinks in hand; voices murmured softly at the Meet and Greet. Cheerful balloons were strung over just about anything that stood still in an attempt to lighten the mood of such a somber event. As Gloria made her way through the crowd, she almost felt like she was at her high school reunion. She caught snippets of conversations as she made her way toward the refreshment table:

"...son's babysitter, so sad..."

"...married for thirty-three years. She loved to..."

"...Davies will fly the search missions. I believe there are other survivors to be found."

The Italian woman stopped at that, turning to see who was making the assertion, for a moment, feeling a glimmer of hope. She wondered whether the finely dressed man had information she didn't have. She went up to the small group of four. "Excuse me, my name is Gloria Vinzetti."

One of the women's eyes got large, her hand going to her open mouth. "Aren't you one of the Lucky Three?" she whispered, referring to the title the press had bestowed on the three rescued passengers. When Gloria nodded, the woman went to pieces, grasping Gloria in a monster hug and nearly pulling the smaller woman off her feet. "I'm so glad someone survived such a horrific tragedy."

Not sure what to say, Gloria smiled shyly. She had been hounded by the media for the first month or so after the rescue, but the furor had all died down as the press turned their attention to other breaking stories. This renewed attention was somewhat disconcerting, especially as the entire group turned toward her. She addressed the handsome man with the sandy colored hair.

"I'm sorry to interrupt, but I overheard your conversation. Were you talking about sending out search planes for 1049?"

Will favored the woman with a charming smile; he'd seen her face a dozen times on the news. He also knew she'd lost a daughter. "Yes, ma'am. I'm Will Ash." He extended a well-manicured hand, enveloping the smaller hand in his. "I'm so sorry for your loss, Mrs. Vinzetti, and I think it's wonderful you were saved."

"Thank you, Mr. Ash."

"Call me Will."

Gloria swallowed, shaking off her response to his charisma so she could think straight. "What is your interest in this, Will? What makes you think you'll find anything?"

"My partner, Dean Ratliff, was on that flight, Mrs. Vinzetti. My heart tells me he's still alive, and I intend to either prove myself right, or," he swallowed, "prove myself wrong."

"The Coast Guard won't help you any further?" one of the men in the group asked, sipping from his drink.

Will turned to him, shaking his head. "I tried every angle until it was suggested to me that I go private. This is where Miss Davies comes in. We've already taken one pass in the general area, but intend to go back out in another month. I heard the author, uh, what was her name..." He snapped his fingers as he tried to recall.

"Rachel Holt," Gloria provided.

"Right. Rachel Holt's husband is supposed to be here today, and I'd like to talk to him. Perhaps with such a high profile victim, we can renew the public interest in this story, maybe get some financial support for rescue efforts."

Matt and Reenie walked in together but quickly separated, with Matt heading toward the cash bar. Reenie took in everything around her, astounded by the number of people the tragedy had touched. How many lives in the room had been ruined by what had happened? The newspapers had recently published new findings from the black box finally found along with wreckage at the bottom of the ocean. Instrument failure, they said. The 767 had been drastically off course, but the pilots had not known it until it was too late. To make matters worse, engine two had given out, causing the plane to make its fiery descent into a watery grave.

There was talk of lawsuits, and no doubt the airline was rallying its own defense team. Reenie couldn't help but smile; she felt they should be scared. Her best friend and favorite client had died because of airline negligence.

She accepted a flute of something amber and bubbly from a passing waiter, nodding her gratitude as she took a sip. She was mildly intrigued by the mixture of souls present, and the disparity in their life status. Some walked around in Armani and Prada, while others walked around in the K-Mart blue light special. Across all the poverty and pomp, there was one thread that wove everyone together — loss.

Total stillness, harsh in its completeness. Visions before her, people walking, gesticulating, expressive and emoting bodies. Tracy Sloan took it all in, eyes wide with curiosity and a mild sense of the fear she always had when entering into an unknown world that she wasn't given time to explore and learn. She felt reassured by the constant touch on her arm, knowing it was Colleen, her interpreter and constant companion since she was seven. Nineteen years later, the older woman was her family.

Colleen had been the one to break the news to Tracy about her mother's death. Next to her mother, Tracy trusted Colleen like no other.

The twenty-six year-old felt a slight tap on her arm, and turned to see Colleen signing to her with swift, graceful fluidity. Tracy nodded in understanding and signed her response. Together they joined the crowd as it headed toward the double doors that opened into the great ballroom.

Standing next to Reenie, Matt was nervous. It would be their turn to shine after the current speaker finished, before the memorial actually started. Reverend Mark Stantz and Rabbi Chaim Halevi were standing by to deliver to their respective messages.

Reenie could feel Matt's nervousness in the way he shifted his weight from foot to foot and cleared his throat more than was necessary. She tried to ignore it and listen to the announcer and promoter of the night's event, Brian Manley, an executive for the airline.

The auditorium was filled to standing room only with hundreds of family members and friends of those lost. The lights dimmed, and a giant screen behind Brian slowly showcased one face after another, candid shots of those passengers who had died, along with their name, age, and city of origin. Sniffles could be heard in the darkened room, random flashes like lightning strikes.

"The lives of these two hundred and sixty-three people are forever linked and live on in our hearts and memories." The last picture to show on the large screen was Rachel Holt, which was Reenie and Matt's segue. "I'd like to introduce to you tonight Reenie Bazilton, Rachel Holt's editor and dear friend, and Matt Frazier, Rachel's husband." Brian Manley stepped aside to thunderous applause as Reenie and Matt stepped into the spotlight.

Matt stared out into the darkness, trying not to think about the hundreds of eyes on him, instead focusing on why they were there. He happily left the presentation to Reenie.

"Thank you for coming tonight, ladies and gentlemen. You have no idea how difficult it is for me to stand up here before you." Reenie paused, staring out into the sea of faces, only able to make out the red and green lights of cameras and a few faces up close. "Then again, maybe you do. Rachel Holt was the closest friend I've ever had, and the most talented person I've ever had the pleasure of working with. She bared her heart in every novel she wrote; every word was lovingly applied to the page. Rachel loved her fans and, though this room isn't filled with them now, I know she'd support one hundred percent what I've done."

Reenie stepped aside and looked at the screen behind her, which showed the homepage for the website she'd been steadily working on. "I've created the 1049 Club in Rachel's name. It's a fund that is intended to help the children and needy families of those who died in the tragedy. Donations from the public have already totaled more than a quarter of a million dollars, and that is in addition to the two million with which the fund was started."

Matt had heard all of this before, but he still couldn't keep the smile from his face, knowing just how pleased Rachel would be that her money was being put to such good use. Pride filled his chest. After he had heard the terms of Rachel's will, he had pegged Reenie as a greedy, scheming bitch who'd likely influenced Rachel's disposition of her estate. But, after finding out about Reene's plans for the money, he realized that he was wrong.

There was a smattering of applause and many gasps of surprise, and Reenie glanced back at the people assembled. "Every passenger is listed on the website." She turned back to the screen, which changed to show the page she had mentioned. "I've gathered information from the authorities, and will be opening special pages for each of you to write in about your loved one, and to leave a special message for others to read." The screen changed again. "Here you can write to Matt and me personally, describing any financial problems you face from the loss of a spouse, parent, guardian, etcetera." She paused for a moment. "I am already aware of many ways in which this has devastated people's lives: a husband who was killed and had no insurance, so that now his family is going under; children who lost both parents.

"Hearing that my best friend died in this crash has affected me in ways I never imagined. Though it has nothing to do with my financial situation, my life has been changed forever. Deeply, deeply changed. That is why I'm hoping that this money can help, even if just a little."

Tears glistening in her dark eyes, Gloria listened, stunned at the woman's kindness of spirit. As the speaker wrapped it up, once again a larger than life picture of Rachel Holt appeared on the screen. Gloria had never seen that picture. Rachel was smiling, her eyes twinkling and the most beautiful color of green. All her pictures on her books were in black and white. Gloria studied the picture for long moments, feeling more tears spring to her eyes. *What an utter waste of all these lives lost.*

His face hurt. His hand hurt. Hell, even his *hair* hurt. Conrad Dupree sat in the hard chair outside the principal's office, waiting. He wanted to rest his chin on his fist, but even that hurt, so he rested his head back against the wall instead. His grandma was inside talking to Mrs. Caster, no doubt, about what a bad boy he was and how he needed to change and watch his temper. *Whatever.*

Conrad jumped as the office door was opened, his principal stepping only halfway out, just far enough to get his attention, beckoning him inside. Conrad sighed heavily as he flopped down in the chair next to his grandma, though he tried his best not to wince, 'cause even *that* hurt.

"Conrad, do you have anything to say for yourself?" Mrs. Denise Caster leaned slightly forward on her desk, gray eyes focused on the slumped form before her. Conrad said nothing, didn't even meet her eyes as he shook his head.

"Conrad, this is the third time this semester," Meredith reminded, her brow knit as she studied her grandson. Nearly at her wit's end with him, she winced when she saw the bruise on his jaw and the one eye beginning to darken. Come the light of day, he'd look like he'd been through a battle. *Walter is going to hang the boy out to dry!* "What happened?" she asked, her voice softer as she reached over to brush a few blond strands out of his eyes. Conrad jerked away, breaking her heart.

"You need to tell us what happened, Conrad," Principal Caster said. "Nick isn't telling us anything, so you'll have to."

"Nick's a jerk," Conrad finally muttered, almost into his chest, his head had fallen so low.

"Why is he a jerk, honey?" Meredith asked.

Conrad could see it again, plain as day. He'd been walking down the hall, trying to get to his math class, when suddenly Nick Stavros had stepped away from the lockers in the sixth grader hall, arms spread out wide like bird wings, making airplane sounds then running into the locker with a verbal imitation of an explosion. Conrad Dupree had immediately felt tears sting his eyes, but couldn't allow Nick to see them. Instead he'd jumped the kid, nearly beating him to a pulp before the gym teacher, Mr. Martinez, separated them.

Conrad sniffled as quietly as he could, but the principal didn't miss it. Her gaze met that of the boy's grandmother to see if she'd heard it too. The look of profound sadness in Meredith's eyes told her all she needed to know.

"I'm going to suspend you for one day, Conrad, so you can think about what you did." The principal felt horrible for having to dole out punishment, but she couldn't dismiss the beating of another student without consequences. Even so, she'd given the Dupree boy a much lighter punishment than the Stavros boy would get. "You're dismissed, Conrad."

Meredith turned to her grandson, who sat slouched in his seat, arms crossed defiantly over his chest. "Jennifer and I are going to go visit your mom and dad's graves. Want to go?" she asked, eyes flicking over Conrad before turning back to the road.

"No."

Chapter 9

"Damn pain in the ass," Pam muttered, almost falling head first into the bush from which she was extracting the food masher. Holding the dildo by the base between thumb and forefinger, she studied it, shaking it slightly to rid the flesh colored device of the leaves that stuck to it.

Running up the beach toward the older woman, Mia panted, "No luck, Pam." When Pam turned to face her, the food masher held up, Mia stifled a giggle at the look of utter disgust on Pam's face. "Oh."

"Little bastard better have cleaned it." She marched toward the fire ring, Mia in tow. Denny and Rachel, who were twisting vine into rope, glanced up, both snickering.

"You think this is funny?" Pam asked, one dark eyebrow arched. Both women tried to look solemn. "Fine. You two get to do the mashing."

Pam threw the masher down and marched back into the dense foliage. Mia chewed uncertainly on her lower lip, then hastily followed Pam.

"Methinks someone's going off in search of the big leaves," Denny whispered, a sable eyebrow raised.

Rachel chuckled and nodded. "Methinks you're right."

They finished the rest of the vine in companionable silence before moving over to the fire ring and the berries Pam and Mia had gathered.

"So what were you muttering about the other day?" Denny asked, trying not to grimace as she picked up the food masher, surreptitiously smelling it to see how thoroughly it needed to be washed. She quickly boiled some water to sterilize the masher.

"Muttering about?" Rachel's eyebrows drew closer together, indicating her confusion. Her fingers continued to remove stems from the berries, throwing the discards in the cold ash in the center of the rocks.

"Yeah. The other day, you were roaming around, muttering about something. I could only catch a word or two now and then, carried on the breeze. At first I thought you were singing, but I don't think so."

"Oh." Rachel blushed. Sometimes she hated how small the island could be. Much of the island's three mile radius was too dense for habitation, so the small amount remaining made it difficult for one to get any true privacy. "I was working on a story, talking it out." She glanced shyly at Denny then turned back to her task.

"Talking it out?" Denny winced as the steam from the simmering water scorched her fingertips as she lowered the masher into the makeshift pot.

Rachel nodded. "You should see me when I'm at home." She grinned. "I used to love doing the dishes, because it's mindless work, you know? You stand there at the sink, your hands in nice, soothing hot water, and nothing to do but think. I'd talk out dialogue and story plots, and figure out my characters' psychological profiles. Good times."

Denny laughed as she took the berries from Rachel and mashed the hell out of them with the cleaned dildo, scraping the remnants off onto the leaves Pam would use to wrap the fish.

"You're always asking about me, but trust me, my writing rituals *aren't* that interesting. What about you?" Rachel glanced over at the brunette, whose attention was fully on mashing a stubborn berry that insisted on rolling instead of becoming purple mush. "Why a coffee shop?"

"Why not?" Denny raised a challenging eyebrow. The glare she got made her chuckle. Denny wasn't fond of talking about herself, always far more curious about other people, but she knew her captive audience wouldn't let her get away with her typical pat answers. She cleared her throat as she got serious. "My folks and I didn't get along that well. They're devout Catholics, and I'm...not. Even before they knew I was gay, I was a disgrace in their eyes."

Rachel listened, noting that her usually upbeat companion refused to meet her gaze. She felt the uncharacteristic need to reach out and touch Denny, lay a comforting hand on her arm or hand, but decided against it. It was almost as though Denny had closed herself and her personal space off with yellow tape: Do Not Cross.

"I used to love to dance. Me and my friends used to go out all the time, fake I.D.s and all." She chuckled at the memories. "Needless to say, dancing led to drinking which led to smoking, which led to me breaking a whole laundry list of commandments. Bad daughter, sinner, must exorcise the demons."

Denny sighed, staring out into the darkening day and absently eyeing the pregnant clouds above. "Anyway, so I was out and had to get my own life. I got a job at a local hangout called Mile, and my boss, Joni, saw potential, I guess. Either that or I was the only one who showed up for my shifts on time." Denny grinned at Rachel. "Anyway, I found that I was good at it, enjoyed it, so I decided to get a place of my own."

"Do you see your parents now?"

Denny shook her head. "Nope." She slammed the food masher down until it suctioned itself to the rock, the body doinging back and forth, making both women snicker. "Sometimes when your biological family fucks you over, you go out and make your own."

"Hannah?"

"Hannah." Denny couldn't keep the smile from her face. "And what about you? Do you miss your husband?"

Rachel was about to open her mouth, coming up with some sort of lame, superficial response, when they heard a loud whoop. Relieved, she turned toward the shore, getting to her feet to meet the men coming in, holding up a bag full of fish.

"Victory at sea!" Michael yelled, pumping his fish-gripping fist in the air. Dean grinned from ear to ear next to him, grunting as they pulled the raft ashore.

"We're eating good tonight, ladies!" Dean said, nearly falling back on his butt as the raft got stuck on a small fissure in the sand. Regaining his footing again, his grin reappeared.

Mia laughed at the robust belch Michael just released. "Oh, that was charming."

The group chuckled, sitting around the roaring fire, the only light in the deep, dark night. Distant rumbling was heard and everyone was surprised the sky hadn't yet split open to drench them. It had been threatening to all day, the sky heavy and foreboding.

"You know, if we ever make it home, I will never touch fish again," Pam joked, licking her fingers of the juices from the wonderful dinner.

"Amen!" Denny echoed, reaching for second helping. They hadn't eaten so well in weeks.

They all chuckled, knowing full well they would be eating fish the following day, and the day after that, and the day after that...*ad nauseum.*

"Look at me, though," Dean said, rising to his feet and striking a pose. He gave them all a profile, showing off his flattened stomach and shapely legs. "Now I look like some twink in New York."

Denny burst into laughter while everyone else looked on with confusion. "I know. Check this out." She jumped to her feet, displaying her own sleek and toned body. She'd never been in such great shape in her life. It was just sad that it took being stranded with barely anything to eat for her to lose the fifteen or twenty pounds she'd been wanting to drop. She raised her arms, flexing and growling as she changed poses. Someone threw up a high-pitched whistle and Dean cheered.

"You go, you big ol' dyke!"

Rachel sat back, grinning like a fool as she watched Dean and Denny. Her eyes brushed over Denny's body. She'd already noticed the woman's belly had disappeared. Now she saw smooth skin painted in gold and shadow by the firelight.

"Hey, now," Pam said, the skin jiggling slightly as she smacked her own belly. "I'm finally finding the six pack under my two liter." That set everyone off again.

"Well, us Texans are just born gorgeous," Michael said with a wink, heading off into the darkness to relieve his bladder.

Denny sat back down, catching green eyes as she did. She grinned at Rachel, getting a raised coconut shell cup in salute.

The wind howled, shaking the very fibers of the women's structure. The whistling that seeped between the woven leaves was unnerving, and the air was cold.

Denny pulled her legs up closer to her chest, almost into the fetal position. The woven grass mats they each usually slept on were now being used as coverings, but even that wasn't keeping them warm. She felt a shiver rush through her and listened as the rain began. The drops were not yet falling through the trees above into their sanctuary, but she could hear the sand being pelted. She shivered again, about to pull her face down toward her chest under the mat, but stopped when she noticed Rachel was awake, an arm raised and holding up her own mat in invitation. The blonde was also curled in on herself. Denny looked at her, a slight feeling of panic settling over her as she thought about how her body had reacted after their tug-of-war game. She also recalled her feelings of guilt and the loneliness of not having Hannah's touch.

Denny's own emotional tug-of-war came to an abrupt halt when she saw Rachel's arm waver, her eyes confused and hurt. Deciding she was being ridiculous, Denny scooted the couple of feet over to Rachel, turning her back toward her.

"It's getting colder at night," Rachel whispered against her ear, causing a different kind of shiver in Denny.

She nodded mutely, feeling the blonde curl up against her back. Soon with body heat combined, the two women drifted off into comfortable sleep.

Rachel felt warmth, completely enveloped in it, causing her to smile and wiggle back into it. She felt protected. Safe. Warm. Held. *Held!* Green eyes popped open. Rachel, disoriented and suddenly struck with fear, heard the roar of the world around her enter her reality. She was lying on her left side, Denny nearly wrapped around her from behind, a long arm across Rachel's stomach, holding her close against the warm body behind her. She only had a moment to soak that in when cries outside rent the air, as did a recurrence of the deafening roar that had first woken her.

"Fuck! Help me, Michael!" Dean screamed at the top of his lungs, desperately trying to gather as much gear into his arms as the driving wind and rain would allow.

The Texan barely heard him over the sound of the storm, the waves swelling and breaking on the beach, almost knocking him off his feet. Sputtering, he tried to shake the rain out of his eyes, only able to see the struggling man when another crack of lightning split the sky in two.

"What's happening?" Pam yelled as she shot out of the women's hut, looking around frantically.

"We got washed out!" Michael hollered back, grabbing for Dean, who had slipped, losing half of the things he'd so far managed to grab. Their nail clippers, knife, and three shirts were instantly washed away as another set of waves crashed ashore, nearly pulling all three of them with it as it receded into the angry ocean.

"Jesus Christ!" Pam yelled, holding on to a tree for dear life. She felt a hand on her back and turned to see a wind and rain swept Denny, spitting water out of her mouth.

"We've got to get to higher ground!" Denny yelled, her words swallowed by the loudest crack of thunder any of them had ever heard. When the noise had diminished from impossible to just ridiculous, she repeated herself.

Pam nodded then turned back to Michael, who no longer stood next to her. She was barely able to make out the outline of the two men, screaming into the wind, down by the shore.

"Grab it! Fuckin' grab it!" Michael yelled, teeth bared as he tried to get hold of the edge of the raft, which was being pulled out to sea. "We can't lose this!"

"Michael, I can't hold on!" Dean yelled, losing his grip. He grasped desperately for some sort of purchase, but the rain-slicked rubber and forceful winds and waves were making it nearly impossible. "I can't—"

"No! Hold on, goddamn it! We can't lose this, goddamn you!" Michael felt frantic, as though their only hope of ever leaving the island was literally slipping through his fingers. He felt like crying; he was losing his grip too. "No!"

"Michael!" Dean's heart sank when a strong wave crashed over them, taking the raft and Michael back out to sea with it. Without a second thought, Dean threw himself at the larger man, managing to grab his legs and refusing to let go. "Hold on, Michael! I've got you!"

Michael spat out a mouthful of salt water, feeling it burn his eyes and the insides of his nose and throat. Another wave crashed down over him, making him panic at being unable to breathe or move. He felt something tight around his legs, almost painfully so. Over the roar of the surf he could make out a word now and then – *got you...swim...help me!*

Dean grappled with all his might, finally able to gain his feet during a very short reprieve from the pounding surf, though he could see the waves building again.

"We've got to help him!" Pam cried, about to run out to the beach, but she was stopped by a hand on her shoulder and another grabbing a handful of her pant leg.

"No!" Mia stared the older woman down as Pam turned to see who had dared to stop her. She was face to face with fierce, dark eyes. "We need to save ourselves! What good is it if we all die? We have to survive!"

The older woman was so stunned all she could do was nod dumbly. Snapping into action, she could just barely see Denny and Rachel disappearing into the jungle, a wet, slimy trail of mud and leaves turning to mush in their wake. With one last glance over her shoulder, she saw Dean was managing to pull Michael into waist-deep water.

"I'm not going to let you die, damn it!" Dean screamed into the wind, using every ounce of muscle and adrenaline he had to pull the Texan to shore before the next wave got to them. Using fear induced, super-human strength, he swung the larger man back to shallower depths, quickly splashing after Michael and grabbing him around the waist, hoisting him to his shoulders like a fireman and then slogging back onto shore, ignoring the wrenching pain in his back and legs, and the fury of the rain and wind.

Finally making it into the jungle, Dean dropped Michael on his butt under an overhang then collapsed down next to him.

Denny crawled forward from the small hiding nook where the other three women still huddled. The water cascaded down over the rocks in a torrent, the usually calm, almost soothing waterfall seeming angry and violent. She stepped out from behind the waterfall and peered into the darkness, searching anxiously for any sign of Michael and Dean. She knew yelling out their names would be useless; the roar of the storm and the waterfall were deafening. She saw nothing, nothing but roaring blackness.

"Shit." She returned to the cave behind the water. Though she was unable to make out the faces of her companions, she figured they would want to know, so she shook her head. Then realizing that chances were good they couldn't see her, either, she said, "Nothing."

Mia sighed, clutching tighter to Pam, who rested her cheek on the girl's head. Rachel met Denny halfway across the nook, reaching out blindly to make sure the black spot on the slightly less black background was Denny. "You okay?" she asked.

"Yeah. I'm just hoping with every bit of my being that they made it. I should have stayed. Helped." Denny's head fell forward, the long, wet strands of her hair falling to form a black curtain over her face.

"Hey." Rachel put a comforting arm around Denny's shoulder and squeezed lightly. "There's nothing any of us could have done, nothing." Rachel could feel Denny's shoulder shaking. It took her a moment to realize Denny was crying. "Come here."

Denny went willingly into Rachel's arms, resting her head on her shoulder, feeling the chilled skin against her cheek. Deceptively strong arms wrapped around her, holding her close. Denny had no idea why she was crying. It seemed as if all her emotions were firing at once: grief, fear, anger, loneliness.

"It's okay," Rachel whispered in her ear.

After a few moments, Denny shuddered and took a deep breath. She felt ridiculous, laughing at herself to ease her nerves. "Sorry," she murmured, wiping at her eyes and stepping away from Rachel.

"Don't apologize. I think we've all lost it more than once here." Rachel smiled, her eyes adjusting to the darkness enough to make out the pale shape of Denny's face. "Come on. Let's go sit down." She took the brunette's hand and led her back toward Pam and Mia, tugging until Denny sat down with her.

"No doubt everything's been washed away. We're going to need to rebuild," Pam said, her voice devoid of emotion as she stared out into the night.

It sounded as if the rain might be easing up a bit, but no one said anything; there wasn't much use. It wasn't like they could be easily heard anyway.

As she watched the vicious beauty of Mother Nature, Rachel's mind flickered back to her rude awakening, which seemed like hours ago but in reality was no more than half an hour earlier. Her sleep had been disrupted by voices, then the rain, as it inevitably broke through the thick foliage above their shelter and poured through the woven leaves, drenching them all. She'd woken up with Denny wrapped around her, and Rachel had relished the protective warmth. And that was strange. She recalled times when Matt had tried to hold her and she had refused. More often than not, they'd end up with his head on her shoulder, or him just rolling over, angry and hurt.

It was silly, she knew, and completely psychological, but Rachel felt weak when she allowed herself to be held. Her life had always been about ensuring she had complete control over herself, her mind, her emotions, and her craft. Growing up with an obsessively controlling father and a mother who was too weak to stand up to him, the Holt girls had struggled to take any amount of control over their own lives they could, which meant mainly in their own minds. The degree to which her childhood was supervised and regulated had sent Rachel into her own head at a young age. There she had created an entire world she alone could build or destroy.

Now she wondered why she had allowed Denny to hold her. Yes, she had been asleep, and good sleep was hard to get on the hard, cold ground, but their shared body heat had apparently sent them both off into a deep sleep. Rachel didn't think Denny would have held her otherwise. Glancing at her now, she didn't think Denny even knew what she'd done; when Denny was awakened by the storm, Rachel was already running out of the shelter.

Rachel realized that her tolerating, even welcoming, Denny's embrace probably boiled down to being very tired, warm, and content for the first time in months, and the easy, trustworthy persona that was Denny. Green eyes closed as Rachel rested her head against the wall.

Cold. So very cold. His knees already pressing uncomfortably against his ribs, Dean tried to pull his legs even tighter against his body. He was wet, covered in mud, and tired. *Does the blasted rain ever end?!* He ducked his head out of the tiny hiding place he and Michael had found, looking up into the sky beginning to lighten. The rain was still falling, but now at a much less threatening rate. It had become more like a pleasant afternoon drizzle.

"If I don't see rain again any time soon, it will be fine by me," Michael grumbled, eyes closed and his head resting back against the trunk of a tree.

Dean sighed heavily. "Amen to that."

Eyes sliding open, Michael glanced over at the man sitting no more than a foot away. He was amazed to find he no longer felt any of the contempt for the smaller man he'd felt just the day before. Now, looking at the miserable attorney, he felt a sense of pride and camaraderie with the little guy.

Feeling eyes on him, Dean met the Texan's gaze. He was surprised to see a smile on Michael's rugged features.

"We ain't so different, are we?" Michael's deep voice was filled with pleasant surprise.

Dean shook his head. "Nope. Guess not."

"Thanks, man." Michael held out a large hand, which was quickly grasped. With one firm handshake, an understanding of sorts was forged and all assumptions fell to the wayside.

"You're welcome." Dean's chest filled with a sense of a job well done. He released Michael's hand and tucked his own under one of his armpits. "What a mess," he said at length, looking out over the destruction.

"Ain't that the truth. Reckon that was a hurricane, or at least a pretty damn ugly tropical storm," Michael said, remembering the storms of his childhood. Hell, Katrina still woke him with nightmares, and now the existence they had managed to scrape out on the island had been destroyed. Everything was gone; they'd have to start over.

"Wonder what happened to the women." Dean worried they mightn't have fared well. The thought of being stuck on the island with only Michael, with no buffer, made him cringe. No matter what kind of understanding they'd reached, he didn't think that would be wise. Michael was a good looking guy, with a real cute butt, but Dean knew he'd be murdered with Michael's bare hands if he were to even *think* like that. With an instinct for self preservation, he tossed any such thoughts out of his head.

"Don't know. Did you see them?" When Dean shook his head, Michael dragged himself to his feet, though his body was screaming. He was cold, hungry, tired, and beyond sore from battling the elements. "Come on, Dean. Let's get this over with. We'd better check out the damage."

Dean groaned as he stood, surprised by the steadying hand on his arm. Smiling his thanks, he followed the Texan out to the beach. To the horror of both men, as expected, the beach was in ruins. The normally flawless sand was marred by deep ruts filled with small oceans of their own. Tree and plant parts littered the sands, and the spot where their shelters had stood now held only a toppled palm.

Michael whistled through his teeth, shaking his head as he tucked his hands into the back pockets of his jeans. The wet, muddy denim felt like a vise around him.

The storm's aftermath reminded Dean of the destruction of Ground Zero in the months after the terrorist attacks, which took place not far from Will's office. "This is unreal," he said, his voice soft and thick with unshed tears.

"Let's explore, see if we can find the girls and anything that can be salvaged."

Dean started to follow Michael then stopped as he noticed movement out of the corner of his eye. His laughter was so sudden, so completely unexpected, it startled Michael. The Texan's gaze shot to where Dean was trotting off, his own amusement bubbling up until his laughter mingled with Dean's.

Green eyes slowly slid open, and for the second time in five hours, Rachel wasn't sure why. Warmth engulfed her on either side, insulating her from the cold behind and beneath her. She was sitting against the back wall of the recess behind the waterfall, legs stretched out and crossed at the ankles. *Okay, that explains the coldness under my ass.*

Glancing to her right, she found herself facing very dark hair. An inspection of her left side revealed the same. It seemed Mia and Denny had found her shoulders to be comfy as pillows. Smiling to herself, Rachel was loath to disturb either of them, but then what had wakened her made itself clear.

"Shit," she muttered, her bladder demanding relief. All the wonderful fish and water she'd had the night before was making its last curtain call. Her physical need outweighing her emotional one, Rachel gently extricated herself from the sleeping duo that flanked her. Checking to see they had stayed asleep, the blonde scurried out of their dry spot and into the drizzle beginning to warm with the rising sun.

Despite the devastation the storm had wrought, Rachel was amazed by the intense brightness of color around her. The plants seemed to have brightened their neon hues by at least fifty percent overnight. It would have been breathtaking if the broken leaves, pummeled flowers, and snapped trees hadn't been a part of the picture.

Her bladder urgently reminded her of its intention to let loose at any moment, which drew Rachel's focus back to the reason why she was out wandering in the wild in the first place. She picked her way around what was usually a deep pond but was now a veritable lake, trying to find a good bush still in one piece. Zeroing in on one such bush, she pushed down what was left of her jeans, sighing in relief and then yelping when a rogue leaf tickled her in a spot where she hadn't been tickled for quite some time.

As Rachel relieved herself, she wondered where they'd build their next shelter, certainly further up from the beach and deeper into the jungle. It would take some effort from everyone. That led her thoughts to Michael and Dean, and she prayed they had survived. She smiled slightly, remembering Dean's easy smile and somewhat tempestuous personality, while Michael was gruff and rugged, yet had a heart of gold. She wondered what Melissa was like. *What kind of woman had tamed the beast of Texas and managed to mine her way to that gold?*

Rachel snapped out of her musings with a shriek as something smacked her in the shoulder. Stopping mid-pee, she shot to her feet, looking around fearfully for a snake. What she found was long and could be slimy, but it wasn't any snake.

Blue eyes flew open as a shrill scream rent the air. Confused and disoriented, Denny scrambled to her feet and ran out of the little alcove, doing her damnedest to run on wet, slick rock and dirt without falling into the brand new ocean that had developed on the island overnight. She briefly wondered what the eighth ocean would be called. Her amusement was short lived as she heard another scream.

Holding her pants closed, Rachel bent over and picked up the flesh colored object that had bounced off her shoulder and landed in a tumble of leaves and branches. She screamed again as something pinched her ass. Spinning around, eyes wide, Rachel's heart swelled with her relief. "Dean!"

She threw herself at him, as covered in mud as he was; she didn't care. In fact, she wondered how the rather fussy man was handling the grime. It didn't matter; she was just relieved to see him. "You made it," she breathed, as he wrapped his arms around her, hugging her tight. She felt the sting of tears behind her eyes and quickly forced them down, though they welled again when she saw the tears in Dean's eyes. "What about—"

"I'm here, too, darlin'."

Rachel let out another small cry when she found herself pulled into an almost painfully tight hug, breathing her sigh of relief against Michael's chest. "Oh, thank God!" Pulling away just enough to look up into his face, she gave him a relieved, watery smile. "We were all so worried."

"Rachel!" Denny yelled, running through the foliage, trying to find her friend, who sounded as if she was in trouble. "Rach—" She cut herself off mid-yell when she saw the grinning trio. "Son of a..." She ran headlong to the two men, grabbing both in a headlock, relief and anger clashing for supremacy. "Do you two have *any* idea how goddamned worried I was?"

Dean and Michael were taken aback by Denny's reaction, having only seen her get fired up the one time, back when Michael called Dean a name.

"Don't you ever do that again, you got it?"

"Michael! Dean!" Mia exclaimed.

Within moments everyone was crying at the happy reunion, all hugs and smiles.

"Anyone up for breakfast?" Dean finally asked, waving the retrieved dildo in the air for emphasis.

Chapter 10

Tiffany Riley sipped from her clear plastic cup, her upper lip stained with red drops from the fruit punch being served. Her eyes, coal black, studied the brunette across the room talking to Jim Lopez, one of the district managers. The new accountant wiped her red punch mustache with a napkin adorned with a colorful turkey and wishes for a happy Thanksgiving. She couldn't keep her eyes off of Hannah, knowing full well what had happened to the woman over the summer, her loss. Tiffany was reluctant to approach her, though she wanted to get to know her.

It had been a month since the shorter woman started with the company, and Hannah Donnelly had caught her eye right away. Tiffany had lacked the courage to so much as speak to her, but figured today she'd take the risk.

Running a hand through short auburn hair, Tiffany let out a long breath and set her plastic cup down on the refreshment table. She straightened her suit jacket, thrusting her shoulders back in a feigned sense of confidence. She walked slowly toward Hannah, smiling slightly in relief as Jim Lopez squeezed the beautiful woman's arm then moved toward the buffet table to fill a plate with the turkey dinner provided smorgasbord style. Left alone, Hannah sipped her punch, watching her co-workers.

"Nice get together, huh?" Tiffany asked, standing at Hannah's side.

The brunette glanced at her and nodded. "Nicer than last year. We got cold cuts." Hannah chuckled along with the shorter woman, whom she'd noticed in the office on and off. She thought she was new, but didn't know her name.

"At my last job, over at Hoff and Curtman, they handed out hard candy."

Hannah chuckled again, shaking her head. "That's terrible. A slap in the face." They stood in silence for a moment until Tiffany introduced herself. The researcher took the offered hand and replied, "Hannah," then dropped Tiffany's hand, but not before she had noted the softness of it. She blocked it out of her mind.

"So, any plans for the long weekend?" Tiffany asked at length, feeling her palms sweat as she tried to bolster her courage.

"Not really." For a moment, Hannah looked profoundly sad. "Hang around the house, maybe do some spring cleaning."

"In the autumn?"

"Yeah. Kind of like Christmas in July, I suppose."

They shared a small smile before turning their attention back to the room filled with people, murmurs of conversation, and the occasional peal of laughter. Tiffany tried to think of a way to get to know Hannah outside of work, some way to casually invite her out without it seeming as if she was *asking* her out.

"I don't know about you, but I'm kind of thinking this turkey they're serving is a little gross. I'm not a dark meat gal."

"Yeah." Hannah glanced down at the remnants of her mostly uneaten dinner on the table next to her.

"I was thinking about maybe grabbing a sandwich at Rocky's."

"Ohhh." Hannah grinned. "I love Rocky's. Their meatball sandwiches are to die for."

"Mm, yeah." Tiffany's eyes brightened, as if the idea had just struck her. "Want to go get one?"

Hannah was surprised by the offer, but couldn't help the small smile that turned up the edges her lips, or the nod she gave. She couldn't get her four day weekend to start soon enough. It was her first Thanksgiving without Denny, and she just wanted to curl up in her flannel pjs and shut out the world. Maybe a little socializing first would be good for her. "Sure."

The winter air was well and truly settling over Buffalo, New York. Both women tugged their jackets tighter around their bodies, braving the fierce wind to walk the one block to the popular deli. Nearly blown inside, they welcomed the warmth and calm of the small place, which was nearly empty on the late Wednesday afternoon.

"Hey, ladies. What can I get for you?" the man behind the counter asked, resting his hands on the counter on either side of the register. After taking their orders and ringing up their money, he said, "Grab a seat, I'll bring your orders out to you."

"I think this is the emptiest I've ever seen this place," Tiffany commented, dragging her scarf from around her neck. The absence of its warmth made her shiver slightly.

Hannah nodded. "I know. If only it was always like this."

She has such a beautiful smile. Tiffany cleared her throat, smiling at the man as he brought their drinks. One thing she didn't like about Rocky's was the "no refills" policy. She often wished she could take a full cup back to the office with her.

As Hannah held her cup of coffee between chilled palms, blowing over the black beverage, Tiffany spared a glance at her, trying to study her face in the split second she allowed herself. She made a note to herself to start asking around about the beautiful brunette more than she already had.

I won't get sick. I won't get sick. I won't get sick.

"You okay, Will?" Garrison asked, her voice tinny in the headset they each wore. Will nodded vigorously, though his face got more green as they flew out over the water. The pilot tried not to chuckle, hoping he wouldn't puke in the Bell 407. The seven-seater was flying low, the waves rushing beneath them. The bubble cockpit made it easy to see a good distance around the chopper. After stopping to refuel, they were at last on their way for mission number two.

Will swallowed his sickness down, not liking the height thing at *all*. There was no way he wasn't going to be with Garrison for the flight, just in case. It was the holiday season, and he had vacation time to take before the end of the year, so he was using it wisely. Will had come to respect, and like, Garrison Davies more than a little. She was a good person with a big heart. During their last flight, she had told him all about her partner, Keller, and their ward, Keller's much younger sister, who Garrison referred to as her daughter. In a nutshell, Will had discovered that Garrison had saved the girls from a savagely abusive father, she and Keller had fallen in love and started a life together, raising Parker together.

Will was touched by the story; it made him respect the pilot even more. Watching the obvious love between the two pilots — Keller also flew with Davies' Hangar — Will had become that much more determined in his search for Dean. The memorial back in October had been a success for his goal of getting Rachel Holt's husband on board with his wild idea. Sure enough, the high profile backing had mustered financial support for the mission to find any additional survivors.

Garrison felt guilty about accepting money under potentially false pretenses from the dear man sitting beside her, but she'd promised to help him, though she felt it was a fool's errand. Knowing the power channeling through an aircraft, she had been stunned to hear there had been any survivors at all. She thought it unlikely more were out there somewhere; she didn't have the heart to tell that to Will.

During the first trip, Garrison had covered charted territory, but now was going off the beaten path, checking in with the closest tower every few minutes to give her location and direction. The cockpit remained silent for some time, both occupants of the plane keeping their eyes focused on the sea below, praying to see anything indicative of...well...anything.

"I can't believe how much water there is down there," Will noted, squinting at what he realized was a fisherman's vessel below, which they quickly passed.

Garrison nodded. "There sure is. A shit load of ice melting, huh?"

Will chuckled. "Isn't that the truth."

"Shit!" Dean muttered a few other choice words as he sputtered salt water out of his nose, his sinuses burning from the unexpected swim.

"Son-of-a-bitch, bastard, piece of shit. Shit!" Treading water, he noted the bobbing pieces of wood, almost taunting him, as they floated close by, slowly drifting further and further away from one another as vines dangled lamely from the trunk around which they'd been secured.

"Guess that didn't work." Michael grinned, chuckling at his companion's glare of death. The Texan had been pissed off, oh Lordy, yes! But as soon as he'd seen how upset Dean was, he figured one of them had to keep a level head. He swam over to one of the logs, grabbed onto it then swam back toward Dean, floating it toward his irate companion. "Hold on to that," he instructed, swimming toward the other three logs moving further away. He figured one of them would just have to get away, as he only had two hands and didn't want to swim too far out.

Dean did as he was told, watching as Michael swam toward the other logs, wrapping powerful arms around two and grunting as he turned them around, holding on as he kicked back toward shore. Dean followed with his single log.

"Well, hell, doesn't seem that worked all that well," Pam snickered, shielding her eyes with a deeply tanned hand, watching the men return from their aborted fishing trip. She heard Denny chuckle behind her.

"Nope. Don't you hate it when a plan falls apart at the seams?"

"I told them to use the double knot—"

"And tie the vine around the other way, too," Denny added as the women headed back into the jungle, sharing a knowing grin. "Men."

"No doubt you're the smart one," Pam said with a roll of her eyes, drawing a laugh from her equally tanned friend.

Rachel sat perched in a tree, watching out over the beach and ocean, legs drawn up and sheets of stiff paper resting on her thigh. Her hand was poised over the page, unmoving, as she watched Denny and Pam approach. Green eyes rested on the lithe figure of the brunette, noting yet again how Denny's eyes nearly glowed electric blue against the sun-darkened skin of her face. When she smiled, as she did at the moment, her teeth were like a lit mega-watt light bulb. In a word, she was stunning.

Dragging her eyes from Denny, she turned her attention back to the page she'd been working on all morning. Rachel had no idea she could write so tiny, but space on a page was a precious commodity. She had figured her supply of stationery wasn't going to last much past the end of the year, and they were in late November already. Thanksgiving was some time soon, or past, but they'd decided to celebrate it that night. Michael and Dean were out shaking down their newest watercraft, since their former fishing raft had been swept away long ago by the violent tropical storm that had stripped them of everything they'd originally managed to salvage.

Even that had turned out okay; what they had rebuilt was new and improved. They'd learned a heavy lesson, and used that knowledge productively. Just beyond a small cluster of palms to Rachel's left were their new, larger shelters, built with ingenuity and practicality. The same basic model had been used — Pam, Rachel, and Dean painstakingly weaving grasses and leaves to wrap around trunks of trees to form the shape of the dwellings. The massive number of fallen trees and branches provided the ideal building materials, which they were able to use to reinforce their structures and make sturdier walls and roofs. That helped keep out the cold night wind and winter rains.

Rachel brushed her bangs out of her face, growling when they fell back into her eyes. Her uncut hair fell in shaggy golden waves around her shoulders, her bangs just long enough to be a menace. As she finished recording her creative thought on paper, she blew up a breath to move the annoying hair out of her eyes. *What I wouldn't give for a pair of scissors!*

The blonde's attention was distracted from her story when she heard a muffled groan coming from near the waterfall. Curious, Rachel climbed down from her perch with the swift grace of hours of climbing to find food or hunt for the perfect leaf. With stealthy steps and hops over fallen trees, she followed the noise, which had turned into a deep moan.

Rachel felt her stomach flutter in anticipation of what she might find, but her curiosity had a firm grip on her. She knew she probably should turn right back around and mind her own business, but just in case it wasn't what she thought, and there was a problem, she decided to proceed. Just before rounding the bend into a slight clearing beside the new river they had in the middle of their island, Rachel stopped. The moaning was getting slightly louder.

Biting her lip, Rachel reviewed the current location of everyone she'd seen recently: Michael and Dean were playing surfer boys with their fallen logs, and Denny and Pam were talking quietly between themselves somewhere near the women's hut. That left Mia.

Green eyes wide, Rachel peeked from her hiding place behind a tree, seeing the waterfall and nook behind it. Beyond the roaring water, the barest hint of flesh color was visible, as was a slight movement. A loud groan followed by a gasp sent Rachel loping back into the safe anonymity of the dense foliage, her heart pounding.

I can't believe I did that. That was so *bad. Peeping at Mia in, well, less than public circumstances.*

As she headed out of the jungle, Rachel's own horribly neglected nether regions let her know in no uncertain terms they could also use a little attention.

"I'm such a letch," she muttered, noting Dean and Michael dragging what was left of their mighty fishing vessel to shore. "You guys didn't wrap that second vine around, did you?" she called, grateful for an interruption of her thoughts, and for her cheeks returning to their natural color.

Dean glared but didn't answer. Michael sighed, pushing his hair off his forehead and rubbing at his beard. "Really thought it'd work," he muttered defensively, staring down at the remnants.

Rachel snorted. "I know." She patted the man on his freckled shoulder and headed off toward the women's hut. "Hey," she said, ducking so she wouldn't knock her head again on the low-rise door frame.

Denny, who sat alone in the center of the hut, looked up from the coconut shell she was scooping. "Hey. Want some?"

She held out the half shell to Rachel, who took it, happily scooping out two fingers full of the pure white coconut jelly. She hummed as she sucked first one finger, then the second, tongue licking off the cool coconut. Denny's eyes were locked on her mouth and finger, blue eyes unable to look away. *Oh, God.*

Denny forced herself to look away, concentrating on her lunch of coconut and water instead. She could feel Rachel's presence as she sank down to sit next to her, her sun-kissed skin, her very presence. *Damn it!*

"So what do you—" Rachel cut herself off, stunned when her friend suddenly disappeared through the grass flap of their shelter. Confused, and a little worried, Rachel followed, afraid that maybe Denny had heard something, a problem. When Rachel examined the dense foliage around her, she saw no hint of the other woman. Nor was she on the beach. It was like the brunette had vanished.

"You lost, blondie?" Dean asked, on his way to the waterfall to rinse off the sticky salt water.

"No," Rachel said absently. "Have you seen Denny?"

Dean turned in a small circle, scanning his surroundings. "Nope. Sorry, Rach."

"'S'kay." A small sense of disappointment and, even crazier, *hurt*, filling her, she headed back to the shelter for her afternoon nap.

Denny took several deep breaths, allowing the heavy humid air to fill her lungs and ease the tension in her body. From her vantage point in the tree, she could see out over the entire island and to the ocean beyond, though the pounding of the surf was muted by distance. Her heart was pounding, her palms sweating.

Abstinence was not in Denny's makeup, and she was torn by the fierce battle being waged inside. Every day it seemed she was drawn more to Rachel, and she found herself fighting to keep the image of Hannah alive. She tried to close her eyes and bring up her partner's face, her voice, her body, a certain time they'd made love... When she had it, when the image would come into focus, it would ripple and shatter, replaced by beautiful green eyes.

"I can't do this." Hannah had been, *was,* the love of her life, and Denny couldn't forget that fact, nor could she just allow her body's urges to overrule her heart or her sense of what was right. She tried to deny the attraction to Rachel Holt, telling herself it was base need that made her skin tingle every time the blonde was around her, but Denny found she couldn't lie to herself anymore. "Shit, shit, shit!"

Dinner had been a rare treat of roasted birds, two of them, for dinner rather than fish, of which everyone was tired. No matter how many different ways they found to cook the catch of the day, it was still fish. Pam had taken extra care over the meal, preparing a special beverage, as well. She saved berries all week, crushing them and mixing them with water, creating a weak Kool Aid, of sorts, which everyone had sucked down with desperation for something different, even in small amounts.

Stomach full, body partially warm, but her mind troubled by what had happened earlier in the day, Rachel lay awake. She was deeply bothered by Denny hurrying out of the shelter, then disappearing until it was time to help with dinner. Even during the meal, which had been filled with not only good food, but laughter and horror stories of Thanksgivings past, Denny had been strangely quiet, never once meeting Rachel's concerned gaze. Even their usual exchange of wishes for a good night's sleep had been skipped.

Rachel turned onto her side, pulling the newly woven grass mat further up her body and sneezing when a blade tickled her nose. The sound caused the opening of two blue eyes, which stared into Rachel's. Their proximity gave Rachel the opportunity she had been denied all day. Mindful of the two women sleeping behind her, she whispered, "Did I piss you off?"

Denny, who slept next to a wall, sighed quietly as she shook her head. She could see the hurt in Rachel's eyes, and it pained her that she'd put it there. "No," she finally whispered back.

"Then why have you been avoiding me all day?"

She had Denny there. *Why indeed? So I wouldn't do something stupid to make you hate me, or me hate myself.* Knowing she couldn't confess that to Rachel, Denny wracked her brain for a good excuse and, also, a way to not let it show that the author made her blood burn.

"I just needed some time alone today, that's all."

In some part of Rachel's mind the explanation made sense, but for some reason she didn't believe Denny. Even so, she didn't push it. She was silent for a moment, watching the brunette's face, Denny's blue eyes turning away from the scrutiny. Rachel decided Denny was perhaps the most beautiful woman she'd ever seen, a beauty that both intimidated her and drew her closer. Suddenly, for the first time in her life, Rachel felt the need to be physically close, to share personal space with someone. She wasn't sure if it was to somehow comfort the troubled Denny, or herself.

"Cold night," she whispered, feeling manipulative. Yes, it was definitely cooling off, but the blonde knew she could sleep just fine.

Denny's eyes flickered up to meet Rachel's, her heart beginning to pound in her throat. She knew what the blonde was asking, and she knew she couldn't deny her. Rachel was cold, and wanted to be warmed. With a small nod, Denny lifted her arm in invitation, much like Rachel had done for her the night of the storm, and the last time they'd shared body heat.

Rachel glanced over her shoulder, making sure Pam and Mia were still asleep. For some reason, she felt like what she was about to do was...wrong. Turning back to Denny, Rachel clutched her mat to herself as she scooted the short distance between them, turning to her other side to present her back to the taller woman.

Denny tried not to make it too obvious as she inhaled Rachel's natural scent. "Comfortable?" she whispered into the nearby ear. Receiving a nod, Denny allowed herself to relax, concentrating on keeping her companion warm and ignoring her own raging hormones.

Rachel was indeed comfortable, too comfortable for her own liking. She was beginning to wonder whether the closeness had been a bad idea, and then she felt a peace wash through her as Denny's hand came to rest lightly on her waist with the barest brush of the tops of long thighs against the back of Rachel's legs. Without her knowledge or permission, Rachel suddenly realized her own hand had covered Denny's, pulling gently until their joined hands came to rest on her stomach, this move forcing the brunette a bit closer.

Denny squeezed her eyes shut, willing her fingers to remain still and the throbbing in her nether regions to stop.

Rachel felt deeply comforted, as though everything was okay. She closed her eyes, sighing softly as she fell into sleep, with no idea her sleep-mate was wide awake, and praying to Apollo, the sun god, that he would arrive soon. She also missed a pair of dark eyes, half lidded under dark lashes, watching.

Chapter 11

Matt took in the elegance of the restaurant around him. He'd never been to Boston, though he'd had a few opportunities with Rachel. Now he wished he'd taken her up on those. It didn't help matters that the last time Rachel had been to Bean Town, Matt had declined to accompany her so he could get to know Diane better.

"There she is." Will pushed back from the table when he spotted Garrison, waving her over.

Garrison smiled when she saw them, weaving her way through the busy establishment, accepting Will's offered hand, then Matt's.

"Hey, gentlemen." Allowing Will to push her chair in for her, the blonde studied her two companions. When the waiter suddenly appeared, she smiled at him and gave her drink order before turning back to her clients. "I've contacted a friend of my father's, Jake Potter, who is a cartographer. He made maps during the Korean War. He's charted that area of the Atlantic for me."

"How did he do that?" Matt asked, dark eyebrows drawn as he brought up his beer for a sip.

"He researched every map he could find of the area and basically made a compilation map for us." Thanking the waiter as he set her seven and seven on the table before her, Garrison picked it up and took a long pull before she continued. "I'm thinking it would be better to wait out the holidays, maybe give it another go come spring—"

"Spring?" Instant anger gripped Will. Leaning forward on the table and lowering his voice, though the intent was clear, he hissed, "Garrison, if we wait until spring, we won't find a goddamn thing!"

"Will—" Matt began.

"No." Will was determined to make his point. "If we're going to find anything, we've got to do it now. What if Dean is drifting out there somewhere, on some..." he stumbled over his thoughts, rage and profound grief clogging his throat, "...some floating seat cushion! If we wait, he'll be dead."

Garrison reached across the table for Will's hand, but it was yanked away. Eyes turned to the sound of scraping as he shoved his chair back and stormed toward the front door.

"Shit." Garrison pushed her chair back, leaving Matt alone at the table, wide-eyed and wondering what the hell to do.

Will heard his name called as he headed out into the winter wonderland that was Boston, the noisy city crashing in around him.

"Damn it, stop!" Garrison ran after the man who had much longer legs, but finally she caught up to him, snagging the arm of his London

Fog and whirling him around. Sad, tired eyes looked down at her. Before she knew what hit her, Garrison found a sobbing Will in her arms. She held him, rubbing soothing circles on his back, feeling an amazing amount of affection and sympathy for the sweet man as he cried. Suddenly she got it, and it made her more determined than ever to help him. "Okay, Will. Okay."

"All right, what have we got here?" Keller Davies scooped up some salsa on a corn chip and tossed it into her mouth. Her eyes met those of the two men and her partner, who stood around the dining room table in Will's suite.

"I'm thinking that we start mapping out some of the land masses," Garrison said, settling back in her chair, ankles crossed and resting on the edge of the table. She steepled her fingers atop her stomach as Keller nodded in agreement.

"Maybe Jake can help out, or any number of Frank's war buddies."

Matt watched the two women making plans, their harmony obvious as they seemed to read the other's mind, even to the point of finishing each other's sentences. It was a foreign concept to him, and he wondered whether he and Rachel could have ever had that.

"One thing, Will," Garrison said, a note of apology in her voice, "this is our busiest season right now, so you have to understand that we have other obligations, as well."

Will nodded, munching on his own salsa-doused chip. "I do."

"Okay. So," she clapped her hands together as her booted feet hit the ground with a thud, "I think we've got a plan of action. I'll make some calls and see what I can come up with." Garrison got to her feet as Keller began rolling up the map Jake had prepared for them.

"Wait." Matt spoke up for the first time. Something was niggling at him. "What's to say *we* can find anything when the authorities couldn't?" His eyes darted back and forth between the two pilots, who stared at each other across the table. Finally Keller's blue eyes settled on him.

"Because we're the best."

Hannah wiped her mouth, her giggling causing more Pepsi to spout out from between her lips. "I'm sorry," she managed, watching in amused embarrassment as Tiffany wiped her sweater and shot over a good-natured glare.

"I'll forgive you. *This* time." It was mostly her fault anyway. She'd made Hannah laugh by doing an impression of George W. Bush, and that was when Hannah had spat the soda on her.

"Oh, this time, huh?" Hannah chuckled, resting back against Tiffany's couch, feet curled up under her. They'd spent an amazing day together, Christmas shopping and laughing. Oh, how Hannah needed to laugh! Tiffany was one of the funniest people she'd ever met, and had the rare ability to reach inside Hannah's well-guarded heart, making her forget about her problems and giving her life a bit of the light that had gone out when Denny died. "And if it happens again?" *Am I flirting?* She felt giddy at the thought, and slightly panicked. She knew she could trust Tiffany. They had become great friends, and it felt good.

"Ohhh," Tiffany purred, "I'm sure I can think of something."

Hannah was taken aback at the look in the redhead's dark eyes. *Desire.* She swallowed hard, dropping her eyes and sipping from her soda, feeling it burn all the way down her throat.

She's nervous. Tiffany studied the beauty before her carefully, noting the subtleties of her body language. Only moments before Hannah had been laughing, light and airy. At the first sign of serious, she closed up. Tiffany decided a change of subject was in order.

Getting to her feet, Tiffany scurried to her bedroom then hurried back, a small bundle hidden behind her back. "Okay, I'm always giving you shit about being a nerdy researcher for computers, so I saw this the other day and just *had* to get it for you." With a huge grin, she brought the little guy out from behind her back, holding him under the arms.

"Ohhh!" Hannah cooed at the adorable brown teddy bear, dressed in a white researcher's jacket with big, wire rimmed glasses over black, glossy eyes. Tiffany had even written *Hannah* over the left breast pocket in magic marker. "He's so cute! Thank you."

Tiffany basked in the tight hug, feeling Hannah's breasts pressed against her own, the warmth of her body and smell of her perfume invading her every cell. "You smell so good," she whispered into Hannah's neck, surprised she'd spoken it out loud.

Hannah trembled at the contact and the softness of Tiffany's words. Her eyes slid closed as the hug continued, soft hands making lazy circles on her back. She shivered at the sigh that blew through the short hairs at her neck. "Thank you," she said unnecessarily in delayed response to the compliment.

Tiffany pulled back just enough to be able to see into Hannah's eyes, which were filled with unease and...something else. Tiffany brought up a hand, gently brushing a few dark strands out of the equally dark eyes. *This has been so hard on her.* The redhead's hand found its way to Hannah's jaw, caressing the soft skin with her thumb.

Hannah's breath caught, her heart pounded with need and fear, she was gripped by guilt. Before she could voice her thoughts, soft lips pressed against her own.

Tiffany felt the brunette respond to what she'd had no intention of doing, but couldn't resist. Hannah's lips softened, her breathing shallow as the kiss began to deepen. When Tiffany's tongue caressed Hannah's, the spell was broken.

Pulling away with a gasp, Hannah's hand went to her lips, feeling the very place where Tiffany's had just been.

"I, I can't do this, Tiffany," she whispered, her eyes filled with hurt. She almost felt betrayed, though whether it was by Tiffany or herself, she wasn't sure. She rose to her feet, almost knocking Tiffany over in her haste to escape.

"Wait, Hannah..." Recovering her bearings, the redhead jumped off the couch, hurrying after Hannah, who had already reached the front door. "I'm sorry." She caught up to her, placing a hand on Hannah's shoulder, turning her away from the door. "I'm so sorry. I didn't mean to do that. I swear, I'm sorry."

Hannah was unable to meet the dark gaze. "I'll call you tomorrow, okay?"

Tiffany nodded, though she had the feeling she wouldn't be hearing from the woman who had come to mean a great deal to her in the past month. "Okay." Her voice was quiet, defeated.

"Good night." Hannah slipped out the door, still clutching the teddy bear in her arms.

Chapter 12

"Go long!" Michael yelled, arm cocked back, ready to let the coconut fly. He chuckled as he watched his little buddy try and run down the sand, which was no easy feat, especially in Gucci loafers. "Dumb fairy," the Texan said, then chuckled with affection.

Dean glanced over his shoulder, trying to keep Michael in sight as he ran, waiting for the Texan to throw another one of his bombs. *Oh shit, oh shit, oh shit,* he chanted mentally as the big man let 'er rip, the coconut flying through the air at a dizzying speed. Dean's eyes followed it all the way into the surf, throwing himself into the incoming wave to make the grab and almost drowning in his shock at actually catching the damn thing.

He broke through the surface, getting to his feet, half sputtering, half laughing as he raised the prize high overhead. He could hear Michael cheering from where he stood far down the beach. Dean was about the spike the "ball" when he stopped. Brow creasing in a frown as he concentrated, he looked up into the sky, trying to figure out what he was hearing.

"Dean!" Denny whined, waiting for her turn as the receiver.

"Wait," he said, still looking up into the sky, holding a hand up to forestall any further talking. "A hum," he said softly to himself, "like, like," he concentrated, listening, listening... "Plane! It's engines!"

Denny and Michael ran over to him, almost running him over as they, too, studied the skies, trying to hear what Dean was hearing.

"Don't you hear it?" Dean was beside himself. "Yes, yes, it's engines. Like a plane, but not quite..."

Denny listened, straining, a vibration of sorts. Like, "A helicopter."

"Yes! That's what it is!" Dean was almost jumping up and down. "Light the fires! Light the fires!" he yelled, running toward the signal logs.

"Wait, Dean; hold on now, buddy. Let's wait," Michael cautioned.

"For what!"

"Until we see it." Michael was frantically scanning the sky. It was bright blue, not a cloud to be seen or a glint of metal. "Don't be wastin' the wood 'til we have something to signal."

"No! We need to light it!" Dean's hands shook with excitement and nervousness, and he cursed as he dropped the wood bow.

"Do you guys hear that?" Pam asked, running full speed out of the dense jungle, her eyes already pinned to the sky, Mia at her heels. "Do you?"

"Yeah!" Denny spun in a circle, squinting against the glare. Oh, what she'd give for a pair of sunglasses!

"Are they coming for us?" Mia asked, her voice a whisper of subdued hope.

"I don't know, darlin'." Michael's Adam's apple bobbed as he swallowed hard. "I just don't know."

Rachel looked up from her newest project, Christmas gifts in the making, eyes shaded against the intense blue of the sky. She set down the coconut shell she'd been working with and rose to her feet. She could hear it, a motor of some type, disturbing the still, afternoon air.

"What is that?" she whispered, walking over to her favorite spot on the ledge near the waterfall, getting as close to the edge as she dared, the ocean waiting below. "Is that an airplane?" She craned her neck back as far as she could, searching, hoping, her heart pounding in anticipation.

"Come on, you bastard!" Dean yelled, dropping the bow again. Finally he managed to get all the parts together, gasping with relief at the smoke that began to rise. "Light, you bastard. Light!" The kindling caught fire and Dean smiled as the small flame flickered to life. Glancing up at the skies again, he jumped to his feet, running into the foliage, toward his hut.

"Where're you going, Dean?" Denny asked, taking her eyes off the sky for only a moment.

"To pack! We have to be ready!"

"Dean, no," she shouted after him, returning her gaze to the heavens. The sound was getting softer, further away. "It's leaving." She slumped as disappointment gripped her, hard and painful. Soon the sound was nothing but a brief memory of hope.

"Where is it? I'm ready," Dean said, panting from the exertion and excitement, his few meager belongings in his hands. Wide eyes looked everywhere, as though he expected a helicopter to be landing on the beach.

"It's gone," Pam said harshly, head hanging as she turned away from the sky, disgusted and disheartened. She walked over to the fire that was quickly spreading on the pyre, angrily kicking sand on it to douse the flames. "Fucking gone!"

"No." Dean ran toward the water's edge where he'd first heard the chopper. "No, it can't be gone." Desperation filled him as he searched the sky, two coconuts clutched to his chest, along with his one extra sarong. "No! Goddamn it, where did they go?"

No one said a word, each dealing with their own devastation. Dean turned to face each one in turn. "Where did it go?" he asked again, voice rising in pitch with his panic. Still everyone remained silent. Frustrated and beyond upset, Dean kicked at the sand with a growl, throwing his worldly possessions to the ground and stalking off into the jungle.

"Well," Michael said at length, "that's that." He sighed heavily, reaching for the coconut they'd been using as a ball earlier. "Denny, it's your turn," he said flatly, his heart not in it.

"Yeah." Denny easily caught the toss, fiddling with it in her hands, lost in her own disappointment. She wanted to cry, break down and scream at the sky, the Fates, and everyone on the God-forsaken island, but she knew it would do no good. She needed to keep it together. After all, they had everything on the island they could want, right? Except their freedom.

Hearing the silence after the sound of the motor faded, Rachel felt the silent tears sliding down her cheeks and she brushed at them absently. With a dejected sigh, she turned back to her project, starting another small fire.

Never in her life had Denny seen such a quiet group of people, nor had she seen the island so quiet, save for the first day she arrived, when she'd been alone. She left everyone to their own devices, knowing that each needed to get through their disappointment in their own way. If any of them were thinking along the same lines she was, then they were remembering their lives before the crash, realizing how close they'd come to going home, and how dreadfully far away they still were.

Denny walked along the beach on the back side of the island, feeling the chill as night fell. The waves crashed upon the rocky shore, but she paid them no mind. She did notice a lone fire up on Rachel's ledge. Realizing she hadn't seen Rachel since early afternoon, she followed the beacon, climbing rapidly with calloused hands and feet. At times like this, she felt like Jungle Jane.

Rachel's golden hair glowed orange in the small fire, her features painted in eerie pockets of dancing shadow. Rachel looked over at Denny, eyes turning a golden gray in the firelight.

"Hey," Rachel said, her voice soft, eyes glancing back at her fire as an unfortunate bug flew into the flame, popping and fizzling.

"Hi. Is this okay?" Denny asked, awaiting permission to join Rachel on the ledge. The golden hair bobbed and Denny sat down, eyeing the six coconut shell halves that were lined up in front of them, four of them filled with a strange material. The color was hard to distinguish in the fire light. "What is all this?"

"I'm making soap."

Denny's eyes widened, her spirits lifting. "Soap!"

"Shh." Rachel put a finger to her lips. "Christmas gifts. The other night it hit me. I had to research soap making when I wrote *Willing To*

Conquer, so I figured I'd give it a try. I just hope I remembered all of the ingredients." Her grin was sheepish.

"Well, after today we all need something to pick us up. This is a brilliant idea, Rachel. So these are the molds?" She fingered one of the coconut shells. At the blonde's nod, she continued. "What's in it?"

Rachel raised a honey colored eyebrow. "Oh, come on, Denny. Don't hurt my feelings by telling me you didn't read the book."

Chuckling, Denny nodded. "I did read it."

"Saponaria officinalis." Rachel stuck a finger in the mixture in one of the coconut shells, testing the texture. She glanced up with a playful smirk. "Better known as soapwart. Watch and learn."

Rachel took a handful of already peeled roots and leaves, poured a bit of water over her hand then rubbed vigorously. Denny's eyes were pinned to the sight as froth began to seep out from between the blonde's palms. Her skin and scalp itching at the sight of fresh soap, she let out a long breath. "Share?"

Rachel chuckled, opening her hands to Denny's outstretched ones. "It doesn't smell particularly wonderful, but it's something."

"Oh, yes!" Denny lathered the slightly prickly foam between her hands; in their circumstances, the soap was worth more than gold. She closed her eyes as she brought it up to her face, inhaling the natural, slightly bitter scent. "This beats out the smell of Dean's sweat any day."

"That's no lie." Rachel poured water over Denny's soapy hands, smiling at the contented sigh that elicited. Her demeanor changed and her voice was low and flat as she tossed more petals and stems of the soapwart into the shell over the small fire. "Did you hear it today?"

At first Denny was confused by the sudden deflation, but then she understood the reference. "We all did. I think Dean was the most devastated."

"I don't know about that." After a moment, Rachel gave her friend a sad smile, her eyes quickly flickering away. "What would be the first thing you'd do, if we were all able to go home?"

Denny leaned back on her hands and stared out into the darkness, a black wall that seemed to close them in on three sides, the jungle and more rock to their backs. Grimacing as she ran a clean hand through her greasy hair, she considered the question. She was surprised by the first thought that popped into her head, and what the first thought *wasn't*. "Sleep on a bed." She smiled.

"Oh, that sounds *so* good," Rachel purred, eyes half-hooded in anticipatory bliss. "Do you think they were looking for us today?"

"I doubt it. It's been a long, long time. No doubt everyone thinks we're dead by now. It kills me, putting Hannah through all this for nothing." Denny sighed heavily, lying back on the cool rock, hands tucked behind her head.

"I know." Rachel thought of her husband. She hadn't thought of him in a long time, and she wondered whether that was wrong.

"Rachel?"

The softness of Denny's voice got Rachel's attention. She met the lazy blue gaze.

"How come you don't talk about your husband?"

Rachel thought about that for a moment. She knew why she didn't talk about Matt, but was trying to decide whether she wanted to share something so personal with Denny. Looking into concerned eyes, she felt she could trust the brunette completely. Rachel was amazed by the realization; she didn't even trust Reenie as much as she wanted to trust Denny. Finally she sighed, setting down the newest batch of "soap" she'd mixed to let it harden like the others.

When she spoke, her voice was soft, almost as though she were telling her secrets to the night. "The reason I was on that flight was because, yes, I was going to Italy to start researching my next book. But the timing was because..." She hesitated. Her heart pounded, the old pain surging back in a bright burst. She looked down at her hands, feeling like a failure yet again.

Denny saw the transformation instantly, and for a moment regretted asking, but then decided maybe Rachel needed to talk about it. She scooted closer to the author, giving her silent support.

"Four days before I got on that plane, I went out to meet with a local vendor about a book signing, and when I came home, I found Matt in bed with a woman named Diane. She lived down the street."

"Oh, Rachel." Denny's heart broke for her friend. She pushed herself up into a sitting position, moving so she was sitting beside her friend, her right thigh touching Rachel's.

"I guess I should've known something was going on; all the signs were there. You know — him coming home later and later, the sudden purchasing of cologne." She shrugged, unable to meet Denny's eyes. She knew if she saw the concern that she knew she'd find there, she'd lose it and start crying again. The betrayal was still raw. "I called my best friend in New York, asked if I could visit for a few days. Reenie let me mope around her loft for a while, though I think she was about to kill me." Rachel grinned, only then able to meet Denny's gaze. "When I decided that she needed her space back and I needed some of my own, I hopped a plane for Milan. The rest is tragic history."

"You've been keeping that bottled up inside all this time?" Denny's voice was soft, soothing. She saw a nod from Rachel, who looked away. "Why?" she asked, bringing a hand up to run her fingers through shaggy blonde hair.

"I'm okay."

Rachel shrugged, though it was not believable in the least, and Denny wasn't falling for it. "You're full of shit." She scooted back against the rock face and reached for Rachel. "C'mere."

Rachel nearly flew over to the offered solace. She didn't want to talk about Matt and his infidelity, but she supposed she might feel better if she did. She certainly couldn't feel worse. Maybe if she talked it out, she might come to some sense of understanding. That would certainly make it easier when, *if,* they ever made it back. Rachel found herself engulfed in a strong embrace, her body cradled against Denny's chest.

"Talk to me," Denny said, once her friend was settled.

Rachel was quiet for a long time, so long Denny wondered if maybe she'd fallen asleep. Tilting her head to see Rachel's face, she saw green eyes blinking away tears. Denny rested her head back against the wall, bringing up a hand and absently running her fingers through Rachel's hair. She loved the golden color, the softness. Even before she knew Rachel, Denny could remember — when she'd seen pictures in magazines, or the one talk show interview she'd done — being mesmerized by the color, wondering if it was real. She blushed as she thought about how she knew it *was* natural. Stranded on an island, modesty was not an option.

"I didn't want to marry Matt, Denny. I've never said that out loud before." She'd always harbored a great deal of guilt over that. Rachel swiped at an errant tear.

"So why did you?" Denny whispered, resting her chin atop the golden hair.

"Honestly? It seemed like the right thing to do." Rachel sniffled, tears flowing freely down her cheeks. "I saw it as an experience. My whole life I've lived to gain experiences, something to write about, story fodder." Her voice lowered to a whisper, shame filling her as she finally admitted to herself, "I married Matt for story ideas."

Cringing inside, Denny tried not to react. No doubt Matt knew it, or knew something was not right between them. It wasn't her place to judge, so she made no comment, silently providing support and friendship.

"I cared about him, I may have even loved him in some way, but I know now it wasn't how it should have been. God, no wonder he cheated." Rachel buried her face in her hands, the tears cascading in earnest.

"Hey, hey." Denny tightened her grasp, placing a soft kiss on the top of Rachel's head. "If he was unhappy, or unsatisfied, he should have left, not brought another woman into your home."

"I agree, of course, but it's not so simple when your life is legally bound to someone else's." Rachel's laugh was bitter and short. "I looked into it."

"You were going to leave him?"

"I thought about it. The public scrutiny and tabloids would have been awful. I had decided to give our marriage more time, maybe another year, to see if we could be happy together." She sighed heavily, her tears slowing. "Then I caught him with Diane." Rachel stared out over the edge of the rock ledge that dropped off into the sea. "You know what I think upset me the most about finding him with another woman?"

"What?" Denny whispered.

"Knowing that I pushed him into it. I took for granted that Matt would stick around. No matter what, that *I* controlled the future of our marriage. It never occurred to me that *he* would get tired of *me* and move on. I can't blame him, really."

Denny understood both Matt and Rachel's positions. Hannah had been in a similar situation with her husband, marrying when she was nineteen because it was the proper thing to do. Still, Denny could see how angry and hurt Matt must have been. She knew if she were with Rachel, she'd want all of her too, not just what the woman was willing to give.

Her feelings of guilt coloring her interpretation, Rachel took Denny's prolonged silence for judgment. "You must think I'm a real bitch." She forced herself to listen with an open ear, trusting whatever Denny said, it would be her concept of the truth.

"No, Rachel, I don't. I think you..." *What do I think?* Taking a deep breath, she decided to be honest. "It undoubtedly wasn't a great idea to marry when you weren't ready, but since you go through life looking for experiences, you should know that you learn and grow from those experiences, good or bad."

Rachel found herself getting lost in the low, velvety quality of Denny's voice and the gentle, absolving words. "I've had a lot of time to think about this since we've been here. I honestly don't think that it was a deliberate decision for me to be so cold, so heartless as to marry him for a goddamn story." Tears started again.

"Hey, I don't think you have it in you to be so calculating on a conscious level, Rachel," Denny said into her ear, brushing long bangs out of green eyes.

Rachel had nothing left to say, so she cuddled closer into the warm body wrapped around her. She was struck by her need for Denny's comfort and the effortless way Denny got her to drop her defenses. Only Daisy could ever do that. She was the only one who truly understood Rachel, or tried to. Until now.

Dean cursed as he pushed his way through the foliage, stomping a path until he finally realized he had no idea where he was. He looked around. One tree, plant, vine, patch of dark soil, all looked like the next.

"Shit." Deciding not to panic — after all, how could he get lost on a three mile island? — the attorney decided to give himself time to vent his profound disappointment at not being rescued before returning to the others, *if* he returned to the others. He was tired of this, tired of the island, seeing the same thing every day, the same faces every day. Tired of the wind, the surf, and the ruination of his skin. Dean ran shaking hands through his stringy hair, which pissed him off all over again. He wanted his shower back home, with the three massive heads that sprayed his body with precious hot water from three angles. He missed picking the day's shampoo from the array they kept on hand, the feel of soft skin, lotion, and a goddamned shave.

The blade, in the shaver found in the washed up baggage, had long ago gone dull and been used for something else, and now even *that* was gone, victim to the wrath of Mother Nature. Why was he being punished? Was being an attorney really *that* bad? His eyes rose to the heavens as if he would find answers in the clear blue sky, which oddly, matched the color of Denny's eyes.

Dean's thoughts turned to Will. It was funny. During the first part of their incarceration, he could only think of Will's body, his incredibly talented mouth and tongue, and how good Will felt against him. But now, all he wanted was a hug from the man he loved more than life itself. He wanted to be able to look into Will's beautiful eyes and know he was home.

Dean sniffled, swiping angrily at fresh tears. He had a feeling of dread in the pit of his stomach that he'd never see his Will again, never step foot into his favorite boutiques or the bagel shop on the corner, never again be able to use their season tickets to the theater.

Finding a small clearing, Dean plopped down and buried his face in his hands.

Chapter 13

"Buon Natale!"

Gloria rolled her eyes as she was hugged by yet another cousin she hadn't seen in twenty years. She wouldn't have been seeing them *this* year, either, if not for everyone feeling the need to coddle her and surround her with joy and cheer. They had wheedled until she had made this trip to Italy.

"Buon Natale," she said, accepting a kiss on each cheek, then providing the obligatory hug to each of Cousin Bernard's six children. *Stick your Merry Christmas up your ass.*

"Gloria! Come help. Nonna needs your help."

Gloria was happy to leave the receiving line and help her grandmother set the table. The Vinzetti women had been cooking for six days, anticipating having to feed at least thirty-seven relatives. She had no idea where in her grandparents' very small cottage these people were going to go.

Christmas had been Gloria's favorite holiday, but not any more, not with Mia gone. She had never dreaded a day so much in her life. She knew her family was trying to be there for her, trying to help her forget. Despite their well-intentioned efforts, there was no way she could forget she was celebrating a day of family and love *without* her only child. She faked it as best she could, smiling and participating in mindless chatter and catching up, wishing she were back in New York, curled up with a whiskey and cable TV. The only thing she was thankful for was the chance to spend time with her grandfather, who was getting weaker as his cancer took its toll.

The previous day, Gloria had gone with her grandparents to see the doctor. The sobering news was that this would likely be Paolo's last Christmas. Gloria felt sick Mia wasn't able to see her Pappo one last time, or vice versa. But then she realized, Mia and her Pappo would be together soon enough.

Naomi studied her brother-in-law — the bright red Santa hat perched slightly askew on his head, his tailored pants and white button up shirt, festive Christmas tree bow tie. He smiled, he joked, he even took seconds of the delicious catered dinner. All of it was for appearances. He was dying inside.

"Hey, you," Will said, raising his glass in a holiday salute to his favorite female.

Naomi smiled back, hip bumping him as she sipped from her eggnog. "Hey, yourself. Great party."

"I thought so," Will agreed proudly, looking over his guests, who were merry and jubilant, just as he'd planned. "The plum pudding made quite the splash, I must say. I wasn't sure." He wrinkled his nose, sipping from his own goblet of thick, rich eggnog. Crossing one arm over his stomach, he rested his other elbow atop it, tapping his chin with a finger.

"So are you going to introduce me to your new friends? After all, they *did* fly all the way from Massachusetts to join us."

Will met twinkling dark eyes, then grinned. "But of course. Follow me." He took Naomi by the hand. "You'll love Parker, their fifteen year-old. She's darling!"

"Come on, Walter. The kids are ready to open their presents. Slowest damn man on the planet," Meredith Adams muttered, arranging the last of the cookies she and Jennifer had baked the week before and then frozen to keep them fresh. "Come on, kids. Jennifer, pour everyone something to drink. Alan, get the fire banked. Conrad, help me carry this stuff in." Meredith felt like she was parceling out instructions to thin air, as there was no movement as a result. She sighed. "I have to do everything myself."

Slamming the last cookie down on the tray, Meredith wiped her hands on a dish towel and stormed up the stairs. She was dismayed to find Jennifer's door closed, thinking the girl had been on the stairs. She swore she'd heard her. Knocking on her granddaughter's bedroom door then opening it, she saw that the girl sat at the small writing desk, working feverishly on a paper for her tenth grade history class.

"Did you hear me? I need some help downstairs to get dinner on the table."

"Hang on, Grandma. I'm almost done," the girl said, scribbling the last of her notes.

Meredith went to the desk and peered over her granddaughter's shoulder. "Is your paper on that female king? What was it, The Donald?"

Jennifer chucked, glancing up. "*Donal*, Grandma. Yeah, she was a female ruler."

"Well, whoever she was, get your little butt downstairs so we can start Christmas."

"Come on, boys," Walter said, walking by the family room where Alan and Conrad continued to play video games, despite their grandmother's summons, which were loud enough to be heard, but had been completely ignored.

"Come on, Con," Alan said, tossing his controller to the floor and pushing up from the couch. The stubborn thirteen-year-old remained in front of the TV, focused on killing the bad guy, again and again and again.

About to make his way to the living room, Walter stopped, noting the youngest boy still playing games. "Conrad," he barked, "get off your ass and do as your grandmother says."

"Why? *You* don't," the boy muttered, not taking his eyes off the screen, lip curled in rage as he shot the zombie, watching in satisfaction as it blew apart, blood and gore spraying the screen.

Having no patience for the defiant attitude, Walter felt anger wash through him. He and his wife had taken the kids in out of a sense of duty, and he was getting damn tired of their bullshit. He wanted his old, peaceful life back. And his little girl.

Conrad yelped in surprise as large hands gripped him under the arms and dragged him away from the TV. Kicking angrily, the boy tried to get away from his formidable grandfather. "Let me go! Let me go!"

Hearing the struggle from the other room, Meredith and Alan ran in to find Walter and Conrad grappling, the boy about to launch a physical attack on his grandfather as his temper flew out of hand.

"Con!" Alan grabbed the boy, pinning his arms to his side, lifting the boy off his feet as Conrad struggled against him. "Stop it, stop it!"

Conrad stilled, the sound of his brother's voice penetrating the fog of anger that constantly clouded his judgment and thoughts.

"This is not gonna bring Mom and Dad back!" Alan felt his little brother go limp in his arms, so he put Conrad back on his feet then he turned the boy around. Conrad had grown so much over the past year the older Dupree couldn't even use the kid's head as an armrest anymore. Alan knew Conrad would later be ashamed of the tears that streamed down his face. Their dad had always taught them to be men, and men didn't cry. "Come on," he muttered, leading the boy outside.

Profound disappointment filled Meredith. All she'd wanted was a good Christmas for the kids. Suddenly her husband's arms were around her, his plaid shirt absorbing her tears of frustration.

"Here. Thought you might want this."

Matt looked up as the unexpected voice of his partner broke the stillness of the squad room. "What are you doing here, Burt? And all dressed up." He sat back in his chair, taking the steaming coffee the large man had set on his desk.

"Look pretty sharp, don't I?" Langley grinned, adjusting his tie under the roll of his double chin. "Going to Mass with the wife. Thought I'd stop by on the way to give ya this." He set a festive plastic tray filled with Christmas goodies and wrapped in green cellophane in the center of the detective's desk.

"Tell Rita I said thanks. This'll be dinner."

Burt's smile, weak to begin with, slid off his face. "That invite still stands, Matt. Nobody should be alone on Christmas."

"I've got work to do."

"Yeah, well, dinner's at six if'n you change your mind. Gotta go — the Communion wine is calling." With a wink, Burt headed out, leaving Matt alone with his thoughts.

The cop grabbed a pencil from the holder at the corner of his desk and twisted it between his cigarette-stained fingers. Rachel would kill him if she knew he'd picked up the habit again, but some days it was the only thing that calmed him. He was working ridiculous hours every day, sometimes seven days a week. His captain had already warned him, so to appease her he'd taken the weekend off, but was back sitting at his desk on Christmas Day. "Deck the halls," he muttered, turning back to his computer.

"You have *got* to be kidding me!" Reenie gawked, watching the two women dancing across her spacious living room. Hair whipping around, the little blonde in Beth's arms looked wonderful, and their dancing together was one of the most sensuous things Reenie had ever seen.

Furniture pushed aside and rug rolled up, Beth and her castmate, Christian, were doing their best not to giggle as they dirty danced, then Beth whirled the blonde away, watching as Christian launched into the air, landing silently on her knees, head snapping back.

"Bravo!" Reenie cried, clapping loudly as the two ladies bowed deeply. "You two can be the Christmas entertainment *any* time!"

The two dancers hugged in triumph as the dark eyed woman fanned herself. Beth had met the amazingly talented dancer in San Francisco, where they'd worked together briefly. They had become fast friends, keeping in contact over the years, even as Christian moved from state to state and country to country, performing for audiences all over the world. Beth was thrilled to have her back in the U.S., and was in New York to support her friend in her newest role in *Midnight Run*.

"Miss Scott." Reenie handed the dancer a rose from a Christmas basket she'd received at work.

"Oh, why thank you." With a grin, Christian bowed deeply again as she accepted the gesture of appreciation.

"And Miss Sayers."

"Madame." Beth's bow was all flourish as she accepted her rose.

Chuckling, Reenie moved toward the kitchen. "Come on, you two. Dinner's ready."

Christian did not have enough time off to fly to Sterling, Colorado to spend the holiday with her elderly aunt and uncle, so Beth had invited her to join her and Reenie for a quiet, low key dinner with the girls. Though she had performed in New York many times before, she was a new resident and didn't yet have many friends, so Christian had eagerly accepted.

Beth knew a holiday away from family was tough on her longtime friend, so she'd done her best to keep the evening light and filled with laughter. A wonderful person and good company, Christian had hit it off with Reenie, just as Beth figured they would. Instead of wallowing in sadness or loss, thinking about Christmas without seeing Rachel, or at least talking to her for half the day over the phone, Reenie listened and laughed at the two entertainers' stories of success and dismal failure on stage, of breaking legs, figuratively and literally. It was more fun than Reenie had had in six months.

It had been a hard decision. It had been a *very* hard decision, but Tracy liked her new surroundings, enjoying the snow falling around the ranch in Billings, Montana. When her mother's insurance and self-funded retirement savings had been cashed in, Tracy took the money, quit her job, and bought the small ranch out west. She was tired of the East Coast, having lived there most of her life, save for the four wonderful years she'd gone to college in Idaho. She'd fallen in love with the dry climate, the people, and the unbelievable openness of the land. Back in New York, everything and everyone was crammed into such tight spaces. She wanted her son to grow up in Montana, where both of them would be able to ride every day, not just on weekends when they could get to the stable horses.

Colleen decided against making the move west. Her elderly parents lived in New Jersey and she wanted to stay near them. It had been a painful parting, but Tracy understood. Colleen and Tracy had talked about it at length, and decided Tracy would get a hearing dog, trained to be an aide for the deaf. Besides, Luke, now seven, could help. It was scary, but necessary. Tracy needed a new start and new surroundings, where she wouldn't be haunted by the specter of her mother. There had been many unresolved issues between them when her mother's plane had gone down.

Tracy had been a junior at Lampley, a college for the deaf in Idaho, when she met Samson Tackle, a professor who was hearing impaired. Tracy had become pregnant that spring, and Pam had been livid. She had worked long, hard hours to pay for her daughter's education, and to her mind Tracy was throwing that away, with an instructor to boot. An instructor who didn't stay around to face up to his responsibilities. Mother and daughter had never gotten along afterwards, and Pam had a difficult time accepting her grandson. Still, Tracy knew over the past couple of years, her mother had tried her best, and she and her mother had gotten closer, but nowhere near as close as they'd been before Tracy left for college.

Now, watching her son tear into a gift from his dad, who had come back into Luke's life when the boy was two, Tracy felt a sense of peace. She would always have regrets, and would always yearn for the mother who had withdrawn emotionally and then died before they could fix things between them.

Tracy's attention was captured by movement, an automatic smile returning to her face at her son's excitement over the huge fire engine. She clapped her hands to let him know she was happy for him.

She released her lip then pulled back in, this time even, white teeth chewing lightly. Hannah ran her thumb over the cool glass; Denny's beautiful face smiled up at her. The picture had been taken during their trip to Kauai. Denny was sitting on the trunk of their rental car in the strangely wooded area at "The end of the road", the beach at one end of Kauai's only highway, and where they'd spent a great deal of their time.

Hannah felt her heart pounding in her ears as she questioned her decisions of the past month. *Tiffany.* After the redhead had kissed her, Hannah had run, and run far. The kiss had felt so right and yet, so terribly wrong. She'd gone home and cried, cradling one of Denny's shirts to her chest. It reminded her of Denny, which made her cry harder.

After long talks with her mother, Hannah had come to the conclusion she couldn't live her life grieving. She had to live for what she felt was right for her. She loved Denny, would always love Denny, but ultimately she knew Denny would want her to move forward and be happy. Hannah felt as if she had a shot at happiness and decided to take it.

"I love you, Denny," she whispered, kissing the glass then placing the photograph in the box with the rest of Denny's things. She carried the final box to the garage and stacked it with the rest.

Chapter 14

Rachel chuckled as the parade of freshly cleaned bodies walked by, each person sporting a huge grin. It had been so difficult to keep her gift a surprise for everyone until what they surmised was actually Christmas Day, but she had managed with Denny's help.

> *"Can I give it to them now?"*
> *"No, Rachel, it's not time yet."*
> *"But—"*
> *"No! Come on, Rachel. Stay strong."*

"What are you grinning at?" Denny asked.

Rachel shook her head, brushing overly long bangs out of her eyes. She couldn't wait until she could actually tuck them behind her ears. "Just glad everyone enjoyed their Christmas gift, that's all."

"Ohhhh," Denny purred, sniffing at her own skin, which wasn't Irish Spring fresh but was no longer oily and smelled of nature. "You have *no* idea."

"I think I do, if Dean's antics are any indication." They both laughed, remembering how he had run to the shore, whipped off his sarong, and waggled his business to God and the sea with a whoop. "I've never seen such white ass cheeks in all my life."

"Giggling girls make me nervous," the owner of the white ass cheeks said with a raised eyebrow, walking up to the couple.

Though no one had said a word to Rachel and Denny about their status, everyone on the island was seeing the two women now as a couple. It was obvious to anyone with eyes something had been growing between the two almost since day one. Pam told Dean and Michael about their nights — how Denny and Rachel would glance over at their two housemates and make sure they were asleep, then Rachel would cuddle up with Denny who wrapped her body around the blonde, both quickly falling asleep.

"Yeah, well your peanut flapping in the wind makes *me* nervous," Denny said, eyes wide as she prodded her chest with her thumb.

Dean chuckled. "Eh, you're suffering from dildo loss."

"Yeah, 'cause you keep stealing it."

Rachel lost it as a blush crept slowly up Dean's deeply tanned chest, burning his cheeks and ears until, finally, without another word, he raised his chin in defiance and marched off. Blue eyes met Rachel's green, and both women dissolved in fits of laughter.

The back beach, where Pam, Mia, and Rachel had landed was covered in dangerous rocks and reef. Pam stood on what had become known as The Rock. She was freshly washed, her skin tingling and her hand absently running over a naked breast. She was missing Austin, her thoughts drifting to him for the first time in several months. They hadn't dated long so the emotional attachment wasn't there, but she still missed him and was deeply sorry he'd lost his life in the crash. She knew though his death had been gruesome, at least it had been quick.

Closing her eyes, her thoughts returned to the sensation of her hand on her skin, highly sensitive skin, and wanting it to spread through her body. She'd kept her body's needs under control, but she was feeling them keenly at the moment. She didn't know if it was because she was clean, or because she simply needed physical release. Whatever the reason, she gasped as her hand brushed across one of her rigid nipples, arousal gathering between her thighs, which moved together restlessly as her weight shifted from one hip to the other.

Michael hummed under his breath, his deep voice almost gravelly in his song. He was searching for more vines to make the women necklaces for Christmas. He was amused at himself. Being stranded on an island had done nothing to improve his tendency to procrastinate at the holidays. The Texan spotted exactly what he was looking for — the bright white and pink flowers winking at him in sunlight and shadow through the trees. He could hear the crashing of waves on rocks getting louder as he neared The Rock.

Pam's eyes remained closed as her hand squeezed her breast, then her palm rubbed over the tightening nipple. Her other hand slid down over a newly flattened belly to undo the tie of her sarong. The skin hot to her touch, she was aching now as her mind brought up fantasies and memories of being touched.

"Oh," she sighed, the material of her clothing sliding down her thighs, pooling at her bare feet. Her fingers slid further down, brushing the wiry hair between her legs, surprised by how wet she was.

Michael's hum turned to a soft whistle as he broke through the line of trees, stopping dead in his tracks when he saw a naked Pam standing on the beach. Her hands were blocked from his sight, but he thought he saw slight movement from between her legs.

Michael Dupree had an unusually potent sex drive, and the island had been like a death sentence to his manhood. He'd sneaked off into the jungle many a night, groaning quietly at the quick release, but nothing would ever replace the softness of a woman, the feel of her heat surrounding him in a pocket of softness. He felt himself growing hard at the thought and at the vision before him. He knew he should walk away, go jack off in the trees, then finish his vine gathering, but he was rooted to the spot, unable to take his eyes off Pam obviously pleasuring herself, soft sighs and groans audible above the sounds of the surf.

Suddenly getting the feeling she was being watched, Pam froze. Embarrassment filled her as she took her fingers away from her clit and covered herself as best she could. Turning, she gasped at seeing Michael standing in the shadows. His presence spoke to Pam's need, and she felt new wetness gathering.

Without a word, she slowly uncrossed her arms in silent invitation. Michael walked onto the beach, hands reaching down to his fly to swiftly unzip what was left of his jeans, his intent clear.

Pam felt her heart pounding, her breathing quickening as she slowly backed up, her eyes locked on his, indicating he should follow. In a heartbeat, Michael pounced, his mouth roughly taking hers, feeling hands pushing at his pants. One of his big hands reached down to wrap around the back of her leg, roughly pulling it up, Pam's heel latching onto the back of his thigh.

Pam groaned loudly at the intense heat as Michael entered her in one quick thrust. Both were breathing harshly as they basked in the bliss of human contact and sexuality. Never in her life had Pam experienced anything so satisfying, brief though it was. Michael groaned into her neck as he thrust one last time, their bodies plastered together by sweat and desire.

After a moment, they began to recover and realized what they'd done. Michael pulled out, turning his back on Pam as he resettled himself. Pam ran a shaking hand through her hair as she watched his changing demeanor.

"Michael," she said softly, grabbing her sarong and retying it. She placed a hand on his back. "Michael," she said again. He glanced over his shoulder at her and she said, "Please don't feel guilty. It just happened."

"I promised," he said, his voice shaky.

"Promised?"

"Promised my wife I'd never do that again." He dropped his gaze, hating his weakness.

"Honey, Melissa is gone." Pam gently turned the big man around until he was facing her, his eyes sad. "Don't beat yourself up over this."

He nodded, but that didn't convince Pam. Without a word, she gathered him in a strong embrace, holding him as he dealt with the pain and guilt of his sense of having betrayed his wife. Pam rubbed his back, thinking about what they'd done and how she felt about it. She knew it was a simple act of physical release and nothing more, and Michael should feel the same way.

The sky was perfect, absolutely perfect — black velvet with stars that looked like diamonds and the moon a giant pearl. Sapphire blue eyes studied the stars and sky, hands tucked behind her head as Denny lay on the cool soft sand. The sound of the ocean twenty yards away was soothing.

She thought back over her Christmas and how vastly different it was from the year before. She'd been thrilled over gifts of seashells, soap, and vines, where twelve months ago, she'd happily opened a new espresso machine for the house, clothes, and a pair of Columbia boots. She and Hannah had spent the rest of the day making love and just enjoying each other's company. This Christmas had started out with the routine of survival: gathering food, making repairs to the shelters, and washing out in the open in the cold waters of the waterfall and pond. She'd created and eaten dinner with five people who had been total strangers to her this time last year, but who had become her family. They fought together, played together, and survived together.

Denny sometimes wondered whether, if they did get rescued and returned to their lives in New York, Texas, and Oregon, they would remain in each other's lives or disappear into distant memory.

"Looks serious."

Denny glanced up into Rachel's smiling face. She smiled back and nodded. "Oh, it is."

"Do tell." Rachel gracefully settled to her knees then sat on the sand, legs stretched out and supporting herself on her hands.

Denny tore her gaze from the blonde and turned it back to the sky. "Just thinking about this time last year and how amazing it is just how quickly your life can change." She snapped her fingers. "Just like that."

"Thinking about Hannah?" Rachel was surprised at the sound of her own question, a bit harsher than it should have been. Tucking her bottom lip between her teeth, she hoped Denny didn't pick up on her tone.

"No," Denny said softly. "Not totally." She had been questioning her own feelings over the past month or two. Hannah had occupied fewer and fewer of her thoughts, though Denny didn't want to admit what, or *who* had been occupying them instead. She glanced over at Rachel who was staring at the ocean, watching as the moon capped waves danced their eternal dance.

Rachel felt eyes on her and looked down, meeting Denny's gaze. Denny looked deeply confused about something. As she continued to study the beautiful features, Rachel felt the attraction, the attraction she'd been feeling almost since day one. It was a physical pull and a spiritual one, something that tugged at her higher being. She felt her weight shifting to the arm closest to Denny, body leaning, but stopped it, sitting up and pulling her knees to her chest, closing herself off.

"So, was it me or was there some tension at dinner?" Rachel asked at length, keeping her eyes on the sea.

"I felt it, too. I wonder if Michael and Pam had a fight or something. Hell, he refused to even *look* at her. Must have been a doozy."

"I hope they can get past it. This isn't the place to be feuding with someone." Rachel rested her chin on her knees.

Silence reigned, though Denny kept stealing glances at Rachel, the curve of her back, the moonlight glinting off the smooth skin, the perfection broken only by the strap of her bra. Her gaze strayed to the sides of Rachel's breasts, pressed against her folded legs, thighs strong and tanned. Denny thought she was perfectly beautiful.

"Denny?" came Rachel's soft, almost wistful voice.

Denny tore her gaze away. "Yeah?"

"If we make it back home, do you think we'll all stay in contact?" She glanced over at Denny, who sighed.

"I don't know. I was thinking about that too. I hope so. It's like everyone has become part of me. We've bonded in a way that people just don't in normal living circumstances, you know?"

"Yeah. I know. Denny?"

Denny shivered at the softness of Rachel's voice, letting it fill her. She loved Rachel's voice. She said nothing, just met the green gaze.

"Do you..." Rachel swallowed, not sure whether to finish her question.

"What? Do I what, Rachel?"

"Do you miss Hannah's touch?"

Denny was surprised by the question, and noted Rachel could no longer keep eye contact, instead dropping her gaze to the sand between them. "I miss being touched," Denny finally said, her voice just as soft.

"Do you like to be touched?" To Denny, Rachel sounded anxious.

"Yes," Denny whispered. "Very much." She slowly pushed herself up to her elbows, noting a change in Rachel's breathing that matched the change in her own. Damn it all to hell, she was so drawn to Rachel! "Do you?"

Rachel's smile was sad and somewhat rueful. "I didn't, we didn't..." She sighed, looking away. "Matt and I hadn't been together for months before I left."

"Oh, Rachel. I'm sorry." Denny scooted over to Rachel's side, their shoulders nearly touching as the brunette mirrored Rachel's position.

"I'm not even sure I ever really liked sex. It never reached me on a level that I needed it to. It was just physicality. I don't know." Rachel shrugged. "Maybe that's all it's supposed to be."

"It's not. Trust me, it's not. When a relationship is right, and you've connected with that person on more levels than just skin on skin, it's incredible."

Rachel turned her head, resting her chin on her shoulder to look into Denny's eyes. "It sounds wonderful."

"It is."

Only two words, but so telling. Denny heard Rachel's breath catch as she studied Denny's lips.

Denny fell further into needy green eyes, losing all sense of self and propriety. Hannah was dangerously far from her mind, her head filled with the vision of beauty before her. Not realizing she'd brought a hand up until it already rested against Rachel's flushed cheeks, Denny was surprised to feel flesh against her fingertips. "You're shaking," she said, and Rachel nodded. "Are you cold?" Again the blonde nodded, but they both knew she was lying. All the same, it was a good excuse to abort what Denny so badly wanted to do. "Maybe we should get some sleep then."

"Sure." Rachel's voice was hoarse. Denny helped Rachel to her feet then watched as Rachel brushed the sand from the back of her sarong. Silently the two women made their way to the shelter, where Mia and Pam were already getting situated for the night. Pam looked up as they entered, noting in the light of the small fire in the corner, the flush on Rachel's features, a flush very similar to the one she had been sporting earlier in the day. Twin eyebrows rose in question, but neither woman would meet her eye.

Her steps were sure, her intent obvious. Pam stalked over to where Michael, Dean, and Mia were cleaning fish; she grabbed the big man by an ear and yanked him to his feet.

"Jesus, woman!" he barked, pulling away.

He wasn't going to get free that easily. Pam was on a mission. Michael found himself dragged away from his task until he and Pam were alone, just inside the jungle. He stared down at her, arms crossed over his barrel chest. "You wanna tell me just why you pulled me away like a child?"

"Sure," Pam said, mirroring his posture. "As soon as you tell *me* why you've felt the need to be an asshole for the past two weeks. It happened, Michael, get over it! We both had a need and we took care of it. That's no reason to sulk around here, making everyone uncomfortable. There's only the six of us and we all have a role to play. When one of us decides not to play, it throws the entire symbiosis off. You got me?" She poked the deeply tanned chest.

Michael was affected by the tirade. Unable to maintain his defensive posture, his hands fell to his sides. Sighing heavily, he ran his fingers over his thick beard.

Pam could almost read his unspoken thoughts. "Michael, you can't let guilt over past actions run your life. Even if we're stuck here until we all die, it won't do you any good; it'll just eat you up inside. If we do get home, your kids are going to need their dad, and they're going to need him to be whole." She was taken off guard by the Texan's reaction to her lecture. A hand strayed to her hip as his laughter bubbled up from deep in his throat.

"Woman, you sure are a force of nature."

Pam grinned. "Can you believe my husbands called me controlling?"

"No."

"I know. It was hard for me to believe, too." Pam grinned, reaching a hand up to cup the side of his face, suddenly sobering at the obvious pain in his eyes. "Don't let Melissa's memory hold you back from being a human being, Michael. We all make mistakes, but she knew you loved her."

Michael nodded, eyes falling. He knew Pam was right. Though he was loath to admit it, he knew he was using what had happened with her as an excuse to be angry for his own past misdeeds. Far too many nights he'd left the bar with a woman not his wife. Melissa had been hurt deeply in those years, and he'd made a solemn promise to her it would never happen again. Guilt was a mean monster.

"Come here, you big pain in the ass." Pam pulled Michael into a hug and her brow furrowed. "Are you happy to see me, or do you have a banana in your pocket?" She pulled away just far enough to let Michael sheepishly pull the short fruit out of his pocket. Their laughter startled the birds nearby.

Mia glanced over at Dean, wondering whether he knew what the exchange between Pam and Michael had been about. He just shrugged slim shoulders, turning back to his rather nasty task.

"When I get home, I swear I will never eat fish as long as I live," he muttered, placing the freshly shredded strips of meat onto the flat rock used for just that purpose.

"I've never been a fish person actually." Mia shrugged, squinting as she studied what she thought was a tiny bone buried in the meat. Carefully she picked it out. "I don't know, I kind of like it now." She set the boned meat aside for Dean to cut up with the sharpened rock. She remained quiet for a moment, mind wandering in a few different directions. "Dean?"

"Yeah, Sweets?"

"How did you know you were gay?"

The question about his sexuality surprised him, especially coming from the young girl of whom all of them had become extremely protective. "Don't tell me I've got another lesbo on my hands. I've already got two."

"Two?" Mia cocked her head, studying the grinning man, who waved her off.

"Never mind. But, you're not...?" He eyed her.

"No!" Mia wasn't offended, just shocked at the question. That drew even more laughter from her companion. She smacked him playfully on the arm. "I'm just curious, you goof."

"Okay, okay. I don't know." Dean swiped his forearm across his forehead, wiping away the sweat from the midday sun. It might have been January, but oy! "I think somewhere inside I always knew, since I was a boy — crushes on this actor or that actor; loving to watch the Olympics, especially the men's gymnastics." He winked at her conspiratorially. "I remember getting my first woody the year Mary Lou took the gold." He sat back, a slight smile on his lips.

"Who?"

Again, Dean waved her off; unimportant details. "I just loved the boys, loved looking at them, fantasizing about them, jerking off to them—"

"Ew! Dean!"

"Sorry, Sweets. Just part of every growing queer's maturation process." They were quiet for a long time, each lost in their own thoughts. Dean glanced at Mia. "You got a boyfriend back home?"

Mia grinned, her head lowering so her curtain of dark hair covered her burning cheeks.

"Ohhhh! Daddy like! Tell me about him."

"His name is Abraham Schwartz."

"Mm, Jewish boy. Don't believe what they say about circumcision, Mia," Dean whispered, leaning over to the giggling teen. "Foreskin has its plusses, too."

"God, Dean, you're so gross!"

"That may be, but I'm also an expert on such things. So? Is the boy cut?"

"Cut?" Mia was confused for a moment, but then the meaning hit her and her cheeks flamed. "Dean!" The heat in her face persisted, partly from embarrassment and partly from memories of the little bit of experimenting she and Abe had done.

Dean was thoroughly enjoying the conversation and the reactions of his young friend. His virgin alarm was humming steadily. All the better to torment her.

"I'm sorry, Sweets," he said with an unrepentant chuckle.

"We hadn't gotten that far," Mia admitted, almost ashamed to tell this man — who obviously knew so much about the carnal world in all its forms — that she was inexperienced.

Dean sensed her discomfort and immediately felt remorseful. "Mia," he said, voice soft as he reached over and raised her face with a finger under her chin. Once he had her dark gaze, he smiled. "Be proud. It's nothing to be ashamed of. This Abraham obviously wasn't the right guy, or it wasn't the right time." He shrugged. "Or, you're old-fashioned enough to do that whole 'no sex before marriage' thing. Which, of course, is fine, too."

Mia rolled her eyes, then smiled shyly and nodded. She still felt embarrassed, but not quite as badly.

"I'm a pig," Dean continued, dropping his hand and turning back to his task. "Always have been a pig, always will be a pig, but you, dear Mia, are a beautiful lady."

"Awww, you're so sweet, Dean! Cheesy and queer, but sweet."

Dean chuckled, nodding. "You got that right, Sweets. It sucks being here with only Michael." They both snickered at Dean's enforced celibacy.

"Can I ask you something?"

"Anything."

"Am I crazy, or is there something going on between Denny and Rachel?" Mia had been wondering about it for months and now she glanced over at her friend, worried he'd laugh at her, that she was all wrong about their relationship. She was surprised by Dean's soft smile.

"Oh, I think so. Definitely." Dean nodded emphasis. "Those two share a very special bond, I think, Mia. If I didn't know better, I'd say they were very much in love."

"Really?" Mia's voice was soft, wistful.

Dean nodded. "It's beautiful to watch, isn't it?" His smile turned sad. "I think Denny is fighting it though."

"Why?" Being a romantic at heart, the teen couldn't understand not grabbing at love with both hands.

"Hannah."

"Oh." Mia's heart fell, understanding all the implications behind that one word. "But what if we're stuck here?"

"I don't know, Sweets." Dean sighed, cringing at the very thought of being stuck on the island for the rest of his natural life. He knew his loafers certainly wouldn't make it, nor would his libido. "Then we can only hope that Denny sees reason."

The night was quiet, unusually so. It was almost as though the entire island had fallen asleep, all except Denny. She lay on her side, facing Rachel, who also lay on her side, facing Denny. They were no more than six inches apart, the blonde's face relaxed and peaceful. Denny studied that face, so beautiful. Dark blonde eyebrows arched slightly over amazing green eyes, and it wasn't just the color. No matter how hard the author tried to hide herself, Denny could read all of Rachel's emotions in the green depths. Ironically, the eyes of a famous author read like an open book. Denny didn't understand why no one else could read Rachel, why her own husband couldn't see everything, because it was all there in plain view. All one had to do was pay attention.

Thinking about what she'd seen in Rachel's eyes over the past several weeks nearly took Denny's breath away. No doubt she saw her own feelings reflected back at her, and it scared her half to death. She hated to admit it, but the guilt was steadily seeping from her, replaced by a longing so strong it was sometimes painful. She felt Rachel in every part of her being, but how could she dare act on her attraction? It wasn't fair to Rachel, who seemed to be quite confused about the feelings of her own heart.

Who was she kidding? And why was she putting her own issues on Rachel's shoulders? When it all boiled down to it, Denny was scared. What was she afraid of? She knew love; she understood its beauty and its complications. She had taken a huge gamble on Hannah, and it had paid off in eight years of wonder and deep love. Perhaps she was scared because Rachel had entered her life and the love she felt for Hannah seemed to have been swept away. No, not swept away. Denny would *always* love Hannah, no matter what, even if she was stuck on the island for the rest of her life. But she had to admit that her heart was big enough to allow for more than one love in her life. And she did love Rachel; that much she grudgingly admitted to herself.

Rachel felt like she was being watched, her brow knitting for a moment as she was pulled from sleep. Eyes opening, she found herself staring into an unwavering blue gaze. She said nothing, but smiled in greeting, though her smile quickly faded at the intensity in Denny's eyes. She studied those eyes, looking deeply within, almost able to read Denny's thoughts. She wanted to blush at what she saw there, a shiver of heat flowing through her body. Though married for three years, with Matt for four — well, it would have been nearly five now — his touch had never aroused her desire, at least not to the degree caused by a simple look from Denny.

Denny reached out a hand, needing to touch the softness that was Rachel. Green eyes closed as the backs of her fingers brushed Rachel's cheek, her hand turning over so her fingertips traced her brow, down the straight line of her nose, and over soft, full lips, which brushed her fingers in passing. The hand trailed its way down along the jaw and opened to cup the side of Rachel's face.

Rachel's heart beat an insane cadence, her skin tingling where Denny touched her, lips slightly parted as her eyes opened, noting where Denny's eyes rested. *I want to kiss her, too.*

Denny licked her lips, as though readying herself for a big, juicy steak, as if her very life depended on kissing Rachel. She held Rachel's gaze, her own breathing beginning to hitch, her blood racing through her, warming her in the most wonderful ways.

Rachel reached out a hand and touched the soft, warm skin of Denny's shoulder, tracing the valleys and hills of muscle, skin, and bone, awed at just how soft the brunette was, so very different from

Matt and the few other men she'd been with. She allowed her fingers to trace over the smooth yet hard skin covering the muscle leading toward Denny's neck.

Denny fought a shiver at Rachel's soft, teasing fingers, her own hand finding its way down the blonde's side and finally tucking itself behind Rachel's back.

Rachel felt the slight tug at her back, but wasn't sure if that was what propelled her to move, or if it was her own uncontrollable need for closeness. Bodies a hair's width apart, Rachel looked up into Denny's eyes, feeling the soft warmth of the brunette's breath on her face. Rachel swallowed, suddenly nervous and uncertain. *What am I doing?* No longer able to look into those intense eyes, she closed her own, tucking her head under Denny's chin. She felt strong arms wrap around her, and she snuggled in as close as she could against Denny's chest.

Denny was grateful when Rachel snuggled up against her, taking the temptation of her lips away, allowing her to just hold Rachel and feel her close. Their breasts and stomachs were pressed together, the warmth electrifying. Denny sighed deeply as she held Rachel as close as she dared. She had a lot to think about, a lot to consider, but she didn't want to think about it now, knowing it would leave her with troubled dreams. Closing her eyes, she fell into a deep, easy sleep.

Chapter 15

"Where do you want these, Hannah?" Lisa Baker lifted the box filled with napkin dispensers in her arms.

Hannah walked over and looked into the box. "Uh, those can go in the truck. Tyson doesn't want any of the decorative stuff with DeRisio's stamped on it."

"'Kay." The high school student chomped on her gum as she took the box outside.

"The tables are staying, right?" Tiffany asked, entering the kitchen where her friend was packing up ingredients: bottles of syrups and chocolates; espresso beans, ground and un-ground.

"Yeah," Hannah said absently, marking off on Denny's order forms what was presently in stock.

The redhead stood beside her, watching for a moment, studying Hannah's profile.

"How are you doing?" Tiffany asked softly.

Hannah sighed, shrugging tired shoulders. "Okay, I guess." She met the concerned gaze. They'd not been intimate — Hannah knew she wasn't quite ready for that — but her heart was slowly beginning to mend. It was a matter of time before she took a chance on Tiffany. "I absolutely *hate* selling the shop, but I just can't do all this. Plus, this was Denny's dream, you know?"

Tiffany nodded. "I can understand that." She felt guilty sometimes for being so tired of hearing about the dead Denny DeRisio. At the same time, Hannah's previous love seemed like someone she would have liked to know. They probably would have been good friends. The workers at DeRisio's adored their boss; the entire place was still grieving over Denny's loss. It seemed as if everyone in the woman's life was.

Dark eyes landed on Hannah again, noting the way she chewed on her lower lip as she turned a bottle of peach flavoring in her hands, gauging whether there was enough to save or should she just dump the remnants in the huge, stainless steel sink.

"Okay, I think this is the last of it." Deciding to dump the peach, Hannah grabbed the ever present roll of tape, sealed up the box, and handed it to Josh Townsend, an employee of DeRisio's since its inception almost nine years ago. "Thanks, Josh."

He refused to answer, taking the box and scurrying away. Hannah knew he was angry at her for closing the coffee shop and felt that she was betraying Denny by doing so. Hannah had run into that a lot since she'd made the announcement about the closing a month earlier. It had been one of the most difficult decisions of her life, but one that needed to be made.

She'd done her damnedest to find a buyer willing to take over the location and keep it as a coffee shop, even keep the name DeRisio's, but she had no luck. Ultimately, Hannah had to sell to the highest bidder, her heart breaking when she realized the place her dead partner had put her heart and soul into was to be turned into a French bakery.

As she and Tiffany gathered up the rest of the equipment in the back room, she was grateful for Tiffany's presence and comforting support. No doubt the process was hard on Tiffany, but she had stuck by Hannah, doing everything she was asked. They'd talked about the kiss that had yet to be repeated, deciding that their relationship was moving beyond friendship, but Tiffany understood Hannah wasn't quite ready for intimacy.

Matt slid a hand through his hair, fussing with it to make sure it looked properly messy, the casual ease of his look belying the hour it had taken him to attain it. Samantha liked it; he was willing to do it for her. Today they were going for a fun day playing miniature golf and go carts. He liked Sam; she was fun, young, and hot. He grabbed his sunglasses and keys, checked his breath one last time, and locked the house behind him.

He had struggled for a long time, trying to decide what was appropriate: was he supposed to play the single, grieving husband? Was he allowed to date? Truth be told — and he had told no one — since Rachel's death he had realized just how unhappy they had been as a couple, and the relief within his heart was immeasurable. He loved Rachel while she was alive, he had no doubt, but through her absence, he also found he hadn't liked the man he'd become while married to her. He had spent such a long time trying unsuccessfully to make her happy, that after a while, he hadn't given a damn, and he'd let himself go, ignoring his wants and needs until he'd given in with Diane and got caught red-handed. Though it was tragic how their marriage had come to an end, with the benefit of hindsight he could see that Rachel had already known that they were over. That was why she had left the bulk of her estate to Reenie and her sisters. His anger had fizzled over time, realizing that it didn't matter in the long run. He needed to make himself happy, and Rachel's money wasn't about to do that.

Matt had stopped by the cemetery two weeks ago, putting flowers into the bronze container next to Rachel's large stone, her memorial erected beside her sister Daisy's, just as she'd have wanted. He had sat on the grass that was gaining new life as spring inched its way toward summer. He'd talked to Rachel for hours, sharing his thoughts about what he wanted for his life and what he planned to do. He begged for her forgiveness concerning his infidelity, but hoped she'd understand that he needed to move on with his life. Matt wasn't sure how often he'd return to the marker, but he assured her he loved her and always would.

With a spring in his step, Matt climbed into his brand new SUV, started the engine, and listened with satisfaction as it rumbled to life. Buckling himself in, he pulled slowly out of the garage, letting it buzz closed behind him.

Meredith Adams listened to the guidance counselor, periodically glancing through the office window to the waiting area where her grandson sat tapping the arms of his chair. "I'm sorry, what was that last part?" she asked, shaking away distracting thoughts of his increasingly hostile behavior over the past month.

"I said I'll need to see him twice a week for two to three months. If we make any progress, we can reduce it to once a week. Mrs. Adams, that is one angry boy," Lynn Mason said unnecessarily.

The older woman nodded somberly. "I know. These past eight months have been trying for all of us. We just don't know what to do with him. My husband Walter is giving me ultimatums."

"Giving you ultimatums?" The counselor didn't like the sound of that, and her body language spoke volumes as she crossed her arms over her ample chest.

"Yes. He said that if Conrad gets into one more fight, he's out of the house," Meredith revealed. "I don't know what to do!"

"I hope that I can get Conrad talking about this. He hasn't dealt with the death of his parents. Keeping it bottled up inside is extremely dangerous, and counterproductive, as you've seen." She placed a hand on the older woman's arm and led her to the door, a gentle indication that their session about Conrad's latest infraction was over. "I'll see him back here day after tomorrow. Mary can schedule an appointment for you."

"Thank you." She went into the anteroom and turned to her grandson. "Come on, Conrad." Meredith tugged her purse strap over her shoulder, waited for the boy to drag himself from the chair, then followed him out the office door. She glanced at him as they made their way to the receptionist's desk. "How did your meeting with Mrs. Mason go?" she asked.

Conrad shrugged. "This is stupid."

"I'm sorry you think that." Meredith made an appointment for him, taking the reminder card from the gray-haired woman behind the desk and tucking it into her purse. "You have got to make an effort, Conrad. You have *got* to stop this fighting. Your grandfather is so upset with you." She unlocked her side of the car, reaching across the bench seat to unlock Conrad's. The boy surreptitiously massaged his jaw. Wade Pickett could sure throw a mean right hook.

"What's got you so sad, pretty girl?" Denny asked, settling herself down beside Mia, who sat on the beach, the shore washing up to cover her wiggling toes. Mia had been sitting there for the better part of an hour, staring out to sea, long, dark hair blowing in the salty breeze.

"Do you think we're ever going to get home?" the teen asked, her voice soft, wistful.

Denny was without an answer for a moment. Mia was simply stating aloud what everyone else was thinking. "Sure we will." She smiled, but she knew the weak attempt at reassurance was not very convincing. Denny's heart broke as she watched the girl's face crumple then disappear behind her hands.

"I'm gonna die a virgin!" Mia cried, her voice muffled.

Denny tried to hide her smile as she placed an arm around Mia's shaking shoulders and pulled her close. "Shh," Denny cooed, kissing the side of Mia's head. Denny had kept track of their time on the island for the first hundred and seventy-two days, but then it began to depress her more than keep her up to date, so she stopped. She had absolutely no idea what month it was, though the weather was becoming warmer. The nights weren't quite as cold, and the rains had turned warmer and become more frequent.

"I want to go home, Denny," Mia said, sniffling as she rested her head against the strong shoulder.

"I do too."

Mia was quiet for a moment, watching the waves come in, then flow out, just like they had done every day since they'd arrived on the desolate island. She was beginning to hate the island. The light in her eyes faded along with her hope. "Do you think they had funerals for us?"

Denny's shivered at the morbid thought and she took a deep breath. "I don't know. Probably. They think we're dead."

"I bet we die here, Denny. I bet one by one we're going to die until there's only one left, and then that one person will have to try and fend for themselves until they die, too."

"Why are you saying all this, Mia?"

"Because it's true. Tell me you haven't thought about it, too." The girl raised her head, meeting troubled blue eyes. "Part of me feels guilty for thinking this way because I know I should be grateful for surviving the crash and everything. But what's the good of surviving the crash if we're doomed to die here?"

"I don't know." *I wonder the same thing, kid.* "But I have to think that the six of us surviving has to be for a reason, right? Maybe we're supposed to live on, whether it's here, or if we get home, making the best of the second chance we're given."

Denny's voice was soft and soothing as she spoke in the girl's ear, fingers running absently through long, soft hair. Mia was almost lost in the sensation of the comforting gesture. Her mother used to do that.

"I'm not going to give up, Mia, and don't you either. There's a reason for everything, and there is a reason we all survived."

Mia was quiet for a moment. She respected Denny, and so respected what she had said. At length, the girl cleared her throat. "Denny?"

"Yes, honey?"

"If we do get home, can we stay in contact?"

Denny smiled, pulling the girl in closer and placing a soft kiss on the side of her head. "Of course."

There was silence for a moment then Mia said, "Denny, are you and Rachel fighting?"

Denny sighed deeply. "No. Why do you ask?"

Mia shrugged. "I don't know. Guess you guys aren't together all the time like you used to be. I saw her crying the other day, over by the waterfall, not sure why, and I felt like I was intruding, so I left."

"Crying?" Denny felt a pain shoot to her heart. No, they weren't fighting, but, yes, they were spending less time together, compliments of Denny's avoidance. It was a hard thing to do on an island three miles across, but it was necessary. After that night in the shelter, she realized she needed to put some physical space between her and Rachel, needed to allow her heart and head to clear. Denny *needed* to believe they would get home some day, and there was no way she could face Hannah knowing that she hadn't been true to her.

"She loves you."

Denny wasn't sure she'd heard right. "What?"

"That's what Dean says. He says you guys love each other, and that you need to get your head out of your ass and open your eyes."

Denny would have laughed if she hadn't been stung by Dean's words. "Well, maybe Dean should mind his own fucking business."

Uh oh. Mia raised her head from Denny's shoulder, turning enough to look into the older woman's face, which had hardened. "I'm sorry, Denny. I didn't mean to upset you."

"You didn't." Denny smiled, raising a hand and gently cupping the girl's face before dropping her hand to her own lap. She sighed heavily, running a hand through her too long hair. "I can't allow myself to..." She hesitated, unsure of exactly what she was trying to say.

"To?" Mia encouraged.

"To follow my heart. These are hard circumstances, and the feelings I have aren't honest ones. I think ultimately Rachel would get hurt."

"And what about you?"

Denny met wide, innocent brown eyes. "What about me?"

"I see it." Mia brought her own hand up, thumbing one of Denny's eyebrows. "You look so sad when you look at Rachel." Mia felt sad as blue eyes disappeared behind dark lashes. "Denny?" Her gaze was again met by piercing blue. "We may not get out of here. Don't keep hurting you and Rachel."

"You don't understand, Mia." Denny's voice was thick with emotion. Yes, she was hurting Rachel. She saw it every time she dared to look at the blonde, which wasn't often. At night, Denny turned to her side, with her back to Rachel, effectively cutting herself off physically and emotionally. The few times Rachel had tried to snuggle up behind her and she got no response, she'd given up, curling up into a little ball. It had broken Denny's heart, but she had to do it, had to protect herself and her goddamn super-sized sense of what was right and what was wrong.

Mia had a feeling she was only making her friend mad, and she didn't want to do that. "Denny?"

"Yes?" Denny could feel her jaw clenching, trying to think of a way to tell the girl to drop the damn subject without hurting her feelings. She was eternally grateful when she heard the next softly spoken words.

"If we get back to New York, will you make me a mocha breve at your shop?"

Denny grinned, unable to help it. Her eyes moist, she pulled the teenager against her again. "Of course."

She was so damn angry she almost couldn't stand herself! Rachel splashed in the water, scrubbing at her skin until it was raw from the scratchy plant lather. Sniffling, she ducked her entire body, pushing her medium-length hair from her face, finally able to keep her damn bangs behind her damn ears and out of her damn eyes.

"That's some pretty fierce washing."

Rachel whipped around, green eyes flaring as she spotted Dean sitting on one of the rocks around the pool, arms crossed over his chest.

"Do you mind, Dean? I'm trying to take a bath."

"It looked like you were trying to kill the soap, your skin, the water—"

"Fuck off, Dean." She turned her back to him, quickly swiping at her eyes, only to get more frustrated as the water made her nose itch. The more she tried to scratch at it with wet fingers, the worse she made it itch. "Damn it!" She waded over to where she'd laid her sarong, which had become shorter when she ripped off the bottom third to make a covering for her breasts. Her bra had given out two months ago, literally falling apart.

"Hey." Dean rested his hand atop hers as she reached for the garment to dry her face with it. "Slow down, Rach," he said, taking the sarong from her hand and gently wiping at her nose, then tenderly wiping her eyes. His concern and compassion only made more tears fall. She tried to turn away, but he wasn't about to allow that. "Come here, you. Play the tough butch later."

Rachel allowed herself to be drawn into a warm, scratchy embrace. It reminded her briefly of Matt, and her mind flew to a comparison of the coarser male skin and Denny's smooth skin. The thought made her tears fall harder.

"Shh, sweetie," Dean cooed. "It's okay, Rachel. It's ooookay." He rubbed her back in comforting circles, rocking her gently. His heart ached for the two. He knew what the problem was, but decided to get Rachel to talk about it. She lived so much of her time inside her own head, it was no wonder she was falling apart.

Once Rachel had herself under control, Dean waited while she dressed and then took her by the hand and led the way to her favorite ledge.

Rachel knew what was coming and tried to brace for it, her mind swarming with ideas and excuses, any diversion to avoid talking about Denny.

Dean got himself comfortable and patted the rock beside him. Once Rachel was situated, he placed an arm around her shoulders, absently stroking her muscled shoulder, a testament to the hard lifestyle of survival. None of them had an ounce of body fat on them now; they were lean and fit. Even Pam had lost all of her excess mid-section. Dean often ran his fingers over the hard bumps and valleys that were now his stomach, amazed at the transformation.

"This is kind of nice," he commented, squeezing Rachel's shoulder. "Reminds me of the first and last time I played peek-a-boo with a vagina."

Rachel exploded into laughter, her tone thick and nasally from crying. She stared at him, incredulous. "Dean!"

"What?" He glanced over at his companion. "It's true." He smiled and winked. "Now, tell me what happened."

Knowing there was no way to get around talking, Rachel swallowed and readied herself for humiliation. "I don't know. I think I've pissed Denny off in some way, or hurt her, or—"

"Made her fall in love with you."

Stunned, Rachel's head whipped around until she was looking at Dean's profile. When he turned and met her gaze, she croaked, "What did you say?"

"I said she's in love with you, and scared shitless."

Rachel blew out a deep breath. "*She's* scared shitless?"

"Honey, she's got a partner back home who she loves dearly, and then her heart has the nerve to fall in love with another woman? Shit, that's a lot for a dyke to deal with."

"She can't be in love with me," Rachel insisted stubbornly.

"Why not? You're in love with her."

"No, Dean. I am *not* in love with Denny. I can't be."

"Why? Because you have a husband back home, or because you're straight?"

Rachel looked down at the hands that fidgeted in her lap. "Because I don't know how to love. That's pretty clear from the way I totally screwed up my marriage."

He had no idea what Rachel was talking about, but decided to wait her out, let her explain in her own time. He didn't have to wait long.

"I'm so confused, Dean. Never in my life have I felt anything like what I feel when she's around." Rachel was shocked by the words coming from her mouth. She couldn't take them back, so she tucked her bottom lip between her teeth to keep anything else unexpected locked inside.

Dean hadn't been expecting Rachel's declaration, but was glad she hadn't required prodding. They were at the core of the issue. "What do you feel, Rachel?"

"I don't know. It's like my day brightens, my skin tingles, and my stomach flutters. It's like, it's like nothing else matters, you know? Just the fact that she's close to me. I want to touch her; I want her to touch me." She hesitated, searching the sea below them for answers. "It's like I *need* her to touch me."

"Honey, can I ask you a question?" Dean's voice was soft, filled with understanding. When she nodded, he asked, "Have you two..."

"No." Rachel smiled sadly, shaking her head. "I thought for sure one night she was going to kiss me, but...she didn't."

"What if you kissed her?"

Rachel snorted, hand swiping at an errant tear. "I think she would freak out. She won't talk to me; it's like she can't stand to be around me. It hurts, Dean, and there's not a goddamn thing I can do about it."

"Give her time, Rachel. I think Denny's pretty conflicted right now. She's got a good heart and is obviously loyal to Hannah, even if it's not necessary anymore. No doubt she's pushing you away because she's struggling with a fight between her heart and her head."

"Really? You think so?"

"I do."

Rachel sighed heavily and leaned against Dean's shoulder. "This would all make such a great book."

Dean frowned, confused. "What do you mean?"

The blonde chuckled. "Never mind."

Chapter 16

Will pulled a face as he adjusted the headset again. Those things just weren't meant to be comfortable. He wondered how his pilots did it every day, day in and day out, and still managed to have magnificent hair. Keller sat beside him, the tall, powerful brunette in full command of the Cessna they were using. Garrison was using the Bell 407 today, and couldn't get away. Before they took off, she had warned Keller not to "kill her baby", whatever that meant, some sort of private joke between the two women, no doubt. Keller was a good pilot, adept and graceful, but she seemed to take more chances than her partner. She'd get an evil twinkle in those baby blues and Will knew he was in trouble. She'd apologized profusely for making him lose his lunch the last time they flew together, and so far she was behaving this trip.

It was their fifth trip, fifth fruitless trip, and Will was beginning to think maybe Garrison was right, that it was a fool's dream to think anyone else could have survived the crash and be living on a modern day *Gilligan's Island*. Will was a stubborn man, and very tenacious, but even he was starting to wonder when enough was enough. Even with donations from the public, the trips were draining him financially, and hope could only hold out so long. The worst part though, was his own hope was fading; resignation was settling in. Dean was most likely dead, and his heart had been lying to him for almost a year, an entire year without his feisty, picky, fussy, prima donna lover.

Sighing heavily, Will looked down at the map that Garrison's friend had drawn up for them. Little red squiggles and circles all over it marked where they'd been. The map was a testament to how much he loved Dean, but also, and perhaps most sad of all, his refusal to believe what seemed so clear to everyone else: Dean was gone, and no amount of stubborn determination was going to bring him back.

"Look at those waves," Keller said, eyeing the sea below, which was starting to curl in on itself. "Looks like a storm is brewing. We should probably turn back soon, Will."

He nodded mutely, noting the cresting of the waters below. It was early May, and hurricane season was just around the corner.

Keller glanced over at her passenger, noting the touch of gray at his temples and the lines around his mouth and eyes that had started to form over the past year. Disappointment was having a profound effect on the man, and she just wanted to grab him and protect him from his own heart and hopes, which any fool could see were fading.

She remembered when Garrison would come home at night after the first couple of turns, and she'd be exasperated with Will. His demands and earnest belief were exhausting and pushing the pilot to her limit. Now, Keller could see the toll the year had taken on Will; he wasn't quite the man he had been when his search had started.

Keller reached across the small cockpit and comfortingly squeezed his hand, which rested on the map splayed out on his lap. His sad gaze met hers and they shared a moment, understanding and affection passing between them. Will squeezed her hand back and then released it. Her message had been clear and he was appreciative. Even after the search was over with, he wanted to keep Keller and her family in his life. He'd never known more kind, honest, and just all around wonderful people.

"Nonna, give me that." Gloria took the heavy box from her stubborn grandmother, placing it atop the others in the storage unit she had rented.

After her grandfather died, there was no way Gloria was going to let her Nonna live all alone in Milan, and she couldn't leave her life in New York. Having only a two bedroom apartment, Gloria had made the difficult decision to pack up Mia's room and bring her Nonna to live with her. She couldn't bring herself to part with her daughter's belongings, so they were being stored.

"Watch yourself."

Lizbeth stepped back, watching as her granddaughter slid the storage door shut and locked it with a yank to the lock. The past year had been a difficult one, watching Gloria fall apart. When she'd lost Mia, Gloria had shrunken inside then put herself back together, only to fall apart once more when Paolo had inevitably succumbed to his cancer. Lizbeth was amazed Gloria still had a job to come back to, so much time off she'd had to take. Gloria wasn't the same woman she was at this time the year before. Now she was just a machine who walked through each day doing what must be done. She was existing.

"Gloria," Lizbeth said, her voice soft, accent lilting. When she had her granddaughter's attention, she continued. "Why you no have some fun on this lovely summer day, eh? I can take care of myself."

"No, Nonna." Gloria shook her head, sighing deeply as she hailed them a taxi. There was no way she was going to make her grandmother, only in town a week, ride the train. "I've got to work."

Lizbeth shook her head sadly, groaning slightly as she tucked herself into the back of the Yellow Cab.

Denny stood bent at the waist, resting her hands on her knees and taking deep breaths to ease her racing heart and burning lungs. The island so early in the morning was an incredible sight — the colors sparkling over the water, white sand beaches almost glowing pale in the birth of a new day. Rising to her full height, she rested her hands on her hips, the gentle summer breeze drying sweaty hair and making her shiver. Never a runner back home, on the island she found it to be calming. It also gave her time to herself, a chance to think and to find joyous, and rare, solitude.

Blowing out a breath, she watched in awe as the sun slowly broke the surface of the watery horizon, making her squint at its brilliance. If someone didn't believe in God, such a sunrise would make them think about changing their mind. It seemed only a divine entity could create such breathtaking beauty. No wonder so many crazy stories were created to account for the unexplainable mysteries of life in Greek, Roman, and Christian mythology. Never in Buffalo had she seen anything even half as spectacular.

Reaching behind herself, she untied the material forming her pseudo bra, allowing her breasts the freedom to dry uninhibited. She was large breasted, and the lack of a real, structured bra had taken its toll. Her breasts ached and her back complained from time to time. How on earth had women coped before the invention of the brassiere? Smiling at the thought, she slapped the damp garment over a piece of driftwood that was usually used as a seat, then untied the sarong at her waist and let it fall to the sand at her feet.

The cool waters of the ocean felt marvelous against her heated skin. Denny dove down into the depths, allowing her muscles to stretch and her body to soar. She caught sight of a few fish, their bright colors muted by the depths.

Having learned the hard way not to stray too far from shore in the early morning hours, Denny swam back toward the beach. The sight of a dorsal fin, not thirty yards from her during a late night swim had cured her of *ever* wanting to see *Jaws* again.

Like Aphrodite emerging from the waters, Denny broke the surface, water trailing down her long body in rivulets kissed by the golden sunlight of dawn. She ran her hands over her face, then her hair, pushing the wet strands back to flop against her back. She marveled at the way the rising rays cast sharp shadows against the foliage that formed a barricade behind the beach, the rock facings winking in shadow and moss-covered landscapes.

"Wow," she breathed, taking it all in. *Truly a masterpiece.*

Rinsed off, Denny decided to go bathe and start her day before the mad dash for privacy began, everyone trying to get to the waterfall first. Grabbing her sarong and top, she flopped them over her shoulder and walked naked to the rock on which she'd set her soap. Finally she headed into the jungle, heavily calloused feet barely registering any change in terrain. The warming months had brought warm rain with them, and the waterfall was swollen with the overflow. The spill could be heard up to half a mile away before the sound was eaten up by the dense foliage. Humming softly to herself, Denny noted the island coming to life — a few colorful birds watching her from their high perches, as well as unseen rodents scurrying into hiding.

Denny's steps faltered as she heard whistling not too far up the path ahead of her. Quickly tying her sarong and top in place, she broke through the trees then froze to the spot. Rachel stood just beside the rock ledges that curved around to the wall of the waterfall, her bare back toward Denny. She still wore her sarong, but was about to untie it when she stopped, cocking her head to the side almost as though she knew she were being watched. Denny watched with bated breath as Rachel's green eyes met her own, Rachel slowly turning to fully face her, her top in her hands. They stared at each other for long moments, neither one moving or saying a word.

Months ago Denny had started pulling away. She had gotten so far she had no idea how to make her way back. Now, standing face to face with the woman who haunted her waking and sleeping moments, Denny could do nothing but stay rooted to the spot, hungry eyes drinking in the sight. Rachel made no move to cover her exposed flesh, and blue eyes took her in — beautiful, perfectly shaped breasts, small enough to remain firm, but large enough to make Denny's mouth water. The skin was pale, rosy tips slightly puckered. Rachel breathed heavily, breasts heaving with every intake and exhale.

Rachel couldn't take her eyes off Denny's. The hunger and desperate want she saw in their turbulent depths both scared her and aroused her beyond anything she'd ever felt. Her body was responding in ways that shocked her. Denny had made no move, as though she were frozen, which surprised Rachel. She expected Denny to run off like a frightened deer, as she'd been doing since Christmas. Something inside spoke to Rachel, telling her to move, to go to Denny, so she did. Denny swallowed visibly as Rachel got closer, until they were standing toe to toe.

Denny looked down into Rachel's eyes, which seemed remarkably calm, though they were alive and burning. Denny wanted to speak, to say something to defuse the intensity of the moment, but it was almost as if her brain had shut down. Her throat was parched and her lips numb. A hand came up and rested against her jaw, and Denny's own hands betrayed her as they encircled a slim waist, feeling the softness of Rachel's naked flesh. Denny had no idea who initiated it, but her eyes closed as she felt soft lips against her own, just a touch, then a return touch, this time more solid, the fullness of Rachel's lips pressing into her own.

Rachel's fingers gently twined themselves into the long, wet strands of hair made stiff by saltwater. The fit of their lips was perfect, softness like Rachel had never known. She could taste salt upon Denny's lips, wanted to taste more, but she had no idea how to proceed.

The warm hands at her waist moved, sliding up the length of Rachel's back, kneading the skin and muscle as they went until finally those hands and fingers were running through Rachel's hair, running to the length, allowing the strands to fall back between Rachel's shoulder blades before capturing the back of her head, the kiss deepening.

Denny stepped closer, feeling the warm softness of Rachel's breasts pressed against her. Rachel gasped slightly at the rough brush of Denny's top on tender flesh. Tongue teasing trembling lips, Denny silently asked for permission to enter, and the lips parted.

Rachel sighed into the kiss, feeling her heart become lighter even as her body tensed. Waves of budding pleasure spread through her as she pressed their bodies together, needing to feel the steady strength of Denny against her.

Denny was vividly aware of the pulsing in her own body, and knew she had to stop before she *couldn't* stop it. Breaking the kiss, she rested her forehead against Rachel's, both breathing heavily. "Damn it," she groaned, eyes closed as her fingers continued to play in the golden strands.

"I know." Rachel stroked the tanned skin of Denny's shoulders and upper back.

"I'm sorry, Rachel," Denny said, a whimper in her voice. Her body was thrumming with need, but her brain made her say, "I just can't."

Rachel could hear the pain in Denny's voice, knew that Denny needed her to be strong and understanding. "I know. I know." She gently cupped Denny's head and settled it against her shoulder, holding her close. Squeezing her eyes shut, Rachel ignored her racing heart and the ache between her legs. Her erect nipples had become even harder by the contact with the cold, wet material of Denny's top, and now they were highly sensitive. *How could heaven feel like such hell?*

Denny allowed herself to be comforted, guilt of two varieties waging a battle inside her. How could she do this to Hannah? How could she do this to Rachel? She tried to pull away, but was held fast, Rachel whispering for her to stay, so she did. She basked in the warmth, needing it more than ever. After a few moments of just clinging to Rachel, her thoughts bubbled to the surface and spilled out her mouth. "Do you think Hannah has moved on?"

The question was so unexpected, Rachel almost missed it. She thought about her answer for a moment. "I don't know, Denny. We've been gone so long. Surely no one has put their lives on hold for us. They can't."

Finally Denny did pull away, but only far enough to look into eyes so filled with compassion and...love? Denny threw that thought out of her head. It didn't matter right then. "Am I a fool to hold on, Rachel?" she whispered, desperation in her voice.

Rachel brushed a drying strand of hair away from the beloved face. "No. I think you're a wonderfully loyal, loving woman, and Hannah would be a fool to move on from you." She met the troubled blue gaze. "But ultimately you'll have to understand that things have changed, for everyone. None of us are the people we were when we got here, and I'd wager no one back home is either." She returned the small smile that rose on the full lips that had been so wonderfully intimate only moments before. "Wash my back?"

"I'd better not." Denny chuckled, stepping away. "I'm going to start gathering breakfast."

Rachel nodded, her own body still buzzing. "Okay." She watched until Denny disappeared through the trees, then with a heavy sigh, returned to her morning shower.

Chapter 17

"It has been one year today since the tragic crash of Flight 1049. Hundreds of miles off course due to instrument failure, it was ultimately determined that engine failure was responsible for the deaths of almost all of the passengers and crew. What has become of the Lucky Three in the twelve months since they were pulled from the waters of the Atlantic? Have they been able to resume their lives? How are they dealing with the loss of their loved ones who were consigned to a watery grave? From coast to coast, hundreds are attending private memorials to commemorate the deaths of the two hundred and sixty-three people who lost their lives in one of the most deadly plane crashes since Flight 800. Join us tonight on Action News at—"

Reenie pushed the power button on the remote control, clicking the TV off. Turning back to her guests, she sighed sadly. "I can't believe it's been a year."

"I know," Gloria Vinzetti said, nodding. They turned to see Will, the man who had brought them all together, staring out the window of Reenie's high rise loft. "You okay, Will?" she asked, sipping from her bottle of spring water.

He nodded, but didn't answer. They were all there to decide what, if anything, they wanted to do concerning the rescue expeditions. Should they continue, should they give up and accept the fact that their loved ones were gone for good? Along with their original core of supporters they were joined by Milton Bryce, a man they'd met at October's memorial who had lost his wife and two daughters on Flight 1049.

"Well, I need to get to work soon, so let's get talking," Milton said, his voice breaking. Like the others in the room, his eyes were sad and empty. He'd lost his world on that plane.

Will sighed heavily, feeling the three pairs of eyes boring into his back. He knew they were all waiting for the report on his and Keller's last flight. Turning away from the window, he rested his hands on his hips. "I think we should stop."

The silence filled Reenie's loft like the quiet of a tomb, each in shock at Will's calm, firm announcement.

"I've been thinking a lot about this. Five trips." He held up his hand, fingers spread wide. "Five. All that time, energy, and money, and for what? We've found nothing. Hell, we haven't even found *nothing*. It's all just bleak, dark, cold, and empty ocean. There's nothing there."

Reenie's heart fell. Though she had felt it a fool's errand to even start searching, one small bit of hope had persisted. Hell, if three could survive the crash, why not three more? *One* more? Swallowing, she contained her disappointment. "What do the rest of you think?" she asked, looking at Gloria and Milton in turn. "Do you think we should stop?"

Milton's anger bubbled up and exploded. His face red and the veins standing out on his neck, he shouted, "Goddamn it, Will! You got us all stirred up with this hair-brained idea of yours, and now you just wanna give it up?"

"I don't see any other choice. I can't keep doing this every damn time. Do you have *any* idea what it's like to go up there in that helicopter or airplane, your hopes flying as high as the engines will allow, only to fall short of anything but profound disappointment? Well, I can't do it anymore. If any of you would like to volunteer to take a trip or two, then fine, do it. But I can't. I *won't*."

"We need to make a decision. Garrison and Keller will be here soon," Gloria prompted.

"She's right." Reenie sensed a fight could break out between the two men in the room. They had to deliver a decision to those funding the expeditions, and who had added their hopes and prayers to those of the small group leading the mission.

It hurt like hell to say it, but it needed to be said. The rising hopes followed by the inevitable disappointments were eating him alive. "I say we stop," Will said, shoving his hands in his pockets. "I think it's done."

"Okay." Gloria's agreement was soft. They all knew none of the attempts would have been made if not for Will's determination, so she was willing to accept his recommendation. Reenie also nodded.

Milton shoved away from the table and stomped out onto Reenie's balcony. The other three were silent, awash in an assortment of emotions and feelings. Guilt — were they giving up too soon? Foolishness — was it crazy to ever think anyone else survived? Grief — the final connection to hope was being cut as they sat and deliberated.

With relief and dread, Reenie answered the knock at her door, knowing it was Garrison and Keller, coming to get the committee's decision. She smiled as she ushered in the pilots and the fifteen year-old, Parker. "Come on in, ladies." With a heavy sigh, she closed the door and leaned against it, eyes briefly squeezing shut before pushing herself to join the others.

Assessing the looks on the faces of the foursome — especially Milton Bryce, who stood in the doorway of the French doors leading to the balcony, a lit cigarette dangling from his fingertips — Garrison had a pretty good idea of what had been said before they arrived.

"You've decided to call off any further searching," she said, meeting each gaze in turn. Most looked away or simply nodded. Garrison was surprised to feel the pang of loss. She had been hoping that the group would decide to continue. She wanted so desperately to find something, *anything* for them, even if it was just a piece of luggage for a last physical link with their lost loved ones. Sighing, she sank onto a chair, Keller standing behind her and rubbing her shoulders.

"Are you sure?" Garrison said. When no one answered, she accepted the finality of their decision. "Okay."

"You are so full of crap, Dean! You did too move that piece when I went to the bathroom," Mia complained, staring down at the checkerboard they'd made in the sand, using rocks as their checkers.

"I did not!" he defended hotly, looking to Denny and Rachel, busy eating bananas and staring at each other. "Ladies? Can you defend me here, or are you too busy making googly eyes at each other?"

"Huh?" Denny blushed deeply, knowing full well she'd been busted watching Rachel's lips as she ate her lunch, the soft, pink tongue poking out now and then to snag a bit of runaway banana from her lip. "Oh, uh, didn't see it."

Denny felt like a kid caught with her hand in the cookie jar. She had no idea she was so transparent. She and Rachel had kissed more than two weeks ago, and it hadn't happened again, but she still felt that kiss all the way down to her toes. She just couldn't let it go, no matter how hard she tried. Though she and Rachel were spending time together again, she made sure it was with at least one other person there with them. She didn't trust herself. "Sorry, Dean. I wasn't watching the game," she repeated.

"Small wonder," Dean groused, Mia giggling behind her hand.

Rachel was also an atypical shade of red. "Sorry, guys."

"Y'all might wanna consider folding everything up. Looks like we got ourselves an ugly coming."

At Michael's words of warning, everyone looked up into the sky. The clouds were dark and brewing, distant rumbling indicative of the storm to come.

"Oh, man," Dean whined with a heavy sigh. Looking back to the board, he saw Mia take out three of his men. "Hey!" he yelped. The girl gave him a shit-eating grin and he petulantly brushed out their board, muttering, "Storm's coming."

"Sore loser."

"Better than being just a plain loser," he mumbled, getting to his feet.

"Oh, *that's* mature." Mia followed him toward their shelters. They were learned in the art of escaping a big storm now, though every time one came in, they all held their breath, hoping it wasn't a hurricane or a tropical storm bigger than the first one that had blown in. More than likely, nothing on the island would survive a blow of either magnitude.

Everyone gathered what mattered most to them, which boiled down to their soap and the few scraps of clothing they had left. The few tools they'd made from stones and sticks were also gathered and taken to the shallow cave behind the waterfall to wait out the storm. It wasn't long before the island was inundated by severe rain and winds. It was nearly impossible to see through the deluge. The skies opened up with a roar of thunder.

As everyone settled in to ride out the storm, Michael said, "Do y'all think we'll ever get off here?"

Pam sighed heavily. "I sure hope so. My grandson is bound to be about two feet taller than when I saw him last." That earned a round of chuckles.

"What do y'all say about making a boat again?"

"To fish with?" Dean asked, having a sinking feeling that wasn't what the Texan had in mind.

"No. A boat to load us all up on, with water and food, and get the hell out of here. Find civilization somewheres." He studied everyone in turn. "Anyone agree?"

Pam's eyebrows raised in surprise. "Are you suggesting we leave the safety of the island and take a homemade boat out into the middle of the Atlantic Ocean?"

"I'm sayin' that I don't want to stay here forever, Pam. What if one of us got sick?" He eyed her suspiciously. "Or something else?" The non-specific question hung in the air between them.

"Sick, yes, something else, no," Pam answered with a slight shake of her head.

Michael's relief was visible, but it didn't sway him. "Either way, we gotta get outta here. Who's with me?" He was surprised by their silence. "Come on, guys! Do you really wanna rot here?"

"We could still be rescued," Dean said, his voice quiet, almost shy for clinging to the hope.

"Do you really think that, Dean? Can you honestly look me in the eye." The Texan pointed at his own face. "And tell me y'all think some big boat is gonna float on up to the shore tomorrow and bam!" He clapped his hands, startling everyone. "Saved!"

"Don't be an asshole, Michael," Pam said, her voice a low growl. "We can talk about this without the theatrics. I mean, isn't Dean here the drama queen?" She raised a single eyebrow.

Michael grinned at the chuckles from the group, but his smile quickly disappeared. "We've got to be thinking, folks. If y'all wanna stay here, then stay. But I'm gonna start thinking outside this damn island. I want to go home."

"I'm with you, Michael," Mia said, nodding with conviction. She turned hopeful eyes to Denny and Rachel. Rachel met her gaze, but said nothing.

"Why now, Michael?" Denny asked, bringing her legs up to wrap her arms around, resting her chin on her knees.

"I heard engines again the other day," he said, looking bashful.

"What!" Dean shot up from where his lounging position against the wall. "Why didn't you say anything?"

"'Cause I didn't want any of y'all to get upset."

"Great!" Dean exploded. "We could all have looked for it, waved it down, something!"

"Dean, stop it." Pam glared at him and turned back to the Texan. "What's your plan, Michael?"

"As I see it, they gotta have a base around here somewheres in order to be out there." He indicated the world beyond their cave. "I figure we've got a shot to find them."

"I don't know if it's wise, Michael. We don't have anything that will hold water. The only way to get fish to keep is to salt it, and that would make our thirst worse. We certainly can't fish while on our raft and then eat them raw; we'd get sick. I just don't know if the idea is practical."

Michael sighed, stubbornly crossing large arms over his chest. He was irritated. He'd thought that more than Mia would stand behind him on the idea of leaving the island. Not wanting to admit they were right, he was still determined. "I still think we should build a boat."

"Okay, how about this." Denny tucked her legs under her and leaned forward to be heard over the sound of the storm. "Let's compromise. If no one has found us by, what," she looked to the others, "say, six months, we start considering our options."

"That's a lot of hash marks on a wall," Rachel muttered.

"Three months," Michael countered, ignoring Rachel. The women and Dean exchanged looks.

"Okay. Three months, and a shit load of hash marks."

"I'm glad that storm's over."

Rachel glanced over, watching as Denny climbed up on her ledge. "Me, too. It didn't seem to do much damage."

"We'll have to make some repairs to the shelter tomorrow, but other than that..." Denny settled in next to Rachel, sighing as she leaned back on her hands and looked out over the sunset.

"I'm not sure whether Michael did more damage or more good with his outburst tonight," Rachel said thoughtfully.

"Why?"

"Because now he's got everyone thinking."

"Including you?" Denny tucked her chin into her shoulder to look at the other woman, who sat cross-legged.

"Yeah. I guess including me. I don't know." Rachel picked at some loose vegetation swept onto the ledge during the storm. "I've been thinking a lot about Matt over the past months, and I think it's best I let him go once I get back. Let him find a woman who can be what he needs her to be."

"And what about you?" Denny had no idea why she asked that question. She knew when she got back, *if* she got back, she would make an attempt to reclaim her life with Hannah and get back into the swing of things with DeRisio's. She would have no room in her life for unanswered questions concerning Rachel Holt.

"What about me? Good question, Denny." Rachel mirrored the brunette's position, basking in the coolness of the night. It was humid and the air was heavy after the rain, but the breeze coming in off the ocean was cool and refreshing. The daytime temperatures were definitely getting hotter and hotter. "I guess I'd rebuild my career, decide where I want to live."

"Will you stay in Oregon?"

"I honestly don't know. My best friend Reenie has been trying to get me to move to New York, but..." She shrugged a shoulder. "I don't know if I want to do that. I'm just not made for the big city." She glanced over at Denny. "You'd go back to Buffalo."

It was a statement and Denny accepted it as such. "Yeah. I would."

"You know, I wish I could have met you back home, me on some trip to New York to meet with my publisher, or something."

Denny smiled. "Yeah. You walked into DeRisio's, and I fell all over myself, unsure what the hell to do with a celebrity in my humble coffee shop."

Rachel chuckled. "I'm hardly a celebrity, Denny." Rachel had been able to forget about that unwelcome part of her life while on the island. No one knew she was anyone other than Rachel, a member of their island family.

"Bullshit! You've been on more covers of *People* magazine than Julia Roberts." Denny liked the blush that covered the blonde's face. She found it adorable. "No, I would have been honored to make a caramel macchiato for the great author, Rachel Holt."

"I'm just me, Denny. Nothing special."

"That's not true, Rachel." Denny's voice was soft, like a whisper on a breeze. She met Rachel's gaze and almost got lost in it. Clearing her throat and looking out toward the ocean again, she said, "You know, I was sitting next to Mia and her mom on the plane."

"You're kidding!"

Denny shook her head. "Ironically enough, we were talking about you during the flight." Again she met Rachel's gaze. "Gloria was a huge fan of yours, too."

Rachel had to look away, sudden emotion rising to sting her eyes. She wasn't sure what she felt, knowing Gloria was now dead and Mia had no idea who Rachel was.

"I didn't mean to make you cry, Rachel. I'm sorry." Denny reached over and patted the blonde's shoulder.

"No, I don't know why that touched me so. God, that poor girl." Rachel took several deep breaths to calm. She knew she was getting close to her week of fig leaves, and that was probably a large part of why she was feeling overwhelmed by sudden fear and grief. What if she did make it back home? What did she have to go back to? She struggled for control, feeling silly and insecure. Wiping her eyes, she took a deep breath.

"I was wondering if maybe you'd talk to her, you know," Denny shrugged, "tell her. It might help for Mia to be able to talk about her mother. She really hasn't so far."

"Do you think that it might be a little too much for her to deal with?"

Denny shrugged. "I don't know. I really worry about her. She doesn't talk about anyone back home, other than her great grandparents in Milan. I don't know if she has anyone else."

"Yeah." Rachel nodded. "Mia doesn't deserve this, but then again, none of us do." She looked at Denny. "You should be home with Hannah, cuddling in front of the TV or something."

Denny sighed. The crazy thing was, in the fantasy Rachel described, she only saw Rachel in it. "Why did all this happen? They say things happen for a reason; what was the reason for all this?" She waved her hand, indicating them and the island around them. "Why did all those people die?"

"I don't know. You want to know the crazy thing, though?"

"Hmm?"

"I'm so sorry for everyone who died, and for those left behind, including everyone's families, but as for me, I don't know." She fell back to lie prone, hands tucked behind her head. "I feel like this whole thing, as nutty as it sounds, has been good for me. I don't know... I feel like I've grown in some way, as a person."

"If you stop growing, you die," Denny said, her voice soft as darkness crept over them, that time of night when secrets seemed to be more safe and honesty more abundant.

"That's true. I always thought that's what happened to my parents. They were too afraid to grow, too afraid to discover what the world was really like outside religion and rigidity." They fell into companionable silence for a moment, surrounded by the sounds of the island as the small wildlife began to return after the storm. "Denny?"

"Yeah?" She could no longer see Rachel, but could feel the heat radiating off her smaller body, could feel her own body responding.

"I probably shouldn't say this, in light of what we've been talking about tonight, but..." Rachel paused, almost at an uncharacteristic loss for words to convey what she needed to say. "I really loved kissing you.

I don't know, it, it just made me feel so..." Her brow knit. An author who had no words. "It just made me *feel*."

"You don't get to feel very often, do you?"

"No." Rachel's response was like a whisper on the wind, filled with sadness and longing. "I know we shouldn't have done that. I know you have Hannah back home, and I know you love her, but I wanted to say 'thank you' for that. It was beautiful."

"It was." Denny wished she could see Rachel's eyes at that moment. She loved those eyes, not just because of their amazing color, but because she could read Rachel in them, see exactly what she was feeling and thinking. She tentatively reached out a hand, so as not to frighten Rachel with the sudden touch, and also to make sure she wasn't going to accidentally grab something she shouldn't be grabbing.

Rachel gasped at the feel of warm fingers brushing across her cheek. She brought her own hand up, covering that hand and closing her eyes; the touch was pure bliss. She heard movement then suddenly the side of her body was engulfed in heat as Denny scooted beside her.

Denny couldn't deny herself the feel of Rachel's skin, the smoothness of her face, inhaling the fragrance that was all Rachel. "How do you always smell so good?" she whispered, the breath from her words making Rachel shiver.

"Hardly. I haven't had a stick of deodorant in months."

Denny smiled at that. "It must just be you then."

Rachel could tell Denny was near, could feel her breath against the side of her neck, gently blowing her hair off her face. Her hand left Denny's and followed along the arm until eventually she was touching a shoulder, then a neck, then her fingers curled around the back of Denny's head. "Denny?"

"Yeah?"

"I'd really like it if you'd kiss me again."

Denny said nothing, instead leaning in, intending to drop a soft, brief kiss on full lips, but she was a fool to think she wouldn't lose herself again. The hand at the back of her head moved to the back of her neck, squeezing slightly as Denny was pulled closer, as Rachel's breast brushed against her arm. At first the kiss was a simple touching of lips, softness brushing against softness, exploring.

"Please," Rachel whispered against Denny's lips. She felt Denny lower herself slightly, their upper bodies almost making full contact. Rachel opened her mouth, inviting Denny inside, sighing at the feel of the soft tongue caressing her own.

Denny pushed everything out of her head, only allowing herself to take in what she was feeling and tasting. Her brain threatened to pull the plug on her bliss by bringing up images of Hannah's face, taunting her with the realization that she was having trouble remembering just how her partner tasted and felt, replacing those thoughts with how

Rachel tasted and how soft she felt. Even as she pushed that part of herself down, the part who screamed *traitor,* she couldn't help but be frightened by just how badly she wanted to make love to Rachel, how badly she wanted to show Rachel she could feel a hell of a lot more than just a simple kiss.

Rachel's neck arched back instinctively as soft lips left her own and began to trail along her jaw. Denny's heavy breathing in her ear was followed by a wet tongue flicking at her earlobe. Those touches made Rachel's eyes shoot open, her fingers clutching Denny's shoulders.

"Denny," she whispered, half moan, half plea. "Denny, baby, wait."

"What?" As soon as the word was out of her mouth, Denny knew why Rachel had gotten her attention. Sighing with frustrated resignation, her forehead fell to Rachel's shoulder, her body still thrumming, electrified. "God, this is torture."

"I'm sorry. I don't want you to do something you'd regret. I'm sorry, Denny. I never should have said anything." Rachel felt suddenly cold as Denny scooted away to put a little distance between them.

"No." Denny scrubbed her face with her hands before running them through her hair. "I'm sorry. God, that was dumb."

Denny's taste still fresh on her tongue, Rachel took a deep breath. "Maybe we should get some sleep."

"You go ahead. I'll be in later." Denny climbed down the rocks, disappearing into the inky darkness.

"Keller, calm down."

"Calm down? Why the hell should I calm down?" Despite her protest, she did feel herself regaining control of her emotions. She stopped pacing, looking to her partner, who was already in bed, sitting up against the headboard, sheet tucked at her waist. "Why the hell would he give up? I don't understand this."

"Because we haven't found anything in a year. What do you expect the poor man to do? We've given him the best discount we can, basically only charging for the gas, but it's still expensive. Plus, to be honest, I think Will's dying inside. He's a sensitive guy, and I don't think he can take any more." Garrison's voice remained matter-of-fact to try and keep her excitable partner from flying off the handle again. It was a trick she'd learned over the years. It usually worked.

"I just..." Keller plopped down on her side of the bed, stretching out and facing Garrison. "My gut tells me to keep going. I don't know why, but it does."

"You really think so?"

"I do." Keller nodded, reaching out to play with the hem of Garrison's tank top. "I think we should make one more pass, one last go of it. We only have one or two places left on the map, anyway."

"True. But I doubt Will would go for it," Garrison warned, reaching out to smooth dark strands of hair out of Keller's eyes.

"So then, let's just do it, Garrison. We can afford this one trip, on us, just to close the books. It would make me feel a hell of a lot better." She studied her partner's eyes, knowing that ultimately it was Garrison's decision. She handled the financial end of their business. To her relief, her partner nodded.

"We can."

"So let's do it, baby." She scrambled up to straddle Garrison's legs, caressing the side of her face with calloused fingertips. "Just one last flight to ease my gut."

"Or I could just get you a shot of Pepto Bismol." Garrison grinned, kissing the fingers that grazed over her lips.

"Cute."

"We've got summer rushes, baby. When are we going to find the time?"

"I don't know. It may not happen tomorrow, but sometime soon, within the next couple of months, I really want to do this."

Garrison looked into Keller's eyes and saw the depth of her sincerity. She really believed in this, and Keller wasn't one to be frivolous. Finally she nodded. "Okay. We'll do it for Will." Her partner grinned that adorable lopsided grin which made Garrison's heart melt, even after more than ten years together.

"Yeah. We'll do it for Will."

"I love you," Garrison said.

"I love you more."

Chapter 18

Michael could feel the sweat dripping down his temples, and used the back of his arm to wipe it away before it stung his eyes. He looked over what he had achieved so far. Five logs or huge branches had been dragged from the jungle and laid out on the beach for his examination. He had a visual in his head of what he thought would make the raft stay together this time, and was determined to make it work.

"You gonna actually use a second tie this time?" Dean asked, strolling onto the beach, doing one of his twice daily teeth picks with a fishbone from their dinner.

"Fuck off, pain in the ass, unless y'all plan to help."

Dean chuckled, continuing on his way to the waterfall. "Whatever, Red." Feeling something warm and grainy seeping into his shoe, Dean stopped and bent down to examine his footwear. "Aw, damn." Through a small hole in the loafer, he could see his pinky toe wiggling. Grumbling to himself, he marched off to take his daily bath, passing Mia and Rachel on his way.

"Wonder who started his tighty whiteys on fire," Rachel murmured, making Mia giggle as they proceeded to the far side of the beach. In the three days since Denny had confided that Gloria had been a fan of her work, Rachel had thought a lot about Mia and whether it would make things better or worse to tell the teen who she was. Ultimately, she decided she should tell her. "Want to sit?"

"Sure." Mia sat, crossing her legs in front of her and resting her arms on her knees. She liked Rachel. Like Denny, Rachel was enough older than Mia to gain her respect and admiration. *Plus the Denny and Rachel are really cool!*

"It's hot today," Rachel commented, watching a sea bird diving for its lunch.

"Yeah. I can only imagine how hot it is back home." The girl rolled her eyes at the thought of the hot, humid nights. At least here they had the breezes rolling off the ocean to cool things down.

Slightly embarrassed, Rachel wasn't sure how to bring the subject up without feeling like she was trying to throw her name around. Finally she decided to approach the connection obliquely. "Are you a reader, Mia?"

"I used to read from time to time. Not *half* the reader my mom was, though."

Handed the perfect opening, Rachel swallowed and asked, "Did she have a favorite author?" She couldn't look at Mia; she felt like she was manipulating her.

"Oh, yeah! Rachel Holt. Hands down."

The author couldn't help the slight shiver of pride, but it passed quickly as she realized it had come at the expense of a dead woman. "Oh, yeah?"

"Yeah." Mia smiled, remembering the hours and hours her mom had spent reading all those books, many more than once. She looked at the woman sitting next to her and found herself staring into intense green eyes. "Why?"

Rachel looked away, wishing she had decided not to speak to Mia. But Denny had said it might help Mia to talk about her mother, so, determined to follow through with what she had started, she said, "Thanks for sharing that, Mia. I like to know people enjoy my books."

What? Mia stared at her friend's profile in confusion, dark eyebrows drawn as she tried to process what Rachel was saying. *Wait. Rachel. Blonde hair. Young. No way.* Mia shook her head, not sure whether to laugh or be angry at Rachel's audacity in making such a claim. The blonde met her gaze evenly. "You're trying to tell me..." Again, Mia shook her head. "No way, Rachel." Despite her protests, Mia stared into Rachel's green eyes, picturing them in black and white, and Rachel with short hair. "No way," she breathed.

Rachel nodded. "Yeah."

Mia's hand flew to her mouth, eyes open wide as she studied the author, not sure what to say or think. Instead of doing either, she pushed up from the sand and ran off into the privacy of the jungle.

"Shit." Rachel hopped up, turning to run after her. "Mia!" She could hear the girl's muted sobs as she followed the well-worn path through to The Rock. "Mia, stop, please!"

Mia stopped at the water's edge, her tears nearly blinding her as she thought about her mother's admiration for Rachel Holt, and the way she'd gone on and on about her work and wondered what kind of person the author was.

"Why didn't you tell me?" she yelled, hearing the blonde break through the trees behind her.

"I didn't tell anyone, Mia. Denny recognized me. I had no idea about your mom being a fan, I swear." She walked over and put an arm around the girl. "I'm sorry. I didn't mean to hurt you, honey. I just wanted you to know that your mom's appreciation of my work means a great deal to me, and I'm very grateful for it. That was all."

Still crying, Mia allowed herself to be pulled into a warm embrace, her head resting upon Rachel's shoulder. "I can't get over the irony," she said at last, sniffling. "My mom would've crapped her pants if she'd realized her beloved Rachel Holt was on the plane with us. I mean, back at the beginning, when we were trying to find out what skills everyone had to contribute to our survival here, you just said that you did a little research and a little writing. I always thought you wrote for a newspaper or something. You said Denny told you about my mother being a fan; when did Denny know? Why didn't *she* tell me?"

"Denny recognized me when she got on the plane. I don't know why she hasn't said anything to anyone else. I guess she was trying to respect my privacy, which I'm grateful for. I don't need all that crap, Mia. I'm just me, just Rachel, and I happen to love to write stories. We had enough to deal with here, without buzzing about who I was."

The voice was soft, calming, and Mia found herself burrowing into Rachel's arms. She loved to listen to Rachel talk, always had. She had such an aura of peace and calmness about her she couldn't help but be affected by it.

"If we ever get back home, can I have you autograph one of my mom's books for me?"

"Of course, honey."

Mia grinned, pulling back just enough to look into caring green eyes. "I can't believe one of the people I care about most is a famous author."

Rachel smiled warmly, brushing strands of dark hair off tear-streaked cheeks. "I'm just me, Mia. No better, no worse."

"I'll have to tell my mom about this tonight, when I pray to her."

"Tell her I said hello."

Mia laughed, clasping Rachel in another hug.

"Hey, Monk," Tony Smith called out, seeing his boss walk into the hangar. Crew and mechanics at Davies' Hangar used the owner's childhood nickname: Monk, short for grease monkey.

"Hey, Smitty. How's it hangin' today?" Garrison mouthed the words along with Smith as he gave the same response as always: *straight and slightly to the left.* "Walk into that every damn time."

She went directly to her office to use the phone. Keller had contacted Garrison by radio up in the Cessna, so Garrison had promised to call her when she got in. "Hey, baby. What's up?" Garrison plugged her other ear to try and hear through the ruckus of a drill across the hall in the hangar. "What?" She nodded as she pieced together the words, broken up by a bad connection on Keller's cell phone. A quick goodbye, and Garrison flopped down into the chair behind her desk, whipping off the doo-rag she'd been wearing to cover her blonde hair, fluffing it with her hand.

Using what time they had between jobs, they'd been working on their plan for a month. Summer was the busiest time for the pilots and their cargo business, but Keller was determined, so Garrison supported her. Keller had found them a seaplane to use, a G21-A Goose, to be exact. A vintage plane made in the last year of World War II, it seated six, with additional seating for pilot and co-pilot. If they needed the passenger room at all, Garrison hoped the plane would be large enough.

Grabbing a pencil out of the small army of them held in a coffee cup on her desk, she twisted it in her fingers. Only one of them would be flying to Canada to pick up the Goose. They had a standing agreement they'd never fly together, unless Parker was with them. If something happened and a plane went down, Parker would not be orphaned again. The three of them had a bond stronger than any Garrison had ever known, especially since she had lost both of her own parents way too early.

It was love for her own family that had driven Garrison to help Will in the first place, and then to persist even when their searches had proven fruitless. She and Keller were determined to finish searching all of the remaining grids, no matter what the outcome.

They planned their final search mission for the last weekend of July. Garrison was free that date and she would be flying the Goose on their last ditch run. The spots on the map where they had yet to cover were too far away for the Bell to safely search and return to land, and Keller would be using the Cessna for her scheduled flight, so the Goose would be ideal. Garrison had called in a favor from Duke Wingom, a long-time friend and flying peer. He had agreed to fly with her, as she was shaky on seaplanes, having only flown one a few times.

"Everyone move together!" Denny grunted, the weight of her end of Michael's raft nearly immovable. She could see from everyone else's face that they were struggling, too. "Jesus, Michael! Did you use an entire forest?"

The Texan grinned then glanced over his shoulder to make sure he wouldn't trip as he stepped back into the water. He felt a small wave break on the back of his legs, but he was counting on them getting bigger and stronger. "Set it down," he instructed, feeling they were in deep enough water that the raft should float on its own. A round of relieved groans sounded with the splash of the heavy raft hitting the surface of the water. They all watched with bated breath as the raft bobbed on the oncoming waves. Michael climbed on top, the oar he'd carved from branches in hand. Dean and Mia followed.

"I think they're going to kill themselves instead of just catching fish for tonight," Rachel muttered, stepping up beside Denny, their arms touching. The brunette nodded absently, amused as she watched the three trying to get their paddling in sync. "I talked to Mia yesterday, about her mom and who I am."

Denny looked over at Rachel, catching her profile before the wind whipped long, blonde strands around her head. "And?"

Rachel tucked the wayward hair behind her ears, meeting the blue gaze. "She was upset, but then we talked, I mean *really* talked, about Gloria, and about Mia's fears of going home. She doesn't have a father,

Denny. The only people she has are her great grandparents in Italy, and she doesn't want to live in Italy."

The brunette sighed, brushing her own hair out of her mouth. "I've thought about that. Hell, I'd be willing to take her in."

"Really?"

"Sure. I've got the room at my place; I could even give her a job at the shop." She shrugged. "It's not much, but it would keep her somewhat close to home, and with someone who cares about her."

"Poor kid. She's such a sweet thing. I'm actually impressed with how well she's handled all this. She seems like a sheltered girl, somewhat naïve."

Denny nodded in agreement. "I know." Before she realized what she was doing, her arm had snaked around Rachel's waist, pulling the blonde against her as they continued to watch the three drift further out, Michael's deep voice barely audible as he barked out orders to the other two. Rachel stepped into her personal space, moving to stand in front of Denny, arms wrapping around her neck. She rested her head on Denny's shoulder, sighing heavily at the feel of the body against her — the warmth, the softness.

Denny lowered her nose to Rachel's neck, inhaling her scent, forgetting herself and where they were. The warmth of the blonde's bare stomach pressed against her own; only two thin cotton layers separated their breasts. She closed her eyes as she felt warm breath against her neck, causing a shiver to rustle up her spine. Soon the breath was replaced by soft lips. Denny sighed at the sensation, one of her hands coming dangerously close to the top of Rachel's sarong, her fingers itching to slide underneath.

Rachel started when she heard cat calls, her head whipping around to see Dean making less than gentlemanly gestures and Michael whistling around two fingers.

"Oh, God." Rachel hid her blush against Denny's neck. "I'm sorry."

Denny hugged her close, placing a soft kiss on the top of her head. "Come on. Before we get knocked over by a wave."

"You okay?" Rachel asked, her voice soft as she climbed up onto the ledge and saw Denny lying on her back, an arm over her eyes. "Another of your headaches?"

"Yeah." Since Denny lost her contacts in the plane crash, the eye strain of the past year had played havoc with her head. She suffered almost weekly headaches, sometimes badly enough to make her physically ill.

"I'm sorry, Denny. Want me to leave you alone?"

"No." One blue eye peeked out from a toned arm.

"Okay." Rachel settled next to her, brushing some hair from her face and studying her with concerned eyes. "Can I do anything for you, honey?"

"A cool rag?"

"Okay."

Denny closed her eyes again as she heard her friend scamper away. She hadn't realized just how much Tylenol meant to her until she had none. They were lucky that no one had been sick or hurt badly enough to require serious medicines, but Denny was plagued by these horrendous headaches and she was tired of them. There was very little she could do to counteract them, except try and sleep or lie in utter blackness and quiet. She'd left dinner early that night, bidding everyone a good night, then slipping away to the ledge to suffer in solitude missing most of the celebration of the raft's success. Truth was, she was glad Rachel had sought her out.

"Here we go," Rachel said, as though stepping out of Denny's thoughts. "How's that?"

Denny gasped as the cool cloth laid across her forehead, gentle fingers cool against her heated skin. "Better. Thank you." She closed her eyes, the sudden cold causing the pounding to become worse for a moment before it began to ease slightly. The pain calmed to a mere marching band inside her skull rather than a series of atomic bombs exploding.

"Do you want me to go, Denny?" Rachel asked, gently caressing the brunette's arm.

"No." She was silent for a moment before asking something that had been on her mind. She also hoped a change of subject would help her to ignore the headache. It might also extend the time she was getting alone with Rachel. "What were you writing before you ran out of paper?" Denny smiled weakly.

"A novel. Who knew bleached magazine pages would work so well?" They both smiled. "I finished it in my head. Actually, I'm still revising it."

"Tell me?"

"Okay."

Denny listened to Rachel's voice, the soft, soothing tones affecting her like it did Mia, the sound having an instant calming affect, allowing Denny to relax and listen. The novel was about strangers, trapped on an island. She smiled, listening to the characterizations of the six of them, including Dean's antics over the endless days. As she knew it would kill her head, Denny tried to keep herself from laughing outright at the mention of the fictional character's struggles with a private pleasure device.

Enjoying talking about her tale, as Rachel spoke, her fingers stroked the soft skin of Denny's arms. Her voice never hesitated as she smiled, noting how Denny turned her arm over, silently encouraging the caressing of the sensitive, paler underside of her arm.

Denny sighed, the exquisite touch filling her with pleasant sensations sending a shiver down her spine. Between the touching and the soft voice and the story it was relating, Denny was almost able to forget about the pain in her head.

Rachel paused for a moment, her fingers touching the damp cloth on Denny's forehead. "How are you feeling?"

"Better. Please don't stop; I love listening to you talk. Have you ever considered reading books on tape?"

Rachel smiled. "No." She leaned down and placed a soft kiss on Denny's damp hair. "Shall I continue?"

"Please." Denny leaned into the touch as fingers left her arm and resumed stroking her hair. She loved Rachel's touch.

As Rachel continued her tale, weaving her story as well as discussing details of it, it was almost as though she'd forgotten Denny was there, though her fingers continued to play in the thick, dark hair. Denny knew the questions posed weren't for answering, but just simply the author's mind at work. She was enthralled to hear the thoughts and questions slowly mutate themselves into ideas, then visions, then scenes, and finally they were smoothed over to fit into the story, molded and gently sculpted around the edges until the progression was seamless.

Rachel was lost in the world she knew well, the one in which she felt most comfortable, a world of her own making, a work in her own head — the world of creation. She had no worries about what people thought of her, or how they might complain or try and pick apart her story. In the world of creation, she was the boss, she made the decisions, and she could make things beautiful. Rachel grunted slightly as she pushed herself down to her side, her thigh brushing Denny's. "I'm thinking of calling this *Lost in Paradise*."

"I like that." Denny smiled, eyes still closed. The pounding in her head had lessened substantially, making her want to kiss Rachel in gratitude. "Will you take it to your publisher?"

"I don't know." Rachel shrugged a shoulder, her hand moving from Denny's hair to rest on her naked stomach. A larger hand covered it, entwining their fingers. "This may just be for me. Not sure yet." Finished with her tale, she grew silent, studying Denny's features. "You know, you are a truly beautiful woman." The blonde's voice was soft, almost awed. "Truly," she said at the blue eye that studied her. "It's just amazing." Rachel shook her head in wonder. "I think someone sculpted you."

"Stop!" Denny protested as loud as her headache would allow. "You're making me blush." Her eye closed and she heard a soft chuckle.

"Not trying to. I thought that from the moment I laid eyes on you on the plane." Soft fingers brushed over softer skin on a forehead, trailing down prominent cheekbones to a proud jaw. "I have an artist friend who I bet would love to paint you."

Her whispered words crept straight into Denny's heart, warming her from the inside out. "You are a silver tongued devil," Denny whispered, the slightest up curve of her lips exposing her pleasure at Rachel's words.

"That I am. But this devil speaks the truth." Rachel leaned down, placing the softest of kisses on Denny's lips, just a brush for emphasis then she withdrew. She was silent for a few moments, pushing herself up to a sitting position again, nudging Denny to lay her head in her lap. The brunette grimaced slightly, the movement unsettling her easing headache. "Relax," Rachel whispered, fingers finding her temples and gently massaging.

Initially the pressure hurt, but eventually began to ease the pain in Denny's head. "That feels good," Denny whispered, sighing in relief at the magic in Rachel's cool fingers.

"I'm sorry you hurt," Rachel whispered back. "I wish I could take all of your pain away."

"You are." Denny brought an arm up, snaking it around one of Rachel's thighs, fingers lazily caressing the skin she found there.

The touch made Rachel self-conscious. "I can't wait to shave," she said, her fingers changing their position just slightly, still massaging the delicate bones of Denny's face.

"Me, too."

"The cloth is getting warm. Want me to refresh it?"

"Yes, please," Denny said as she shook her head no, making Rachel grin, bemused. "Don't want you to move. I'm comfy; but my head feels like it's boiling."

"I'll be right back, then you can have the best of both worlds, 'kay?"

"'Kay." Denny moaned as Rachel slowly slid out from underneath her, almost purring when she returned. She gasped as the cold rag was placed across her forehead, Rachel inching it down so it covered her eyes, too. "Ohhh, that's nice." She turned her head, lips almost touching Rachel's bare stomach.

"How are you doing? Need anything else?"

"Just keep talking," Denny murmured. "Your voice is so soothing."

"You want to hear something crazy?" Rachel hesitated, looking out over the darkened night. "I can't believe I'm actually going to say this out loud." She resumed her gentle combing of Denny's hair. "There's a part of me that doesn't want to go home. I mean, sure, I miss all the comforts of civilization. I miss Reenie, my two sisters, and even Matt. But..." Sighing heavily, she looked down at the woman whose head rested in her lap. Denny's breathing was even and slow, her body relaxed in sleep. Rachel smiled, leaned down and placed a soft kiss on slightly parted lips. "I don't want to leave you guys."

Going, going, almost gone...gone. Will sipped his wine, one leg crossed over the other as he sat on the Italian leather sofa he and Dean had bought together three months before his partner boarded the doomed flight. Reaching to the table in front of the couch, he grabbed the bottle, pouring what was left of the expensive red into his glass.

Had he done the right thing? It was too late now, for certain, but it plagued him. Coming home from Reenie's loft almost two months ago, he had stared at Dean's picture for a long time, memorizing every tiny detail of his partner's face, remembering the sound of his laughter, his voice, the way he smelled. He had to smile, even now, remembering Dean's aversion to *anything* dirty, or what he felt to be unsanitary. Even at the club, when they'd go play racquetball, Dean refused to walk barefoot in the locker room, his ever-present slippers there to protect his feet.

The sun was going down, not only on the day, but also on the summer, a summer Will had prayed would bring joyous news, or at least some sort of closure. The other day he'd seen ads on television for school supplies, always the first indication fall was, indeed, on the way. Another holiday season without Dean, the second of many to come. Will wasn't so sure he could handle it again. Sure, he'd put on a happy, smiling face, even his Christmas bowtie, but those closest to him knew it was a façade. Will never was a good liar. After all, Dean was the attorney, not him.

The wine had ceased to taste like anything, the strong drink frosting Will's brain, dulling his senses but making his thoughts sharper, his pain more acute. Alcohol was funny that way. Perhaps he should switch to something stronger.

Mind trailing back to Reenie's loft, Will remembered the look on Keller's face when he told them they were finished, would not be continuing the search. Hell, she'd looked almost more crestfallen than he had felt himself. He really needed to do something spectacular for Keller and Garrison. They'd put their heart into the searching, not taking money for anything more than fuel and maintenance of their planes. *Real troopers.* He often wondered what Dean would think of the ladies, grease monkeys, both of them. More than once Will had seen a smudge of the black goo on Garrison's cheek, and the women's hands were definitely more calloused than those of all the men in Will's architectural firm. Dean would probably initially have turned his nose up at the pilots' rough and sometimes unkempt appearance, but Will thought his partner would have liked those two.

Sighing heavily, Will drank the last of the wine.

Lizbeth Vinzetti hummed an old Italian lullaby her mother used to sing to her almost eighty years ago. She could recall her mother's lilting voice singing to her and her eight siblings as they hid during the bombings in World War II. At twelve, Lizbeth had been second oldest, and she and her older sister, Rose, had been expected to help care for the other seven. Those had been hard times.

She had already vacuumed her granddaughter's small apartment, trying to help. Gloria worked so hard — working at the courthouse all day, then at night, working part-time at the diner. Gloria was even considering taking on a third job. Though she tried to say it was because they could use the money, Lizbeth knew better. Her Gloria was trying not to think, trying to work herself into an early grave. The elder Vinzetti knew the trick all too well. When she and Paolo had lost Gloria's mother, thirty years earlier, Lizbeth thought she would die right along with her. Somehow she needed to convince her granddaughter life did go on, that no matter how hard she fought it, she would not win.

Part humming and part singing the words, Lizbeth held the picture in her hands, the picture she had found in the drawer. Smiling at the beautiful face of her great-granddaughter, Lizbeth placed the picture in its place of honor among the other family photos, arranging them so Mia would have pride of place.

Lizbeth smiled, knowing they'd go through the same routine tomorrow. When Gloria got home at an ungodly hour, she'd put Mia's photo away, and the next day Lizbeth would bring it out. She wasn't going to let Gloria forget. She *couldn't* let her forget.

Tiffany sipped her morning coffee as she looked out the window. She was trying not to be angry, but her emotions were starting to get the better of her, starting to override her rational side. It had been almost eight months, *eight* months! She promised Hannah she'd be patient. She understood her need to deal with all the radical changes in her life. She promised Hannah she'd be there for her, support her, and be her friend first, girlfriend second.

Eight months ago, Valentine's Day had been their first mutual kiss (mutual, compared to when Tiffany had surprisingly kissed Hannah and had ruined that wonderful day of Christmas shopping), and Tiffany was fine with that. She'd kept the holiday low-key, not pushing anything onto Hannah she wasn't ready for. There had been flowers, a nice dinner, and a moonlit stroll. They had done a lot of talking that night, about their dreams and hopes, what Hannah planned to do with her life now that she was suddenly a *me* instead of an *us*. When Tiffany had dropped the enigmatic brunette off at her house, she'd been surprised when Hannah had leaned across the seat, giving her a soft, wonderful kiss. Tiffany had responded, but all too soon it was over.

Time moved on, as it does, and still Hannah was keeping Tiffany at a distance. Understanding could only go so far, and Tiffany was starting to run out. *If she's not over Denny's death, fine! But don't drag me into the quagmire.*

Last night Hannah had opted to spend the night, a first time event. Tiffany had been surprised but elated. She hoped it would be an opportunity to show Hannah she was serious about her and wanted to give them a chance. They'd kissed. Hannah had even taken Tiffany's hand and placed it on her breast, outside her t-shirt, but it was something. Tiffany's body was on fire when suddenly Hannah had stopped her, apologized, then quickly left.

Another sleepless night. Tiffany had tossed and turned, weary and emotionally exhausted. She'd been a fool. The thing was, as angry at Hannah as she wanted to be, she couldn't quite muster up the energy to get past the anger at herself. She should have known better. It was time for her to really evaluate their situation and decide whether it was worth pursuing. She didn't think Hannah was trying to play with her emotions, not at all. But she did think Hannah should have given herself more time, more time to grieve and truly put Denny's memory to rest.

She remembered the day when everything had been final, the sale of DeRisio's complete and the shop emptied, Hannah had cried in Tiffany's arms for hours.

"Did I act too soon, Tiffany?" Hannah cried, wishing she hadn't acted so rashly. "I guess I felt it was the only way for me to move on. I can't keep seeing Denny at every turn. Driving by that damn coffee shop or going in to check on it," she shook her head, wiping at her eyes, "I couldn't do it anymore."

Hannah had said she couldn't keep seeing Denny at every turn. Tiffany chuckled ruefully. It didn't seem that Hannah was anywhere near getting over Denny enough to move on with her life, whether she saw her at every turn or not.

"Hell, I don't know," Tiffany whispered, sipping from her coffee, watching as the paperboy rode by on his bicycle, tossing a thick, rolled paper on her front lawn.

Jennifer Dupree sat in the idling car, waiting. Her grandmother had sent her to pick up Conrad from his weekly counseling session. Her little brother had always been a handful, but one word or look from their dad and he had straightened right up. Grandpa was a lot like their dad was, but that seemed to make Conrad even more rebellious. Maybe he felt Grandpa was trying to take their father's place.

Her fingers tightened around the steering wheel. She'd been nervous about taking Meredith Adams' car, but her mom's car, which was now hers, was still in the shop. Her grandparents were having it painted and detailed for her seventeenth birthday, coming up in September. She couldn't wait to have her own car, though every time she got in it she wanted to cry. She and her mom had been close; Jennifer could still see her mother's sparkling eyes and hear her boisterous laugh.

Resting her head back against the headrest, Jennifer began to daydream about her parents. It had been one year, one month, and nineteen days. The only daughter of Michael and Melissa Dupree had been keeping a calendar since the day of the plane crash, used for marking off each day that passed with a red X. She missed them terribly. Her mother had started to teach her about wearing make-up, Jennifer finally allowed at fifteen. Her dad, the big ol' dork that he was, had been pacing out in the hallway outside the bathroom, glancing in from time to time. The girl had asked her mother what his problem was, and her mom had explained he didn't like the fact his baby girl was growing up.

Jennifer looked into the rearview mirror, studying the reflection becoming more and more like her mom's. She had the same hair color and eye color, but her dad's height. He had been a big man, strong and sturdy. A hug from him had been like nothing else in the whole wide world. Jennifer smiled at the memory of how warm and comforted he could make her feel. Yet, oh boy! If you made him angry...wow. Her father always made her think of that country song by Holly Dunn, *Daddy's Hands*. It was about how a father could be hard and stoic one moment, then soft and a big teddy bear the next.

That was her father to a "T". She could see his big smile, so handsome with his Stetson on.

"Hey, dork. Why are you crying?"

Jennifer was startled out of her reminiscences by her brother's voice and the slamming of the car door. Swiping at her tears, she sniffled and got the car started. "How was your appointment?" she asked, carefully looking in all her mirrors and over her shoulder before merging into traffic. She'd only had her license for nine months and was still nervous, especially with a passenger in the car.

Conrad shrugged. "It was okay, I guess."

Jennifer could tell her brother didn't want to talk about it, so she dropped it. "Grandma is making a big dinner for Alan's visit," she said conversationally.

"So?"

"Don't be such a jerk, Con. They're just trying to do right by Mom and Dad." She glanced over at her brother who refused to look at her, his body slumped against the door.

"Yeah, well, they're not Mom and Dad, and never will be."

"Good luck, baby," Keller said against Garrison's lips.

"Thanks, darlin'. I love you." Turning to the back of the Cessna, Garrison reached around and squeezed Parker's knee. "Love you, honey. Have fun today."

"Thanks!" Ignoring her family, she turned back to her laptop, writing frantically on her newest story, this one a whole fifty pages.

"I love you, too." Keller watched her partner climb out of the Cessna; Duke Wingom waiting for her. "Call me and let me know what happens, either way," she called out. "I should be home by nine tonight." She smiled at Garrison's salute and returned the blown kiss.

"Hello, Monk." Duke slapped Garrison on the back. "Good to see you." He led her toward the hangar, where the G21-A Goose was already fueled and ready to go. They stepped into an office in the large hangar, Garrison shrugging out of her backpack and unzipping it to pull out the map.

"This is where we've been so far," she explained, pointing to all the red marked areas. "I'm thinking here." She ran her finger around in a circle on the smooth paper. "I know we went over this on the phone, but I had a couple of thoughts last night. This is our last shot, so we've got to make it count." She met the grizzled man's gaze, waiting for his assessment.

He stroked his salt and pepper beard. "What's your plan to get there?"

As Garrison went over her strategy with him, as well as the figures she'd made for fuel and flight time the night before, the older pilot nodded in understanding. His mind flitted to a flight he'd taken with his uncle years ago, just the outline of a memory, so faded over time he wasn't even sure that it hadn't been a story. He shoved it into the back of his brain, focusing on what Garrison was saying.

"It's a bit chancy to make these last minute changes, kid, but," he grinned with mischief, "your chutzpah is one reason why I always liked ya."

Denny groaned slightly as she tried to move. Her headache was gone, but now she had a whole new ache to keep her company throughout the day. Her back was punishing her for sleeping on the hard stone of the ledge all night. She must have overslept after talking long into the night.

"I thought those grass mats were bad," she muttered, eyes blinking open, envying the others the relative comfort of their shelter. It didn't help that there was extra added weight either. Rachel was lying practically on top of her, head tucked under Denny's chin, one hand tucked under Denny's shoulder, the other resting on her upper chest. Denny noticed something else, too.

Glancing down, she saw the side of Rachel's breast, where it was pressed against her stomach. The other side was the same. *Why the hell is Rachel half-naked?* This thought led to another: *it feels wonderful.* Her hands, resting on the slight waist, began to move, wanting to feel the smooth skin of the entire expanse of Rachel's back. The skin was warm, soft. Rachel sighed in her sleep, her upper body adjusting slightly as Denny's fingers ran up her spine.

Denny closed her eyes, allowing her fingers to do the walking in a tactile journey. Her fingertips grazed up and over slightly pronounced shoulder blades, gently pushing blonde hair aside as they danced across the back of a slim neck, Rachel shivering slightly as they passed. A soft smile graced Denny's lips. Her fingers continued over smooth, strong shoulders, down the warm skin of Rachel's sides, ribs, barely brushing the sides of soft roundness before returning to the back.

Slowly, Rachel rose to wakefulness, sighing at the sensation of being touched. She kept her eyes closed, allowing the feelings to stream through all of her nerve endings, making her shiver. The hand wrapped around Denny's shoulder began to move, fingers squeezing and massaging the skin, letting Denny know she was awake and very okay with the exploring fingers. For a brief moment Rachel panicked, remembering she was topless; she'd used the material for Denny's cool rag. She quickly shoved embarrassment aside as the magic fingers spread out into warm palms, running all over her back, gliding down to her hips before returning upwards to her neck and shoulders, then coming dangerously close to the sides of her breasts.

Denny sighed at the feel of soft lips against her upper chest. Her hands grew bolder, her mind filled with sensation; at that moment, nothing else mattered. She felt the soft material of the cotton sarong wrapped around Rachel's hips, her finger daring to brush underneath, making Rachel gasp in surprise. That was quickly followed by a soft, almost sighed moan. Her large hands cupped Rachel's butt, feeling the muscles underneath tense in response.

Rachel lifted her head and upper body, resting on her elbows as she pulled herself up so her face was level with Denny's. Without thought, without a single twinge of conscience, she leaned in and took Denny's mouth in a kiss that deepened quickly, her nipples hardening as they brushed against the material that still covered Denny's chest.

"Oh, Rachel," Denny whispered into her mouth, hands sliding up Rachel's back and curving around until she reached between their bodies and cupped the bare breasts.

"Oh, Jesus," Rachel gasped. Arching her back, her eyes closed as Denny's palms pressed against her nipples. Her entire body burst into life, every fiber of her being alive and buzzing. She exhaled shakily as lips and tongue attended to her exposed throat, her arms trembling as she tried to hold herself up against the onslaught of sensation.

Denny could not recall ever wanting anyone as badly as she wanted Rachel Holt in that moment. The taste of her skin was exquisite, as was the texture and weight of her breasts, the feel of her wet heat through the thin sarong she wore. She wanted to make love to her, *needed* to make love to her. She knew there was no way she could resist what was happening between them. She'd been blessed with a second chance in a situation that was otherwise a tragic curse. She'd be a fool to let it pass, when chances were good she'd never set foot home again. This was her life now, so why deny her body and heart?

Gently pushing Rachel onto her back, Denny leaned over her, looking into her face. *Such a beautiful, beautiful face.* She ran the backs of her fingers down the side of the sculpted cheek, over the jaw, and finally down the side of Rachel's neck. Her gaze drifted down over Rachel's face, following the path her fingers had just traced until finally she took in Rachel's breasts.

"You called me beautiful, but I don't think you've looked at yourself," Denny whispered, looking into Rachel's hooded gaze as her fingers inched toward the round underside of a breast. "You're so amazingly gorgeous, Rachel, inside and out. So wonderful. So soft." She leaned down and placed a soft kiss on waiting lips. "Thank you for last night," she murmured.

"Any time. I hate seeing you in pain."

"I'm cured."

"For now," Rachel smiled, her fingers weaving into thick, dark hair, gently pulling Denny closer.

"And *I'm* telling you I think you're out of your mind." Mia glanced over her shoulder at Dean, who scowled behind her.

"You don't think I have the ears of an eagle?"

"No, I don't."

He stopped mid-step, hands on hips. "And why not?"

"Well," the girl laughed, "mainly because I'm not quite sure eagles even *have* ears." She laughed harder as Dean stomped past her, grumbling to himself about what he knew he had heard. "Come on, Dean." Mia jogged to catch up with his longer stride. "Don't do this to yourself again. I think you heard what you wanted to hear." Her voice had softened, not wanting to hurt him but trying to be honest.

Dean stopped and waited for her; he knew she hadn't meant it that way. "Do you really think that's what I'm doing — playing tricks on myself, hearing things?"

"I don't know, Dean, but I don't want to see you get so upset again." She placed a hand on his shoulder and leaned up to place a soft kiss on his cheek. "Come on. Pam ordered us to get her some water, so let's get her some water."

Headset firmly in place, Garrison looked out the side window and watched their tiny shadow move along the waves, then turned to her co-pilot. "I can't believe how differently she handles than my Cessna."

Duke grinned, nodding, his response tinny in her headphones. "Different animal entirely. I'm surprised Davies' doesn't have a seaplane."

"Dad wanted to get one years ago, but it didn't work out. We do pretty well with the Bell, Cessna, and Herc. I would like to possibly expand and bring in a few seaplanes."

"Aren't you just the little entrepreneur?" he teased.

Garrison chuckled. "Hey, I've got college to pay for, and soon!"

"Om on, eice o it!" Michael muttered around the "knife" held between his teeth, polished wood with razor sharp reef tied on. Grinning with the tool between his teeth, he looked like some sort of psychotic jungle serial killer. He squeezed powerful thighs around the tree to free both hands, reaching up and grunting as he tried to dislodge the stubborn group of coconuts. Finally he gave it a good whack with his fist, watching in satisfaction as the shells fell to the ground below. Turning to the other side of the tree and the goodies it held, the Texan stopped, cocking his head to the side as he listened. *What's that?* Like...like...a swarm. Bees? Locusts?

Climbing higher, Michael craned his neck to try and see above the treetops. He cried out as he started to slip, fingers digging into the bark as his thighs tightened. Heart pounding, the mechanic resumed climbing, determined to get a look out to sea, or the sky.

"Any time now would be just peachy!" Pam hollered, the lunch catch already beginning to sizzle. She had sent Dean and Mia out on the simple errand of getting fresh water, and Michael was to supply coconut milk. How hard was that? Climbing to her feet, she was prepared to launch an all out fit when she stopped, turning toward the ocean. "What is that?" Bringing a hand up, she shielded her eyes from the intense overhead sun, still squinting. A buzzing, like an annoying mosquito...

Chapter 19

Duke veered off to the left, following the flight pattern they'd registered before leaving that morning. They'd gotten a later start than he'd wanted, but such was the life of a pilot. He felt like he was entering the memory that had eluded him when Garrison had arrived. Familiar, something niggling at him. What was it? What was he trying to remember? On instinct, he veered slightly off their charted path.

"What are you doing?" Garrison asked, noting that Duke was heading them west.

"I don't know. Something...I feel like there's something out this way. I think I remember...something..."

Trusting her old friend, Garrison turned back to the window, keying the radio to call in their new coordinates.

Rachel's head fell back as she felt fingers inching closer to her breast, her nipples straining with arousal, desperate to be touched. About to grab Denny for another earth-shattering kiss, she suddenly froze, ears straining.

"Wait, Denny, wait." She pushed up, holding herself up on her hands.

Surprised, Denny also pushed herself up to her knees. "What is it?"

"Wait, listen." If Rachel could have perked up her ears, she would have. Eyes closed, she tried to concentrate fully on hearing. "Hear it?" she asked excitedly.

"I don't—" Denny stopped, suddenly...yes, yes, she... Jumping to her feet, she spun around in a full circle on the ledge. She was joined by Rachel, who was quickly tying her top into place. Their gazes settled out to sea.

"Oh, my God."

Michael nearly fell out of the tree in his haste to get down, forgetting about the coconuts he'd struggled for as he ran headlong toward the beach, powerful body pumping as fast as it could go. Breaking through the trees, he saw Pam at the water's edge, standing stock still, hand raised to shade her eyes. The Texan stopped mid-beach, eyes glued to the sky.

"Oh, my God!" Duke cried out, startling his co-pilot, making what was a dangerous turn, but he didn't care. He was an experienced pilot and knew what he was doing. Garrison, caught off guard by his unusual carelessness, was about to holler at him, but then she saw it, and then she saw *them*.

"They see us! They fucking see us!" Dean was nearly tripping over his loafers as he ran out of the jungle, Mia right behind him. "Hey!" he yelled, waving his arms frantically, half yelling, half crying as the beautiful glint of steel and glass in the sky headed straight for them. "They see us!"

Mia was crying as she ran to join Pam and Michael, throwing her arms around Pam, who was also sobbing.

"What's happening? Oh, my God," Denny breathed, breaking through the trees, Rachel beside her. They watched as if in a daze as the seaplane made several spins high above the island, coming in closer each time, dropping low enough to make a landing.

Garrison was beside herself, tears streaming down her face as she tried to relay what they were seeing through the radio wires. Her voice was shrill and almost unintelligible.

"We found someone! Oh, my God, we found someone! *Lots* of someones!"

The six islanders stood together in a huddle, mixed emotions flowing through each as they watched the white and blue plane make a graceful landing on the ocean surface and taxi over to them.

Denny felt Rachel's hand take hers and she squeezed it. "I can't believe they found us," Denny whispered, her voice thick with emotion.

"I know." Rachel couldn't decide whether she'd ever been happier in her life, relief washing through her and threatening to erupt in a windfall of emotion, or whether she was scared. She thought of the life she was going back to, as well as the leaving of the family she'd made. And she'd have to leave Denny, who would undoubtedly go back to Hannah.

Unable to help himself, Dean fell to his knees. He could no longer see, his vision shrouded by a solid sheet of tears. He heard the propellers and engines winding down, then the squeak of doors opening, and a woman's voice.

"Ahoy, there!" Garrison stood on the floater above the wheel, waving an arm at the stunned group that watched from the beach. She jumped into the water, which reached her waist, and sloshed her way toward the beach. The closer she got, the more easily she could tell these people had been there for a while, but obviously weren't natives.

Mia was crying steadily, holding on to Pam for support. She couldn't think, couldn't feel anything but ultimate relief, and that maybe her mother had been right all along — there was a God.

"Hello!" Michael hurried into the surf to grab the small pilot in a massive, bone-crushing hug. "Jesus, God are we glad to see y'all," he whispered into the sweetest smelling hair.

Garrison couldn't keep her own emotions in check; she looked up at the big man with tears in her eyes, which spilled down her cheeks at the look in his eyes.

"We thought y'all forgot all about us," he whispered, voice choking on the last word.

"Why are you here?" the pilot asked, hope flaring.

"We was all on that flight that went down." His brow scrunched in thought. "What day is it?"

"It's July 30."

"We been here for more than a year?" he asked, eyes wide.

"You guys were on flight 1049?" Garrison asked, bursting into tears at his nod. *Oh, Will.* She threw her arms around the castaway's neck, feeling his arms wrap around her waist. *You were right all along.*

Denny wiped at her eyes, though it didn't seem to help. Her vision was blurred as the tears continued to fall. She watched Michael escort the pilot to the beach.

The woman looked from one to another to the next in disbelief. "All of you?" she asked, meeting six pairs of eyes and matching nods. "What are your names?"

"I'm Denny DeRisio, this is Rachel Holt—"

Garrison's eyes got huge as Reenie's face popped into her mind. "Oh, God!" Her hands went to her mouth, fresh tears threatening to fall.

"Mia Vinzetti," Denny continued, surprised when the blonde hurried over to Mia and wrapped her in strong arms.

"Oh, honey," Garrison cried, unable to control herself. "Oh, honey," she said again. "Someone is going to be so happy to see you."

Mia clung to the stranger, crying at the thought of going home, finally going home. "I'm excited to see my great-grandparents, too," she managed.

Garrison sniffled, shaking her head as she pulled back just enough to look into the girl's dark eyes. "No, honey. Oh, Mia, your mom is waiting for you."

"What? No," Mia shook her head, heart breaking all over again at having to say it out loud. "My mom was on the flight with me."

"Gloria Vinzetti. Mia, she survived." Garrison clutched the girl's arms, shaking her slightly for emphasis.

"Oh, Sweets!" Dean tugged Mia from Garrison's embrace and held her close as the girl sobbed.

Feeling like Santa Claus, Garrison looked into the eyes all around her. "Who else do I have here?" She looked at Michael then at Dean and Pam. "Anyone here related to Will Ash?"

Dean started. "Will?" The name was like a balm on his tongue. "Will Ash? Have you seen him?" He pulled away from Mia, leaving her to Pam's arms. As though in a dream, he walked over to Garrison.

Eager to confirm that she was right, Garrison placed a hand on his arm. "Are you Dean Ratliff?" At his confirming nod, Garrison's face broke into a huge smile. "Oh, Dean," she whispered, "it's because of you that we're here."

Tears leaked out of his red-rimmed eyes. "What do you mean?"

"Will never gave up hope of finding you. We've been searching for you since September." Garrison took the slender man into a warm embrace, letting him cry on her shoulder.

"We're going home," he whispered. At the pilot's nod, Dean finally was able to let go of the grief and fear, loss and isolation. Garrison held him, whispering to him, telling him how much Will loved and needed him.

Denny was sobbing, almost numb on sensation overload.

"Garrison?" Duke stepped up on shore. He felt bad about interrupting, but they had pressing business. "We've got storms moving in; we need to get moving." The co-pilot looked at each of the survivors, calculating the added weight of six adults and the estimated flying time from the fuel they had left. Making a decision which he knew Garrison wasn't going to like, he said, "We can take half of you today and come back for half in the morning."

Garrison opened her mouth to protest, but then her years of experience took over. She knew Duke was right. Sighing sadly as she pulled away from Dean, she faced the small gathering. "I'm afraid that what he means is that we can't chance this much extra weight and still be sure of getting back safely."

"I'll stay," Michael said, stepping back. "Let Mia and Dean go." He motioned toward them, and their gratitude was plain in their eyes.

Duke nodded his approval. "One more."

"Go," Denny said, turning to Rachel.

She shook her head. "No. Not without you."

"Please go," Denny leaned her forehead against Rachel's. "Please." She needed to break it off now, to make it hurt less later. "Please, just go with them."

Rachel threw her arms around Denny's neck, hugging her tightly. Eyes squeezed shut, she breathed in the familiar scent, memorizing everything about her. Finally she released Denny. Looking into the deep blue eyes, she looked inside Denny's soul and saw herself reflected. Nodding in acknowledgment of the things they dared not say, she placed a soft kiss on Denny's lips then let her go.

"I'm going to miss you," Pam said, hugging Mia close. "I'm so happy for you, honey. So very happy." She smiled at the light she saw shining for the first time in those dark eyes. "Goodbye."

"Thank you, Pam. For everything." Mia leaned in close. "Tell your daughter you love her," she whispered in the older woman's ear then she was gone.

Denny tried to hold in her own overwhelming flood of emotion as she watched the goodbyes. Mia walked over to her and took her in her arms. "I will never forget you."

"You won't have to," Denny whispered, squeezing Mia tight. "I promise we'll have that mocha breve someday, you and me."

Mia nodded, giving the brunette one last squeeze before letting her go. She studied the sad blue eyes. "Denny?"

"Yeah?"

"Follow your heart."

The girl nodded over to where Rachel was saying her goodbyes and Denny smiled sheepishly. If only Mia understood how hard that was. "Be sure and tell your mom hi for me, okay?"

"Oh, I will!" Mia thrilled to the knowledge her mother was alive. She had no idea how, but she didn't care. Nothing mattered except that she was alive.

"All right, Red, you're finally free of me," Dean said, grinning up at the large Texan.

Michael chuckled. "Yeah. Maybe we'll finally have some peace on this damn island."

Dean laughed, almost giddy in his unbridled excitement. He extended a hand. Michael looked down at it for a moment then Dean was pulled into a bone-crushing hug.

"You take care of yourself," Michael said.

"You, too, big guy." Dean stepped back, hand still resting on Michael's shoulder. "Go take care of your kids. They need their dad."

Michael, Pam, and Denny watched as half their family boarded the small plane. Garrison gave them a thumbs up before the powerful engine and propellers rocked the stillness of the day.

Denny could see Rachel sitting next to a window, the blonde's face pressed to the glass, eyes on her. Denny raised a hand and waved, and before the plane carried the others from their island life, she saw Rachel do the same.

Chapter 20

Dark brows knit, Keller pushed the replay button on the answering machine and listened to the message again. She held the small phone to her ear, holding up a hand to forestall whatever Parker was about to tell her so she could concentrate again on the hysterical message from Garrison.

"Keller! Get you and Parker up here ASAP! WefoundDeanand fiveothers, ohmyGod, Keller, wefuckingfoundhim!"

Keller stood slack-jawed as the meaning of the words registered. Turning stunned eyes to an expectant Parker, she swallowed. "Go pack a bag for Canada, Parker." The teenager ran back up the stairs.

Keller walked over to a kitchen chair and fell into it. Shaking herself out of her daze, she quickly dialed the familiar number of Garrison's cell phone. It was picked up after half a ring.

"Keller? Oh, thank God!" Garrison ran a hand through her hair. "Oh, baby, we did it. Oh, Keller..."

"Whoa, whoa, honey, finish a sentence." Realizing that she, too, needed to pack a bag, she got up from her chair and hurried up to their bedroom.

"We found six survivors on an island, Keller! And Dean was one of them."

Keller faltered at the top of the stairs, nearly landing face first on the landing. "What?"

"Yes. Mia Vinzetti, Rachel-friggin'-Holt! Oh, God, Keller. Please hurry. I need you here."

"I'm coming, baby. Parker's packing a bag now, and I'm on my way to pack mine." She pushed through the door into their room, looking around frantically for an overnight bag, holding the cell to her ear with her shoulder.

"Thank you, Keller."

"For what?"

"For having faith and wanting to make one more run. All those people would have been stuck there for God only knows how long."

"I can't believe so many survived. Nine people! That's unheard of!"

"I know."

"Where are you?"

"We're at Duke's house. We could only ferry three of the survivors, so we're heading back out in the morning."

"Who all do you have?"

Garrison was getting impatient. She needed to see Keller, and she needed to see her *now*. After seeing what Will and the others had gone through, then finding the survivors, it made her realize how important cherishing her own little family was. "Less talk, more fly!"

Keller chuckled. "I love you. See you in a few hours."

Rachel ran her hands over her face, wiping the water out of her eyes. She turned off the shower, wishing she could stand underneath the water all night, but she knew there were other people in the house besides her and Dean and Mia. She was surprised there was any hot water left after Dean's marathon shower. She was the last, the other two already swathed in clothing volunteered by Duke and his family. Rachel's own borrowed sweats and t-shirt, gloriously clean, were waiting for her on the toilet seat.

Stepping out of the shower stall, she blew out a breath, feeling utterly exhausted. It had been one of the most emotionally draining days since the day of the crash. The flight back to Canada had taken forever though it was probably far shorter than it had seemed. Rachel had looked out the windows, part of her terrified to be in the air, the other part amazed to feel padded seating again. She smiled, remembering their landing.

Rachel and Dean and Mia exchanged looks of uncertainty when they looked out the windows and saw a large group waiting for them when they landed — employees and crews from the hangar and small, attached airport.

They unbuckled themselves and made their way off the plane, immediately swarmed by cheering and hollering people as the three refugees disembarked. Rachel tried to keep her emotions under wraps as she was hugged by one person after another, Dean and Mia given the same treatment. They'd been offered food, drink, anything they desired. The first word out of all of their mouths was, "Shower!"

Duke, his wife Eva, and their three sons were kind and generous, opening their home to the survivors, who had quickly become dubbed The Island Six, until they could be transported back to their own homes.

Home. That was a foreign and confusing concept for Rachel, who had no idea where she wanted to go. Her world had turned completely upside down during the past fourteen months. Looking in the mirror over the sink before stepping into the shower, Rachel hadn't recognized herself. Her hair had grown out, her body was hairier and she needed a serious eyebrow wax, but the changes she saw had little to do with her physical appearance. It was all in her eyes. Unable to look in their depths and view the altered soul within, Rachel had to look away.

How was it she could discover herself on a small island, yet back in civilization she felt so incredibly lost? It was as though nothing made sense, nothing she had known for twenty-eight years seemed like the truth; her life was a lie.

Rachel wrapped herself up in a fluffy towel, inhaling the fragrances that danced all around her nose in the steam-filled room: laundry soap, shampoo, steam-enhanced body soap. She nearly moaned in pleasure as she rubbed lotion onto shaved legs; the smooth skin felt wonderful beneath her palms and fingers. Rachel almost felt overwhelmed by the luxuries all around her. Just peeing in a real toilet and not having to bury her waste in rock-infested dirt had been the highlight of her day!

Passing her hand over the smooth, steam-opaque glass of the mirror, she studied herself, noting how thin she'd gotten. She could almost hear Reenie chewing her out, all the while trying to fatten her up. *Reenie.* Rachel smiled, suddenly filled with a sense of giddiness. On the flight back to Canada, the pilot, Garrison, had explained what had been happening over the months since the crash. The 1049 Club established by Reenie and Matt, and the committee, led by Will Ash, set up to generate search missions to try and find any remaining survivors.

Garrison had offered the use of her cell phone to the trio. Rachel felt a mixture of nervous energy and elation at the prospect. She couldn't wait to hear Reenie's voice again and let her know she was okay.

Mia took a deep breath, grateful for the hair band Duke's wife had loaned her. Her hair had gotten long and unruly on the island, and it was bliss to have it out of her face. She closed her eyes as she took a large bite of the cheeseburger, chewing with slow reverence, allowing all the flavors — ketchup, mayonnaise, mustard, and pickles — to burst in her mouth, along with the taste of the grilled meat and soft bun. What she had once taken for granted as Tuesday night dinner had become a delicacy of the richest variety.

When Mia opened her eyes, she felt sheepish, as every pair of eyes at the table was on her. Dropping her gaze down to her plate, she ran a French fry through the puddle of ketchup.

Garrison was fascinated at the relish with which Dean and Mia were digging into their dinners. It reminded her of Parker as a little girl, when she had been introduced to chocolate milk. She smiled at the memory, realizing she was staring when she heard a throat clearing. "Sorry," she muttered, looking away from Dean's raised eyebrow. "So, Dean, are you *sure* you don't want to call him?"

"Positive." Dean grinned, wiping his hands on a napkin. "I want to give Will the surprise of his life! Me!"

"I think you're going to manage that just fine, my friend," Duke chuckled, chewing on the tender skin of a tomato slice. "Bound to give the guy a heart attack."

Duke couldn't believe he was playing a part in such an amazing, momentous event; he would be grateful to Garrison all the rest of his days for giving him the opportunity. He couldn't wait to go get the other three the next morning. They planned to take off just after daybreak.

"Isn't that the truth." Mia grinned then gulped from her glass of milk, eyes closing at the wonderful cool smoothness.

Duke chuckled. "There's plenty where that came from, Mia. Don't make yourself sick."

"Do you have *any* idea what it's like to only have water and coconut milk to drink for an entire year?"

"And the berry water Pam made from time to time," Dean added.

"True. From berries crushed using the food masher." The teen's eyes filled with evil delight. Rachel held back her laughter, curious to see what Dean's reaction would be.

The others around the table looked baffled at what was obviously a private joke between the survivors. Dean actually looked embarrassed as he turned his attention to his plate. "A man's gotta do what a man's gotta do, Sweets."

Mia chuckled. She was about to ask Garrison's permission to use the phone, as offered, when there was a knock at the door.

Garrison jumped up, quickly following Duke's wife through the house. To her relief, Keller and Parker stood on the other side. "Oh, thank God!" She took her partner in her arms, feeling the craziness of the past few hours receding.

"Oh, Garrison," Keller said, her voice unusually deep. When she pulled back from the hug, her blue eyes were filled with tears. "We did it?"

Garrison grinned, her own eyes watery. "We did it," she whispered. "Show me."

The sun was beginning to set, the blazing red sizzling into the ocean depths. It was beautiful, but Denny wasn't paying any attention. She sat on the ledge she'd shared with Rachel the night before, the place where they'd had some of the best talks she'd had with anyone. It was the ledge where she'd gotten to know Rachel, to understand and to love her.

Surprised to feel moisture on her fingertip as it brushed under her eye, Denny looked at it then rubbed it into her thumb with a sigh. So they were to be rescued, saved, brought forth from exile. How amazingly bitter sweet. Was she a monster to feel that way? Should she be jumping up and down for joy, as Pam and Mia had been doing earlier on the beach? Should she be howling to the moon above, thankful to the goddess of good luck?

She felt none of those things. All she felt was confusion and desperate loneliness. Off in the distance she could hear Michael and Pam laughing, singing ridiculous songs and reveling in their impending freedom. Did she want it? Of course she did. She had to go back to her life, reestablish herself in the world of civilized society, and all that came with it. There was no other choice.

Telling Rachel to get on that plane had been one of the hardest things she'd ever had to do, but she knew it was for the best. One of them had to be strong, had to be practical. Denny cursed her damn practical nature. *Hannah.* She had to focus on Hannah and getting their life back together. What had Hannah done all this time? Denny knew her partner was a strong woman, but she also knew Hannah was extraordinarily sensitive. She couldn't even imagine how Hannah had managed to cope with her grief.

Knowing Hannah, who didn't like to deal with things, she'd probably put all of Denny's things in one of the spare bedrooms, closed the door, and hadn't been able to look in there since. Denny smiled at the thought then she thought about the kind of pain Hannah had been put through, and all for nothing. Would Hannah be angry? Losing so much of herself in grieving for Denny, as Denny knew she would have, or would she be so relieved at Denny's reappearance that it wouldn't matter? Had Hannah moved on?

Denny rolled that thought around her brain, tasting the slight bitterness. How would she feel if Hannah had moved on? If she had died in the crash, looking down at her partner, she knew she would want to see Hannah happy, and would be thankful for whatever it took to make her that way. But she wasn't dead. She was very much alive, and heading home.

Then there was Rachel. Denny felt like such a hypocrite, daring to think she might possibly be hurt or angry if Hannah were dating someone else, when she, herself, had fallen in love with another woman while away from Hannah. She had tried to fight it, knowing if Hannah and her situations were reversed, Hannah would have done the same — she would have waited. Still, Denny could control what her body did, almost; however, there had been no way to stop her heart from following its own path. And it had boarded that plane with Rachel Holt.

Denny was so tired, her eyes burning almost as much as her heart ached. She wished she could just close her eyes and go back to her world before the crash, before the name Rachel Holt meant more to her than just an attractive face and an impersonal author.

Michael sat back, hands tucked behind his head and an unshakable smile plastered on his face. It hadn't waned since he'd spotted the plane earlier that day. Pam's was just as big as she lay in the sand on the other side of the small fire.

"What's the first thing you're going to do?" Pam asked, not taking her eyes from the constellations in the night sky, knowing this would be the last time she would see them so clearly.

"That's easy," Michael said, his voice soft and wistful. "Give my kids the biggest damn hug they ever had."

Pam smiled at that, picturing it well. "Yeah. Me, too. My daughter and my grandson."

"Grandkids." He whistled through his teeth. "Can't even imagine, though my oldest boy could very well be a daddy by now. He's twenty-two. I was a daddy by then."

"Tracy became a mother younger than that." Pam sighed, happy and satisfied, though admittedly a little scared and uncertain about what she might find when she rejoined the world. "Michael?"

"Hmm?"

"Do you think they forgot about us?" She glanced over at Michael; his eyes reflected the flames. "Our families?"

"Nah," he said after some thought. "If'n they had, we'd never have been found."

"I can't believe Dean's partner is the reason for all this." More tears choked her and Pam did her best to swallow them down. She hadn't cried as much in the past two years as she had in that one afternoon. "He must really love that little pain in the ass."

Michael snorted. "Some love, indeed. Maybe them queers got the right idea." He thought of Will and Dean, Denny and Hannah. Hell, even Rachel, it seemed, the way she was always carrying on with Denny. After a heartbeat of silence, he and Pam glanced at each other. "Nah."

Pam chuckled, as did Michael. They had never again talked about what happened between them, and on one level, that bothered Pam. She wanted Michael to know that she would never forget it, or him. They had managed to comfort each other that day in a way no one else could. "Michael?"

"Yeah?"

"About what happened between us..."

He was surprised Pam was bringing it up, but she apparently needed to talk, so he gave her his full attention. "Yeah?"

"You and I have our own lives to return to, and you'll have a lot to deal with — the kids and their grief at losing their mother..." She studied his face for a moment. "I just want you to know it meant something to me. It wasn't just some mindless fuck to this lonely old veterinarian. I mean, it was, but it wasn't. I care about you, Michael. That said..." Both understanding what she'd left unsaid. It was a mutual need, and they'd taken care of it.

Michael was surprisingly touched by the declaration. Pushing himself up to his knees, he crawled around to her side of the fire and took her by the hand. Pam nestled into the hug, resting her head on his shoulder, relishing their last bit of closeness on the island. They sat silently on the sand in each other's arms, staring into the fire.

"More martinis are on the way," Reenie yelled from the kitchen. Tossing an olive into her mouth, she chewed happily, shaking the last of the drinks and pouring the mixture into the waiting glass.

"Hey, Reen?" Quinn said, pushing the swinging door open and sticking his head into the kitchen.

"Yeah?" she said absently, loading drinks onto the tray.

"Your cell is ringing." He handed her the phone.

"Thanks. Take these out, will you? I'll be out in a sec."

"Sure." Quinn, one of Reenie's copy editors, grabbed the tray in steady hands and butted his way back through the door.

Reenie looked at the small window on the phone; it was flashing a strange number. She decided to let it go to voicemail and rejoin her party. Tossing the phone to the counter, she was about to push through the door but then decided better of it. She had a new author she was working with, and it might be her.

Snatching up the phone, she flipped it open and put it to her ear. "Hello?" There was silence on the other end, though it was obvious the line was open. "Hello?" she repeated impatiently, dark eyebrows drawn. Finally she heard someone take a breath.

"I understand I owe a great debt of gratitude to you and Will Ash."

Reenie's heart skipped a beat. She knew the voice like she knew her own face, but...there was no way. "Who is this?"

"Don't you recognize the voice of your favorite client anymore, Reenie? I haven't been gone *that* long."

"Rachel?" She whispered the name, falling onto a nearby stool, her face paling, hand beginning to tremble as she pressed the tiny phone closer to her ear.

"It's me, Reen. I'm alive. A little thin and with the best tan of my life, but I'm alive."

Reenie's gasp was part whimper, part cry, and she was shaking her head. "Oh, my God. Oh, my God. This can't be!"

"It is, Reen. I swear. And if I didn't know any better, I'd say you're having your end of month, Friday night martini party. Am I right?"

"Oh, God, Rachel!" Reenie felt something explode in her chest — shock, profound relief, and joy. "Where are you? How did this happen? Who found you? Where are you!"

"Whoa!" Rachel laughed, swiping at her eyes, amazed how relieved she was to hear a familiar voice. For just a moment she felt normal again. She had to keep blowing her nose and wiping her eyes as she explained what had happened and where she had been.

Reenie interrupted often, with tons of questions or words of astonishment. Before Rachel could finish her tale, Reenie interrupted her yet again. "I'm coming to get you. I'm on with the airlines right now, getting us tickets."

Rachel felt her heart skip a beat, realizing she was about to reenter her life and she'd have to deal with the mess she had left behind. "Wait, Reenie." Running a trembling hand through her hair, she sighed. "I can't get on a plane. I don't have anything — no money, no identification, nothing. Not even a passport to get back into my own country."

"Shit. You're right. Jesus Christ, Rachel! You're alive!" Reenie felt another burst of realization flood through her, bringing with it a new torrent of watershed.

Rachel smiled, feeling her own eyes brim again. "Crazy, isn't it?"

"Yeah. I've *got* to get you here. I've got to see you, Rachel. Give me the number where you're at— Wait, I have it on my phone. Stay put! I'm going to call Carrie."

"Why? We certainly have no need of a publisher right now."

"Because she can get us a charter. Honey, we've got to get you here. Carrie is going to shit her shorts!" Reenie paused, taking a deep breath. "Honey, your contracts have all been rewritten with your heirs. You *need* to talk with Carrie, get all this straightened out."

Rachel took a deep breath, nodding with a sigh. "Okay."

"You're alive!"

Rachel smiled. "Mostly."

The entire house was up in arms, the damn dogs barking like mad. Sighing in irritation, Carrie Tillman tugged her robe tighter around her body as she stumbled down the hall toward the front door. She growled in her throat as the bell rang again. "Damn people know how I like my sleep. I go to bed early in order to get an early start each day. This had better be something that is so important that it couldn't wait until morning."

Shocked to see one of her editors on the stoop, Carrie unlocked the locks, chains, and deadbolts, yanking open the door of her brownstone. "Reenie? Are you okay? What the hell are you doing here at..." She looked at her wrist, irritated anew when she realized she wasn't wearing her watch.

"It's almost nine." Reenie breezed by the surprised woman, who quickly closed the door and relocked it. Carrie followed her employee into the living room, waiting not-too-patiently for an explanation. "You're not going to believe what I have to tell you, but I need you to listen. Okay?"

"You okay?" Keller laid a comforting hand on Mia's shoulder. The girl nodded, but she was still trembling; she'd dropped the cell phone three times. "Here. Let me help," she said softly, taking the small phone from the girl's hand.

Mia laughed nervously. "I'm sorry."

Keller asked for the number, dialing as Mia told her. The line was ringing as Keller brought the phone to her ear. Picked up on the fourth ring, she was taken by surprise as a woman began speaking in a language that was definitely not English. She gave Mia a questioning look. "Uh, is Gloria Vinzetti there?"

Lizbeth was beside herself that someone would have the *audacity* to call so late. "How dare you wake me up!" she shouted into the phone, her words slightly slurred with sleep. She could not understand the caller's words, her English sketchy at best. The only thing she was able to pick out was her granddaughter's name. "She works! Unlike you."

The phone was slammed down, ringing in Keller's ear. Closing the cell phone, Keller looked at Mia. "She hung up on me."

"What?" Baffled, Mia looked at the cell as though it held the answer.

"Some older lady; it sounded like she was speaking Italian or something."

"Italian?" Mia was trying to make sense of this. It was nine-thirty, and her mother was always home and awake at that time. She prayed that Gloria hadn't moved, changed her number, or— Gasping, Mia covered her mouth with her hand, dark eyes wide. "My great-grandmother," she whispered. It was the only thing that made sense.

Taking the tiny phone from Keller's hand, Mia quickly dialed her home phone number again, the number she'd known since she was a child, the only phone number she'd ever known. As the line kept ringing, dark eyes closed, the girl silently prayed that if it was, in fact, her great-grandmother, she'd answer.

Keller sat back, watching Mia as the girl toed a dog toy, her nerves flowing through her in waves. She couldn't help but wonder what was going through the girl's mind at that moment. What was making her so nervous? Keller couldn't help but put herself in the shoes of the survivors. What were they facing going back to their lives? Did they have lives to go back to? She hadn't had much chance to talk to Rachel or Dean, Dean was too busy thrilling the gathered family with tales of life as an islander. She wasn't quite sure what to make of the attorney, though she couldn't wait to hear how Will reacted to finding out his partner was still alive. Apparently Rachel's publisher was sending a chartered plane for her in the morning. Dean was going to leave with her.

Keller's thoughts were drawn back to Mia when she heard the girl begin to speak in her mother's native tongue.

Mia blushed at the unkind names being directed at her through the phone line. When the old woman took a breath, she spoke. "Grandmamma, it's Mia."

About to slam the phone down again, Lizbeth stopped, at first because of the Italian spoken back to her, then at the voice, then lastly because of the name. She stopped dead in her tracks, stunned, as though her heart had stopped beating. When her voice returned to her, it was barely a whisper. "You are a cruel demon to play such a trick."

"It's no trick, Grandmamma, I swear." Mia felt a smile spread across her lips at the sound of her great-grandmother's voice; she was that much closer to her mother. "I survived the crash, Grandmamma."

"I do not understand." Lizbeth slowly fell into a nearby chair, hand gripping the handset for dear life, the other grasping the small gold crucifix around her neck. Surely this had to be a trick. Surely.

"We were rescued today," Mia said, her voice thick with rising emotions, images of her great-grandmother and mother swimming before her eyes. "They found us, finally."

"But..." Lizbeth was trying to wrap her mind around this miracle, her eyes beginning to sting as moisture gathered, hands shaking. "They said..."

Mia smiled through her tears. "I know."

"Oh, Mia! Mia, Mia, where are you, child?!" Lizbeth loosened her grip on the crucifix, easing the strain she was putting on the chain with her desperate clutching. "Thank God!" She looked to the heavens, but saw only the water stain in the corner above the bookcase. "Oh, Mia!"

"Where's Mom, Grandmamma? They said—" Mia was suddenly afraid to finish her sentence. What if it had all been one big lie, and Lizbeth and Paolo were just clearing out their dead granddaughter's apartment?

"She's at work, my child."

Mia gasped. *So it is true!* "She's alive?"

"Oh, yes, child, though barely." Lizbeth was scurrying around the apartment, grunting as she threw on her clothes, trying to see through her tears of relief and joy. Managing to climb into the dress she'd so carefully removed earlier, she nearly dropped the phone, sliding a gout-swollen foot into her shoe. "Oh, child, your mamma will be so happy!" Lizbeth Vinzetti almost forgot to lock the door on her way out.

Gloria sighed heavily. It had been a long day and just seemed to be getting longer. Her shift at the diner would end in less than two hours but it felt like a lifetime. She began to hum softly to herself, figuring if she had to concentrate on the tune, she'd be able to stay awake.

The waitress knew she was slowly killing herself, working fifteen hour days five days a week, then any overtime she could get on her days off. She couldn't stand being at the apartment, even though she was thrilled to have her Nonna at home waiting for her. The problem was home wasn't home anymore. Something had died inside her the day of the crash, and Gloria felt a cold presence inside of her, slowly taking over until there was nothing left but a woman in her mid-thirties, grown old before her time.

"Gloria!"

"Yeah, Joe?" she called from the back room, where she was chopping tomatoes for a salad.

"Someone here for ya!"

Gloria set down her knife and wiped her hands on a towel. She had absolutely no idea who would be coming into work to see her.

"Gloria!" Lizbeth yelled, trying to push past the man who refused to allow her into the back kitchen. *Doesn't he understand what is happening?!* She hissed nonsense at him in Italian, his face registering only confusion and anger.

"Nonna," Gloria said, shocked to see her grandmother standing there, and in her slippers, no less! "What are you doing here?"

The seventy-seven year-old heart was pounding wildly. "Take this!" Lizbeth held out the cell phone she'd clutched to her chest the entire three blocks she'd puffed her way to the diner.

Gloria stepped out from around the breakfast counter, leading the old woman away from prying ears, just in case Lizbeth Vinzetti was starting to lose her mind. "Nonna," Gloria said softly, trying to keep her anger in check, "you ran here in your house shoes for a *phone call?*"

"You must take this, child. Here! Take it." She shoved the phone at her granddaughter, fire burning brightly in her eyes.

That intrigued Gloria, though she still felt her grandmother was losing her marbles. Taking the tiny phone, Gloria put it to her ear. "This is Gloria." She heard a sniffle, then a miracle.

"Mom? It's me!"

Gloria stood stock still, her mind trying to catch up with what she'd just heard. *It can't be.* "Who is this?" Her voice was low and deep, filled with warning.

"It's me, Mia. I'm okay. I'm coming home in the morning."

Gloria felt tears of grief sting behind her eyelids. She sat on a stool at the breakfast counter. "I don't know who this is, but you are a monster to play such a cruel prank."

Mia felt her heart pounding. She was elated her mother was truly alive and yet deeply disappointed at not hearing the reaction she'd hoped for. Tears streamed down Mia's cheeks. Before she knew what had happened, the phone was taken from her.

"Gloria? This is Keller."

Gloria gasped at the sound of the pilot's voice. Hope was beginning to trickle through her anger.

"I have Mia sitting here beside me, and she's one upset kid who needs her mom."

"Keller...I don't understand."

"She's alive, Gloria," Keller said softly.

"We stopped looking," Gloria whispered, a trembling hand fluttering to her mouth. Overwhelmed, she didn't even notice the small group of curious coworkers and diner regulars that had begun to gather, a proud Lizbeth standing in the midst of them.

"Well, uh," Keller picked at her jeans, "yeah, about that..."

"I don't care! Give me my baby back!" Gloria lifted her phone away from her ear. "My baby's alive!" She was crying now. "Mia? Honey, are you there?"

"I'm here, Mamma," the girl sobbed, cradling the phone against her ear. She heard her mother's sob at the endearment Mia hadn't used since she was a small child. She felt like a small child again — lost and utterly vulnerable.

Garrison was leaning against a wall, watching, arms crossed over her chest and a smile on her lips. She couldn't help feeling she and Keller had participated in the most important event of their lives. She caught her partner's eye and beckoned Keller over to her, giving Mia privacy. Keller hurried over to her, taking the blonde in her arms and burying her face in the familiar hair.

"I've never been so happy in my life," Keller whispered, feeling Garrison's nod of agreement. "We should go to bed, baby. You and Duke have an early morning."

"I know." Garrison rested her head against Keller's shoulder, sighing in contentment at the peace that filled her.

"Come on." Kissing the blonde hair, Keller pulled away, taking Garrison by the hand and leading her toward the basement where Duke had set up a room for them.

Chapter 21

Rachel sat cross-legged on the foldout couch trying to adjust to the softness beneath her. At first contact, it had felt wonderful, but her skeletal structure wasn't sure what to make of the unaccustomed padding and luxury. Sleeping and sitting on hard ground for more than a year had been hard on her body. It felt almost as though she'd been running around without stopping for a long time, so busy surviving she didn't feel the strain on her bones and muscles. Now, suddenly stopping, she was beginning to feel the true extent of her aches and pains.

Grimacing as she tried to get comfortable, Rachel laid back, hands behind her head. She stared up at the ceiling, thinking of what would happen in the next eight hours. Reenie had called her back within an hour, with the news that a chartered plane would be ready for take off out of Jean Lesage International Airport, at six in the morning. Rachel, Dean, and Mia would all be on board headed to New York.

Thoughts about her return to society quickly segued into thoughts of Denny. She wished the brunette was with her, holding her. For the first time since they'd been interrupted by the sighting of the plane, she thought about their night on the ledge. When she closed her eyes, she could still feel Denny's hands on her body, her mouth, and could still hear the soft, sensuous words. Never in her life had she been so affected by one single person, and in so many ways: emotionally, physically, and at a soul level that took Rachel's breath away. Feeling Denny's absence acutely, Rachel realized she had never known the kind of longing and loneliness that plagued her.

When Denny insisted Rachel leave the island in the first group, her first instinct was to feel hurt, but looking into the profound sadness in the blue eyes, she understood and could only comply. They had to let go of one another, had to go back to their regularly scheduled lives. Denny was trying to make it as quick and painless as possible. *Quick, for certain; painless, not in this lifetime.*

Turning over on her side, Rachel curled her hands up under her chin, staring at the furniture moved aside to make room for the bed to fold out. She didn't see the end tables in front of her. Instead, she saw the brilliance of Denny's eyes and heard the soft, velvet voice that had come to evoke so much more than just comfort. Rachel's heart hurt, a burning inside she was afraid might consume her.

Rachel forced her thoughts away from Denny; they were far too painful to be her bedmate. Instead she made herself take a look at the reality in front of her, with an eye to deciding what needed to be done.

There was Matt. She knew in her heart their marriage was over and she needed to let him go. She needed to be free to explore her own heart. Rachel couldn't think of the direction her heart might lead her in without immediately thinking of Denny, so she concentrated on the rest of her future instead. She had a clean slate, could go wherever she wanted. *Well, when I get hold of some money, I can.*

That thought scared her. From the little Reenie had said, Rachel was without any immediate access to funds unless the publishers took out an option on her next novel. Her own finances were tied up in legalities. She knew she had a place to go. Reenie would never leave her to fend for herself. Still, Rachel was a fiercely independent woman and needed to be alone to think and explore her own heart. Staying with someone, even her best friend, did not appeal to her. Maybe she should find her own damn island somewhere and rot all by herself. But that brought her back to the "needing money" issue. It would be a while before she could reclaim control of her assets. She would have to have a long talk with the insurance company when she got her footing back. She imagined they *all* had long talks with lawyers and banks and the authorities ahead of them.

"Can I ask you something, Denny?" Pam's voice came at Denny through the darkness of the hut. It was almost a relief to Denny to know her house mate also couldn't sleep.

"Sure." Denny had so many thoughts, wanted and unwanted, continuously marching through her brain.

"What happened with you and Rachel?" Denny heard Pam's body turn toward her.

Denny sighed, bringing her hands up under her head. *What happened indeed.* "I fell in love with her."

Pam's next question didn't sound like that much was a surprise. "And what about her?"

"I think so." Denny really didn't want to talk about it. She was about to say as much when Pam spoke first.

"Why did you send her away? Why not give it a go?"

"It's not that simple. She has a husband, I have Hannah." Denny studied the shadow of her friend, then turned back to study the solid darkness of thatched leaves. "I'm sure what happened was a direct consequence of our situation. Back home," she shrugged, "who knows. We may not have felt the same way."

Pam snorted. "Doubt that." Something rustled just outside their shelter. More rustling then the flap was pulled back and a figure loomed in the opening.

"Sorry if I scared ya, ladies," Michael said in a whisper. There was a long pause. "Do y'all mind if I join ya? Kinda lonely over there, ya know."

Utterly charmed, Denny smiled. "Come on in, Michael. We've got plenty of room." Denny scooted over to make room for the big guy, the three settling in once more, finding silence. Denny was amazed at just how cold it felt without Rachel pressed against her. She loved holding the woman, loved the feel of her body, her warmth and smell. They seemed to fit together so perfectly, like two pieces from the same puzzle. As cheesy and clichéd as it seemed, it was the truest truth she'd ever known.

Denny turned her thoughts to home and what she'd find when she got back there. She wasn't sure how she'd be able to face Hannah, knowing in her heart that Hannah no longer was the light of her life. All the same, she would have to resign herself to the fact that what she and Rachel had briefly shared had been a wonderful experience, but could be nothing more.

Closing her eyes, Denny felt a single tear trail down her cheek to settle in her ear, making her shiver.

"Please take care of yourself," Garrison whispered into her hug with Dean. "Will would kill us if anything happens to you before you get home."

Dean smiled, gently pulling away. He gave his rescuer a kiss on the cheek and a blinding smile. "Thank you, Garrison. It seems like such a simple, completely under-whelming phrase, but it comes from the heart."

Garrison chuckled, reaching up to pat the man's clean-shaven cheek. "Tell him hello for us, 'kay?"

Dean nodded. "Will do."

Garrison turned to see Rachel walking toward her and immediately took her into her arms for a quick hug. Parker had been beside herself at being able to spend time with the famous writer. The teen was a budding writer herself, but hadn't been able to find the confidence to truly explore her creative world. Seeing a real flesh and blood author who had been able to make a life of writing, Parker was edging toward her dream. Garrison chuckled when she went in to wake Parker up so the girl could say goodbye to everyone. Parker had a signed copy of Rachel's last novel clutched to her chest.

"Thank you so much, Garrison. Without you and Keller, I can't see how we ever would have made it back."

"It was my pleasure, Rachel." Garrison looked into troubled green eyes. She had no idea what lay behind the pained expression, but hoped the woman could work through it. Perhaps going home would help.

Keller stood back, watching the last of the goodbyes with a broad smile as, one by one, the survivors boarded the plane. She put her arm around Garrison, feeling her partner's head rest on her shoulder. The door was pulled into place as the plane was sealed up and readied for takeoff. Neither pilot could find the words to express how she felt, seeing the first wave of the rescued returning to their lives. They'd cried along with Duke and his family as the three islanders reconnected with their loved ones over the phone. Only Dean didn't make a call, which had been difficult for him. He had paced the house, glancing at every phone he passed.

"Truly amazing," Garrison said at last.

"Yeah. You ready to go back out?"

"Definitely. I wish you could go with us." Garrison sighed, squeezing Keller before letting her go.

"Me, too. We'll be waiting here for you." She gave Garrison a quick kiss and watched as her partner joined Duke at the seaplane to retrieve the remaining survivors. Keller turned back toward the rising sun, its brilliance catching her eyes and making them glow. She watched the small charter plane purr its way along the tarmac, taxiing into position and couldn't help wondering what lay ahead for the occupants. How could they possibly return to life as normal after what they'd been through? Mia had stayed on the phone with her mother until late into the night, laughing, crying, and reacquainting.

As Keller climbed into Duke's truck, ready to head back to his house where Parker was very likely still asleep, she wished she could be a fly on the wall, watching what would undoubtedly be very emotional reunions.

Denny slicked her hair back from her face, bringing the long, wet rope of hair over her shoulder to wring it out. As the cold droplets ran down over her chest, making her gasp, she took in all that surrounded her. The colors and vibrancy of the island had become old hat after daily exposure for so many months, Denny no longer seeing the beauty that was her world. Now, knowing it would all be gone soon, she saw it again through new eyes, trying to memorize every detail, every memory, every bit of luscious growth and natural song.

It had been a restless night for all of them, each of the three lost in reliving the event that had gotten them on the island in the first place, and what might happen when they returned to their lives. Denny was awakened more than once by nightmares she hadn't had in nearly a year. She'd found herself once again strapped in her seat, submerged under millions of gallons of water and heading into black depths. Feeling as though she was suffocating, Denny had woken with a loud gasp, frantically struggling to get to the surface, only to find strong arms wrapped around her and a deep, comforting voice in her ear. *It's alright, darlin'. I gotcha.*

It had taken nearly an hour for her heart to calm and the visions to leave her mind — the screams of panic and fear as the plane headed toward the water, the fear rising up like sour bile in her throat.

Denny climbed up to the ledge to allow her skin to dry in the air which was already warming. She stared up into the sky just beginning to burgeon with color. She'd never look into such a pure sky again and that made her sad. She thought about her hustle and bustle world back in New York and wondered if she'd ever be able to be truly a part of that, now that she knew what it was like to take life in stride, in no hurry, since stressing over things didn't make them happen any sooner. On the island she'd learned to relish smells, textures, and sights. She'd learned that when beauty was ignored, it seldom came around a second time. A bird filled with color and inspiring awe, if not studied and appreciated in the moment, would fly away, perhaps never to be seen again. She'd even caught Dean daydreaming now and then.

Hearing a bird's early call, Denny thought about music. That was one thing she couldn't wait to get back to. It seemed such a simple thing, but one that had always been singularly important to her. She couldn't sing, had no talent for playing an instrument, but music had been a part of her soul since she'd been a small child. Not a day went by she didn't spend at least a few hours filling her soul's need for it. She had found herself humming or singing softly to herself throughout the duration of her stay on the island. It calmed and soothed her frazzled nerves, or eased her bouts of homesickness.

Lying on the ledge, Denny knew she was a short time away from returning to all that she was conditioned to perceive as normal. She felt a nervous flutter in her stomach, various luxuries floating before her mind's eye, things she looked forward to getting back to using or tasting. Or hearing. Her beloved MP3 player had gone down with the plane, a fact that saddened her almost more than losing her contact lenses. Denny chuckled at that. She certainly wouldn't miss the eye-strain headaches.

Michael tossed another pebble into the incoming surf, his other wrist dangling over his bent knee. The sun had come up and a new, fresh day was upon them. Now what? Did he go fish for breakfast? Climb a tree and make it a coconut and berry morning? How much time before the plane came back? Was it coming back?

It had been a long night, thinking about his kids and wondering how they'd managed without either of their parents. No doubt they'd gone to Melissa's parents, which was a good place for them. Michael was worried about his youngest who sometimes seemed unnaturally attached to his mother. How had he handled the news that she was gone?

Michael had no idea how to relate to his children with their mother dead. She had always been the buffer, the nucleus of their family, the one they all revolved around. Now what? How could he face his kids, beaten down with the guilt that he had survived and Melissa had not?

How did he explain that to them? To Mel's parents? To the world? Had he tried hard enough to save her? Had he fought the water and circumstances hard enough, or had he done something horribly wrong, allowing her to die?

He wiped a large hand across his face and then absently tugged at his beard. He couldn't get that thing off soon enough. He wasn't keen on the mountain man look. He had to grin as he imagined that shaving had been the first thing Dean had done when he got back to civilization. He was happy for his friend that Will had never given up searching. Michael wondered if he would have had the same tenacity had it been Melissa who was presumed dead. Or would he have just rolled over in sad resignation?

He hoped one day to meet the man who'd kept Dean going. A strange thought, for sure. Michael had never thought about any man being banged by another guy, and saw queers as the sexual perverts they were perceived and portrayed to be. But one look into Dean's tortured soul and Michael had realized maybe there was more to it than that. Maybe the two men felt about each other the same as he felt for Melissa.

The whole world had turned upside down. Certainly Michael's had. The thought had barely occurred to him when he heard the droning of engines. Pushing to his feet, he walked out toward the water's edge, raising his hand to his eyes, trying to discern which way the plane was coming from.

"I am *not* looking forward to getting on that plane," Pam said softly as she stepped up beside him. He grunted in agreement. The seaplane made a magnificent splash as it touched down then threw plumes of water behind it as it cruised in. Soon they were joined by Denny.

"Guess this is it," she said softly, feeling Pam take her hand.

"Yeah. Guess so."

"I sure am gonna miss you gals," Michael admitted, watching as the plane slowed, the body surging gently over the waves it created.

"Same here." Denny turned to the other two, smiling as they all moved together for a tight group hug. She felt her stomach roiling in waves of nervous excitement.

"Hello!" Garrison yelled as she stepped out onto the floater above the wheel. Her wave evoked three others in response. Once again, she found herself wading through the water toward the island, able to focus more on her surroundings this time. It was beautiful, no doubt, but she just couldn't wrap her mind around trying to survive with nothing more than nature and your own wits. "Are you ready to head back to civilization?" she asked, splashing onto the shore.

"Hell, yes!" Pam said, clutching the pilot in a hearty hug.

"Well, let's get you all home. There are some happy reunions taking place as we speak." Garrison was grinning from ear to ear, thinking that the other three had landed in New York and are involved in wonderful reunions.

Seated in the seaplane, Denny looked out the window. It was so strange to see the island from the other side of the glass. When she looked at the white beach, she didn't see sand and incoming surf. She saw their almost daily game of coconut ball or their nightly campfire. Or Dean prancing around in his sarong, finally clean and ready to tell their limited world about it. Then there was Michael's red face every time he had to use the food masher. She saw Pam's easy smile and the way she had mothered all of them through the most trying times of their lives. She saw again Mia's laughter and tears, and Rachel's lovely eyes and deep insights into the psychology of humanity. She saw them as a family, a unit, and bonded for life in a way no one back home could ever understand.

Pam braced herself as the plane began moving, swallowing hard to keep her newly acquired fear of flying in check. Though she wished a boat could have been sent to get them, she knew the flight was a necessary evil. Her knuckles were white as she grasped the armrests.

"It's gonna be okay," Michael whispered from behind her. She nodded, simply for response rather than because she believed it.

Once they were in the air, Garrison turned around from the copilot's seat. She pushed a blue and white cooler back until it bumped against Denny's bare foot. "Based on how your friends wolfed down cheeseburgers last night, I figured you guys might have a taste for something other than fish." She grinned then turned forward.

Denny unlatched the white plastic lid, her mouth watering at the contents. She held up a can of gloriously cold Coca-Cola, looking around for any takers. Michael nearly jumped out of his seat as he reached over to take it. She handed an identical can to Pam then took a bottle of orange juice for herself. The turkey and cheese sandwiches were gratefully accepted and everyone dug in.

"Welcome back, gang!" Garrison called over the roar of the engines.

Chapter 22

Reenie was almost vibrating, excitement making her body flush, her palms sweating so that she repeatedly wiped them on the thighs of her jeans. Arranging to get Rachel home, Reenie had had almost no sleep the night before, but her mind was wide awake no matter what her exhausted body was feeling. She'd had to fight with herself to not just hop a plane and go to Rachel. She was beside herself with the anticipation of seeing her friend again. It had been a miracle of miracles, and Reenie couldn't keep her emotions under control. She'd been crying off and on since she'd received one of the most important phone calls of her life.

After hanging up with Rachel, Reenie had cleared everyone out of her loft, not saying a word about Rachel's resurrection. She didn't think Rachel would want a media circus when she returned. She had tried to call Gloria, only to get sent directly to the woman's voicemail. After that, she'd hopped into a cab and raced over to Carrie Tillman's. Together they devised a plan. Carrie assured Reenie she'd get Rachel home with as little fanfare as possible, though Reenie was warned that eventually the company would want to milk as much publicity out of her return as possible. Reenie had also left a message on Matt's phone, but he had yet to return her call.

Now here they stood in the airport, waiting impatiently to see their loved ones again. Near her, a very anxious Gloria paced in the tiny terminal for private planes connected to the main airport at LaGuardia. They had been waiting for the past hour. All three, Gloria, Lizbeth, and herself, grew more excited by the minute.

Lizbeth said something to her granddaughter in Italian and Gloria smiled as she turned to see where her Nonna was pointing. Outside the massive airport windows, a plane was coming in for a landing. A small plane. A private plane. Gloria looked over at Reenie and they both drew a deep breath.

"I can't believe this is happening," Gloria whispered, wringing her hands.

"I know. If I didn't believe in God before, I do now," Reenie said.

The three watched in silence as the plane landed, then taxied toward them, crew members out on the flightline directing the small plane to a bright white X painted on the tarmac.

Gloria ached to run out the door and down the stairs to meet the plane, but knew it wasn't allowed. The official who had directed them to the lounge was stern in his instructions that they were to wait in there. He said they weren't even supposed to be there due to tighter airport restrictions after the 9/11 terrorist attack, but circumstances being what they were, the airport had made special concessions.

"Holy God, that must be Dean," Reenie whispered, watching as a thin, very tan, man stepped out of the plane dressed in a simple polo shirt that looked to be a little too large and a pair of cargo shorts. His face was clean shaven, but his dark brown hair was long and shaggy. Reenie held her breath when she saw the sunlight glint off of a white shoe as someone else neared the open door. From the whimper she heard to her left, she knew it was Mia.

Gloria didn't even realize she'd made a sound, her heart pounding, eyes already stinging. She couldn't take her eyes off of her daughter. "Oh, my God," she said, voice cracking. "She's so thin."

"She's alive, child," Lizbeth said, equally unable to take her eyes from the sight.

Next a petite blonde stepped off the plane, her hair blowing around her head and shoulders as a slight breeze caught it. Gloria sucked in a breath. "That's Rachel Holt."

Reenie ran over to the door, her face almost pressed to the glass as she watched the three being led toward the steep, narrow iron staircase. Unable to take her eyes off Rachel, she openly cried. She couldn't believe how long the blonde hair had gotten or that Rachel was so thin. Stepping away from the door only because she had to allow the door to be opened, Reenie flew forward the instant the trio entered.

"Reenie!" Rachel grabbed her best friend and pulled her close. She was stunned to see Reenie's tears, having never seen her cry in all their years of friendship. The display of emotion got her going again, just when she didn't think she had any tears left.

"Oh, Rachel!" Reenie cried, almost crushing Rachel to her. "I thought you were dead." Emotion made her tongue thick and her words were almost unintelligible, and when green eyes rose to meet her own, Reenie was taken aback by the deep sadness that filled them.

"Mamma!" Mia almost bowled Rachel and her friend over in order to get to her mother. Gloria met her halfway, the impact making them both lose their balance. Gloria barely managed to keep them both standing. She crushed Mia to her briefly then pushed her away, needing to see for herself she was okay, that she was *alive!* She touched the girl's face, her hair, saw Mia's overwhelming emotion, much like her own. Pulling Mia to her, she held her tight, rocking her just like she had when she was a child.

The feel of her mother's arms around her, the sight of her even, took Mia back to the days when she had cried over a scraped knee, needing her mother's warm, comforting touch to let her know it was going to be okay. The two were quickly joined by Lizbeth, who was crying and muttering in Italian. Mia grabbed hold of one of her great-grandmother's arms, pulling her into the reunion.

"We had a funeral for you," Reenie cried, pulling back just enough to be able to look into green eyes, shining with tears. "Goddamn you, don't you ever do that again!"

Rachel almost laughed as she was pulled into another bear hug. "Not like I planned it, my friend," she finally whispered. "I've missed you so much."

"I've missed you, too." Sniffling in an attempt to regain control, Reenie smiled through her tears, bringing a hand up to touch the beloved face. "I'm jealous of your tan."

Rachel laughed, leaning into the touch.

"You're so thin, Rach, and your hair is so long." Reenie ran her fingers through it. She just couldn't get her mind to wrap around what was happening — Rachel was alive after being presumed dead for almost fourteen months.

"I know." She looked past Reenie's shoulder at Mia's reunion with her mom. The look on Gloria's face made Rachel tear up all over again. An older woman stepped back from the two, having just enjoyed hugs from Mia. She was watching, a rosary dangling from her clasped fingers.

"Mamma," Mia said, swiping at her face and taking deep breaths, "I want to introduce you to two very important people." Turning, she gestured to Rachel who was standing with a woman with short, dark hair, their arms around each other's waist, and to Dean, who stood off to the side, his face flushed. "This," she reached out for him, "is Dean."

"Oh, Dean..." Gloria took him in her arms. "Thank you, thank you, thank you. Without your Will, I wouldn't have my baby back."

"I'm glad things worked out, for all of our sakes," Dean said softly, squeezing the woman before letting her go with a watery smile. Stepping aside, he made room for Rachel.

"Mamma, I'd like you to meet Rachel Holt." Mia was especially pleased to be able to introduce her mother to her favorite author.

"Your daughter is one of the finest people I've ever known." Rachel found herself lost in another hug. Smiling, she hugged the woman back.

"Can you believe that most of our time on the island, I had no idea who she was?" Mia laughed, wanting bring some relief to the emotional overload. Gloria and Rachel both chuckled then shared another hug.

"Thank you for keeping my daughter safe."

"It was a mutual survival effort, Mrs. Vinzetti. You may be sure that Mia did her part as well." Rachel turned to Mia. "You keep in touch, young lady." Mia saluted with a wide grin.

Turning to Dean, Rachel took his hands, feeling their rough calluses. "Go get him, Dean," she said softly, looking into his eyes, which were as red-rimmed as everyone else's. Dean nodded, past words as he took Rachel into his embrace. He hoped it wouldn't be the last time he saw her, but squeezed her as though it were.

"Take care of yourself, Rachel, and don't let her get away," he whispered into her ear then placed a soft kiss on the side of her neck. Hugging Mia one last time, Dean hurried out toward the door where his limo was waiting, as promised by Reenie. Mia, Lizbeth, and Gloria followed more slowly toward their transportation.

Reenie stepped forward and took Rachel by the arm, leading her out of the small lobby, through the airport, toward the parking garage. As they walked, she kept glancing over at her friend, still unable to believe her eyes.

"What?" Rachel finally asked, feeling Reenie's eyes on her for the sixth time and they hadn't even reached the car yet.

Reenie shook her head. "I don't know. It feels like I'm in a dream, I can't believe you're here." She stopped and grabbed Rachel's arm, pulling her into another hug which was enthusiastically returned. "I'm glad your nightmare is over."

Rachel sighed into the hug, badly in need of the physical affection. She realized that she'd never really thought she'd been without it...until Denny. "I'll tell you about it, Reen. Not now, but I'll tell you everything."

"Aw, son of a bitch," Duke muttered as he began to taxi toward the airport.

"How the hell did they find out?" Garrison eyed the crowd that awaited their return. The cameras and lights were a dead giveaway. "Shit!"

Denny heard the pilots and was curious to see the problem. It didn't take her long to find out. Dozens of reporters and media had massed outside the hangar, just off the tarmac. Vans from local news stations clogged the parking lot, and men were setting up camera equipment as the door to the plane was opened. Immediately the sound of shutters clicking and yelled questions filled the air. The three passengers exchanged looks, their nervousness increasing exponentially.

"Looks like you guys are celebrities," Duke said as he climbed out of the cockpit.

"Goody," Pam muttered.

Hannah closed her eyes, arching her head back to give Tiffany more of her neck to kiss. She moaned softly when her breast was cupped, the nipple growing hard at the warm contact. "Oh, yes," she whispered, lying back on the couch and pulling Tiffany with her.

Their relationship had become physical three weeks earlier when Hannah finally felt ready. The first time they made love had been awkward and tense. Having sex with Tiffany that time had been difficult emotionally as the last person to touch her had been Denny, but ultimately they'd shared a wonderful night. Hannah was convinced she had made the right decision — committing fully to a new life without Denny.

Now, as she felt the wet heat building between her legs, Hannah blocked out thoughts of her previous love, knowing they were a part of her past not her future. Denny would never be forgotten, but her memory had to be put away, stored in a safe place.

"Let's go into the bedroom, baby," Hannah whispered, the noise from the forgotten television program mildly distracting her.

"I'll just shut off the TV," Tiffany murmured against Hannah's neck, and she felt blindly for the remote control. "Shit." Unable to locate it, Tiffany left her pleasurable pursuits and slid to her knees on the floor in front of the couch, reaching underneath. Feeling the smoothness of the control, she was about to pull it out from under the couch when she stopped, her gaze riveted to the TV screen.

The drive from the airport was long, and traffic made it annoying. Reenie kept the radio on, since Rachel, who was quiet by nature, was damn near mute. Sensing something was very wrong, Reenie tried to stay silently supportive, reaching over to squeeze her friend's hand from time to time without prompting her to speak. Reenie figured when Rachel wanted to talk, she would. "Oh fuck!" she muttered as she turned the corner that led to her apartment building.

At Reenie's exclamation, Rachel switched her attention from the clouds to the mob of reporters swarming outside of the building.

"Shit, should I just keep driving? What the hell! Carrie said she'd take care of this!"

Rachel wasn't all that surprised. When she found out her publisher was paying the bill to get everyone home, she knew they'd want some sort of return. "No. They can't follow us inside. Let's just deal with it now."

"Are you sure?" Reenie was taken aback. At one time Rachel would have had them slink off to a hotel for the night.

"Yes."

Trying to swallow down her anger — anger at Carrie for going back on her word, and anger at the damn gossip hungry public who would do anything for news — Reenie gunned the engine as she pulled up in front of the building, startling a few of the reporters. A valet was right there to meet her.

"Do *not* let those bastards near my car," she growled, shoving an uncounted wad of bills into the man's hand. She grabbed Rachel's arm, and together they faced the swarm.

Michael had no idea where to look or what to do or say. As they descended the stairs of the plane, they immediately had cameras and microphones in their faces and dozens of questions were being shouted. He kept hearing his name, and when he turned to respond, he was met with another bright flash of light.

"Hey, give them some room!" Garrison yelled, trying to get in front of the three rescued. "Jesus! They just get back to civilization and this is the welcome they get? Get outta here!"

Duke quickly rushed the three into the hangar, the more aggressive journalists following.

Hannah tugged her shirt back into place, eyes riveted on the screen.

"Today, New York has seen an honest-to-goodness miracle. Last summer the country was stunned to hear about the three survivors, dubbed The Lucky Three, who survived the crash of Flight 1049 in the waters of the Atlantic. Fifteen months later, three more survivors, including novelist Rachel Holt, seen here, were rescued from an unmapped island. It is not yet known how the survivors were found, or exactly how many there are."

"Oh, my God," Tiffany breathed, transfixed. She watched the footage of the blonde author, long thought dead, being ushered by a woman with short, dark hair who was holding tight to her arm. Rachel Holt looked dazed and very tired. She ignored all of the questions, hurrying through the throng until she disappeared behind the double glass doors of the building. The newscast moved on to other items of interest. "Let's see if there's any more coverage." She changed channels and was not disappointed.

"Rob, we couldn't get any of the survivors to talk to us today, but we're told that there are..." the reporter glanced down at her notes, *"six survivors total."*

"Do we have any names as of yet?" the anchorman asked.

"We do know that the author Rachel Holt is one of the survivors. Other than that, no, we have no names."

As the reporter's voice became the voiceover of footage shot earlier in the morning, Hannah sprang off the couch, eyes huge as she fell to her knees in front of the TV. She watched as three people disembarked from the small seaplane, two women and a man. She watched as the three were ushered inside, a small, blonde woman trying to keep the reporters at bay. Hannah didn't care about any of that. What caught her eye was the woman with dark hair. She was tall, deeply tanned, and very slim. She thought about Denny and her constant complaining about the last fifteen pounds she wasn't able to lose. This woman's body looked nothing like Denny's, but her hair, the color, longer than Denny's, but...

Hannah's gasp caught Tiffany's attention. Turning to the screen, she saw the tall woman with dark hair had turned, facing the camera, very briefly and yet not briefly enough. "Oh, my God," Tiffany whispered, stunned. "That's Denny, isn't it?" She'd seen enough pictures of the beautiful brunette to know her, though Hannah's reaction had also pointed toward that conclusion. Even now, Hannah could only nod, her hand covering her mouth, eyes filling with tears.

Dean was glad to see a car waiting for him as Reenie had arranged. The door was opened for him and he settled into the backseat. His stomach was churning, making him nauseous as well as anxious. Leaning forward, he noted the time on the dashboard clock. Will would be in his office, probably working on his third cup of decaf.

Will.

Dean let out a long, slow breath at the thought. Running a hand through his hair, which was far too long and heavy for his liking, he closed his eyes for a moment, allowing images to flow through his mind unhindered. He couldn't wait to see him, couldn't wait to inhale Will's cologne, run his fingers through the thick, sandy hair.

During the time he'd been on the island, Dean had thought a lot about their relationship. It was good, had always been good, but he realized just how much they'd taken each other for granted over the decade they'd been together. After more than a year away from Will, Dean couldn't ever imagine taking for granted the fact that, every single day, he could wake up next to Will, see his face, hear his voice, feel his touch. Dean's Town Car couldn't get to Will fast enough.

Denny rested her head back against the headrest of the mini-van seat, breathing out then sucking in a lungful of air. She hadn't been expecting the Welcome Wagon, and could tell Michael and Pam were just as rattled. In the front seat of the van, Garrison and Duke were in a heated discussion about who could have alerted the media.

"I'm telling you, Monk, I made all of my people sign a sworn document. I don't know who talked."

"What about your wife? Any of your kids..."

"I don't know." Duke shrugged. "I can't imagine they would, but I just don't know. It could've been anyone."

Denny allowed their conversation to ease into a constant buzz in the back of her mind, her thoughts returning to her surroundings. She was overwhelmed by the sights, sounds, smells, and feelings flooding her. She felt almost like she'd landed on another planet, gazing in wonder at the cars that passed, the buildings, and people strolling along the sidewalks.

"Feels weird, doesn't it?" Pam whispered beside her.

Denny nodded, grateful for the warmth of Pam's body beside her. "I'm not sure what to look at first."

Rachel was almost pushed into the apartment and then Reenie slammed the door shut behind them, leaning against it.

"Son of a bitch!" She blew dark bangs out of her eyes. "I'm going to fucking kill—" Reenie subsided when a gentle hand pressed against her chest.

"Let it go, Reen. It was bound to happen."

With that, she stepped into her friend's personal space, and Reenie found herself enveloped in a warm hug. She chuckled. "You know, in all the years I've known you, you've never before been the one to initiate a hug."

Desperately in need of the comfort of familiarity, Rachel tightened her arms around her closest friend. "Life changes people."

"What happened to you on that island, Rach? Your eyes..." Reenie pulled away so she could look into Rachel's face. She studied the depths in the usually guarded green eyes, amazed to see just how expressive they were. "Was it bad?" she whispered. She was relieved by the small smile and shake of Rachel's head.

"No. Just..." The woman who made her living with words tried to think of exactly *what* the experience had been. "...just altering." She knew that didn't provide much information, but it was the best she could do.

Will Ash winced as he singed his tongue on his third cup of coffee. "Damn it," he grumbled, setting the mug down on the corner of his desk then walking over to the wet bar. He snatched a paper towel and captured the small amount that dribbled down his chin, glad he'd managed to get to it before it spilled onto his new tie.

Tossing the soiled towel into the trash, Will walked back over to his desk, sighing heavily as he sat in the leather chair, swinging around to face the glassed-in wall of his corner office. It was a beautiful day in Manhattan, not too hot, scattered clouds in the sky. Perhaps he'd take a nice, leisurely walk at lunch.

The Town Car pulled to the curb in front of the skyscraper. With a smile of gratitude for the driver, Dean let himself out of the car and slammed the door behind him. Looking up and down the familiar street, the attorney breathed in the scent of Manhattan in late summer. He couldn't wait to take a walk in Central Park with Will, hand in hand.

Brad Schuester typed the email, fingers flying over the keys at seventy-two words per minute, the light from the reading lamp anchored above his head glinting off the gold ring on his left pinky. He chewed on his bottom lip, wincing as he caught a single hair from his neatly trimmed goatee.

"That should do it," he muttered, tapping the send key and waiting for the sent confirmation. Getting the screen he needed, the assistant twirled his chair around to the filing cabinets behind him, about to tug open the drawer with the files from O to Z; he knew Will would want the Rollings-Homestead file for his meeting at ten that morning.

The door to Will's personal office suite opened, admitting two people, along with a cacophony of shrill protests from the secretary.

"You can't go in there, sir!" Martha Munez objected, running after the man who had sauntered right past her desk and through the door to Will Ash's offices. She managed to get her plump body out from around her desk, short, stubby legs working hard to catch up to him.

Brad sucked in a breath, heart stilling in his chest.

"Brad! This man—"

"It's okay, Martha," he breathed.

Will smoothed down his tie, readjusting the gold clip as he switched on the light over his drafting table and spread out the plans he'd been working on over the weekend. He walked back over to his desk, grabbed a pencil from the cup, and returned to the table. Hearing a shrill voice in the outer office, his attention was drawn toward the door.

The devastatingly handsome man — hair long and shaggy, skin deeply tanned — grinned at Brad. "Dean?" Brad whispered, a manicured hand reaching up to remove the gold rimmed computer glasses from his nose. Brad found himself in a deep fog. His movements were slow, as though he were moving through water. Unsure of what to say or how to react, he threw himself at Dean and was enveloped in a strong embrace.

"Is he here?" Dean asked into the man's ear. At Brad's nod, Dean pulled away and moved toward the door with the polished brass plate that said WILL ASH.

After the shrillness, there was total silence. A niggling feeling tickled at the back of Will's neck, and he tossed his pencil onto the drafting table and hurried toward his office door to make sure everything was all right. Reaching out for the doorknob, he took a startled step backwards as the door swung open, barely missing him. In walked a man dressed in Army green cargo shorts and a gray polo shirt. Will's eyes trailed up tanned arms, noting dark, shaggy hair and dark, twinkling eyes.

The impact hit Will squarely between the eyes, knocking him to his knees. He couldn't breathe, couldn't think, could only stare. He watched as the apparition sank to his knees in front of him, warm, trembling hands capturing Will's cold, clammy ones.

"Hey, baby," Dean whispered, dispelling the cold shock in Will's wide eyes. "It's me. I made it." Hot tears streaked down Dean's cheeks, like those that had begun in Will's eyes.

"I knew you couldn't be dead," Will breathed, finally feeling his heart begin to beat again. "Oh God, Dean!"

Dean was knocked back against the door by a fierce hug. He banged his head, but didn't care. All that mattered was that the man he loved was in his arms again, their tears mingling as Will peppered kisses all over Dean's face, pulling back to look at him, to make sure that he was real.

"I love you," Dean cried, squeezing Will to him, almost painfully.

"I looked so hard," Will sobbed, finally knocking Dean to his back, half lying on top of him. Brushing long strands of hair out of Dean's eyes, he looked at the lean, tanned face, guilt beginning to pool in his stomach. "I don't understand how this happened," he whispered, touching Dean's face, running a thumb over his brow and down his cheek, caressing the skin of his jaw. "We..." Will swallowed hard, his eyes dropping. "We stopped the search."

Dean's heart broke as Will shattered before him. Pushing himself up to a sitting position, he pulled Will against him. "Shh, it's okay," he whispered, rocking the sobbing man. "Keller and Garrison made one last go at it, and they found us, Will. They did it for you."

Will clung to Dean, burying his face against a warm neck. "Oh my Dean."

Rachel leaned against the headboard, Reenie's laptop balanced on her thighs, an empty Word document waiting to be filled. The cursor had been blinking at her for ten minutes, the screen finally going black before it changed to Reenie's screensaver of dancing penguins. Green eyes didn't notice.

It amazed Rachel how she could be in a place that was a second home to her, filled with familiar sights and smells, and filled with the love of her best friend, and yet she felt alone.

The tapping on the closed bedroom door drew Rachel out of her desolate thoughts. "Yes?" Shaking her head, she looked down at the screen as though seeing it for the first time. She ran a finger over the touchpad to make the screensaver disappear.

"Hey. Here." Reenie stepped into the room, a steaming mug in each hand. "Mint fudge hot chocolate."

"Ohh," Rachel purred, setting the laptop aside as she took the proffered mug.

Reenie slid onto the bed beside her friend. "You've been in here for two hours and haven't written a thing?" She met sheepish green eyes. "Honey, that's not like you." Reenie reached up, brushing a long, golden strand out of Rachel's face. "Are you okay?"

Rachel sighed, resting her head against the sympathetic shoulder. "I was fine, Reenie. I was totally focused on my career; my writing was steady and my head clear." Her voice was soft, almost a whisper. She blew on the hot cocoa and then took a sip and swallowed slowly. "My life was fine."

Reenie listened, bringing up a hand to run through the long strands. It was strange for her, expecting to see Rachel's beautiful, short golden hair. The longer style just didn't suit her, somehow. Bringing her focus back to Rachel's words, she cleared her throat.

"What happened, Rachel?" The blonde set her mug on the side table then turned back to her friend, curling up to her side. A comforting arm snaked around her shoulders. "Talk to me."

After a deep sigh, Rachel began, "I met the most amazing soul on that island, Reenie. My eyes and heart have been opened in a way that I just don't know what to do with here, back home. There," she snorted ruefully, "she was just part of my every day." Rachel felt the sting of tears behind her eyes. "I feel so lost," she whispered.

Reenie was stunned. She rested her cheek against the top of Rachel's head and continued to run her fingers through her hair.

"It's not only her. I feel like my entire world, the world I knew, doesn't exist anymore. I'm not sure where to begin to try and find it again."

"I'm so sorry, sweetie." Reenie kissed the golden head. "I can't imagine what you're feeling right now."

"I'm numb. Completely and utterly numb."

"You've been given a second chance, Rach. That has to be for a reason. You're not alone; I'll be here for you every step of the way. You've got to know that."

After a moment, Rachel nodded. "I do." She hesitated. "I'm going to ask Matt for a divorce. I need to set him free."

"I can't believe that son of a bitch cheated on you."

Rachel shook her head. "None of that matters anymore, Reen. I'm over it, and ultimately, I can't say I blame him." She felt Reenie grow stiff as her anger grew. Rachel pushed slightly away, just enough to look at her friend's face. She placed a calming hand on the woman's shoulder. "It doesn't matter. Truly. That's all over with now."

Reenie decided to let it go. "So, tell me about this woman."

Rachel's smile was instant though her heart began to ache. "She's wonderful," the blonde whispered, staring off into a distant place. "She's the most beautiful woman, Reenie. Her heart, it just, it just...glows."

"Rachel?"

"Hmm?"

"Have you ever been attracted to a woman before?" Reenie sipped from her own cooling mug of mint chocolate.

"No. In truth, I've never been really attracted to anyone before. No, not even Matt," Rachel said, forestalling the question. "I feel like I've been reborn."

"Where is she now?"

"I don't know. On her way back to her partner in Buffalo, I imagine."

Silence filled the small room as Reenie lost herself in her thoughts. She was trying to get her mind to accept what she had just been told without reacting. She could feel Rachel's pain, the slight body shaking with the intensity of her emotion.

"It's going to be okay, sweetie," she whispered, placing another kiss on Rachel's head. "It's going to be okay."

Tiffany chewed on the oversized sleeve of her sweatshirt, her body curled up against the arm of the couch. She watched the images on the screen, now just about the only news on TV. She tried not to listen to Hannah's pleading voice on the phone.

"There has got to be *some* way for you to get me through," Hannah demanded of the woman on the other line. Her forehead wrinkled in consternation. "I don't give a shit what the station manager said! One of the survivors that was brought in, and *your* cameras filmed, is my goddamn partner!"

Tiffany was startled by the loud expletive then the sound of the phone slamming into its cradle. "No luck?"

"No." Hannah ran her hands through her hair. She pushed up off the couch, almost tossing Tiffany off with the force of her rising. Walking to the front window of the small house, she blew out another breath, her mind filled with a tempest of thoughts and feelings. She was standing in her girlfriend's house, where they'd spent the past thirty-three hours sharing their bodies and, she believed, Tiffany's heart. So many thoughts and feelings were bombarding her, Hannah wasn't sure which one to latch onto. Deeply entrenched in her thoughts, she cried out in surprise when her cell phone chirped to life in the other room. Hannah hurdled the coffee table in her haste to get to her phone.

"Hello?"

"Hey, baby. It's me."

Hannah blew out a breath, falling to sit on the edge of the bed, eyes squeezed shut. "Oh God, Denny. Oh God. I saw you on the news. I've been trying to get hold of you..."

"I'm here, Hannah. I'm coming home today. I'll be in later tonight."

Hannah sobbed as she heard Denny's voice on the other end of the line.

"Please don't cry," Denny whispered. "I can't stand it when you cry."

Hannah gathered her thoughts and swallowed hard trying to gain her ability to speak.

"God, Denny, I've missed you so much!" Hannah gushed.

"I've missed you too, baby." There was a silence on the other end of the line. Hannah first thought Denny's connection was lost for a second, until she heard Denny's breath as she got ready to speak again. "I can't wait to get home, to you, get my life back."

It had all happened so quickly, like a whirlwind. One minute they'd been lying on the carpet of Will's office, the next they were settled into Will's Lexus, driving home. Dean wasn't able to take his gaze off Will the entire ride, drinking him in like water in the desert. As soon as the car was parked, the two men hurried inside the building. With Will pushed against the elevator wall as the door whooshed shut, Dean couldn't keep his hands and mouth off of him. The year's worth of abstinence catching them up in one fell swoop.

Chapter 23

Peaking with one last gasp, Dean found himself enveloped in a desperate, full-body hug. He tried to get his breath back as he clung to Will, who had begun to string baby kisses along his neck and jaw.

Dean gently pushed at Will's shoulders. "I need a breather, baby," he panted, wrapping his arms around Will's neck and pulling him close. Dark eyes closed as Dean inhaled his partner's scent.

"Mmmm, I missed you," Will whispered, rolling to his back and pulling Dean with him. Dean snuggled in, luxuriating in the feel of skin, the hardness of Will's body, and softness of the bed beneath them. "We're going to have a huge party, invite all our friends, reintroduce you to the world."

Dean sighed, content and sated. "I want to just lie here with you forever, Will."

"We can do that, too."

Dean raised himself on one arm so that his cheek rested in his palm. He studied the handsome face of the man he'd spent all afternoon making love to. At the moment lying in their bed, almost forgotten in Dean's album of memories, nothing else mattered — not the luxury cars, the amazing loft in downtown Manhattan, not even the dozens of pairs of finely polished Gucci loafers lined up in the closet. Gazing into Will's face, brushing sand-colored hair back from his brow, Dean realized his world was complete.

"I love you so much," he said, leaning down to place a soft kiss on Will's lips.

Will smiled. He had always known Dean loved him, but he couldn't remember the last time he'd heard his partner say it, even before he boarded that plane for Milan. "I love you too, Dean. Always."

"And forever."

"Take care of yourself, Mikey." Denny smiled up at the wrinkle that formed between the big man's eyes at the endearment. She leaned up, placing a kiss on his weathered cheek. "Tell those kids of yours hello for me, okay?"

Michael nodded, looking down into moist blue eyes. "Good luck, Denny. I'm gonna miss you, darlin'." He crushed her in a massive hug, squeezing the breath from her lungs. "Be good to yourself."

"You too, big guy." One last painful squeeze and Denny was released. She surreptitiously took a deep breath, watching as the Texan walked over to Pam, clasping her in a similarly tight hug.

Pam reached up and cupped Michael's freshly shaven face. She smiled; he was such a handsome man. "Take care, Michael," she said, placing a soft kiss on his lips.

"You, too. Go make nice with your daughter, Pam. She's all ya got."

Pam nodded, trying to hold back her tears. Her family was slowly slipping away, the last vestiges boarding planes all of them headed to different destinations. She and Denny watched as Michael stepped into the helicopter, one of Duke's staff at the helm. One last wave and the door was pulled closed, and the giant whirlybird lifted gracefully into the air.

The higher Michael soared, the lower Denny felt her heart fall. The world she'd known was dissolving, the people she'd come to know, love, and trust were all gone, scattered to the four winds. She'd been pleased to find the note Mia had left for her at Duke's house, her gratitude written underneath her phone number and address, along with a reminder about that promised mocha breve. She felt a warm hand take her own.

"Your turn, kiddo."

Denny relished Pam's warm hug, tears glazing her cheeks, not for the first time in the past hour. "I'm going to miss you, Pam."

"I'll miss you, too, sweetie. I'm so happy for you and Hannah. I'm sure she's beside herself." Pam felt Denny's pain, could see it in her eyes, and knew it had nothing to do with her partner. She also knew Denny was far too honorable a woman to not do whatever she thought was right.

"Good luck with Tracy, Pam. You two can make it work, okay?"

Pam nodded. She had been shocked to find out from Colleen that Tracy and Luke had moved to Montana. Right then and there, Pam had made the decision to follow them. New York meant nothing to her without her daughter and grandson, a realization that Pam hated herself for not having come to before.

Denny released Pam and walked over to Garrison, who waited beside her partner and the Cessna that would be taking Denny home.

"Garrison, we all owe so much to you and Keller. You are truly phenomenal human beings to keep searching when everyone else had given up hope."

Garrison's face flushed as her gaze dropped. It almost felt like the day after Christmas, a letdown to the long build up as the last of those the media had dubbed The Island Six went home. She accepted a hug, rubbing Denny's back. "Good luck, Denny." She turned to Keller. "Ready?"

"Anytime you are."

Denny gave the two pilots some privacy to say their own goodbyes, ducking as she climbed into the Cessna, taking a deep breath as she buckled herself in. She wasn't keen on another bout of flying, but it was a necessary evil. She took the headset offered by Keller, who settled in beside her.

"This flight will be way more cool." Keller grinned, settling her own headset into place. "The world looks different from the cockpit."

"Okay," Denny said, slightly shaky.

"Let's rock and roll! Get you home!"

Denny managed to get some sleep after a while, overtaken by the exhaustion of a busy, crazy day. They'd been taken to Duke's house, where a nice, hot shower awaited them, with as much soap and shampoo as their bodies could take. And the shower! Denny's lips curved into a small smile as she remembered the sensation of the hot water running down her body, feeling totally clean for the first time in far too long. And the sensation of grainy toothpaste, sadly painful. Her gums were tender, teeth in bad shape. They'd done what they could on the island, chewing on fragrant plants and picking their teeth with the tiny bones of the fish they ate. She knew she would have a smattering of cavities, which pissed her off. She'd always taken pride in her teeth, pleased with their bright white perfection. A dentist was a must, and soon.

Images of Hannah swept through her mind, along with those of their house and neighborhood in Allentown. A nice place, three bedroom house, small but well-kept. She thought about the day they'd bought the house, their excitement at finally having a place of their own. They'd gone out to a home improvement store and picked out wacky paint colors, finally settling on more traditional hues. The fun of painting, splashing each other, eventually making love on the plastic spread out to protect the carpet.

Denny smiled at the memory, wondering whether the house would look the same or if Hannah had made any changes. Was Denny's old Volkswagen bus still working, or had it been parked at the side of the house and left to rust?

"So, are you excited to get home?" Keller's tinny voice asked in the brunette's ear.

Denny thought about the question for a moment, then nodded.

Tracy Sloan looked around the ranch house, making sure it looked perfect. Her heart was pounding and she was filled with a patchwork quilt of emotions, many of which she couldn't put a name to. Colleen had called her the night before, the TTY machine attached to Tracy's phone displaying in green electric letters what Colleen was saying. She had stared at the small screen, falling onto the chair at the desk. Unable to believe what she was reading, deft fingers raced across the small keyboard, asking for clarification. Colleen confirmed that she had Pam on her cell phone, she was alive, had miraculously survived the crash, and was coming home. Apparently Pam had been frantic when Tracy's old number had been disconnected, and she had eventually called Colleen. She was due in Billings in less than six hours; Duke would be flying her in, since he had a cargo drop in Canada, just north of Montana.

After the call, Tracy had cried, head buried in her hands, tears leaking through her fingers. Luke had hurried over to his mommy, hands flying as he asked what was wrong. Tracy had answered with a few simple graceful gestures: Grandma's alive.

Luke wasn't sure what to think. He hadn't seen much of his grandma in the first years of his life, and now, after more than a year without her in his life at all, the eight year-old didn't much care either way. He knew his grandma often made his mom cry, so because of that, he was fiercely protective, being the man of the house and all.

Maybe this time his grandma would be nicer.

Meredith Adams' heart was pounding so loudly, she could barely hear. She hadn't believed it for one minute when the call had come in earlier that morning. It was a lie, a hoax, something. Michael could not be alive, not after all this time. Then, for a split second, her heart had sped up: if Michael was still alive, maybe there was a chance for her daughter. Her heart broke all over again when she got his answer, hope replaced by profound disappointment.

Michael had said he only had a minute, no time to speak to anyone else, just to let them know he'd be in Beaumont within the hour.

Meredith placed her hand over her heart, taking several deep breaths. She had to tell the children. And Walter.

Jennifer had taken Conrad to buy them both some clothes and supplies for school, which would be starting in less than a month. Meredith had to stay home and keep an eye on her cooker, Ball jars all spread out on the countertop, freshly steamed and ready to be filled with the canned tomatoes, peaches, and green beans.

Shaking herself into action, Meredith snatched up the phone and dialed Jennifer's cell phone. It rang three times and Meredith about to give up when Jennifer's breathless voice answered.

"Hello?"

"Jennifer?"

"Grandma? Sorry, I was trying on a pair of jeans. What's up?"

"Honey, I need you to get Conrad and come home pronto."

"What's the matter? Are you okay, Grams? You sound like you've been crying. Is Grandpa okay?"

"We're fine, honey. Just come home. Now."

"Uh, okay. We'll be home in fifteen minutes."

Jennifer Dupree flipped her phone shut. She hoped everything was okay. She hurried into her shorts, tugged her shoes on without tying them then went in search of her little brother, who she found in the mall's arcade. "Con, come on, we have to go."

"No. I'm in the middle of a game," he muttered, never taking his eyes off the screen as he continued to slay the bad guys.

"Now, Conrad. Grandma wants us home right now. Come on."

"Just let me finish—"

"Conrad Michael Dupree, let's go!" She grabbed the stubborn teen by the back of his shirt and dragged him away from the game.

Alan Dupree sighed heavily into the phone. "Grandma, I have work to do. I can't just leave for some family meeting."

"Alan, I really need you to come. I'll talk to your boss if you need me to."

The young man grinned. "Grandma, it's not like school where a note from my mother will do it. I can't just walk out on this job. I shouldn't even be on the phone—"

"Your father's alive."

Alan felt his body stiffen, words of protest stuck in his throat. "What?"

"They've found him. I didn't want to tell you until all three of you were together. You need to come home, Alan."

"Give me ten minutes."

"Conrad! You heathen!" Jennifer yelled, dropping to her haunches to pick up the contents of the shopping bag. Her little demon brother had run by her so fast, he'd knocked the package right out of her hand. Gathering everything up, Jennifer couldn't help but be a little bit nervous. Had one of them done something wrong? Was everything truly okay, or had her grandmother just said that so as not to worry her before she got them safely home? Millions of possibilities raced through her mind as she hurried into the house.

"Grandma?" she called out, heading toward the stairs. She stopped cold when she saw Alan standing in the doorway to the kitchen. They rarely saw their older brother now; he was out on his own, with his own life. His presence was worrisome. His eyes were red-rimmed, yet he was smiling. "Hey," she said, voice uncertain.

"Hey, sis." He walked over to her and took her shopping bags from her hands. "Wouldn't want you to drop these."

"Hello, my little angel."

Jennifer's head snapped up at the deep voice, and the endearment she'd heard her whole life, up until one year, two months and a day ago. Her breath caught as she saw who stood in the kitchen doorway, hair long and shaggy, a neatly trimmed beard covering his handsome face making him look even more rugged than usual.

"Daddy," she breathed, her confusion replaced by relief and happiness. His arms opened and she ran toward him, stopping a foot away to look him over. He sounded like her father, looked like her father, yet there was no way it could *be* her father. "I don't understand," she whispered.

"We were found," Michael said, looking into her eyes, raising a hand to gently brush her hair from her eyes.

With a loud sob, she threw herself at her father, squeezing her eyes tightly shut as she felt him wrap her slight body with his much larger one.

"My little angel," he cooed, cupping her head against his chest. "I missed you so much."

Jennifer couldn't speak, couldn't think, could only feel. She felt like a life that had become dark the day her parents died, had suddenly grown bright, the sun burning away all the inky blackness from her heart. Finally able to breathe again, she pulled away, looking up into his gentle face. "How did this happen? Where's Mom?"

Michael felt his heart crumble, but knew he had to stay strong. For them. "I escaped the wreckage, honey, managed to get to an island. Your mamma..." His voice broke, his emotions precariously balanced. He swallowed. "She didn't make it. I tried."

Jennifer's eyes filled again as her daddy held her close.

It had been something, watching his oldest, Alan, fall apart at the sight of him, but Jennifer, his Jenny Angel, who looked so much like her mother, nearly made him lose it. The big man opened his eyes and saw his third child standing at the foot of the stairs, looking at him in disbelief, his face pale, mouth hanging open.

"Hello, son," Michael said softly, holding out an arm to the boy. He watched in horror as Conrad shook his head slowly then ran out the door.

Hannah had been overcome with a sense of relief when Tiffany called to her after she'd hung up with Denny. Walking into the living room, Hannah had found the few things she had at the redhead's house stacked neatly on the end table by the door.

Tiffany had accepted the possibility Hannah could never truly give her heart, and now with Denny's return, that fact was indisputable. She was letting Hannah go, and asking for the same courtesy in return. It had been a sad parting, but one for which Hannah was grateful. She had a lot to think about and even more to deal with once her partner returned to her.

Now she was walking through the airport on her way to the gate for private planes. Palms sweating, heart pounding, and ears burning,

Hannah hurried past a small gathering of security guards. She read the overhead sign, found her terminal, and rushed to the door.

Denny took a deep breath, running a hand through her hair. She was glad that the plane was on solid ground again. She hated flying now, plus, she just wanted to get settled somewhere. It felt strange glancing over at the airport, thinking back to her life the last time she'd seen Buffalo International Airport, when she caught her flight over to JFK. So much had changed. She had changed.

Unbuckling herself, she noted Keller's wide smile. Denny tried to return it, but nerves and uncertainty made her attempt a weak imitation.

"Everything will be okay," Keller said, as though reading her thoughts. She leaned over and gave her passenger a tight hug. "I wish you the best of luck, Denny. If you need anything, anything at all, you give us a call, okay?"

Denny nodded, pulling away. "Have a safe flight back." Keller nodded as Denny stepped out of the Cessna, one of the tarmac workers holding up his hand to assist her. She smiled her gratitude then took in a lungful of air, filling her chest with the smells of home.

Hannah paced, wringing her hands and then wiping them on the sides of her jeans. She froze when she saw the small white and blue plane taxi in. "Here we go."

Denny climbed the steps, hand running along the smooth, cool metal of the railing, then pulled open the door. The sterile, manufactured air of the airport terminal assailed her nose as her eyes searched. They froze on their target.

Hannah felt her breath catch, melting all over again in the blue of Denny's eyes. Those gorgeous eyes had been the first thing she'd noticed about Denny almost ten years ago, fixing that damn machine, which never seemed to work right.

Denny's eyes closed as she wrapped her arms around Hannah. Nothing was said, no tears, just a seemingly endless embrace of relief and reconnection. Nearly ten minutes later, Denny pulled back, raising a hand to rest on the side of Hannah's head. "You cut your hair," she commented, her voice soft.

Hannah nodded, running a nervous hand through the pixie cut. "It was time."

"It's cute."

"You're so thin, Denny," Hannah whispered, taking a step back to take in all of her partner, dressed in a pair of jeans, which were sagging off her hips, and a plain white t-shirt.

"Borrowed." Denny tugged at the hem.

"Let's go home." Hannah leaned forward, cupping Denny's face and placing a gentle kiss on her chapped lips. "Here," she said against them, holding up a yellow tube of Burt's Bees lip balm.

Denny chuckled, taking it and applying it as they walked back through the airport. Denny glanced over and met Hannah's probing gaze. "What?"

"Nothing." Hannah shook her head, a soft smile on her lips. "I just can't believe you're here." She put a hand on Denny's arm and moved them out of the way of rushing travelers. Pulling Denny into a hug, she buried her face in the long hair. Her mind raced as she considered how to tell Denny about the sale of DeRisio's. Though she knew she had not intentionally done anything wrong, guilt was beginning to gnaw at her and she was nauseous. DeRisio's had been Denny's dream. Hannah had thought it as dead as its owner. The last day the coffee shop was open for business, Denny's old boss and mentor, Joni Sanchez, had come in, calling Hannah just about every name under the sun but murderer for killing Denny's dream.

"I need to talk to you about something," she said into Denny's ear, the breath of warm air making Denny shiver.

"What?" Denny tried to pull away, but was held fast.

"Not here. Later."

Denny nodded, her eyes closing as she tried to concentrate on being happy that she was home. She felt nervous, as though she was entering a new world, unfamiliar and strange. Finally Hannah pulled away and took her by the hand, moving them toward the parking garage.

Chapter 24

Pam had never felt so out of place. Born and raised in New York, spending much of her life in Queens and the Bronx, Montana couldn't have been any more alien to her than if Duke had flown her to the moon. The wide open spaces, endless wilderness, and clear, blue skies were breathtaking, but intimidating.

It was an understatement for Pam to say she had been stunned to find out where Tracy had started a new life for her and Luke. She had no idea what possessed her daughter to move so far west. Regardless, she had, and Pam was going to do her level best to make a relationship work with her daughter and grandson. She'd promised her island family, and herself, that she would.

A woman at the tiny airport, a friend of Duke's, had offered to drive Pam to her daughter's home, as Tracy had to look after Luke.

The small ranch house squatted just ahead, a narrow two-story painted white with dark blue trim. Pam had to admit it was charming. She could feel the nervousness building in her stomach; her parting from her daughter so long ago had not been on good terms. It seemed as if mother and daughter couldn't manage to get on the same page, no matter how hard they tried. That saddened Pam. When Tracy's father, Pam's first husband, had found out they were having a child, they had been thrilled. Theirs had been a marriage of seven barren years, each blaming the other for their inability to conceive. Then like magic, one morning Pam had gotten sick, running from the bed, nearly trampling their Pug, Ralphie, in her efforts to get to the toilet before she vomited. The pregnancy test had been positive, and plans for a new life had begun.

It was pretty quickly evident that Tracy was a miracle baby; Pam would not be having any more. She'd been so excited when the doctor told her she had a girl, the baby's cries filling the delivery room and her mother's heart. By the time Tracy had turned three, they began to realize something was wrong. The toddler was losing her hearing until by age four, it was totally gone. It had been a devastating blow, but one they'd dealt with as best they could, even as Pam and Jack's marriage fell apart. The young mother and the daughter who lived in a world of silence never saw eye to eye. Tracy would move in with her father every couple years or so, until she realized she hated his newest flavor of the month, then she would move back in with her mother, only to dislike her newest stepfather. All part of being a restless teen, who never truly felt understood or accepted by either parent. When Tracy had gone away to college after high school graduation, it had seemed to be the best thing for all involved. Then Luke came.

Pam stared out the window of the bucket of bolts with Ford stamped on the grill. The truck pulled to a stop in front of the house, the front door opened, and curious eyes peered out. Pam was amazed to see how big Luke had grown. His mother stepped up behind him, her hands resting on his narrow shoulders. The boy leaned back into Tracy's body.

Tracy squeezed one shoulder then stepped out from behind Luke, trying to decide which emotion to settle on first. At seeing her mother, she felt a flood of relief, but at the same time, a sense of foreboding washed over her. What would this mean to her and Luke's new life?

Pam quietly thanked Amanda Brody for the ride then climbed down from the large truck, her eyes locked on her daughter as Tracy carefully made her way down the few steps that led up to the porch. Tracy stopped mid-step, then a keening sound rose from her throat and she raced the rest of the way, the little girl inside her winning out over the bitter adult, allowing herself to take comfort in her mother's arms and safe return.

Knowing Tracy could not hear her, still Pam whispered her daughter's name against soft chestnut hair, inhaling the fragrance and essence of her little girl. When she looked down, her grandson was standing next to them, his big, watchful eyes on mother and grandmother.

Sniffling back her relief, Pam swiped a hand across her face then knelt down to look into Luke's face. "Hello, Luke," she said, her voice gentle. "I've missed you, sweetheart." She took the boy's stiff body in her arms, a pang of hurt and regret shooting through her heart. She had a lot to make up for.

"I don't understand," Michael whispered, so as not to wake up Jennifer, who was curled up in his lap. He brushed his fingers through her hair while sipping from a cold can of Miller Walter had brought to him. Now his father-in-law sat across from him on the loveseat, listening to the sounds of a Texas night.

"Don't know. The boy is just filled with so much anger, I don't think he knows what to do with himself no more. Meredith and I have tried everything, counselin', all of it. Nothing is helping."

Michael sighed, staring out into the blackness beyond the living room windows. His heart ached. Conrad had run from the house and had not yet been found. Alan was out looking for him, hoping to knock some sense into the stubborn boy.

"It's been a hard time, Mike. Don't let nobody tell you different. These kids have suffered heaps."

"I know." Michael leaned down and kissed the top of his daughter's head. He couldn't remember the last time he'd done that. "I can't thank y'all enough for what you've done, Walter. These kids needed you and y'all were here for them. Thank you."

Walter nodded, sipping from his own beer. He wasn't comfortable with all the emotional mumbo jumbo. He listened to the sounds of his wife cleaning up the dinner dishes. Normally Jennifer would be helping out, but tonight she wasn't letting her daddy out of her sight so Meredith left her to it.

"Did she suffer?" Walter finally asked, clearing his throat to cover the hitch in his voice.

Michael studied the older, hardened man for a moment then sighed. "No. She went in her sleep. Lost too much blood." Michael could feel his throat constricting. He had put thoughts of Melissa out of his mind for over a year, and talking about her was like losing her all over again.

"Good."

"Look, Walter, Mel—"

"No." The older man stood, waving off Michael's words. "It's late. Gotta get me some sleep." He hurried from the room, the sound of his heavy boots thudding against the wood of the stairs followed by a distant slam of a door.

"Everything okay?" Meredith asked, drying her hands on a dishtowel.

Michael nodded, resting his cheek against Jennifer's head. "Yeah. It's late. I'm gonna get this one to bed." Michael looked down at his daughter's face; she was still deep asleep. Gathering her to his chest, he rose to his feet, holding her safe, and making his way up the stairs in the wake of his father-in-law.

"Daddy?" the teenager mumbled in her sleep, her voice thick.

"I'm here, darlin'. Sleep, Angel." He gently laid her on the bed, pulling the covers around her then tucking her in. With a small kiss on her forehead, Michael turned out the bedside lamp but couldn't leave. He stood next to her bed, staring down into the face of a woman, remembering the little girl he'd left behind. Never in his life had he felt so infused with love and a need to protect another human being. This little girl was the product of his Melissa, all he had left of her.

Reaching out, he brushed a few strands of hair out of her sleeping face, readily seeing Mel, who had been just a bit older than Jenny when he'd first seen her. Jennifer would be a spitting image of her mother, just as beautiful and filled with just as much fire. He smiled at that thought, sending out a silent word of warning to all those boys who would think they could tame her. She'd slowly and quietly tame them, just like her mamma.

Meredith was picking up the beer cans when she heard Michael enter the room. "Out cold," he said, voice hushed. "Let me help you." He took the cans from his mother-in-law, missing the stunned expression on her face as he headed into the kitchen to dump the residual beer into the sink then crushed the cans in his large fist.

"I talked to Leo down at the garage," Meredith said conversationally, wiping down the table again, just to keep busy.

Michael glanced at her over his shoulder. "Yeah?"

"He's real shocked and relieved to hear you're okay. He wants to give you your old job back."

Michael slowly turned to face her. "You're kidding."

"Nope." Meredith smiled; the wrinkles around her eyes had increased ten-fold because of the stresses of the past year. "From all the calls I've had and the gossip going around town since the news broke, you're now our hometown hero, Michael." She walked over to him, placing her hands on his chest, looking up into his eyes. Meredith tried to keep her rising emotions under control, but it was a losing battle. Sobbing quietly, she rested her head against his chest as strong arms enfolded her. "I'm so glad you're alive," she whispered.

"Me too. God, me too."

Matt was tired. It had been a wonderful trip, but exhausting. He and his girlfriend, Jessica, and the guys had been fishing for the past five days, catching just about everything the fish god had to offer, and then some. He set the cooler of iced fish on his counter with a grunt then headed back toward the garage to unload his gear from the back of his SUV. He noticed the number of calls flashing on the answering machine, and wondered who had called him fourteen times.

Dropping his huge duffel bag on the living room carpet, he pushed the play button, jotting down a message from his mother, grinning at the message from Jessica wondering where he was. He had only been forty-five minutes late picking her up, after all. The next message stopped him cold. It was Reenie, and she was almost unintelligible. He hit rewind, listening again, trying to decipher what had the typically calm woman so rattled.

"Matt, oh my God! Where are you? You need to call me right now! Right now, Matt!" BEEP. "Matthew, where are you? It's beyond important. Oh my God, call me!" BEEP.

Matt hit stop on the machine as he picked up the cordless phone, his insides twisting with concern. He waited impatiently for the phone to be picked up, his breath catching when he heard the voice on the other end.

"Hi, Matt. How are you?"

Matt stood silent, rooted to the spot. The voice was familiar. "Rachel?"

"Yes. It's me."

"I don't understand…"

"It's a long story. I'm coming home the day after tomorrow. I'll be flying in with Reenie."

"Okay." Matt ran a hand through his hair, blowing out a breath. He wasn't sure what he was feeling. Was it relief, fear, regret, guilt? Confused as hell? All of the above? One thing he did know — he was in shock.

Denny walked into the house, looking around, curious as to what, if anything, had been changed in her absence. Hannah followed close behind, watching for her reaction and dreading the conversation she knew they had to have. Denny deserved to know the truth right away.

The wall to the right of the stone fireplace was nearly bare. Once it had been covered with pictures of them, trips they'd taken and goofy snapshots taken by friends. The walls had been dark green, the woodwork white. They'd contemplated such a bold color choice for months, Denny finally bringing home cans of paint one Friday night. The rest of the weekend had been spent bickering over which room would get the treatment. Now the walls had been painted off-white.

A couple pieces of the artwork they'd picked out together still accessorized the room, and their small copper Buddha was still sitting on the mantel. The rug under the coffee table was gone, replaced by a large and, Denny thought, mismatched area rug.

The thing Denny noticed above all else was that it was as if any trace of her was gone, leaving only a sterile living space with little warmth or personality.

"It hurt too much to keep some things," Hannah said from behind her, voice tentative. "I had to make a change, Denny. It was the only way to keep my sanity."

Denny nodded. Part of her understood, but the larger part of her was hurt. It was as if she wasn't wanted back, didn't belong there anymore. "I, uh, I'll be right back." Denny hurried from the room, back out the front door and into the cool evening air.

She sat on the stoop, wrapping her arms around her knees, resting her chin on top. Never had she felt so out of place, certainly not in her own home. She felt nervous and unsure, insecurities gripping her in cold fingers of doubt. For a moment she thought about going back inside. She felt bad. She knew Hannah couldn't keep everything as it was, nor would she have expected her to, considering she thought Denny dead. But all the same, she was suddenly overwhelmed — she had returned to her life, but it had obviously changed.

She didn't have time to contemplate that thought. The front screen door squeaked as it was opened, softly banging back into place with a whoosh of air. She glanced over at Hannah, settling next to her on the stoop. "I'm sorry," Denny said, her voice soft. "I guess I just got a little overwhelmed for a moment."

"It's okay. I don't imagine this is easy for you, Denny. I want to try and make this transition as painless as possible for you. What can I do to help? What will make it better?"

"Nothing. I don't know." Denny blew out a breath. "It's all just really surreal. All I could think about was coming home. For the first six months or so, every day I made a mark on a tree, thinking, 'maybe after a few more of these marks, I'll be home'. With you." She looked into concerned brown eyes and shrugged. "As time passed, I stopped marking the tree. I never thought I'd get home anyway, so why keep torturing myself?"

"Oh, Denny." Hannah brushed a long lock of hair out of Denny's eyes. "Was it bad?"

"No." Denny shook her head. "Just different." They were silent for long moments, neither sure what to say as they listened to the summer sounds. Finally Denny took a deep breath. "So, what did you want to talk to me about?"

Panic seized Hannah's heart, her eyes growing wide as she struggled for self-control. Putting a smile on her face and a hand on Denny's arm, she shook her head. "Not now, Denny. Let's get you settled first."

"You sounded pretty serious in the airport." Denny wasn't sure why, but her heart was beating double time. "Just tell me, Hannah. I don't need to be handled with kid gloves. I won't shatter." *I don't think.*

Hannah swallowed. "Okay." She felt the need to explain before she told Denny the plain truth. "When I found out you were dead, it nearly killed me, Denny. I felt like I had lost everything. I was so goddamn angry with your cousins for convincing you to go to Italy." She smiled ruefully. "We argued about you going on that trip alone." Shaking her head, she stared out into the darkening neighborhood. "Anyway, I didn't know what to do with myself, so I kept living, well, existing — going to work, coming home, all to do it again the next day. I was dying inside."

She met steady blue eyes, trying to read what Denny was thinking, but there just didn't seem to be anything there, or it was being well hidden. Hannah had always been able to read her partner like an open book; not this time. "I had to do something, and as the months passed, I realized that being surrounded by you, everything that was you and reminded me of you, was making it worse."

Denny did her best to keep an open mind; she'd want Hannah to do the same for her. She nodded in acknowledgement.

Hannah debated whether or not to tell Denny about Tiffany. Deciding she had enough crushing news to deliver, she left that part out. Maybe she'd tell her later. "One Saturday I decided to take down anything that reminded me of you — pictures, trinkets, whatever. I was amazed to find I had filled six boxes. I guess I hadn't realized just how much our lives were bound together until that moment. No wonder I saw you everywhere." She frowned. "Hell, I even had to take that god-awful troll out of my car. I couldn't help remembering when you had won him for me at the fair.

"Anyway, there was one thing left, one last bit of you that tortured me, that I couldn't just pretend wasn't there. It was the last thing keeping me from moving on with my life." At the look of hurt on Denny's face, Hannah clarified. "I didn't want to forget you, baby; I could never, *ever* forget you. But I had to start a new life, without you in it."

"What was it?" Denny asked, her voice hoarse as fear gripped her.

Hannah took several calming breaths, trying to think of the best way to say it. "Honey, Denny," she took two cool hands in her own, pale in comparison. "I..." Her voice caught and she had to catch her breath. *Forgive me, Denny.* "I sold DeRisio's."

Denny's gut churned. She jumped to her feet, raced back into the house and threw the toilet lid up. Falling to her knees, she grasped the sides of the cool porcelain bowl, waiting for backfire that never came.

"Here." Hannah placed a cool cloth on the back of Denny's neck, gathering the long, thick strands of hair into a rope down her back. "Breathe, baby. Just breathe."

Denny tried to do as instructed, feeling her stomach roil again. Instead of throwing up, she began to sob, the sound echoing in the large bowl. Falling over on her butt, she leaned against the side of the tub, Hannah kneeling in front of her, her own tears washing down her cheeks.

"I'm so sorry, Denny. I didn't know. You know I'd never hurt you on purpose."

Denny heard the words, and somewhere inside even knew they were true, but she couldn't let them penetrate. She buried her face in her hands. Her last vestige of normalcy was gone. Denny's sobs calmed after many minutes, her senses numb, head pounding from the emotional roller coaster that had been her first day back in the civilized world.

"How can I feel so out of place in my own life?" she whispered, not expecting an answer.

"It'll take some time," Hannah responded, reaching out a tentative hand to cup the side of Denny's face. "We've both had a lot of excitement for one day. Why don't we go to bed?"

Denny nodded, not entirely sure what she had just agreed to as she was helped to her feet. She heard more whispered words, Hannah telling her to follow her. Once in the bedroom, Denny's shirt was lifted over her head, her jeans unbuttoned and unzipped, the baggy material sliding down her legs.

"You have a killer tan," Hannah commented, providing a shoulder for Denny to steady herself on as she stepped out of the jeans. "Do these need to be returned?"

"I dunno."

The t-shirt came next, Hannah's gaze roaming across the bared flesh, more toned than she'd ever seen it. She couldn't believe that she could almost count her partner's ribs. Deciding that it wouldn't be a good idea to touch the decidedly skittish Denny, she instead steered Denny to the large four poster bed, their fifth anniversary gift to each other, then undressed herself.

Denny rolled to her side, curling her hands under her chin. She stared into the darkness that was their bedroom as Hannah turned out the light, feeling the mattress shift as her partner climbed on.

Hannah spooned up behind Denny. "Is this okay?" she whispered. In answer, her hand was taken and tucked under Denny's chin.

Michael sighed, flopping to his back again, trying unsuccessfully to get comfortable on the mattress. Sleeping on a bed — once his most anticipated amenity upon returning home — was turning into a huge disappointment. His body wasn't sure what to make of the softness, so long had his bones been adjusted to the hard ground. His mutterings and curses ceased at the soft knock on his bedroom door.

"Daddy?" The door inched open, revealing a dark shadow against a darker night.

"Yeah, Angel?"

"Can I lay down with you?" Jennifer squeezed through the small opening she'd made then softly closed the door behind her. There was rustling as he held up the sheet in invitation. He heard her cross to the bed and felt the mattress dip as she climbed on, immediately snuggling up against her father.

"Can't sleep?" he asked, placing a soft kiss on the crown of her head.

"Not really."

"What's on your mind, Princess? You okay?"

"I'm better than I've been in a while." She smiled into the warm scratchiness of her father's neck. She'd never seen him with facial hair before and wasn't sure she liked it. "I'm so glad you're home. I think I stopped believing in God until today."

Michael chuckled. "Well, don't tell your grandma that. She'd think we hadn't raised a fine, Christian girl."

Jennifer giggled softly. "Who says I am?" She raised her head to meet a hard gaze and giggled again. "I'm teasing." Laying her head down, she sighed in contentment, smelling the laundry detergent used in the shirt her father had borrowed from Alan.

"How is school going?" Michael's brow knit. "What grade are you in?"

"I'm a junior."

Michael's eyes slid shut, his Adam's apple bobbing as he swallowed down his grief at missing an entire year of his daughter's schooling. Jennifer seemed to read his mind. "It's okay, Daddy. It wasn't your fault. I know that; Alan knows that; even Conrad knows that."

"Why is he so angry?"

"I don't know." She shrugged a shoulder. Always a daddy's girl at heart, she reveled in her father's attention. "In some way, I think he feels you abandoned him. It's irrational, but that's how he feels. It's been awful for Grandma and Grandpa. Conrad's in trouble all the time, at school and at home. He's just...mean."

"I'll talk to him tomorrow." He didn't want Jennifer to know just how hurt he was by Conrad's distant behavior. When Alan had marched the fourteen year-old into the house by the collar of his shirt, Conrad wouldn't say anything to his father or pay him any mind.

"Daddy?"

"Yeah, honey?"

"What did Mom die of?"

"Honey, I don't—"

"Please?" Jennifer raised her head again, meeting her father's troubled gaze. "I need to know. I need to know if she was in pain. Did you get to say goodbye?"

Michael studied his daughter's face then a slow smile spread across his lips. He nodded. "Yeah, honey. We got to say goodbye. She..." he cleared his throat, "she died in my arms."

Jennifer laid her head back on his shoulder, feeling better about it, even though tears stung her eyes. She listened to the low rumble of her father's voice as he continued.

"She got a nasty cut on her head. It was just too much for her."

"I wonder if she knows how much she's loved. And missed."

"Oh, she knows, Jenny. She knows."

"Goodnight, Daddy."

"Goodnight, little angel."

Dark eyes blinked open then blinked several more times as the light of day shone in through the large window that led out to the fire escape. Mia turned onto her back, looking around the tiny, cramped room that was her mother's. The bed next to hers was empty, the covers pulled up neatly. Despite the closed bedroom door, she heard humming and could smell the unmistakable scents of Italian sausage frying and coffee brewing. Mia's stomach began to growl.

Gloria flitted from task to task, her chest filled to the breaking point with joy: her little girl was alive! She happily worked over the stove, switching back and forth between preparing the sausage, breakfast potatoes, and Mia's favorite — pancakes.

She had slept beside Mia because she was not about to let her daughter out of her sight. She woke up every two hours or so, making sure Mia was actually there, touching her face and hair, before falling back into the most restful sleep she'd had since the night before the accident. Gloria wasn't sure what to do about sleeping arrangements now that Lizbeth was in Mia's room, but she'd be more than happy to figure it out. Her baby was alive!

"Look at that smile on your face," Lizbeth Vinzetti teased, walking into the tiny kitchen.

Gloria couldn't help beaming at her grandmother with a nod. "I've never felt so happy in all my life, except maybe for the day Mia was born."

"I am glad for you, child." The older woman placed a gentle kiss on Gloria's cheek and patted her arm. She was amazed to see the change in her granddaughter. It looked as though twenty years had melted off of her overnight. Her dark eyes were sparkling and filled with a life that had been missing for far too long. The day Mia had disappeared had been the day that a part of Gloria had died. But with Mia found, Lizbeth no longer feared for her beloved Gloria. "I will move in with your cousin Joseph," she said, uncovering the sausage pan to make sure Gloria wasn't overcooking the patties.

"What?" Gloria blurted in English, shocked. She continued in Italian. "No, Nonna. Why would you do that?"

"Because you and Mia need time to reconnect, Gloria. She has been gone too long."

"Nonna—"

"Besides," Lizbeth placed a dry hand on Gloria's cheek, "there is no room."

"We'll make it work, Nonna. I want you here. I'll worry too much about you if you go back to Milano."

"No, child. You need to focus on Mia now. I am fine."

"Fine with what?" Mia asked, joining them in the kitchen, her stomach announcing her hunger.

Gloria turned at the sound of the girl's voice, the conversation forgotten as she smiled broadly, opening her arms and drawing Mia into them.

"Are you hungry, sweetie?" Gloria asked, face buried in her daughter's hair. She felt Mia nod and slowly pulled away, leaving a soft kiss on Mia's forehead. She began to serve up food as Mia gave her great-grandmother an equally warm hug. "Did you sleep well?" Gloria asked, handing Mia a plate filled with her favorite breakfast foods. Mia's eyes got huge as she went over to the small table tucked into the corner.

"I did, though my body isn't real sure what to think of the change in sleeping accommodations." She grinned. "It's used to the ground and a thin layer of leaves."

Hiding the unexpected pang that went to her heart, Gloria smiled weakly. She sat across from her daughter. "Someday I'd like to know what life on the island was like. Will you tell me?"

Mia nodded enthusiastically. "Definitely." She grew silent and began to eat her breakfast. It surprised her just how lost she felt without her island family, even though her own mother sat quietly talking to her great-grandmother, not three feet away. Mia watched the two women for a moment, unable to keep images of Dean, Denny, Michael, Rachel, and Pam from her mind's eye. She saw the six of them sitting around the morning fire, eating fish or bananas and coconuts, Dean and Michael bickering or Denny and Rachel lost in deep conversation. She had grown to love and respect each of them for their own unique gifts and personalities. It was amazing how much Mia had learned, just how little the pettiness of the world mattered when every day was an adventure in survival.

Mia thought about some of her friends at school and her boyfriend Abe. How simple their problems seemed to her now: pimples, dating, and boys; what one girl was saying about another girl; who was going to make the cheerleading squad that summer. In the larger scheme of things, none of that mattered.

"What are you thinking about over there, looking all serious?" Gloria chewed on a mouthful of pancake as she awaited her daughter's response.

"Oh," Mia shook herself out of her reverie, "nothing important. Just thinking about life, I guess."

Will frowned as he entered the loft. He was nearly run over by Marguerite, the housekeeper, muttering something in her native Cuban as she stormed past. He thought it was something about a crazy white boy. From deeper in the loft came loud tango music, accompanied by Dean's wonderful singing voice in Spanish.

"Dean?" Will called out, setting his briefcase down next to the entry table and shrugging out of his Prada jacket.

"In here, my poco gatito del sexo!"

Will chuckled, though he was leery. Over the week Dean had been home, Will had no idea what to expect each time he walked through the door. Never in all the years they'd been together had his partner been so free with himself, truly living life each moment. It looked like today was to be no exception.

"Honey, why did the doorman look at me like I was nuts, and Marguerite looked like she was being chased by..." Will's words faltered and his eyes opened wide. Dean was bare-chested, a brightly colored sarong tied around his waist and his feet bare, padding around the Mexican tile in the kitchen. "Okay, Dean, why the hell are you wearing a skirt and squashing berries with a dildo?"

"Ah, the misguided," Dean murmured against his partner's lips. "And all these years I thought these things had only one purpose." He held up the purple toy, the tip stained a darker purple from berry juice. Turning back to the counter and the meal he was preparing, he answered, "This is a sarong, my love, and they're amazingly comfortable. You should try one."

"I'll pass," he said into Dean's neck, hugging him from behind. "Mm, you smell good."

"Yeah? Just wait until you smell my berry tart, which will be cooking in five minutes."

"Did Martha Stewart come visit while I was gone?" Will uncapped a bottled water, taking a healthy swig before passing it onto Dean.

"Nope." Dean took a drink of water and passed the bottle back. "I always wanted to try this, so I decided to. Get comfortable, baby, 'cause I've got plans for you later." He grinned saucily over his shoulder, spooning the berry mixture into the dough lining the little tin pans. After another kiss, Will sauntered out of the room to shower and change.

Left alone, Dean returned to his thoughts. Dean's old job at Wheeler & Ferrell was long gone, and he was fine with that. The thought of going back to an office filled with stuffy, pompous assholes, of which he had been at one time, left him cold and feeling empty. Something inside had changed, almost like it had broken, or been repaired. The ostentatious surroundings of his neighborhood made him sad. He wondered if people understood just how useless all the money in the world was if you lost yourself or the meaning of true happiness.

The Island Six. That was a love and a truth that Dean wished for every one of those stuffy bastards who welcomed him back to his face, yet were probably snickering behind his back. He had never realized just how pretentious their world was until he escaped it.

"So, why exactly *are* you using Big Purple to kill the berries?" Will asked, startling Dean out of his thoughts.

"You see the way it bounces?" Dean asked, demonstrating. Will nodded. "It gives just the right amount of bang but bounces before the berries are totally crushed."

"Please tell me you didn't learn *this* on Martha?"

"Nope. You hungry?"

"Famished." Will went into the dining room, puzzled at the seating for eight arrayed on the beautiful polished table.

"Not here," Dean said in his ear from behind. "Follow me."

Though confused, Will followed Dean out the front door and toward the staircase at the back of the hall, which he rarely used. Accepting Dean's extended hand, he allowed himself to be led up the dark staircase until they reached a solid-looking metal door. Dean produced a key, turned it in the lock, and pushed, opening the door with a squeak. The warm, late afternoon air swept over them as they stepped out onto a tar-covered roof, the Manhattan skyline all around them.

"I think you've lost your mind," Will muttered as he was led around a small grove of skylights, then a chimney, and finally to an island paradise ala New York.

"I'm not surprised that Eddie looked at you like you were nuts. Who do you think I put in charge of finding someone to bucket in all this sand?" Dean grinned, reclining back on his hands in the middle of the scene he'd manufactured for their dinner. Thick, soft sand covered ten feet of the roof, a beach umbrella sticking out of it with a folded blanket beneath, ready to be spread out, a single red rose resting atop it. Dean grabbed the flower, placed it between his teeth, and rose to his knees, reaching for Will's hand.

Will chuckled, falling to his knees and accepting the flower, as well as a kiss. "What has gotten into you?"

"Can't a man show the one he loves just how much he loves him?"

"Of course, but, before—"

"Shhhh," Dean whispered, bringing a hand up to silence Will. "Before doesn't matter. That was then, this is now. I've learned a lot over the past months, Will. I never realized what was important, or what was right in front of me. I'll never make that mistake again."

Speechless, Will studied Dean's eyes and then shook his head. "I love you."

"I love you, too. You stay here while I serve dinner." After a quick kiss, Dean was gone, leaving his bewildered partner sitting in the sand.

Will stared up into the sky, a contented smile on his face. His Dean was home. It was still a miracle to him every time he opened his eyes in the morning to see hazel eyes twinkling back at him. For so long Will had cursed the world, and all happiness in it, for taking his life from him. He'd been merely existing over the past year. But now, Dean was back and the world was right again.

Even so, Will could see changes in his partner, things that shocked and sometimes delighted him. Most of all, they baffled him. Things Dean never bothered with before were now interesting and new to him. For instance, they had been in Central Park two days earlier, and Dean had stopped and placed a hand on Will's arm.

"Look at that," Dean breathed, pointing up into the trees.

Will looked, following Dean's finger, but saw nothing out of the ordinary, certainly nothing spectacular enough to stop and take special notice of. "What?"

"Look! The way the sun comes in through the leaves of that tree. Beautiful, isn't it?"

Will shook his head and continued walking.

And this rooftop picnic, homemade food and romance. Another thing Dean had been woefully lacking in their previous years together. Will had long ago accepted Dean the way he was, not expecting or hoping for grand gestures. Now, it seemed Dean couldn't do enough for him, and Will was eating it up.

"What are you thinking about, sweetie?" Dean asked, setting down the basket he'd packed to make carrying their food up to the roof easier.

"Nothing." Will smiled and shook his head. "Absolutely nothing."

Hannah turned over with a soft moan, not ready to face another day, but duty called. Or was that her alarm clock? With a slap of her palm, the annoying beeping was reduced to chirping birds outside the window. Blinking rapidly, Hannah awoke enough to realize that she was alone.

"Denny?" The bedroom was empty, as was the attached bathroom. "Sweetie?" Hannah's feet hit the floor with a thud then she pushed herself from the mattress. "Denny?"

"Yeah?" Denny stepped from around the corner, standing in the doorway to the bedroom.

"Why are you up so early?" Hannah walked over to her partner, taking her in a firm morning hug and placing a soft kiss on her lips. Denny was responsive, kissing her in return, then surprising Hannah by deepening the kiss.

With a happy sigh, Hannah wrapped her arms around Denny's neck, pulling her closer, reveling in her touch. Denny had been somewhat distant in the week since her return. Hannah figured she just needed time to readjust to life. Maybe they had weathered that storm and the physical famine was over.

Denny cupped Hannah's boxer-clad butt, pulling her closer, trying to lose herself in Hannah's familiar taste and feel. As hard as she tried, as much as her body was responding, she couldn't shake one thought from her head: *this is wrong.*

"What's the matter?" Hannah panted as Denny abruptly pulled away.

"Uh, nothing. I'm sorry. Guess I need a little more time." Denny turned away, ashamed and confused. "I've got coffee ready," she spoke over her shoulder as she left the bedroom. Hannah leaned against the wall, chest heaving, body on fire. She tried to shake off the sudden sting of tears behind her eyelids.

Denny closed her eyes as she leaned against the counter. The past week had been a roller coaster, filled with emotions and feelings she didn't know how to deal with. It hurt like hell that her coffee shop was gone. If nothing else, while she tried to deal with her feelings and confusion regarding Hannah, she would've at least been able to lose herself in her business. Hannah had suggested they bring DeRisio's back to life in another building, using the funds from the sale. Denny told her she'd think about it. She wasn't sure of anything anymore.

Two days ago Hannah had showed Denny where all of her belongings were packed into six boxes and stored in the garage. Denny hadn't had the heart to go through them yet, so it had all stayed where it was. Maybe she'd go through it today, once Hannah had gone to work.

Deciding she needed to do something to make up for hurting Hannah just now, as she knew she had, Denny began to make breakfast, trying to hurry and have it done by the time the shower stopped.

"Oh, thank you, baby." Hannah beamed, admiring the bounty that had appeared while she got ready for work.

Denny smiled shyly, putting the finishing touches on the table with folded napkins. "Figured you might want something good to eat to start your day."

Hannah nodded, remembering a time when they had had to choose between eating or making love before work. Denny was typically most amorous in the mornings, so Hannah often stopped at the café down the street from her office for a muffin, nearly running to clock in on time.

"Thanks, baby. That was thoughtful." She smeared a generous spoonful of jelly on her waffle then squirted some Reddi Whip on top, glad Denny remembered how she liked them. "So what are you going to do today?"

Denny shrugged, playing with a sausage link. "I may wander around town for a bit, or maybe do some cleaning."

Hannah's first instinct was to be offended by the cleaning comment, taking it to heart, knowing her cluttered nature was a point of contention between them, but then she remembered cleaning was something Denny enjoyed, and often did, when she had something on her mind. That thought was even more disturbing. For a moment she almost wished the comment *had* been a slight of her housekeeping abilities.

"Sounds good. Al offered to give me a half day off today." She eyed Denny across the table. *Why am I so damn nervous?* "What do you think? Maybe we could do something? Get you caught up on what's been happening in good ol' Buffalo?"

Denny only half heard what Hannah said; her mind was a million miles away. It seemed she couldn't hold a single thought for more than a few moments at a time, and even when something struck her, it was quickly eclipsed by something else. "Oh, uh, yeah. That would be good. Okay."

"Denny?"

"Yeah?"

Hannah didn't know what her question was. Denny's name had just slipped off her tongue. Apparently her mind was more focused than her mouth. "Is—" She stopped herself, sipping from her coffee to decide if she wanted to hear the answer to the question that had finally crystallized.

"What?"

"Well, during the crash, I mean, were you hurt?" *Coward.* Hannah couldn't understand the radical change in Denny's behavior and the thought had occurred on more than one occasion that perhaps Denny had hit her head or suffered some sort of head injury totally throwing her personality out of whack. Or maybe she was just overwhelmed. Either way, Hannah felt ashamed of the thoughts as soon as they had entered her brain. All the same, they plagued her.

"A few scratches. Bruises. Dislocated my shoulder." Denny winced at the memory of Pam setting it for her. It still ached from time to time.

"Ouch."

"Yeah. There was this woman, Pam, she's a veterinarian. She set it for me, and damn." The brunette shook her head at the memory, absently adjusting her shoulder. "Hurt like nothing else."

"I bet. I'm sorry you were hurt, honey."

"Eh." Denny shrugged. "That was nothing compared to what could have happened. All of us were extremely lucky."

"For sure. Did you all get along? Six of you, right?"

"Yes. And, at first, no." She cracked a grin, finally cutting the sausage link into three bite-sized pieces, a comfort washing over her as she settled into thoughts of her island family. "We had our moments of fighting like cats and dogs, a few mismatched personalities. But overall, it wasn't that bad. We formed a family, I guess. It helped us all get through it, I think."

Hannah listened, hanging on every single precious word; she'd heard so few of them over the past days. She rested her chin on her palm as she was regaled by a few choice tales, outright guffawing at the attorney, Dean, and his beloved loafers, worn until the end.

"Oh, but the best part was this dildo we found in a suitcase—"

"Oh, shit!" Hannah shoved back from the table and glanced again at the clock on the wall to confirm the time. "Honey, I'm sorry, but I've got to go. Shit. I'm late." She placed a harried kiss on Denny's lips then gathered her purse and car keys. "We'll talk more when I get home. Okay?"

"Yeah, sure." Denny smiled, but the humor didn't reach her eyes. She watched Hannah rush out the door in a whirlwind of perfume and freshly laundered clothing. Denny marveled at how her sense of smell seemed to have become more acute during her isolation. Certain smells, wonderful smells — perfume, flowers, candles — all delighted her olfactory senses, sending delicious messages to her brain, making her eyes close and a smile spread. She imagined it stemmed from far too many months of the smell of unwashed bodies invading her senses.

Sighing heavily, she began to clean up the breakfast dishes.

Chapter 25

The same trees lined the street; the same houses had the same people living in them. Rachel watched a world pass by that held so much familiarity, yet was an absolute mystery to her now. She no longer understood the importance the world put on the dynamics of a man and wife, and baby makes three. It was a foreign concept; something she no longer cared about.

In the time she'd spent with Reenie in New York, Rachel had kept to herself, trying gamely to refocus her mind and energies into what she knew lay ahead — getting herself reestablished in her life and career. It had been mental gymnastics to keep her thoughts from veering off track, images and memories of Denny never far away.

The meeting with her publisher had gone well, though their every move had been dogged by media, which had nearly turned Reenie into an alcoholic as she drank to settle her nerves. Before the crash, Rachel had a contract for a five book deal, but had only delivered on two. The contract for the other three novels had been voided. When the contract was reinstated, her publisher had been good enough to agree not only to the advance on each novel as designated in the original contract, but also had allotted her an additional small amount. Rachel had been grateful, because she had been shocked to find out she was temporarily virtually penniless. She needed to meet with Matt and her sisters and her attorneys to facilitate recovering her assets, which were ensnarled in a legal quagmire.

Reenie had elaborated about the 1049 Club she and Matt had established, along with the help of many of the family and friends of other victims of the crash, including Dean's partner, Will. She had been awed by her friend's generosity, even if it was with *her* money. It was all material, and when it boiled down to it, it was all earthbound anyway.

"Are you ready to see Matt?" Reenie asked, expertly steering the rental car into the driveway at Rachel's house.

Rachel nodded, taking a deep breath. "As I'll ever be."

"I'm going to drop you off and go on over to the hotel to work on some second edits; that will give you two some time alone. Call when you're ready to be picked up, okay?"

"I will." With a quick hug of gratitude, Rachel climbed out of the car, watching nervously as her husband hurried out onto the porch, then to the driveway, sweeping her up in relieved arms.

Matt had been agonizing over what to do ever since he'd spoken with his wife on the phone two days earlier. He had no idea what the proper etiquette was for a situation like this. Did he break up with his girlfriend and leave the life he'd made for himself, returning to a cold marriage out of duty and honor? Did he tell Rachel he was thrilled she was okay, but their life together had ended the day he thought hers had? With no more insight than he had before hearing Rachel's voice, Matt had decided to just let things happen however they would. He'd see her, which he truly was happy about. He wanted to assure himself she was alive. And she was. Very much alive.

"Wow, what a crazy dream, huh?" he said, pulling away just enough to look into the beautiful green eyes that had captured his attention, after he'd stared at her ass for ten minutes.

"You can say that again." Rachel smiled, her nerves easing at the familiarity of Matt — the same face, same color of hair, though it was shorter and neatly styled. She also noted the clean-shaven face and neatly trimmed sideburns. "You look really good."

"You, too. I can't get over how long your hair is. I've never seen it like that."

"I don't have the heart to cut it," she said. "I kind of like it, and besides, I had to go through the frustration of getting it all one length. I don't want to have to go through that again if I decide to go long."

Matt smiled as he led her inside. "I'm sorry it's messy. I've been working a lot of overtime since coming back from my vacation." Matt grimaced, wanting to take the words back as soon as they were out of his mouth. He didn't want to provoke questions when he didn't have the answers. To his relief, Rachel didn't ask for details.

Rachel looked around the house she had shared with the man standing expectantly next to her. It looked the same, messier, but that was about the only change.

"How are you?" Matt's voice startled her.

She turned, nodding nonchalantly. "Good."

He wasn't buying it. "I mean, how are you *really*?"

Rachel couldn't avoid the direct, detective-interrogating look she was receiving, and chuckled at herself, knowing better than to try. With a sigh, she ran a hand down the length of her ponytail. "I'm coping. That's about the best I can say right now."

Matt understood. Based on his experience from all the disastrous situations he'd seen over the years, he wouldn't be one bit surprised if post-traumatic stress syndrome followed at some point. "Let's sit down."

"All right." Rachel sat and Matt sat next to her. "Listen, Matt, um..." She looked down at her hands fumbling in her lap; her left hand was decidedly bare. The ring hadn't survived the crash. Matt's gaze was drawn to the movement and he noted the missing jewelry. "I think we need to talk. About us." Finally gathering the courage to meet his gaze, Rachel was surprised to see relief there.

"I agree. But can I please say something?"

"Sure."

Matt rubbed his sweating palms over his thighs, swallowing hard, not wanting to bring up such a painful day. "About what happened, before you left... I'm so sorry, Rachel. I don't know what I was thinking. I never meant to hurt—"

"Yes, you did." She held up a hand to forestall an argument. "It's okay, Matt. We were pretty miserable, and I've had a lot of time to think about my part in that. What you did was wrong, no question, but it's forgiven. You did me a favor, really."

"A favor?" His relief was momentarily washed away by the sting to his pride at what he sensed was coming.

"Yes, a favor. Look at you." She placed a hand on the side of his face, smelling the cologne on his skin. "You look so good, better than I've seen you look in years. You're obviously happy, have made a life for yourself — without me." Matt's mouth opened to protest. This time Rachel placed two fingers over his lips. "It's okay," she said softly. "On that island, I came to realize that it wasn't working, and it was time to move on, for both of us. I think you've done that."

His fingers playing with the silver band of his wristwatch, Matt nodded. "Yeah. I have. But I want you to know, thinking you were dead, it hurt like hell, Rachel, especially knowing that you were on that flight because of my stupidity."

Rachel couldn't argue with that, so she didn't try. "I still care about you, Matt, very much. I want you to be happy, and the best way I know for that to happen is by giving you your complete freedom — no guilt, no worries, no hurt feelings."

"You're saying that we should get a divorce?" His voice was thick as his throat constricted. Matt was surprised by his reaction to hearing the solution out loud, though he knew it was the only answer. He was in awe of Rachel's strength and grace in acknowledging they were not good together. Still, he loved her, had once had so many hopes for them.

"Under the circumstances, I think it's the only way. That is, if the state still even sees us as married. I'm not sure how that works, considering they think you're a widower."

Matt weakly returned the small smile. "You're sure about this?"

Rachel was surprised at the pain in his eyes. Taking his hand, she held it between both of hers. "Aren't you, Matt?"

He couldn't remember the last time his wife had initiated any sort of physical contact with him, even in the most innocent of contexts. Caught unawares, he sighed then slowly nodded. "To be honest, it's been on my mind since I found out you were alive. I guess thinking about it and talking about it are two very different things."

"They are," Rachel agreed. Her thumb caressed the back of his hand. "I think it's for the best."

"Is this—" He cleared his throat and tried again. "Is this because of..."

"No." Rachel shook her head. "It certainly wasn't pleasant, what happened with that woman, but no. It might have taken longer for us to get to this awareness, but divorce would have been inevitable at some point, I think."

Matt exhaled sharply. "I think you're right." He looked at her, memorizing her face, wondering how they'd gotten from that first, electrified glance to sitting on the couch, Rachel back from the dead and talking about divorce. "Well, uh, I can be outta here—"

"No." Rachel shook her head. "This is your home, Matt. I have no idea where I'm going to land right now. I'm still just," she shrugged, looking around the living room, unsure exactly what she was trying to say, "trying to figure things out." It was lame, but the best she could come up with. *She* still wasn't entirely sure what she meant.

Matt was confused, but from the look on Rachel's face, he knew she was, too. "If you need to talk, Rach, I'm here. Okay?"

"Thank you. I appreciate that."

"I sure hope you didn't get seasick on that float this mornin'." Jake Bradshaw's chuckle echoed through the giant speakers and over the crowd. He grinned at the guest of honor. Michael looked decidedly uncomfortable standing on the small stage next to the mayor. Jake looked at him expectantly, wanting him to play along with the little joke.

"Uh, no, I'm fine."

The mayor smiled at the gathered crowd, an amazingly high percentage of the population of well over one hundred thousand had turned up to celebrate their local hero.

"The town of Beaumont would like to give you this, Michael, the key to our city." He handed Michael a plaque with a giant brass key affixed and his name engraved into a plate beneath it. Michael held it and smiled beside the mayor while hundreds of flashbulbs went off. The crowd cheered as he looked at the honor in wonderment.

"I really gotta say, I'm shocked. Didn't think I'd done nothin' big enough for y'all to wanna give me an honor like this." He ran a hand over the smooth, cool surface of the key. "Can't say I've ever seen a lock big enough for this key here, neither." That earned him a round of laughter. "Thank y'all. I'm touched. I can't accept this without this belongin' to my wife, Melissa, too. I'd like to ask for a moment of silence in her memory."

"Everyone, if we could have a moment of silence," the mayor said, his voice low and dramatic. The music from the high school band stopped and the square became absolutely quiet.

Melissa, baby, wherever you are, I love you.

After a moment, the mayor raised his hands, indicating festivities should continue.

The parade had been a huge hit, local businesses donating their time and creative efforts to make fun floats, including one for Michael and his family to ride on as they made their slow way through the center of town. Even Walter and Meredith had gotten into the celebration, waving and throwing candy from the large bags given to them before the parade started. At the end of the route, everyone poured into the carnival set up on the Burleson County Fairgrounds. Music, food, and fun awaited the crowd as Michael and Mayor Bradshaw made their way off the stage, engulfed by a sea of well-wishers.

Jennifer stood back, at a loss for words, proud of her father yet deeply sad her mother wasn't there to be included in the celebration. Her dad had been home for almost two weeks, and still she couldn't let him out of her sight, a desperate need for him overwhelming her. Sometimes she felt like a child, clingy and unsure. Luckily, her father seemed to have the same needs as his kids, always keeping her and Alan close. He had tried with Conrad, but her brother was still being obstinate and difficult. However, the other night she had caught him laughing at some of the stories their dad told the family over dinner, about his time on the island and some of the Island Six. *That guy Dean sounds like a hoot.* She'd like to meet him someday, even though it sounded like he and her father couldn't be more polar opposites.

The games, rides, and food were free for the Dupree/Adams family, everyone enjoying themselves and allowing all the stresses of the past year to be released. It had been a hard time, adjusting without Michael and Melissa, and then adjusting to a huge change again when Michael returned. It was a good day.

The garage was filled with old lumber from the shed built four years earlier. The musty smell of dust-covered wood and grease filled Denny's senses. She picked her way past Hannah's parking space to the back where she had been shown where to find the stacked boxes. Sure enough, under an old quilt, she found what was left of her life. Denny brushed a few spider webs out of the way and then pulled the box cutter from her back pocket. Taking the top box, she carefully slit the tape along the sides and top, and pulled the flaps back. Underneath layers of wadded newspaper, she found a framed picture of the two of them during their trip to Kauai. Denny held it in her hands, looking closely at her own face, studying her eyes and the bright smile on her lips. Where had that light gone? The passion she'd felt for life at that time, where did it go? She had been satisfied with her personal and professional life. Now, sitting in the dark, dank garage, she had never felt so lost or disheartened.

Turning her gaze to Hannah in the photo, she saw the love shining in her dark eyes, the happiness. She remembered the day that photo had been taken, the amazing time they'd had together, the way they'd laughed and truly enjoyed each other's company. What had changed? Why did Hannah feel like such a stranger now? Even her eyes were different. Yes, she was kind and understanding and so very gentle with Denny during her readjustment. Yet something was definitely off. Still, it hadn't been very long, and it was an adjustment for both of them, not just Denny. Maybe she just needed to give herself more time. Maybe their relationship would be okay in time.

Then why do I keep thinking about Rachel?

She tried to keep the blonde out of her thoughts, knowing what they had shared on the island was simply a product of their circumstances. They had each temporarily filled the void left by the loss of their families and homes, all that was familiar and comforting. That was all, nothing more. If they met today in the "real" world, what they had felt would soon dissolve into precious memories.

So then why does my heart ache so badly? And why is the void Rachel filled on the island still here now that I've returned to my family and home?

Denny fell against the quilt, leaning against the boxes, a hand over her mouth. She stared out the open garage door into the afternoon, not seeing the woman walking by with the Dalmatian on a leash, or the souped up Acura that roared by.

Tears peppered her cheeks, and she tasted their saltiness as they slid down over the corner of her mouth.

Chapter 26

The street was quiet, the lunch rush not yet started. Denny remembered the time of day well. It was when she and her crew had finally been able to relax and breathe after the morning rush, as well as restocking the pastry cases and starting new brewing rounds. Denny would often disappear into her office to deal with the ordering or other paperwork.

Standing at the corner of Marsh and 14th Street, Denny shoved her hands deep into the back pockets of her jeans and stared up at the corner building, its carved stone face and two big windows, where *DeRisio's* had been prominently displayed. Now that space was filled with the name of the current shop, some sort of bakery.

Denny's hands came up to cover her face as her tears began to fall.

"Can you believe Halloween stuff is already out?" Tracy signed.

Pam chuckled, her fingers signing in response, "Must milk the general public for every penny as quickly as possible. A week after Halloween we'll be seeing Christmas decorations."

Tracy grinned, picking up a heavy piece of orange foam which looked startlingly like a pumpkin with a carved Jack-o-lantern face. "Very cute. Luke would love this." Tracy turned the decoration over to look at the price tag.

Pam tapped her on the shoulder to get her attention. "Wouldn't he enjoy carving a real one better?" Her daughter studied her for a long moment, eyes twinkling with amused astonishment. "What? I think it would be fun."

Tracy beamed. She quickly put the foam pumpkin down and purposefully strode away from the display.

Pam wanted to pump her fist in the air in victory. The past month had had its rough spots; she had been unsure of her place in her daughter's house, or her life. Tracy had invited her to stay with them for as long as she liked, but it was an uneasy truce. Pam tried to keep her tongue in check and not butt in on Tracy's parenting duties, but it was tough sometimes. She was getting to know her grandson and loved him dearly, but was beginning to realize he could be quite a handful. Realizing that just meant that he took after his grandma, she smirked.

"What are you grinning at?"

Pam shook her head. "Nothing."

They shared a companionable silence for a while as they strolled down the aisles of the large discount store. Tracy had been pleasantly surprised at how well things had gone since her mother had returned, though inviting her to stay had largely been out of obligation. It had been a few weeks now and, though they'd had a couple of brief arguments, Tracy could tell that Pam was really trying to make their relationship work, and she appreciated it greatly. In fact, to her shock, she was enjoying the time with her mother. They were rebuilding some of the bridges that had been torched over the years.

Tracy thought about the way her son was responding to the new woman in his life. That alone was in large part responsible for her own change of heart toward the woman who had given birth to her almost twenty-eight years ago, and who, for a long time, she had thought of as a cold, heartless person. Something had happened to Dr. Pam Sloan on that island; it was evident in everything she did, and even in her eyes. They were softer, kinder, and filled with an interest and wonder not there before.

Pam was looking over their shopping list, unaware of the scrutiny. A hand on her arm got her attention. She wanted to cry as her daughter signed, "I'm so glad you're here, Mom."

"So, how has it been? Wonderful, no doubt. It's just fantastic that she's actually alive."

Hannah took a sip from her drink so she wouldn't have to respond. Jill Burbank was a long-time friend.

The tall blonde watched Denny as she stood speaking quietly with her husband, Rod. "How has catching up been? Has she told you what happened on that island?"

Hannah shook her head. "Not really. She's told me some, but," she shrugged, "nothing major. It's been...an adjustment."

Jill could hear the hesitation in Hannah's voice. She wasn't sure what caused it, but it couldn't be good. "Is everything okay?"

Hannah sighed, shaking her head as she, too, watched Denny and Rod in a heated discussion. Turning sad eyes to her friend, Hannah sighed again. "No."

Jill was shocked. Denny and Hannah had always been the golden couple in their small circle of friends, the couple everyone wanted to be like. After eight years the women were still so much in love, it had been an inspiration in Jill's own marriage. Setting her coffee down, Jill took Hannah by the hand and led her toward the door.

"Come on, come outside with me while I have a cigarette."

Hannah settled herself beside her friend on the front stoop. She looked up into the night sky at the few twinkling stars.

"The weather is going to be changing soon," Jill said conversationally as she pulled a smoke out of the pack she kept in her purse. Her companion remained silent. Lighting the cigarette, Jill took a drag then blew out her next question with the smoke. "Talk to me. What's happening?"

"I don't know. It's like something broke inside. Denny..." She glanced behind her to make sure her partner wasn't anywhere near the door, and then lowered her voice. "It's like she's not all here sometimes, like she is distracted, or her mind is a million miles away. Then some days, she's like her old self. Those days we can talk, even laugh. You know, at first, I figured she just needed to readjust to life." She chuckled ruefully. "Hell, at one point I even wondered if she'd sustained a head injury or something."

"Oh, nice." Jill chuckled, taking another drag.

"Well, that's how different she is. Like I said, at first I was okay with it. Confused, maybe, but all right for the most part. I figured that being back together would take some getting used to, but now..." She shrugged. "It's been two months and I still feel like I'm living with a stranger. We haven't made love once. It's almost like I'm afraid to touch her in any way, like she'll break."

"You guys haven't been intimate?" Hannah shook her head. "At all?" Again, Hannah shook her head, pulling her knees up and hugging them to her chest. "Wow." Jill looked out into the night, the cigarette dangling from her fingers. "Do you think this has to do with DeRisio's? I mean, you said she didn't take the sale well, right?"

"She was devastated. I've never felt like more of an asshole than I did that day, Jill. I thought I had done the right thing for me; hell, I *did* do the right thing for me, but Denny was devastated. I've never seen her shattered until that day. She just seems so lost and, yeah, I do wonder whether the sale of the shop has something to do with it."

"Why doesn't she open another shop, maybe something different this time?"

"I've thought about that, even suggested it. We're still dealing with this insurance company business. They paid off on Denny's insurance policy, and now they're trying to decide how to go about getting their money back."

"Oh, shit. What are you going to do?"

"I don't know. The money's gone. We've talked about petitioning the airline to get them to pay it back." She looked at Jill. "I did a lot with that money, helped my parents and sister."

"And the money from the sale of DeRisio's?"

"Most of those proceeds are in the bank."

Jill blew out a puff of smoke, smashed the butt against the stoop, and tossed it into the old coffee can Hannah had set out for just that purpose when she knew Jill and Rod were coming over. That was their deal: they could smoke on the front stoop as long as they threw the butts in the can and didn't sprinkle them over the front walkway or grass.

"I've thought about talking to her about maybe seeing someone, getting some help. Maybe she's just depressed. I don't know. About the only thing I'm at all sure of is that she's certainly not herself."

"You know what I noticed the most?" Jill tucked her hands between her thighs. "Her eyes. Denny had the most gorgeous eyes, and what made them *so* striking was the life in them, that wonderful mischievous twinkle that always seemed to be there."

Hannah smiled, knowing all too well that mischievous twinkle and what it was capable of. She nodded.

"Now, I don't know." Jill blew out a cigarette-scented breath. "It's gone. It's like the lights are on, burning brightly, but no one is home."

"I know what you mean. I know exactly what you mean." Hannah rested her chin on her knees, staring up into the night sky. "I really hope she can bounce back from this. I'm trying to be patient."

"It has only been two months."

"Yeah. It has."

Dinner had been fun with Jill and Rod, Denny thought as she got ready for bed. She pulled back the comforter and blanket, folded them at the end of the bed. The nights were still warm enough for the body heat of two to only need a sheet. Glancing across the bed where Hannah was also getting ready, Denny watched her partner. Hannah had been awfully quiet after returning from outside with Jill. "Everything okay?" she asked, stuffing the clothes she'd worn that night into the hamper.

"Yeah. I'm all right." Hannah smiled, but it was not a happy smile.

Denny headed into the bathroom, heart heavy. She knew that sad look, and knew she'd put it there. It had appeared off and on over the past couple of weeks. As Denny brushed her teeth, still smarting at the three new fillings, she thought about her behavior since her return. She knew it was hurting Hannah, but she just didn't know how to be the same person she used to be, because, when it boiled down to it, she wasn't. Going to see what had once been her baby, her dream, now gone, had affected Denny more than she thought it would. She had been devastated all over again, feeling anger, though surprisingly, not at Hannah. She had come to understand her partner's reasons for doing what she did. Her anger was directed at life, at the world, at the goddamn airlines. She felt they had stolen her life and she wanted it back.

Leaning against the sink, Denny looked into the mirror above it, looking into her eyes, her face, and finally trailing down to take in her upper chest, visible above the low neckline of the tank top in which she slept. Bringing a hand up, she spread her fingers out over the warm skin, her palm resting against her collar bones.

Though her heart hurt and she felt empty and lost, Denny knew she had to make the best of things, had to figure out how to live in her skin. With steely determination, she finished getting ready for bed.

Hannah slid between the sheets, arranging the sheet and her pillow just so, sighing as her body relaxed. She heard the bathroom door open, the lights were turned out, and then Denny climbed in on her side.

"It was good to see Jill and Rod," Denny said, settling on the soft mattress.

"Yeah, it was." She looked over, barely able to see Denny's profile in the darkened bedroom. "Rod said he wants to know the name of the tanning booth you go to."

Denny chuckled, meeting the dark eyes not quite a foot from her. "Well, that's quite a ways away. I don't know if he could do it in a weekend." She smiled at Hannah's laugh. It was a good sound. She decided she wanted to hear it again. "See there's no little goggles and cool glass to keep you safe from the little bits of sunlight captured in light bulbs. No, no, in *my* tanning salon, you get a slab of rock underneath you and a fig leaf over you. You can, however, use coconut shells to cover your breasts, 'cause you know," she lowered her voice to a whisper, "it hurts to have sunburned nipples."

Hannah giggled as she turned on her side, enjoying Denny's lighter side, which had been absent since her return.

"Trust me on this one," Denny continued. "Found that out the hard way."

"Oh did you?"

"I did." Denny stared at Hannah's face, pale against the night, and suddenly she felt a deep need to be close to her, to feel normal again. Reaching out, she pulled Hannah closer, their bodies nearly touching. "I missed you," she said, running her fingers over the soft skin of Hannah's arm.

"I missed you, too, baby." Hannah felt Denny's hot breath against her face and a shiver ran through her body. She whimpered softly when she felt Denny's breasts brush against her own as her lover scooted closer.

Denny pushed Hannah to her back, covering her body with her own as she claimed Hannah's mouth.

It had taken some maneuvering, but Rachel had managed to escape the prying eyes of the media. Only Reenie knew where she was. She didn't even trust her publisher. After all, it was because of them that the media frenzy concerning the Island Six had started in the first place. Her contacts knew how to reach her via email or phone, but that was all they needed to know.

Armed with her laptop, a goodly amount of cash, and keys to the small cottage Reenie had rented for her in Beaver Creek, Colorado — a ski town near Vale — Rachel settled in for an undetermined amount of time and isolation. She needed to think, to write, and to regroup.

Pulling up to the turn which led down a densely tree-lined, single lane road, Rachel looked at the computer printout of the directions to the rental, reviewing the turns she had taken since she'd reached Beaver Creek. Deciding she was at the right junction, she activated her left turn signal, waiting for a large truck to pass before she turned onto the private road, suddenly chilled as the thicket of trees enveloped her rental car in shade before it burst back into sunlight as she neared the small house.

A smile curved Rachel's lips as she pulled the four-wheel drive Explorer to a stop near the front porch, replete with a porch swing and small round table flanked by two wrought iron chairs. Rachel heaved her laptop bag and suitcase out of the back of the rented SUV and mounted the steps to the three room cottage.

The inside was just as charming as the outside. Numerous area rugs covered hardwood floors to protect cold feet in the colder winters. A huge stone fireplace took up one entire wall. The furnishings were rugged, sturdy wood with thick, down throws across the backs.

"This is beautiful," she murmured, turning in a small circle, already imagining the creativity she could summon in the homey space. She set her laptop down on the couch then headed into the bedroom. This space was equally impressive — massive oak bed with thick, homemade quilts, and large, heavy bedroom furniture. The one bathroom was accessed from the bedroom with another door leading back to the living room. Rachel couldn't wait to try out the Jacuzzi. In the meantime, she wanted to get unpacked and to get settled in front of a cozy fire, with a cup of hot tea and an open Word document.

Dinner was leisurely and, afterwards, Rachel sat curled up in the corner of the couch, sipping her tea and staring into the flames. She loved fireplaces and cold weather, something she'd missed dearly living on the island. She couldn't wait for winter and had considered staying in the mountains for the duration of the year, watching the snow covering the Rockies.

Rachel had tucked away the manuscript she'd written on the island; her view of the situation had changed and new ideas had sprouted. She felt far different now than she had when she had started writing it. She needed to write, to vent what was eating her up inside and to sort out her feelings by recreating the events during their exile. Visions were haunting her, demanding to be exorcised.

Setting her cup aside, Rachel opened up the silver laptop, letting it boot up as she took her dinner dishes to the kitchen, rinsed them, and arranged them in the dishwasher. Back in the main living space, she studied the flames, wishing Denny was there. She hadn't seen the brunette in two months, and she missed her. Before Denny, Rachel had had a void inside her, one that had always been there, though she hadn't realized it, and Denny had somehow managed to fill it. When they were separated, the emptiness left by Denny's absence was bleaker than anything Rachel had ever felt.

Reenie had asked Rachel if she thought she was gay, and Rachel hadn't had an answer. She didn't see her feelings for Denny as a "woman" or a "lesbian" issue. Denny was simply the person who made her feel whole, who brought a warmth and joy to her life like no one else; and, she just happened to have a pair of breasts. And Rachel was more than willing to try out those breasts. If that made her a lesbian, she was okay with that.

Rachel sank onto the couch with a sigh, remembering that last morning before the plane had arrived. Denny's hands had been so gentle, her mouth hot, driving Rachel to wild heights of arousal. She'd been desperate for Denny's touch, still was. No matter how hard she tried to keep her out, the beautiful brunette invaded her dreams and her thoughts. It had been most embarrassing when she had been visiting her sisters at Veronica's house in Portland. Danielle had caught her daydreaming, and when her sister had asked what had her flushed, Rachel had been speechless and flustered.

She had thought about making a trip east, visiting Reenie, seeing a good show...*looking up Denny.* That thought had stopped her cold.

Denny was happily married. Their circumstances on the island...that and that alone made Denny stray. Rachel knew she didn't stand a chance against Hannah, nor did she want to put Denny in any sort of position that might ruin the relationship that meant so much to Denny. Besides, Denny was probably crazy busy getting back into her coffee shop and reacquainting herself with her partner.

Rachel forced her thoughts away from Denny and back to the novel she was starting, determined not to leave her retreat until the book was finished.

The night was pitch black; the sun long since disappeared. The only sound breaking the stillness of perfect midnight was the tapping of computer keys, the steady staccato beating a lullaby for the night creatures that inhabited the forests of Beaver Creek, Colorado.

Hannah's breathing was even and slow, her body relaxed and warm. Denny held her, but sleep was far away. It had been nice to give Hannah pleasure, make her feel good, give her what she'd been longing for. Even as she had kissed Hannah, touched her, made love to her, Denny had felt like she was a million miles away, her thoughts wandering, her heart disengaged. She hoped Hannah hadn't noticed; she didn't want to hurt her any more. She didn't want Hannah to doubt herself or her place in Denny's heart. So why did Denny feel sick to her stomach?

With Hannah's sturdy weight all along the right side of her body, Denny stared up at the ceiling. Her eyes followed the subtle pattern made by the brush strokes in the paint. She hadn't allowed Hannah to touch her or try to bring her to release; she knew it wouldn't happen. She felt awful about it, but deep down, Hannah wasn't the woman she wanted touching her.

Shoving that thought aside, she'd told Hannah that tonight it was all about her. Hannah had argued at first, but her body's need finally made her give in. Denny had thought she could do it, thought she could just let herself go, let her body take over and feel the love she and Hannah had shared, the love she knew *had* to still be there, somewhere. Sometimes it was so frustrating it made her want to cry. Since when did making love to the woman she would spend the rest of her life with, had already spent eight years with, become something forced? Denny was confused, and very, very sad.

Michael gazed appreciatively at the set of tools that had been given to him, admiring the chrome sheen and steel perfection. He ran his fingers over the cool metal of a socket wrench, inhaling the smell of greased metal. He loved tools, loved what could be done with them, fixed or created. He looked around the garage, running a hand over the patch that Meredith had sewn on his left breast pocket, feeling the raised stitches that were his name.

Damn, it feels good to be productive again.

Mia studied her textbook, trying her damnedest to not notice the boy and girl sitting at the next table over in the library. He was murmuring some sort of nonsense to her and she was giggling and asking him to stop, though the tone of her voice sent a very different message. Dark eyes rolled for about the tenth time in as many minutes. Finally having enough of the distracting flirting and disgusted at her fellow students not taking their studies as seriously as they should — after all, one never knew when the chance to learn might be snatched away — she slammed the book shut, shoved it into her backpack, and stormed out of the library. She'd find another place to study, a *quiet* place.

For the first time in her life, Mia hated going to school. She loved to learn. She loved what she got from the classes and lessons, but hated the superficiality around her. She wanted to laugh at what her peers thought was the end of the world. *So what, he didn't ask you to the prom? Who cares that your shoes and accessories don't match? And who gives a good goddamn that his fake I.D. isn't as good as his brother's!*

Every day required a pep talk, if not from Mia herself, then from her mother. She wanted to just bypass all of the high school crap and go straight to college. Teenagers had absolutely no idea just how big the world really was, and how small their lives.

Staring down at the book open on the table, Pam ran a hand through her hair and rested her head in the palm of her hand. She was trying to get certified to practice veterinary medicine in Montana, and was having a hell of a time. She hadn't had to worry about tests for so long, she felt like a complete idiot, wondering how she'd ever done it the first time, baby in tow! It wasn't that the material was new to her, but this studying thing was. She would have to pass an exam, and it was stressing her to no end. Much of it was old hat; she'd been doing it for years. However, new techniques had come along that she had to learn, and learning those new techniques was getting to her.

"Because I was thirty years younger," she muttered, testily flipping the page of her notebook, trying to find the notes on the assignment she'd taken in class that afternoon.

After hanging out with Tracy and Luke on the ranch twenty-four hours a day, seven days a week, Tracy had not so subtly suggested Pam try and get back into practice. The older woman knew she was driving her daughter crazy, so had agreed. Besides, she missed her work, loving all the animals like nothing else. The love a cat, or dog, or even pet ferret gave was a love like no other. They asked no questions, wanted nothing from a person but love and care. Perhaps she had been trying a little too hard to force that with Tracy and Luke.

The older woman smiled at the thought, sighing as she found the spot in her notes she was looking for.

"I was thinking that maybe we'd head to Maine, or maybe New Hampshire, see the trees change colors. What do you think?" Will tightened his hold on Dean's arm.

"Mmm," the attorney sighed, "that sounds wonderful. Great idea." He eyed his partner, a smirk curling his lips.

"What?"

"Maybe I'm converting you into a tree hugger after all."

Will rolled his eyes, about to pull away when they were addressed by a young girl wearing a green baseball cap.

"Good afternoon, guys. Care to support your environment?" She held out a flyer. "I'm part of the environmentalist group, WorldWin, and we're asking for donations for our campaign to stop illegal logging, which is destroying our forests at devastating rates."

Dean took the flyer, reading the message as the girl spoke passionately about the negative effects on wildlife and the environment. He could feel Will trying to tug him away, but the attorney in him was intrigued. Glancing up into the girl's animated blue eyes, he smiled. "Tell me more."

Hannah left for work humming. Denny had done her best to play the attentive wife, making breakfast, though she'd made sure she was up before Hannah, not wanting to get cornered in bed. She needed her space.

Now she had it, the house quiet, just the faintest lingering scent of Hannah's perfume. Denny showered then slipped into one of the pairs of jeans she'd bought. Some of her pre-crash clothing had been in the boxes in the garage, but most of it no longer fit her much leaner frame. Buttoning her shirt, she looked into the mirror above the dresser, plucking at a flyaway eyebrow hair, when something in the reflected image of the bedroom behind her caught her eye. Turning, Denny walked over to Hannah's closet, which had been left open in Hannah's haste to leave for work. On the shelf, tucked between a folded blanket and box that she knew held their old love letters, she saw a wooden box, a jewelry box.

Denny chewed on her bottom lip, wondering what to do. She knew she hadn't given the box to Hannah; she'd never seen it before. Curiosity got the better of her and she reached up, taking the delicate box from the shelf and sitting on the end of the bed to examine it. It was a rich mahogany and quite beautiful. Denny ran her fingers over the leaded glass top, tracing the etched flower pattern. The lid squeaked slightly as she lifted it. Inside was a gold watch, also unfamiliar to Denny, and some ticket stubs. Looking at the names of the shows, Denny recognized a couple of the standard Broadway hits — *Chicago, Beauty and the Beast, Phantom of the Opera*, and there were a couple she'd never heard of. Gingerly fingering those aside, she saw a few face-down Polaroids.

Wrestling with her conscience, Denny tried to decide whether to respect Hannah's privacy or satisfy her curiosity. Something inside told her to close the lid of the box, put it away, and continue with her day. Her fingers — frozen in indecision — itched to move, to do something. Taking a deep breath, Denny plucked the pictures from the bottom of the box and turned them over. The first was a scenic picture — boats and water, some sort of harbor, perhaps. Sliding that picture behind the others, the second showed Hannah, her hair in the pixie cut Denny was getting used to and a smile on her face. She was standing next to a woman with medium-length red hair, whose brown eyes gazed at the lens of the camera. The woman was also smiling, though it was closed mouth, more of a smirk.

"Pretty girl," Denny observed. The two women were standing on what looked to be a dock, maybe a dock in the harbor from the first photo. Sliding it behind the first picture, Denny's breath caught, eyes glued to the image on the third Polaroid. Hannah held the redhead in her arms, one hand cupping the back of her head, their foreheads resting against one another's, both grinning broadly in profile. It looked as though the photographer had caught them just before, or after, a kiss.

Her face paled as blood rushed toward her stomach and nausea roiled. She couldn't take her eyes off the picture, her brain turning the still into action: the women's lips met, Hannah's eyes closed as the redhead plundered her mouth, drawing her close.

Denny tried to shake the image, but couldn't. Who was the redhead? Why had Hannah kept the box and pictures? Denny could only guess it had been a gift from the redhead, as had the watch, and that Hannah had gone to the shows with her.

She put the pictures back as they had been, carefully placing the stubs and watch on top of them and then closing the lid. She absently caressed its smooth surface for a moment, lost in thought. *So I'm not the only one who found love.* Though her own culpability was inescapable and technically Hannah had done nothing wrong, it didn't help Denny's nausea or the ache in her heart.

Denny wondered how long had the new relationship been going on. Were they involved when the survivors had miraculously returned from the dead?

Denny dashed to the bathroom and rested her forehead against the cool glass of the mirror, shoulders hunched as she leaned against the sink. Had the redhead touched Hannah the same way Denny had the night before? When was the last time they had been together?

Running a shaky hand through her hair, Denny pushed off the sink and headed toward the kitchen, grabbing her car keys off the hook by the door.

"Hello?"

"Hi." Answered by silence, Hannah said, "I'm sure you don't want to hear from me, but I need to talk. Please, Tiffany, I need a friend." Hannah placed her hand on her pounding forehead, trying to will the pain away.

Tiffany sat back in her chair. After two months without a word as they had agreed, she was surprised to hear from Hannah. It had been difficult, seeing news of the Island Six's return plastered all over every damn TV screen and channel, and knowing Hannah was in the same building, just a few floors away. "Are you okay?"

"Not really. It's Denny. God, I feel like she came back from war or something, shell shocked and changed." Taking a deep breath, Hannah sat back in her chair, wincing as it squeaked. "Last night we made love for the first time—"

Tiffany felt the ache deep in her heart, and her stomach roiled. "Hannah, I really don't want to hear this."

"Please, Tiffany." Hannah heard the heavy sigh indicating her friend's reluctant agreement to listen. "She's not herself. At all. Last night she wouldn't let me touch her, like my touch burned her or something. And even when she touched me, I felt..." Hannah paused to recollect, thinking of what she had felt and thought, even during the bliss of sexual release. "I felt like I was being touched by a robot, some sort of drone. I don't even know if she was truly there," Hannah whispered.

Tiffany squeezed her eyes shut, trying to block out the mental images — Hannah's beautiful body in the throes of ecstasy under another woman's hand. Clearing her throat, she said, "What would you like me to do about this, Hannah?" She didn't want to sound cold, but had no idea what the woman expected of her.

"I want to see you," Hannah whispered desperately.

"Oh, no!" Tiffany shoved away from her desk, eyes wide. "I am *not* going to play that game with you, Hannah. You made your choice."

Hannah nodded dumbly, feeling like a bitch for even having suggested it. "I'm sorry. You're right. I need to go." She carefully replaced the handset into the cradle, tears stinging her eyes.

"You think I don't realize I sell coffee here? As I told you, I'm out of French Nut Surprise at the moment. You can either choose something else, or *go* some*where* else." The vendor's icy gaze nearly froze the rude patron where he stood. Without another breath, he quickly ordered something else then scurried to his seat at the back of Mile. "That's what I thought," Joni Sanchez muttered, hurrying over to the drink station to make up the order. She heard the bells above the door jingle to life. "I'm out of vanilla, whoever you are, so don't even ask."

"Good thing I'm a chocolate kinda gal."

Joni froze, the hair prickling on the back of her neck. "Goddamn, son-of-a-bitch!" Drink creation forgotten, Joni hurried around the counter and grasped Denny in a choking hug. "Wondered when you were going to show up around here." She gave a painful squeeze. "Took you long enough!"

"Yeah, well." Denny had nothing to say as she was led around back into Joni's office.

"Stay. I'll be right back."

Denny sat back in the space she knew well. Even when DeRisio's had become established, Denny had come back to visit Joni from time to time — for advice or just to chat. The office was small, crammed with boxes of syrups and cups that wouldn't fit into the tiny storage room. Joni's desk was covered with papers, purchase orders, and packing slips.

"Had to get Robert from outside to take over," Joni said, breezing back into the office and throwing herself into the squeaky desk chair across from Denny. The older woman sat forward, elbows resting on a small stack of Mile brochures, causing a few to float to the floor. "Can't believe you're back, Denny. Hot damn, what a story."

"Mmhm," the brunette murmured noncommittally.

"How are you doing, Denny?" Joni asked, her voice soft.

"I'm fine."

"No, I mean, how *are* you? You don't look good. You look tired and...haunted."

Denny looked into the narrowed eyes scrutinizing her from head to toe. "You see a lot, Joni." Sighing, she leaned forward, resting her elbows on her thighs.

"What's going on, Den? Everything okay...at home?"

Is everything okay? Her eyes closing, Denny saw the photo again, felt the distance she felt from her own life. Lastly, she saw Rachel's face, felt her touch. *No. Nothing is okay.* Even so, she didn't want to talk about her quandary. She wasn't ready to talk about what she didn't yet understand.

"I'm just trying to adjust, Joni. I had no idea what a huge task that would be. I thought I could come back, rejoin the world, and fall right back into my life." She shook her head. "Harder than I thought."

Joni didn't push. "Well, what are you doing these days to occupy yourself?"

Denny shrugged, sitting back in her chair and jiggling an ankle across her knee. "Cleaning the house, bumming around the neighborhood to reacquaint myself with things..."

"Sounds...exciting."

Denny smirked, shaking her head.

Head cocked nonchalantly, Joni tossed out, "Come work for me here at Mile." Joni thought it would be the best thing for Denny to get out of the house and around something familiar. She had no idea what was going on, but she could tell her friend was deeply disturbed about something.

Denny studied her for long moments, contemplating her offer. Finally she nodded. "Okay."

Joni smiled. "Good. I could use someone around here who knows what the hell they're doing."

"Are you sure about this, Michael? Think maybe you should hold off, get through the holidays?" Meredith asked, hands on hips as she looked around the small house at the packed boxes stacked high.

"No. I need to try and get the kids' lives back to as normal as possible, as quickly as possible." The house he and Melissa had rented had since been re-let. He blew out a breath, pleased to finally have his own house again, even if it was a tiny three bedroom rental at the edge of town. It was rundown and dirty, but affordable. Michael figured he, Jennifer, and Conrad could make themselves a home there. He had been painting, cleaning, and decorating for the upcoming holidays.

"All right, son." The older woman stretched up, giving her son-in-law a kiss on the cheek, then went out to join Walter in the truck.

Michael looked around, trying to decide where to start the unpacking. The kids were still at school. He hadn't wanted them to have to deal with the moving, so their grandparents and a couple of men Michael worked with had helped him move everything into the new house. Jennifer would drive herself and Conrad to their new home after school. Over the weekend he'd take them to the store so they could pick out furnishings for their rooms, personalize them a bit. Maybe he could put up some sports memorabilia in Conrad's room and posters on Jennifer's walls of whatever new actor or singer she liked.

It never ceased to amaze Michael just how much his kids had grown up in such a short time. Granted, he'd been gone for just over a year, but he'd noted big changes in all three of his offspring. Maybe it was the situation, having to grow up because of the loss of their parents, or maybe their maturing was just a natural progression.

He pulled the box cutter out of his back pocket and began to open up boxes that had been kept in storage over the past year and a half. Meredith had put most of their belongings into storage, thinking the kids could make use of them when they were setting up housekeeping. In fact, Alan had a set of their dishes and the downstairs furniture in his house. He was coming over later that night to help unpack and the four of them were going to enjoy a quiet night together, celebrating the new home.

The big Texan got busy unpacking, putting things away and breaking down boxes, getting the kitchen and his own bedroom completely unpacked. He was surprised when he heard car doors slamming outside and the voices of his two youngest. Glancing at his watch, Michael saw he'd been working for more than six hours.

"Daddy?" Jennifer Dupree called out, looking around the small living room as she entered the house. The couch had been set against the paneled wall, a few boxes stacked on top of the cushions, a thick pile of disassembled cardboard on the floor.

"In here, guys!" came the deep, disembodied voice of their father from deeper in the house. She followed his voice back to his bedroom, the smallest, at the back of the house, by the back door. "Hey, angel," he said with a broad smile, placing a soft kiss on her forehead. "Hey, big guy. How was school?" He knew better than to try to touch Conrad, knowing his son would pull away. As it was, he barely stood in the doorway of the room, hands buried deep in the pockets of his baggy jeans, baseball cap perched cockeyed on his head.

"'S'kay," he muttered.

"Good. Well, I left both your rooms alone, except for getting your beds set up. You kids can put your stuff away however you want it. Alan will be over after work, then we can all sit down and eat some pizza. Whaddya think?"

"Sounds great!" Jennifer gave her dad a quick hug then bounced off toward her room. She was so excited they had their own place again. She loved her grandparents, but had never liked staying with them. Her grandfather was unrelentingly grouchy, always had been, and her grandmother seemed overwhelmed most the time. Jennifer hated seeing her that way.

Conrad exited behind her, trudging to his own room.

Chapter 27

"Paramount announced today that they will be producing a feature film based on Willing To Conquer, *a novel by celebrated author, Rachel Holt. The movie is due out next winter."*

Denny looked up from the book she was reading and glanced at the TV, where she saw some file footage of Rachel. Pen in hand, the author was sitting behind a table at what appeared to be a book signing. It was before the crash, Denny was sure. She sat forward, looking into the green eyes. Over the months since their rescue, she'd refused to watch any news footage that included Rachel; she didn't want to be reminded of what they had shared on the island. Seeing the author's face — that beautiful, wonderful face — Denny was amazed to look into her eyes and not see the glowing light she was used to. The eyes were dull, lifeless, the eyes Rachel had had when they'd first landed on the island — the eyes of a woman lost. Denny smiled ruefully; her own eyes looked like that now.

Grabbing the remote control, she turned the television off, trying to turn her attention back to her book. She couldn't concentrate, her mind wandering back to the images on the screen, which then morphed into memories from the island: Rachel's eyes, her face, her voice, the way her body felt... Closing her eyes, Denny allowed her mind to conjure up that last day on their ledge — the taste and feel of Rachel's skin, the sight of her half-naked body, waiting to be made love to, begging to be touched. Denny groaned, her body warming painfully at the memory.

She was abruptly pulled from her reminiscences by the sound of the garage door opening. Pushing herself up from her slouch against the couch cushions, Denny headed to the kitchen where dinner was cooking. Hannah came in through the door from the garage, setting her purse and keys on the counter just inside.

"Hey, baby."

"Hey. You hungry? Dinner'll be ready soon." Denny had to look away; she couldn't help visualizing the redhead standing next to her partner. She felt like a hypocrite as she took a can of peas from the cabinet and used the electric can opener mounted under the cabinet to remove the lid.

"Sure am." Hannah hugged Denny from behind, placing a soft kiss on her bare neck. Closing her eyes, Hannah tried to swallow down the sense of guilt from her brief conversation with Tiffany that morning. She pushed away thoughts of what she might have done, or allowed to happen, had her former lover agreed to meet with her. Instead she concentrated on the smell of Denny's hair and skin, the feel of her body — taller than Tiffany and a very different body type.

"Good. Chicken will be done in about three minutes."

"Smells like cornbread, too. You've been busy."

"I have been. Actually, I went to talk to Joni today."

Hannah's hand froze on the door handle of the fridge. "Oh yeah?" The coffee shop owner had harshly judged Hannah's actions in dealing with Denny's death, and so she had grown hard against Joni, hurt that she could have ever thought that Hannah could just throw Denny away.

"Yeah. She offered me a job."

Hannah turned, but Denny's back was to her as she stirred the peas in a saucepan. "And what did you say?"

"I said yes."

"Honey, we don't need the money. I can support—"

"I know you can, Hannah. And I'm proud of the promotion you got while I was gone." Denny turned to meet Hannah's eyes. "I need this. Sitting around here all day is killing me. I need something for me again."

Though she knew Denny hadn't meant it the way it sounded, the statement stung. She nodded, turning back to the fridge, taking out a bottle of water. "When do you start?"

"I'm probably going to go in tomorrow."

Hannah took a long drink, setting the bottle aside. Sudden anger washed through her. Joni had attacked her character and her love for Denny, and now Denny was taking a job at her coffee shop. Joni might try to poison Denny against her. Or perhaps it was because of her feelings of guilt over selling DeRisio's. "Well, uh, I hope it goes well."

"Thanks." Denny gave her a quick smile then turned back to the stove.

Rachel gasped, her head thrust back into the soft pillow, eyes squeezed tightly...

...Holding her fingers still, Denny tried to catch her breath, her body pulsing.

The blonde's hips bucked as her body convulsed, her breaths shaky.

Denny's control over her emotions hanging from a tenuous thread as she tried to push away the image in her mind, Rachel's face before her eyes, passion shining in her green eyes. "Wait, wait," Denny panted.

"Oh, Denny," Rachel whimpered, the sting of hot tears behind her eyes at the powerful orgasm that had just destroyed her.

Denny covered her eyes with her arm, trying to calm her heaving chest. "Shit."

"What? Are you okay?" Hannah took her hand away, Denny's thighs closing, the brunette turning away. "Denny? What happened? Did I hurt you?"

Denny shook her head. She felt foolish, but couldn't allow Hannah to continue making love to her when all she could see was Rachel's face, her body craving the blonde's touch, not that of the woman who had just been inside her. Sitting up, she covered herself with the sheet as she reached to the end of the bed for the tank top that she had shed moments before.

Hannah moved to her side of the bed, the bitter taste of rejection in her tone. "I'm trying to make this work, Denny," she said at length, unable to look at Denny.

The guilt and confusion that had been her constant companions over the past couple of months consumed Denny. The hurt she heard in Hannah's voice made her feel even worse. Denny was ashamed at what she said next, as her guilt morphed into anger. "Why? Do you feel obligated?"

Hannah's mouth fell open as Denny rose from the bed, snagging her panties from the floor. "No! Because I love you. I missed you."

"Did you?" Denny glared accusingly at her from the doorway of their bedroom then disappeared into the darkened house.

Denny ran her hands through her hair as she stared out of the window in the guest bedroom, her body still humming with adrenaline and un-sated arousal. "What am I doing?" she whispered, hating herself for allowing her tempest of emotions to let her speak before thinking. Hannah hadn't deserved that.

"Shit." Tugging her panties on, she was about to head back to the bedroom to apologize when she almost ran smack into Hannah. "I'm sorry. That was a real asshole thing to say."

"Yeah, it was. I died that day, Denny, and how dare you question that. But you were dead, and I had to learn how to live my life without you." The hurt and anger that had been building over the past two months simmered to the surface. "I'm assuming you were referring to Tiffany?"

Denny said nothing; she had no idea whether that was the woman's name.

"Maybe it was just an ugly remark, but yes, I admit that there was someone. I fought it, but eventually I realized that I had to let you go. Tiffany never had my heart, but she was good to me and helped me get through the most difficult time of my life — your death!" Her hands slapping against Denny's chest, her anger and grief began to trail down her cheeks. "Don't you dare judge me just like Joni. You have *no* idea what it was like for me. None!"

Denny allowed Hannah to let it all go, even took the slight beating she was taking, finally grabbing Hannah by the shoulders and pulling her close. Her heart broke for the woman falling apart before her. For the first time, she thought she could see what Hannah had gone through, and she felt like an asshole.

"Shh. Don't cry. I'm sorry." Blue eyes slid closed as Hannah cried against her, grabbing fistfuls of Denny's shirt, clinging to her. "I'm sorry." Denny kissed Hannah's cheek, cupping the back of her head and rocking her slightly.

"Why did you have to go, Denny?" Hannah cried, finally able to take out her anger on the woman who had caused it. "Goddamn it, why did you have to get on that fucking plane? We were happy! Fuck!" Hannah pushed away, hurrying from the room as realization dawned — it was over. Suddenly she saw it all clearly, what Denny had known, almost from the first day she had returned: Hannah had been holding on to a ghost.

Jennifer's eyebrows drew together as she took a closer look into the water. She brought a finger up, ticking off a stroke in the air for each fish she saw. Only counting nine, she began again, moving around to one side of the tank, then the other, looking for the elusive number ten.

"Hey, Dad?" she called, moving back to her starting position in front of the aquarium.

"Yeah?" Michael walked into the living room, dishtowel in his hand. He and Conrad had been washing and drying the dinner dishes.

"We're missing Rusty."

Michael bent down and grabbed the small green net from the storage compartment under the fifty gallon tank. He squinted into the shipwreck half buried in the white and blue rocks that covered the bottom of the tank.

"Where you at, little guy?" he muttered, sticking the net into the water, waving it around to try and flush the angel fish out of hiding, if he was hiding.

"You don't think he got caught up in the filter, do you?"

"Hope not." He waved the net around again and they both groaned when the body of the fish floated up from where it had settled. "Aw, that sucks," Michael commiserated.

"Conrad," Jennifer called out, still gazing into the tank, "your fish died."

"What? Which one?" the teen asked, stepping into the room.

"Rusty," Michael supplied.

"Figures," the kid snorted, voice dripping with angry sarcasm.

Stomach churning at what might come out of his son's mouth this time, Michael turned to face Conrad, who was eyeing him suspiciously.

"Why would I think you could keep a *fish* alive?"

Jennifer yelped, hands covering her mouth as her brother hit the floor, their father standing over him, hand still stinging. "Don't you ever, *ever* say anything like that again," he growled.

Jennifer watched in shock as her father stepped over the prone boy and slammed out of the house, followed quickly by the banging of his truck door and the roar of the engine. Thoroughly disgusted, the girl looked at her brother, who was starting to pick himself up. "You little bastard," she hissed, tears of rage and grief flowing down her face. "How *dare* you say something like that to him?"

Conrad got to his feet, feeing sick to his stomach. His jaw hurt and deep shame suffused his face. He didn't know why he'd said such a cruel thing to his father; it had just kind of slipped out. Now Jenny was mad at him, and she was the last person he wanted upset with him. In a lot of ways, he felt she was all he had. When they had thought both their parents were dead, he and his sister had gotten very close.

With a heavy sigh, he went to his room, closing the door behind him.

Michael pulled into the parking lot at Stuffy's Bar, shutting down the engine and slamming the heavy metal door behind him. The small bar, which he hadn't been to in over five years, hadn't change a bit — it was smoky, and cheap beer was flowing. Everything seemed to stop as he walked in, all eyes on him. He wasn't in the mood for excitement or for folks to start praising the Almighty because he was alive, having survived some crash.

Ignoring the attention, he took a seat at the bar and ordered a cold one. Once the mug was in his hand, he took a sip, savoring the malt as it slid down his throat. He stared at his reflection in the mirror behind the bar, thick fingers stroking his trimmed beard. Why did Conrad hate him so badly? What had he done to deserve that? He carried enough guilt over Melissa's death. The fact that his son blamed him for that hurt almost as badly as if his wife had slid off the wing all over again.

Running a sandpaper-like hand over his face, Michael's head dropped forward and he stared down into the amber liquid, unsure what he should do. Maybe it would be best for everyone involved if Conrad had someplace else to stay. He couldn't go back to live with Meredith and Walter, things had been tough for the boy — and his grandparents — while he'd stayed there, but maybe Alan would take him in for a while.

Funnily enough, his island family popped into his mind. He thought about Pam, wondering what she would do in such a situation. Michael actually smiled at the thought; no doubt she'd belt the boy into next week. Which made Michael think about what he'd done. Never had he struck any of his children like he just had. Conrad had dropped immediately; Michael's hand still hurt from the contact. He brought his hand up, looking at it, spreading out his fingers before slowly curling them into a fist, noting the reddened skin. His luck, he'd get back to the house to find a police officer waiting for him. Michael sighed again. Not like he wouldn't deserve it.

Opening his wallet, he removed the two folded Polaroids, smoothing them out flat on the bar. In one, Rachel, Dean, and Mia smiled into the camera, just before leaving Duke's house to head home. Dean stood in the middle, grin huge, an arm around the shoulder of each of the two girls flanking him. The other picture was of Pam, Denny, and himself in a similar group photo, though Pam was sitting in a chair between the others. He looked at the faces, all six of them, a smile creasing his grizzled features. It amazed him how much simpler life was when they'd been on the island. He wouldn't give up his kids again for a moment, but he couldn't help wondering how everyone else's lives were going. With any luck, smoother than his.

"Will this work? I know it's not exactly the Taj Mahal, but it's warm and dry, and private."

Denny looked around the tiny room. Boxes, filled with old paperwork to be shredded, were stacked to one side. On the other side was a foldout sofa and small breakfast nook, replete with dorm fridge, wet bar sink, and a hot plate. She nodded, imagining her meager belongings stacked in the corner — all six boxes. "This'll work, Joni. Thanks."

"Great. Well, I need to get back downstairs, so if you need anything, just holler." Joni gave the dazed woman a firm hug then left her alone, her footfalls fading as she hurried down the steep staircase that led to the sidewalk, right next to the entrance of Mile.

Denny blew out a breath, hands in her back pockets as she walked around the small space. There was a window in the wall where the boxes were stacked. She grunted quietly as she pushed it open, hoping to rid the room of some of the mustiness. Denny turned back to the room, running a hand through her hair. She had stayed in the guest bedroom at her house the night before, sleep eluding her. Over a barely touched breakfast, she and Hannah had decided perhaps too much water had gone under the proverbial bridge, and it was time to call it quits. Hannah had cried, which had torn at Denny's heart, but they both knew it was for the best. To make it as easy on Hannah as possible, she waited until Hannah had left for work then loaded up what was left of her belongings in her VW van, gave Joni a call, and left a note behind.

Flopping down on the couch, grimacing at the *boing* of an unhappy spring, Denny buried her face in her hands.

"Hello, my friend!" Reenie took the blonde into her arms, hugging her tight before releasing her and moving aside so Rachel could enter the loft. "Is this all you've got?" She indicated the backpack Rachel had slung over one shoulder.

"Yep. Light packer."

"I guess. Come on in. Beth's here."

"Oh, great!" Rachel had met Reenie's actress friend a time or two before her island exile and always found her enjoyable company.

"Well, it's great to see you!" Beth Sayer rose from where she'd been lounging on the couch and wrapped Rachel in a warm hug, smiling warmly down at her. "What a wonderful thing to happen to a storyteller, huh?" she teased with a wink.

"You have *no* idea." Rachel chuckled. "It's good to see you again, Beth. In town for a show?"

"Yeah. I've got about two weeks left, then I'll be out of this one's hair."

Reenie waved her off. "Sooooo," the editor purred, nodding toward Rachel's laptop, tucked inside her backpack, "you finished?"

"Yep." Rachel grinned proudly. "Martin has it, so you should be getting it soon." Rachel flopped down on the black leather couch. Beth sat next to her, picking up the blanket she'd been wrapped in. "He's looking to get this thing out by the two year anniversary."

"Of the crash or of the rescue?" Reenie asked, handing both women a cup of coffee then folding herself onto the loveseat with her own mug.

"The crash — June 5th."

"Ah, so the media hound strikes again." Reenie was still angry with her employer for sending the dogs after Rachel. It had taken the author disappearing, closed up in a mountain cabin for just a month, to give her the privacy she needed to bounce back. During that time, she'd written some pages that Reenie thought were her best work.

"So are you coming out of your self-imposed isolation? Reen tells me you were in Beaver Creek."

"Sure was," Rachel said with a huge grin.

"It's beautiful up there."

"You've been there?" the blonde asked, relaxing into the corner of the couch. She wrapped chilled fingers around her mug of coffee.

Beth nodded. "I grew up in Pueblo, not all that far."

"No kidding? I didn't know that."

"Yes, ma'am." Beth sipped from her own mug. "I haven't been back in some time, though."

"Does your family still live there?"

"My mom."

Noting how Beth's eyes fell and her shoulders stiffened, Rachel could tell that perhaps a change of subject was in order. "I've actually been puttering around Oregon again, looking to buy a house. I'm ready to go back home."

Beth smiled, her entire face lighting up. "Good for you."

Rachel, who hadn't seen Beth in some time, was struck all over again by the woman's beauty. She found it funny — since she'd accepted her attraction to Denny, she had realized she had always looked at women in degrees of attractiveness. She didn't gauge them in comparison to her own looks, as a lot of women did, but rather as to what sort of character they'd make. Now, after everything she'd shared with Denny, she had to wonder if perhaps she had been assessing them in degrees of how they'd be for *her*.

"So, what's your next novel going to be about?"

Beth's voice drew Rachel from her musings, and she blushed slightly as she looked away, missing the amused gleam in blue eyes. "I'm actually considering something dealing with Pompeii and the eruption of Vesuvius in 79 A.D."

"God, doesn't that require more research?" Reenie asked, resting her head against her closed fist. Rachel nodded vigorously, eyes twinkling. Reenie rolled her eyes. "I don't get it."

"A woman with a brain — it's sexy." Beth grinned. She caught the warning glare Reenie sent her way. *Don't worry, Reen. I know, hands off.*

Rachel blushed again and Reenie changed the subject. "I saw your Island Six on TV the other day," she said, stretching her legs out, resting her crossed ankles on the coffee table.

That caught Rachel's attention. "Really?" She'd been purposely avoiding television and any newspaper articles about the group. She didn't want to see Denny. She already saw enough of her in her dreams.

"Apparently Dean has taken up the cause of environmentalism." Rachel stared at her and Reenie chuckled, amused. "Yep. He's become the pro bono lawyer for WorldWin. Quite the little prizefighter, from what I'm hearing."

"I'll be damned."

"Have you kept in contact with anyone?" Beth asked, getting a refill on her coffee and bringing the carafe over to give the others a warm up.

Rachel shook her head with a heavy sigh. "No."

"Why not?" Beth sat down, tucking her bare feet under her.

"I'd like to say that it's because I've been busy, but to be honest, I don't know. I think a lot of it is because I had so much to deal with when I got home. Hell, everything just kind of..."

Beth nodded in understanding. "Who knows, they may have been able to give you the support you needed."

"In retrospect, that is undoubtedly true. I don't know." She sighed, mind focused on a single image. "I think I needed to get on with my life without memories of what happened there." She looked down at the mug, which she slowly turned in her hands.

Beth studied her movements then glanced at Reenie, who shook her head slowly, as if to say, "Don't ask."

"It's probably best, hon." Reenie reached over to squeeze Rachel's arm. The blonde smiled, but it was forced.

Beth watched the interaction between the two women, and with blue eyes focused on the author again, she saw it plain as day — longing. She knew that look well, knew the heartbreak that went along with it. *Interesting.*

"Beth, would you help me for a second?" Reenie got to her feet and snagged Beth's hand as she passed the couch.

"Uh, sure, Reenie." Beth rolled her eyes at Rachel, who chuckled. "What?"

Reenie waited until the swinging door of the kitchen had shut then turned to her friend. "Listen, Beth, I saw the looks you were giving Rachel in there. I know she's a beautiful woman, but don't even—"

"Reenie?"

"...think...huh?"

More amused than offended, Beth crossed her arms over her chest. "Shush. Do you really think I'd make a play for your best friend?" She saw the embarrassment suffuse Reenie's cheeks. "Listen, Reen, yes, she's beautiful, and well, hot as hell, but something happened on that island, didn't it?"

Reenie looked up, dark eyes surprised. "What do you mean?"

"I'm not stupid and I'm not blind. There was someone on that island special to her, wasn't there?" Beth's eyebrow raised in challenge, daring Reenie to deny it.

The dark-haired woman sighed, running a hand through her short hair. "I can't talk about that, Beth. I'm sorry."

"I understand. It's just," Beth looked down at the tile, nudging at the pattern with her toe, "I know that kind of sadness and loss." She shrugged. "Maybe I could help her."

"Don't!" Reenie's voice was quiet, so Rachel wouldn't overhear, but firm. "She's confused enough as it is."

Beth studied her friend's face for a moment then nodded, the barest hint of the corner of her mouth curling up. "It was a woman, wasn't it?"

"Goddamn you, Beth," Reenie fumed. "How do you read me so goddamn easily?"

Beth threw her head back and laughed. "Oh, honey. You're priceless."

"Uh, ladies, if you'd like to talk about me some more, I will happily leave so you can do it in the comfort of the living room." Two pairs of eyes swiveled furtively to Rachel, who had poked her head in through the door. "Honest, guys, I won't break."

"I'm sorry, sweetie," Reenie said, squeezing Rachel's shoulder. "I was just trying to tell Fido here to behave."

Rachel met Beth's amused gaze and shrugged. She shook her head, walking back out into the living room, followed by the other two.

"Thanks a lot," Beth hissed. She almost growled when she heard Reenie snicker.

Lynn Mason looked over the rims of her glasses, pen paused in mid-air. Clearing her throat, the counselor studied Conrad. "Why do you think your father hates you, Conrad?"

"Because he does," the boy said.

She cocked her head to the side and removed her glass altogether. "Because why?"

Conrad sat on the couch, elbows resting on his thighs, one foot jiggling. He leaned forward, staring out the window at the traffic driving silently by on Ute. His hands dangled between his knees and he stared down at them. He hadn't meant to say it, but it had just come out. It had been three months since his father had struck him, since he'd said...it. Since then, his dad had avoided him, muttering only a few words to him, and only when necessary. Some of the light in his father's eyes seemed to have dimmed that day.

"I said somethin' I shouldn't have said," he finally muttered.

Conrad was surprised at the sting of tears behind his eyes. He cleared his throat, sinking back into the soft cushions, stretching his long legs out in front of him. He'd grown a lot over the past year and a half. He was proud to say he was up to his dad's shoulders now.

"Conrad?"

"Yeah?" the boy croaked. He was trying to keep it in, trying to be a man. He knew what she was wanting, so he pushed himself up in the seat, preparing to talk, when Lynn Mason said magic words.

"It's almost time, Conrad. Do you want to stay and talk about this?" Conrad shook his head, bringing a hand up to quietly wipe *something* from his eye. "All right. I'll see you next week."

Conrad could only nod, afraid that if he said anything, he'd lose it. It became even worse when they walked out of the office to find his dad sitting in the waiting room reading a magazine. Jennifer usually picked him up, and he wasn't expecting to see his father. He figured he'd at least have the ride home to get his emotions back under wraps.

"Ready?" Michael asked, tossing the *Parenting* magazine aside and pushing to his feet. Without waiting for a response, he held open the door for his son, nodding at the receptionist behind the counter.

The walk to the truck was a silent one, Conrad trying to think of a way to talk to his dad. He glanced over at him, noting the way the big man's jaw was working, as though something was on his mind.

Conrad climbed into the truck, tugging at the seatbelt as his dad brought the truck to life. Clicking the buckle into place, the boy stared out the passenger window, his stomach in knots. He tucked his bottom lip in, as if to keep in words he might not be ready to say, not knowing *what* to say. Panic gripped him as he felt the renewed stinging of tears.

Michael whistled softly between his teeth, glancing out at the scenery as it passed by. It was a chilly fifty-nine outside and he was glad he'd brought his coat. He glanced over at his youngest, trying to not feel anger. He was surprised to see Conrad bring up a hand to quickly swipe at his eyes.

"You all right, son?" he asked quietly. When the fourteen year-old broke into uncontrollable sobs, Michael nearly ran the truck into a compact car in shock. Pulling the truck off onto the shoulder of the road, he unbuckled his seatbelt. "Hey, hey, now," he cooed, startled and unsure.

"I'm sorry, Dad!" Conrad yelled, everything he'd bottled up over the past year and a half breaking free. He felt strong arms tug him across the bench seat of the Ford. Unable to resist, Conrad buried his face in the fleece jacket his father wore. "I'm sorry."

His chin resting on his son's head, Michael began to cry. "It's okay," he whispered, eyes squeezing shut. "It's okay."

"Why'd you have to go!" the boy cried, his words muffled, his hand clawing at Michael's chest. "Why'd she have to die!"

"I don't know, son. I just don't know." Michael's sobs were indistinguishable from his son's. "I'm so sorry, I tried, Conrad. I did everything I could under the circumstances. I just couldn't save her."

Conrad felt like a baby again — allowing everything to burst free, feeling safe as his dad tightened strong arms around him, rocking him as they both cried for the life that had been and would never be again.

After long moments, Conrad calmed, his breath becoming warm and even against his father's neck. His father continued to rock him.

"I love you, Dad," Conrad murmured quietly.

"I love you, too, son. Never, ever doubt that. We're gonna be just fine — you, me, Jenny, and Alan."

Denny tossed the last of the trash into the bin in the alley behind the coffee shop. Looking up into the night sky, she smiled weakly. *Snow.* Closing her eyes, she inhaled the cold, wonderful scent of moisture in the air. She figured they'd have a significant accumulation by morning. She took the baseball cap off her head, ran a hand through her flattened bangs, then replaced the cap — maroon, with *Mile* stitched in bold yellow letters.

"Busy day," Joni said from behind her.

Denny turned and nodded as the owner sat on the top stoop. Denny took her place off to the side, one step down. "Never thought it would end."

"Yeah, well, with the better competition gone..." Joni brought out a pack of cigarettes, pounding the tobacco to the bottom of the pack then snagging a smoke between her lips.

"Mind?" Denny asked, grabbing for the pack. Her boss shrugged and handed it to her before lighting the tip of her cigarette.

"Didn't know you'd started back up," Joni commented, the smoke bouncing with each word.

"I didn't. Sounds good though." Denny inhaled and found herself trying not to cough. She'd stopped smoking six years ago. After the first puff, the taste filled her mouth and she grimaced. Tugging the smoke from her mouth, she mashed it on the cement next to her. "Nasty."

Joni chuckled, letting her cigarette dangle between her fingers, which hung over the side rail. Sighing heavily, Denny resumed her examination of the night sky.

"You coming over for Thanksgiving?" Joni asked, taking another drag.

"Not sure. I don't know just how much of the holiday spirit is in me these days, Joni."

"Yep, I could see that. I'm not going to force you, but if you want, you know you're more than welcome. Steve would love to see you."

"Thanks. I'll think about it. Mind if I come over sometime to wash my clothes?"

"Nope. Not one bit."

"I want to know something," Denny said, tugging the cap from her head and swirling it around on a finger. "How did I go from being a successful business owner, living in a beautiful home with a beautiful wife, to living in a ten by ten room and wearing a stupid hat?" She held the hat up to her eyes. "Some days I feel like I'm in prison," she whispered.

Joni reached out and squeezed the thin shoulder. "I don't know, hon. I wish to God I did."

Denny blew out a breath, setting the cap aside and tugging on the hair tie that had held her hair back in a ponytail all day. Running her fingers through the strands, she said nothing, afraid she'd start to cry if she did.

Joni took one last, long drag then flicked the cigarette into a puddle of something wet and very smelly in the alley. She listened for the satisfying hiss of the lighted tip hitting liquid. "I've been thinking about something, Den," she said, folding her hands. She waited until the blue eyes focused on her. "I want to retire soon, within the next six months. I'm tired, *and* I want to enjoy some alone time before Steve retires."

Denny smiled. Knowing how the couple fought like cats and dogs when they spent long periods of time together, she nodded in understanding.

"I've been thinking that maybe you could take this place over, run it."

Denny wasn't surprised by the offer, but as she looked into the face of her long-time friend and one-time mentor, her mind whirled. She imagined herself owning another shop, running Mile, maybe even turning it into another DeRisio's. She imagined living in the neighborhood, maybe tearing down some walls above the shop and creating a nice little apartment for herself. She imagined Buffalo, seeing the same streets for almost thirty-five years, the same faces coming in day after day, asking for the same thing day after day.

Trapped. Denny felt like a rat in a cage, and it had nothing to do with her tiny, spartan living quarters. Something was missing, and she didn't think she'd find it trying to recapture the life she'd left the moment she stepped aboard Flight 1049. Shaking her head ruefully, she met Joni's eyes. "No. it's not for me anymore, Jo."

Joni was only mildly surprised by Denny's answer, but she *was* surprised by the elation that filled her at the rejection. Head nodding, a slow, wrinkly smile rolled across her lips. Denny's smile matched hers.

"What are you thinking about out here all by yourself?"

Rachel turned from where she leaned against the balcony railing, watching Beth shrug into a sweater as she walked toward her.

"Hmm. Nothing much."

"Oh, I don't know about that. Looked pretty serious." Beth rested her forearms against the railing, mirroring the blonde's position.

Rachel looked down at the picture she held in her hands then brought it up for Beth to see. It was a Polaroid that showed three deeply tanned, smiling faces. "This was Dean, Mia, and me just before we left Canada." Beth took the picture from her. "I wish I had one of the other three of our group, but they hadn't been rescued yet."

Beth nodded in understanding, examining the faces closely, settling on the young girl who flanked the other side of the good-looking man with dark hair. "The teenager and...I don't remember — either the Texan or the attorney."

Rachel smiled, taking the picture back. "Dean, the attorney. He'd laugh his ass off if he knew you mistook him for Michael."

"Guess we won't tell him, then."

"Nope. I was just thinking about everyone, wondering where they're all at, how their lives are going. Whether theirs were as crazy as mine started out. Were they happy to be reunited with their families, their lives?"

Beth noted the softening of the author's voice. "Thinking of one in particular, Rachel?" she asked gently. Rachel didn't look at her, but nodded, absently running her thumb over the glossy images. "Do you want to tell me about her?"

Rachel looked over at Beth for a long moment, wondering if Reenie had spilled her secrets.

As though Beth had read her thoughts, she shook her head. "It was a guess. Reenie can't lie to me."

Rachel smiled, nodding. She was aware of her friend's transparency. "Denny. That's her name. The coffeeshop owner," she explained before Beth could ask. "I don't know. We just...clicked somehow."

"By the look in your eyes, I'd say you more than clicked. If I'm off base or out of line, please tell me."

"No. To both." Rachel looked at the picture again, unable to help smiling back at her family. She missed them deeply. She missed Mia's sweet innocence and Dean's fussy good nature. She missed Pam's no-nonsense attitude and Michael's heart of gold. "I've never in my life felt such a wonderful connection, and with her it was almost instantaneous. We were inseparable...'til the end," she whispered.

Beth moved a bit closer, until her shoulder almost brushed Rachel's. "Where is she?"

"At home with her partner, I assume. They live in Buffalo." Her voice caught and she forced a smile. "Denny's probably trying to concoct some new holiday creation at her shop."

"You're going to let her go?"

"What choice do I have, Beth? I can't disrupt her life. She loves Hannah." She shrugged. "I can't deny them their happiness."

Beth was silent for a long time then she inhaled the cold, night air. It would snow soon, no doubt. "Can I tell you something, Rachel? A little wisdom from my experiences."

"Sure."

"When I was nine years old, I met the one person who would change me forever, the love of my life. Emily lived next door to me, and we became best friends almost right away. Somewhere, deep down inside, I knew I was in love with her from the first moment I saw her in that stupid Mickey Mouse shirt she always used to wear." Her smile was painfully wistful. "We did everything together until high school; her parents treated me like one of their own. My folks were caught up in their own problems, and then my dad left us. She got me through it. Without her," she shrugged, "who knows. Anyway, once we hit high school, pressures started, boys and all that. I already knew by then that I liked girls, and that I especially liked *her*. We, uh, we got physical one

New Year's Eve. We were both drunk — we were having a sleepover and I stole a bottle of my mom's — but I have to admit I pretended to be far more drunk than I really was."

Staring out over the railing as she listened, Rachel smiled.

"We were sixteen, I think. Anyway, things began to change. I knew then what I wanted, and who I was. She had no idea, and I think she was terrified to find out. Back and forth, back and forth... Man, that was a hard time. I started getting into drugs, while she poured herself into her studies. She'd always wanted to be a lawyer." Beth smiled, pride shining in her eyes. "And she did it, too. Anyway, I'm getting ahead of myself. Her aunt died, who she was especially close to, and I was there for her, tried to be what she needed. The day of the funeral..." Beth's voice cracked and she cleared her throat a couple of times, trying to get past the obvious pain of the memory. "Things got out of hand in her room and we almost got caught. She was angry with me and told me to never come back."

"Oh, Beth." Rachel placed a warm hand on the woman's back.

Beth smiled gratefully. "I left her house, and then I dropped out of school. I couldn't be there anymore, couldn't be around her. God, it hurt. Well, we ran in into each other again, a year or two later. She had graduated from high school and was set to go off to college. She'd *always* wanted that." Again the smile of pride. "She said goodbye to me, and I watched her go, walking out of my life again. Honestly, I think she hunted me down that day because she wanted to say something to me. You know? It was like, like she'd come to a decision, that she wanted me in her life, but when it came down to it, she left anyway. I wanted so badly to stop her, to beg her to stay with me, or at least let me go with her. I loved her so much, Rachel, and I think she loved me, but I let her go. She walked out of that theater where she'd found me and headed up to Boulder for school."

"Why didn't you?" the blonde asked, entranced by Beth's voice and tale.

"I don't know. I guess I figured if I interfered in her life, she might not follow her dream, all on account of me. And I couldn't do that to her. I felt it was best to let her go, as painful as it was, cut her free."

"Did it work? Have you seen her since?"

Beth raised an eyebrow. "Not done yet."

"Oh. Sorry."

"A couple of years went by, and I traveled around Colorado and did some theater workshops in Utah and Arizona. Finally, I decided to go back home and get serious about my future." Beth grinned. "Got my GED and went to find her. I headed up to Boulder, and by the grace of God, was accepted. I remember how bad my stomach used to lurch every time I'd walk the campus, my eyes always searching for her. I craved seeing her and dreaded it, all at the same time. Then one day it happened. She was working some sort of club table and I saw her, talking to another student. We became friends again then we became *best* friends again. I had pretty much made the decision then that nothing physical would ever happen between us again. Never. She was my best friend, my soul mate, but that would be all. My heart couldn't take her rejection again; I couldn't fall for her only to be destroyed." She sighed long and heavy. "That whole thing about good intentions paving the road to hell..."

"What happened?" Rachel was almost breathless as she waited for more.

"We made love," Beth said simply. "I couldn't resist her anymore. I loved her so much, I guess I needed to show her. It was the most amazing night of my life, Rachel. As long as I live, I'll never forget it."

"What happened?"

"I let her go," Beth said, voice thick with emotion. "I had to."

"But why? You obviously still love her. She loved you, too, right?"

Beth nodded. "You know, that was five years ago and it's something that has haunted me ever since. I think I always looked up to her so much, always admired her drive, her ambition, who she was, that I never thought I measured up, you know? I was so afraid that someday she'd be amazingly successful, practicing law somewhere, and she'd look at me and say, 'Who are you? What have you done with your life?' I couldn't take it if she was ashamed of me, Rachel."

"Do you really think she'd feel that way?" Rachel asked softly, an arm around Beth's shoulders.

"At the time, yes. Now, no. Away from the situation and far more confident in who I am and what I've accomplished, I realize that it was simply the insecurities of a girl who had no idea who she was."

"It's not too late, Beth."

The actress smiled, bringing up a hand to briefly touch Rachel's face in appreciation of the determined fire in her eyes. "I saw her recently, you know. Well, last summer. I was doing a show and I saw her as she left the theater, holding the hand of another woman."

"Oh, Beth. I'm sorry."

"Don't be. The reason I'm telling you all this is because I don't want you to make the same mistake, Rachel. Don't let something that was meant to be get away."

Chapter 28

"Got everything?" Joni looked around the small space Denny had been calling home for five and a half weeks.

"Yep. Everything I'm taking, anyway. Hope you don't mind, but uh, well, your trash bin is preeeeetty full." Denny cracked a grin at the eye roll that earned.

"Where will you go?" All teasing aside, Joni was truly concerned for her friend.

"I'm not sure. I know of one stop I'll make before I leave the state, but..." Denny shrugged. "I'll just keep going until I find a place that feels like home."

"Please be careful," Joni whispered into Denny's ear as she pulled her into a tight hug.

Eyes squeezed shut, Denny nodded. She'd miss the woman who had been a wonderful friend to her. "I will. I promise." Released, Denny gave her old friend a brave smile. Joni walked her out to her packed van, a cooler filled with food and drink in the passenger seat, a box of CDs on the floor. Joni opened the door for her and Denny settled in.

"Take care, sweet girl," Joni said, leaning in through the open window to kiss Denny's cheek. She felt like her little girl was leaving her again, just when she'd gotten her back in her life.

Denny buckled her seatbelt and adjusted her rearview mirror, checking her side mirror as well before she pulled out into traffic with a last wave to Joni. She'd never done anything so crazy, but she felt good about it. Keeping an eye on the road, Denny fumbled the glove compartment open and dug around for her sunglasses, slicing her finger on something. Stopping at a red light, she leaned over to see what it was, surprised to see a sealed, plump envelope. Plucking it from the glovebox, she held it up. Her name was printed in neat block letters on the front. Tearing the envelope open, she saw a note written in the same neat writing, and ten one hundred dollar bills. Tears came to her eyes as she read:

DENNY—
YOU'VE BEEN THROUGH SO MUCH AND YOU DESERVE TO BE HAPPY. I KNOW YOU GOT THE MONEY FROM THE SALE OF DERISIO'S, BUT STEVE AND I WISH YOU THE VERY BEST, AND MAY YOU FIND WHATEVER HAS BEEN MISSING SINCE YOU CAME BACK TO US. KNOW THAT YOU WILL ALWAYS HAVE US AS A BEACON

YOU CAN RELY ON WHEREVER YOUR LONG, DARK
NIGHT MIGHT TAKE YOU.
LOVE,
JONI & STEVE

Mia chewed on her lip as she flipped the page to make sure she was
working on the right practice problem. She felt a hand run through her
hair and rested her head against her mother's side.

Gloria wrapped a casual arm around the girl's shoulders. She truly
was a beautiful young woman. "How's it going?"

"Okay."

Gloria sat down at the small table, watching the yellow #2 race
across the provided work space as Mia's tongue barely peeked out from
the corner of her mouth. The older Vinzetti couldn't take her eyes off
her daughter. Before they'd left for Milan, Mia had begun to show signs
of typical teenage behavior — apathy and attitude. Since she'd been
back, Mia was filled with a focus, a determination to live a full life.

Mia had decided to take her GED. She said high school was petty
and stupid, and she felt she was beyond that. Gloria was *not* thrilled, to
say the least, but after listening to Mia's argument — she could start
college early, graduate by twenty-one, or even twenty if she went to
summer school — she was convinced that it was the right decision for
her daughter.

"What?" Mia asked, feeling her mother's eyes on her.

Gloria shook her head. "Nothing. I'm just so proud of you, honey,
working on your college entrance exams."

"Yeah, well, be proud when I get in."

"You will, sweetheart. I have absolutely no doubt."

Mia smiled. "Thanks, Ma." She turned back to her studies,
knowing full well that her mother was still watching her, but she didn't
mind. They had clung to each other after her return, each having faced
the ultimate loss and determined to use their reunion as a new start, a
second chance, not to be squandered. Her mother could get a bit clingy
at times, always having to know where Mia was going and when she'd
be back, but the girl understood. She was often the same way in return.

She was applying to local schools; community college was probably
a good way to get started. She wasn't sure what she wanted to do
exactly, but was leaning toward law. Dean had made a huge impact on
her. One thing she knew for sure — she wanted to get herself and her
mom out of the tenement, out of the Bronx. She wanted her mom to be
able to quit her jobs.

At the sound of the knocker, Gloria pushed back from the table.
Looking through the peephole, she was momentarily confused. Taking
a second look, she gasped, quickly working to undo the many locks. "Oh

my gosh." She opened the door and pulled the visitor into a warm, welcoming embrace.

A grinning Denny was careful not to spill her offering. "Is she here?" she asked as she was released.

Gloria nodded. "Follow me." She led the guest through the living room toward the kitchen. "Mia, honey. It's for you." The girl looked up, pencil poised over the page, frozen as her eyes widened.

"I got your note." Denny smirked, holding up the paper Mia had left for her at Duke's. "Told you I'd bring you a mocha breve." Denny held up the paper cup.

"Oh my God," Mia breathed, nearly knocking the chair over backward in her haste to get to her friend. "Denny!"

Gloria barely managed to snag the cup out of Denny's hands before she was engulfed by an excited seventeen year-old.

"Hey, kiddo," Denny whispered, holding the teenager. She pushed her away just far enough to look at her, take in her flushed features, beautiful long hair, casual dress, and bare feet. "You look great." She beamed from ear to ear. A missing piece of her life had clicked back into place.

"So do you, Denny," Mia fibbed. What she didn't say was that Denny looked decidedly unhappy. "I can't believe you're here!"

"Well, I'm on my way out of state, so I figured I'd drop by and say hello first."

"On your way out of New York?" Dark eyebrows drew together. "Where are you going?"

Not wishing to intrude on the reunion, Gloria slipped away to her bedroom to finish reading a Rachel Holt novel.

Denny sighed, running a hand through her hair as she followed Mia's lead and took a seat at the kitchen table. She watched as the girl closed a thick textbook and shoved it aside.

"So, where are you going? Is Hannah waiting for you?" Her grin huge, Mia grabbed the cardboard container of coffee from the table, lifted the lid and inhaled the strong, mocha fragrance. "I can't believe you remembered."

"I never forget a promise to a friend." Denny squeezed the girl's hand, then steepled her own fingers in front of her on the table. "No, Mia, Hannah's not with me."

Mia could see that things had gone terribly wrong. Denny looked too thin and like she hadn't slept well in far too long. "What happened? Are you okay?"

"Can I ask you something, Mia? Kind of a strange question."

"Of course."

"When you came back, you know, back into your life, here, was it easy? I mean, did you feel..." Denny chewed on her lip for a moment, trying to find the words to describe her emotions. She didn't have to; a soft touch on her arm stopped her.

"I didn't know if I was coming or going, Denny. At school, everything seemed so foolish, like all these kids could worry about was what color lipstick to wear, when there was such a larger picture out there. Nothing felt right, tasted right, or even *smelled* right. I think my mom was really worried for a while."

Denny was relieved to hear that she wasn't the only one who hadn't slotted right back into the life she'd left. "I know what you mean, Mia. I felt so out of place, like I was a stranger in my own life."

"You were, Denny. I don't think any of us came back as the same people we were when we left. I know I didn't."

"Me, neither." Denny's eyes dropped.

"Denny, where's Hannah? You wanted to get home to her." The pain in Denny's eyes was so powerfully expressive, Mia thought she knew the answer before Denny spoke.

"I..." Denny swallowed, surprised at what she was about to say. "I moved on, Mia. I got back here, and I'd look at Hannah... Yes, I cared and, yes, I still loved her, but, my heart wasn't there anymore." Denny ran her hands through her hair. "I feel like I left some part of me back on that island."

"More like you gave that part of yourself away, and it's probably in Oregon somewhere."

Denny was stunned as she looked into dark eyes, far too wise and aged for the youthful face.

"We all knew," Mia continued. "Everyone saw it except you two."

Denny looked at her, a smile beginning to grow. "Who made you so smart?"

"Born that way." Mia grinned and sipped her coffee.

Denny chuckled at the whipped cream mustache, grabbing a napkin from the dispenser in the middle of the table and wiping it away. For all of Mia's almost adult nature, there was still a young girl inside.

"Thanks. So where are you going?"

"Not sure. I need some new scenery, a new start somewhere."

Mia studied the tired eyes and too thin frame. "I think that's a great idea, Denny. I really hope you can find happiness. You're an amazing person and you deserve nothing less."

Touched by the words, Denny squeezed her hand in gratitude.

November 30 Denny DeRisio's Diary:

I'm not entirely sure how to do this, never having written in a journal before. Do I write to this...diary, itself? Am I writing to myself? To someone in the future? Hell, I don't know. Guess I'll just start.

Well, I left Mia and Gloria Vinzetti's place today. After talking until pretty late, Mia talked me into crashing on their couch. Then Gloria made us the most amazing breakfast this morning. It was nice to spend some time with Mia and her mom — good people. They wished me well on my journey, which I've begun. I had no real direction in mind, just got on the road and drove. Right now I'm in Cherry Hill, NJ, sitting in a Barnes & Noble, drinking a caramel macchiato. I was just chatting with the woman behind the counter. Her nametag said Debbie. Lived here for about 30 years, she said. Nice lady.

I have absolutely no idea where I'm headed from here — thinking Philly. Deb said I'm not too far from it, like half an hour or something. Why not? Maybe I'll stay there tonight, or keep going.

December 13 Denny DeRisio's Diary:

Guess I've been a little remiss about writing. Not used to this whole diary thing. I've been traveling at random. I hit the City of Brotherly Love, always liked Philadelphia. Wandered around the streets a bit, visited the Liberty Bell and a few other historic sites. Did you know Philadelphia has some friggin' awesome cemeteries, Diary?? Wow.

December 24 Denny DeRisio's Diary:

It's Christmas Eve. To be honest, I'm extremely sad, very lonely. I don't even really want to write tonight, but it seems, Diary, you are my only companion at the moment. I've looked at my cell phone I don't know how many times tonight. But who would I call? Joni? Make her worry? Nah. Besides, knowing her, she's put a tracking device in my van and will march her ass up here to Huron, Ohio.

Earlier today I was standing on the shore of Lake Erie. Man, it was cooooold! I bet it's beautiful in the fall. A woman there, I think she said her name was Laura, told me that during the summer, spring, and fall you can watch the ships coming in, carrying iron ore. I bet that's pretty cool to see. Sometimes, with the way technology is today, I'm surprised ships and trains are still used.

I can't help but think about this time last year, last Christmas on the island. Rachel was making soap for all of us. It was a difficult time, but a good one. I still feel lost, but what makes it easier this time is at least I actually am alone. It's pretty painful to be lonely when you're surrounded by people.

All right, I'm depressing myself even worse. I'm going to bed. Night, Diary.

February 5 Denny DeRisio's Diary:

Winter has definitely hit the Midwest. I've been stuck in Oronogo, Missouri for a month. They got hit hard this year, so I'm here for a while. Somehow I don't think a VW van was made for plunging through waist-high snow. A nice lady named Vicki has actually given me some temporary work, shoveling her walk and drive when it's necessary, in exchange for a warm bed and food. I was staying in my van, trying to conserve resources, but for some reason, she didn't like that very much. Maybe it was because I got stuck in a drift in front of her house. *snicker*

I had absolutely no idea there were a bunch of mines dotting the Missouri landscape! Go figure. Vicki has been telling me all about them, and something locals call the "circle cave". She told me I should stick around until spring and see for myself, but I think I'll be gone by then. This just doesn't feel like home. I'm actually starting to get a bit of cabin fever. I've been on the road for over two months, and I'm enjoying the trip. The holidays were tough, but they're over now. I'm ready to move on, see what else lies ahead.

I truly had no idea what a cool country I live in. The people I've met are amazing. I'm glad I bought that disposable camera back in Hershey, PA. I can't wait to get the pictures developed and see what I got!

February 26 Denny DeRisio's Diary:

The snow has stopped! I am so outta here. Vicki, it's been great, but I just gotta move! I can't even begin to tell you how much snow I shoveled in the past two months. But I must admit — it's gorgeous. I love snow, but am anxious to move into a little warmer climate, or at least a different one. I've never lived in any state other than New York. And on some uncharted island in the middle of the Atlantic.

I've figured out that people are rarely happy. On the island, I prayed daily for snow, knowing damn well it would never happen. Now I'm in a winter wonderland, and I'd love to have the sun beating down on my skin.

I think I'll head west.

March 3 Denny DeRisio's Diary:

You know, I haven't quite decided yet why I keep writing that it's Denny DeRisio's Diary. Who the hell else's would it be??

March 7 Denny DeRisio's (no shit!) Diary:

Okay, so I mean absolutely no offense to the fine people of Kansas, but JESUS! The longest eight hours of my life sitting behind the wheel of my van. Even singing show tunes didn't help the time pass any quicker. I counted shrubbery as I pass it, giggling at the little tufts atop some of the hills, thinking how much they look like nipples on breasts. Told you I was bored. I'm not sure where I'm headed, but I thought Colorado sounded good. I've always wanted to see the Rockies.

So today I allowed myself to indulge a bit. I bought *Willing To Conquer* on audio. As it was read, the man's voice smooth and velvety, I couldn't help but think back to that night on our ledge, when I had my migraine, listening to Rachel talk about her story. Knowing how she sounded, her reverence for her characters and their situations, it wasn't hard for me to imagine her voice instead, allowing it to fill me — her words, her thoughts, the wonderful way her mind works.

I'm a little ashamed to admit I ended up in tears. Now that I'm totally removed from Hannah and my guilt over leaving, guilt over falling out of love with her, and guilt for falling for another woman, I'm allowing myself to think about that other woman. It hurts, but at the same time, it puts a smile on my face. I'm surprised that after all these months I'm still able to see Rachel's face so clearly in my mind. I can still hear her voice — soft and unbelievably comforting. You know, sometimes as I lie in my van, or when I decide to indulge in a hotel room, I have the strangest thoughts: what would it be like to have coffee with her? You know, like go to some outdoor café or something, just us, sitting at one of those small, round wrought iron tables with the matching wrought iron chairs. What kinds of things would we talk about? What would I see in her eyes?

Even now, sitting here in my hotel (too damn cold for the van tonight) in Sterling, Colorado, I'm staring up at the ceiling, hands behind my head. I've got you, dear diary, lying face down on my stomach, waiting there so I can write down all of my wonderful pearls of wisdom...er...something. I wonder what would have happened if Rachel and I had met under different circumstances — a book signing or a chance meeting in some elevator. Would we have started to talk? Would we have noticed each other? Like, if she wasn't some famous author and we were just two regular people doing regular things. No doubt I would have noticed her. She's gorgeous! Would I have spoken to her? Had the courage to? Would she have spoken to me?

While flipping through stations on the radio one day, I had caught that Rachel Holt had basically disappeared off the radar. Rumor had it she'd moved to Europe. Did she make a trip to Milan after all? What was she doing right now at...9:37 p.m. Mountain Time? If she were still in Oregon, it would be, what, 8:37? Doubtful she was in bed. Was she up, fingers racing across a keyboard, working on her latest masterpiece? Was she curled up on the couch, watching TV? Did she ever think of me?

I was so grateful for the Polaroids we were given. Mine is still in my bag — I hadn't dug it out tonight yet. Thought about getting up now to grab it, but I'm too tired. My butt hurts from so much sitting, but I wanted to make it through Kansas before stopping. Time for bed, I think. At least time for my brain to go to bed. Maybe I'll watch some meaningless TV. Maybe take a hot bath.

Either way, goodnight.

March 20 Denny DeRisio's Diary:

Man, that's high! Today I walked across the Royal Gorge Bridge in Canon City, Colorado. At 1,053 feet, it's the tallest suspension bridge in the world. When you're standing on those wooden planks, which I swear will break in half at any second! you can't help but look down, seeing the itty bitty Arkansas River below, like really far below, and thinking morbid thoughts.

Apparently the bridge is a favored suicide spot for folks in Fremont County, or even beyond the county. Some guy told me that a few years back, a guy from England jumped off the bridge. Turned out he was wanted in Oklahoma for child molestation charges. Poof! He was gone, leaving his girlfriend standing there, stunned when she turned around and found him gone.

Canon City is an interesting place. I've been here for about two weeks. Small town, twenty thousand or so. I'm kind of creeped out, though, as I sit here in Mr. Ed's — local greasy spoon. This place was the headquarters for the KKK years back. Lovely. The area sure has some beautiful cathedrals, though. The one with the copper roof is gorgeous, especially when the sun hits it just right... Oh, another creep-o-meter fact — this town is home to, like, nine prisons! What the hell?! Think I may have to pull up stakes.

The other day I went into the prison museum, which is the former women's prison. The cells are all still there, and each cell houses a different historical fact about a specific inmate or a lynching, or the like. The museum is right next to Territorial Correctional Facility, which is the oldest prison in the state, and still very much in use. It is strange to hear the men talking and laughing, or the radio of a guard, when you're at the prison museum. Looking at those high, stucco walls, the towers, all of it, I keep expecting a scene from Shawshank Redemption or Bad Boys with Sean Penn. I wonder if my license plates came from a prison.

And what the hell is it with these western states, where it takes an entire day just to get out of the state? And where are the trees? It's beautiful here, but wow, so different. The dirt, rocks, and...holy shit! That was an actual tumbleweed! I thought those were just in old John Wayne movies! How crazy is that? Joni would never believe me. Wish I'd gotten a picture of it.

I'm sitting here looking at a map of this entire country as I sip my very strong coffee, deciding where I want to go next. I've been moving on a pretty general westerly route. Maybe I should shoot up north, check out Idaho, or maybe even Washington State. Hmmmm. California?

Carrie Tillman glanced up, irritated at her assistant's interruption. "Yes, Tom?"

"I brought this for you to look at." He tossed the test copy of Rachel Holt's pending novel onto her desk then leaned on the VP's desk, waiting until she looked up at him again. "And, I've got an incredible idea."

"Do you?" Carrie picked up the novel and leaned back in her chair. She examined the cover, running a finger over the raised letters of Rachel Holt's name.

"I do." Tom grinned, flopping down in the chair across from his boss. "You are going to *love* this!"

"Welcome to Lone Pine, California," Denny read, her van passing the sign as she drove on 395. The highway stretched out into what looked to be an exceptionally small town, sprawling about six blocks in one direction and five in the other. *Tiny!* She had to admit, it was a nice change from the craziness that was Las Vegas. "What the hell?" Denny glanced in her rearview mirror to make sure she'd seen what she thought she'd seen. An anatomically correct horse stood sentinel in front of a place called Lloyd's Shoe Store. Chuckling, she slowed down to take in her surroundings. She pulled off into the parking lot of the Dow Villa Motel, opting to give her van a break for the day. The engine had been overheating of late, and Denny didn't want to push it.

In the motel office, she was greeted with a smile from the woman behind the counter. "Can I help you?" she asked.

Denny read her nametag: Cathi. "Yes. I need a room for the night."

"All right."

Looking around the small area as the clerk processed the paperwork, Denny noticed a couple of framed pictures of John Wayne. "What's with the pictures of the Duke?" she asked, leaning against the counter.

"Back in the Forties and Fifties, a lot of westerns were filmed around here. This is where John Wayne stayed when he was in town," Cathi explained.

"No kidding? Hmm." Denny handed over the requested amount of money, accepting her room key and directions to it in exchange. "Any good places to eat?"

"Well, we've got the Mount Whitney diner down that way, Lauten's that way," she offered pointing, "or Bo-Bo's Bonanza over there."

Denny stared at the woman, making sure she was actually serious. She didn't see even a crack of a smile. "All right. Thank you." With a smile, Denny shrugged her overnight bag higher onto her shoulder and proceeded to her room.

The small room was like any other in the dozens of hotels and motels Denny had stayed in throughout the winter. The single bed was covered in the typical motel bedspread, the TV was bolted to the long dresser, and the small bathroom was illuminated by a flickering light bulb. Reaching up, she screwed it in a little tighter, exorcising the disco feel.

Denny was tired, she was very, very tired — tired of driving and sitting for hours on end, tired of living out of a suitcase and cooler on the front seat, tired of being alone. She felt ready to start rejoining the human race. The heavy burden of loss and grief had slowly lifted during the months she'd been traveling, and for the first time since boarding Flight 1049, Denny felt like there was a light at the end of the tunnel, and she would find her whole self waiting on the other side. Maybe it was time to find a place to put down some roots, time to start over.

Will stood in the corner, champagne flute twisting in his fingers. He couldn't take his eyes off Dean who was involved in an animated discussion with one of the partners in Will's architectural firm.

"He's changed," a voice said from his left.

Will hummed an agreement as he turned to find Martin Budd also watching Dean. An attorney who worked in another part of Will's building, Martin's nose was slightly wrinkled and a salt and pepper eyebrow was raised in disdain. Will was surprised at the apparent distaste. He and Dean had attended many dinner parties with Martin and his wife. "What do you mean by that, Martin?"

"Just look at him! He leaves here a well respected attorney with one of the most prestigious firms in the city, a man on the rise in his career. And now look at him." He shook his head in disapproval. "He looks like a clown in that red jacket. What happened to him on that island, Will? He has come back as some sort of liberal tree-hugger."

Martin's comments hit Will in the gut. He'd had a sense that some of their friends didn't approve of Dean's choices and new attitude since returning, but no one had said anything to him. Hand clutching the crystal flute in a firm grip, he wasn't sure how to respond.

"Listen, Will, I didn't mean to upset—"

"Enjoy your evening, Martin." Will handed the attorney his glass and strode over to Dean, grabbing his arm to get his attention. "Are you ready to go?"

Surprised, Dean looked around to see whether there was someone chasing his partner. Finding no one, he looked back into Will's handsome face. "Uh, sure. I guess."

"Excuse us," Will said to the small group to which Dean had been talking, and grabbed Dean's hand, weaving their way through the crowd until they hit the cool April night air.

"Will, where's the fire?" Dean exclaimed, trying to keep up. He'd never seen his partner make such an abrupt exit, and it worried him. Will didn't answer, holding the door of the taxi open for Dean, then climbing in beside him. Dean glanced over at Will from time to time as Will stared out at the traffic on their way home.

Later, Will stood out on the balcony off their bedroom, sipping from his beer. Suit jacket thrown over the armchair in the living room, tie loosened, he leaned on the railing, looking down at the city below and around him. Martin had hit a nerve with his comments. So much had changed since Dean had returned to him last summer. He hadn't wanted to admit it to himself, but he was also wondering about the drastic changes in Dean's behaviors.

Will was torn. The Dean he saw now was the Dean he'd fallen in love with almost fifteen years ago — loving, carefree, and true to himself. Will had always been the sensible one, the one to keep Dean's wild impulses in check. Somewhere along the way, Dean had bought into the world in which they'd found themselves — a world of high-priced living, pomp, and pretension. Eventually all that Dean had been had died, leaving an ambitious, pompous ass in its stead. Will was swimming in the same waters with the same high-powered sharks, so he hadn't seen the beach for the grains of sand. Now, Dean had reverted to his true self — a man who enjoyed life, who loved the law, and what it could do for people — while Will was still stuck in a world of superficial judgments and expensive expectations.

Martin's words had made Will recognize something within himself that made the architect very uncomfortable. Had he been responsible for the same judgments against Dean? Had he supported his partner as much as he should in his decision to change his life?

"You okay?" Dean asked, stepping up beside Will, wrapping chilled fingers around his coffee mug. When Will remained silent, he probed, "Something happened at the party, didn't it?" Will nodded, looking down at his hands, still wrapped around the nearly empty beer bottle. "Tell me."

Will debated whether or not to say anything. Looking into Dean's concerned eyes, he decided to be honest. "People are talking...about you."

"Okay. And what are they saying?"

"They can't come to terms with what you're doing. Your work with WorldWin...they don't understand the drastic changes in you." Will tipped the bottle back, draining the rest of the lager.

"Okay." Dean let that sink in, trying to ignore his own swell of emotion. Despite the fact that he no longer ascribed to the life he'd been leading before the crash, he still considered those people his friends, and their criticism hurt. But what mattered the most, what *bothered* him the most, was Will. Very few things upset Will as he was obviously upset tonight. "And what do *you* think?"

"I think I don't understand you either." He held up a hand to forestall anything Dean might say, so he could explain. "What I mean by that is, how do you turn your back on all that you know...knew? How can you look these guys in the face and raise your head high, saying you don't give a damn what they think? I don't understand."

"Will, on that island, everything was stripped from me — Gucci, Prada, Fifth Avenue, all of it. It was gone," he snapped his fingers, "just like that. I had to watch my fine, expensive clothing deteriorate, my belt and other possessions used for implements of survival. I found that good conversation and company meant more to me than some pretentious party, where what you were wearing or the deal you'd made that week determined whether or not you were the guest of honor. I hate to simplify things, but basically I was living with the salt of the earth over there — the bare necessities to live with and eat, and you know what I missed out of that huge closet?" Will shook his head. "Not one thing. Nothing. The only thing I missed on that island was you. All of this," Dean waved his arm out over the city, "it's a delusion, Will. If you lost your job tomorrow and we had to get ourselves a hovel in Queens, which one of those bastards would be there for us, to help us?"

"None of them."

Dean nodded. "That's right. Not a single one. My priorities have changed, honey. All we have is this one shot at life, and if we blow it on the stupid things, well," Dean shrugged, "at the end of the day, we haven't really lived at all. So you ask me, how doesn't it bother me, how do I turn my back on the life I knew? It's easy, Will. None of it matters. The only thing that matters is you, and what you think of me. But even if," Dean swallowed, not wanting to say the words he was about to say but knowing that he had to, "if you didn't approve, it would hurt like hell, but even then, I wouldn't change who I am, not anymore, not for anyone. I learned that I need to be true to myself first. The world can be damned."

Will felt himself falling in love with Dean all over again. He tugged the shorter man into his arms, sighing in contented relief. "Let's go to bed." As they headed inside, they heard the ringing of the phone.

Seeing her grandson running past the kitchen, arms loaded with a quilt that was almost as big as he was, Pam called out, "Luke, run that into my bedroom, please."

"Okay, Grandma!" he called from further inside the house.

Pam smiled. After talking late into the night over the Christmas holiday, she and her daughter had decided it would be best if Pam — newly licensed in Montana — got her own space. She'd bought a pre-fabricated house and had it built on the property that she now jointly owned with Tracy. This way she was close enough for Luke, who had become a grandma's boy, to spend time back and forth between the two houses if he wished, as well as for Pam and Tracy to see each other on a regular basis without being on top of one another.

Looking around the spacious three-bedroom, Pam couldn't help feeling a sense of pride. The modular was more space than she'd ever had all to herself. The apartment back in New York had been tiny, but it was what she'd always had, so it hadn't seemed out of the ordinary. Now she felt as if she could have Luke and all his friends play a game of football in her living room!

"Grandma, can I stay over tonight?" Luke asked, suddenly standing next to her, where she was putting some finishing touches on her paint job in the kitchen.

"Of course you can, sweetie. You need to ask your mom, though, okay?" The boy nodded vigorously, then was gone like a shot. Pam chuckled. Returning to the detail work near the counter, she couldn't help but smile at what her life had become. She never, ever had imagined that she'd be happy in the open, cold spaces of Montana, so far from what she'd known her whole life. But now, she had her own three bedroom home and twelve hundred square feet all to herself. She had a relationship with her daughter, the likes of which she hadn't had since Tracy had been in her early teens. And, most importantly, she had her grandson, for whom she thanked God every day. Luke made her life so much more fulfilled, almost as though she was being given a second chance with him to correct what she'd done wrong with Tracy. She adored the boy. It brightened her whole day to hear his sweet little voice telling her he loved her or asking if he could stay the night.

Life was good. Pam turned when Luke burst through the front door.

"Grandma, Mom says you have a phone call at our house."

"Okay, honey." Pam rested her hand on Luke's shoulder as they walked back across the large yard to Tracy's house.

"Hey, sweetie. How was your day?" Gloria asked, wiping down one of the tables at the diner.

"Hey, Mom. It was good." She gave her mother a quick kiss on the cheek then sat down in a nearby booth. Like magic, a Coke and piece of apple pie appeared before Mia. "Ohhhh, you are all that is good and holy!"

Gloria chuckled. "I don't know about that, but just for saying it, I'll put a dollop of ice cream on top." Returning with the promised addition, Gloria slid into the booth across from her daughter. "How're classes going?"

"Good." Mia unzipped her backpack and brought out her biology text. "We got our grades back today. I kicked butt on the test last week."

"Figured you would. You studied hard enough." With a quick squeeze of her daughter's hand, Gloria got to her feet and went back to work.

Mia chewed happily on a bite of the pie, tapping a pencil against the Formica table. She had started attending Bronx Community College with the spring semester, and she loved it. It had been the smartest move she'd ever made. The semester would be over in less than a month and a half, and she had aced all of her classes thus far. Not wanting the girl to start out her life with bills, Gloria insisted on paying for at least part of Mia's tuition at the community college.

Grabbing for the workbook that went with the class, Mia heard the ringtones from her cell phone. She unzipped a side pocket and pulled it out. "Hello?" She listened to the voice at the other end, eyes growing wide.

"Run!" Michael was on his feet, cheering along with his daughter, both laughing as Conrad fell ass over appetite and landed on his back. The boy held onto the ball, his friends gathering around him, helping him to his feet.

"Oh man, that was funny." Jennifer chuckled, leaning back on her hands. Her boyfriend, Toby, sat on one side, her father on the other.

"Kid needs to grow into those boats on the end of his legs," Michael said with a smile. He couldn't believe his youngest would be fifteen that summer and Jennifer had almost finished high school. It was nearly May, and the days were definitely warming up, an indication that summer was on its way.

"Dad, your phone's ringing," Jenny said, glancing back to their truck, parked at the curb beside the field.

Michael groaned slightly as he got to his feet and hurried over to the open driver's side door and snatched the small phone from the car charger.

"Hey, Den, you need some help?" Foster Phelps asked, sitting at the counter of the new espresso shop that had opened in Lone Pine.

"Yeah, Foster. That'd be great," the brunette said, almost breathless as she tried to keep up with the orders coming in. The kids from one of Bishop's high schools were in town to play against the local high school, and Bishop, being a larger town with more to offer, brought in the business. The shop's business depended mainly on the tourists passing through, or on the patronage from high school athletic events. A lot of the locals weren't yet sure about the new coffee shop, or about that espresso stuff.

Denny had called Lone Pine home for two months, and for the most part she had enjoyed it. It certainly wasn't where she wanted to stay — a closed minded, conservative town with more churches than taverns, and more pairs of eyes watching Denny's every move than if she'd been a rat in a cage. As an outsider come to invade their bailiwick, she wasn't trusted. What had made the decision for her was when her van officially died, coughing out its last exhaust only three days after Denny arrived in town.

Not wanting to dip into her bankroll for starting fresh when the time came, she had decided to get a job and stay just long enough to earn the money to buy a secondhand car and move on. She was thinking of heading to the northern part of California or maybe southern Oregon. Hell, maybe even Seattle. Wherever she went, she needed to find a place that she could settle down, buy a house, and start a new career.

Lone Pine had been impressed by her extensive knowledge of the coffee industry and, against the local opinion, had hired her on at the espresso shop. Denny knew that coffee and food wasn't in her future career plans, but for the time being, it got her a familiar job and a few extra bucks to put away.

After work, Denny flopped down on her bed, the same room she'd rented the night she arrived in town. Her cell phone was beside the lamp. 1 NEW VOICE MESSAGE blinked in the window. She rarely got calls. Picking up the small device, dark brows drawn, Denny listened to the message and her heart began to pound.

Chapter 29

Rachel sat in the chair, trying to be as still as possible as the girl put the last touches on her face; her hair was already coiffed to perfection. The young make-up artist took a step back, admiring her handiwork.

"Are you ready, Miss Holt?" the production assistant asked, clipboard in hand.

The author nodded, feeling her palms beginning to sweat. "I'm ready."

"Welcome back, and thanks for joining me on *Conifer Talks*. I'm sitting next to one of the hottest young authors of her generation, Rachel Holt." The talk show hostess turned to look at her guest. "Now, Rachel, before the break, you mentioned that you'd recently bought a house."

"That's right. I bought a home in the northwest."

"You disappeared for quite some time," Maureen Conifer said, chin resting on a loosely curled fist. "Where did you go?"

Rachel tried not to squirm in the armchair, as always hating the intense scrutiny on her. She had wanted to turn down Maureen's invitation to promote her new book on the show, but her publisher wouldn't hear of it.

"Things were pretty crazy when we got back. I needed some time to myself." Rachel crossed one leg over the other, hand absently straightening her skirt as she did.

"And where did you go? Your editor, Reenie Bazilton is based in New York, and you two are pretty good friends, right?"

"Yes," Rachel hedged. One thing she hated most about interviews was all the personal questions. She was a very private person and didn't like having to stay on her toes for an hour. Even so, Maureen Conifer was the only journalist she'd ever allowed to interview her, trusting her ethics and their mutual respect.

"Well, I wondered if perhaps you had escaped to the Big Apple to throw off the hounds for a bit."

The talk show hostess smiled. Rachel chuckled, shaking her head. "No. I actually rented a small cottage in Colorado for a while. It gave me a chance to write in peace."

"Speaking of which..." Maureen plucked Rachel's book from the small table placed between their armchairs. "*Lost In Paradise*, your newest novel, will be out on shelves Tuesday." The hostess turned to the audience. "And everyone in the audience will be getting a signed copy today." She waited until the enthusiastic applause died down before continuing. "In my opinion, this novel is your best work to date, Rachel."

She felt a little embarrassed at the praise. "Thank you."

"Today is the two year anniversary of the crash. What are your thoughts, all this time later? I mean, this time last year, you and the other Island Six were still considered lost."

Rachel nodded, sipping from the glass of water provided by the prop man. "It's strange. I was actually thinking about that very same thing this morning when I arrived in LA. So much has changed since I boarded Flight 1049. My life has certainly changed." She rested a hand against her chest, mindful of the microphone clipped to her shirt there. "It's been a time of growth and healing for me."

"I think that shines through in your writing, Rachel. This novel, I'm assuming, is a fictitious account of your time with what you've been quoted as calling, your 'island family'. So tell me," Maureen said, a twinkle in her blue eyes, "what parts are true?"

"Oh, no, no, no!" Rachel laughed, sitting back in her seat. "I am *not* going to tell you that."

"Oh, come on!" the talk show hostess urged. "The kite made with fig leaves? The masher? What is real and what came from your imagination?"

Rachel grinned. "My lips are sealed."

"Okay, okay. I see I'm not going to get anywhere with that. Tell me a little about your time there, Rachel. Was it paradise, or more like hell?"

"Which day?" Chuckles rippled through the crowd. "We had days where it was amazing, the most beautiful place in the world. And," she shrugged, "we had days where it was really difficult. The day you got a skull-splitting headache and there wasn't a thing you could do about it. Or days when you missed your family so badly you ached with the longing to see them, especially those among us who had children back home who were thinking their parent was dead — it was particularly hard on them."

"No doubt. Why the title, why *Lost In Paradise*?"

"I don't know." Rachel's voice turned wistful as she thought back to her state of mind during the writing of the novel. "I guess because I felt like I did lose parts of myself those fourteen months. When I got back, I wasn't quite sure who I was anymore."

"And it must have had a harsh effect on your life. Not long after you returned, you and your husband, Matt Frazier, split up."

Rachel cleared her throat. "I'm not going to talk about that, Maureen. That part of my life is over, and it's a private matter."

"Fair enough. All right, well, let me ask you one final thing."

Rachel nodded, despite her concern about what the talk show hostess might try to ferret out of her. She steeled herself.

"What do you miss most about the island, if anything?"

The blonde smiled, her answer automatic, no thought required. "The Island Six. I miss my island family."

"We miss you, too, darlin'." The deep twang resonated through the studio over a loudspeaker.

Eyes wide, Rachel turned in her chair, looking about for the owner of the voice. The crowd's uproar finally made Rachel turn to her right, and her hand flew to her mouth. Michael walked out onto the stage, a grin on his face and a single red rose in his hand. Dressed in Wranglers, flannel shirt, and Stetson, the handsome Texan opened his arms wide, and Rachel flew into them.

"Oh my God, I've missed you!" she exclaimed, voice muffled against his broad chest. Feeling a tap on her shoulder, she started. Pulling away slightly from Michael's embrace, Rachel's eyes filled with tears when a grinning Mia handed her a second rose. Engulfed by the girl, Rachel became overwhelmed as Dean sauntered onto the stage, rose between his perfect teeth. Rachel laughed through her tears, taking the flower from him and accepting a kiss and hug. Pam walked out, arms already opened wide, ready to draw her surrogate child into her arms. Rachel cried against her shoulder.

"Hello, sweetheart," Pam said into her ear, Rachel barely able to hear above the cheers from the audience.

Rachel pulled away, trying to brush the tears from her eyes. Her breath caught as she caught sight of the final guest over Pam's shoulder. "Denny."

Her own rose twisting between her thumb and forefinger, Denny couldn't take her eyes off of Rachel. Rachel hurried over to her, almost knocking the breath out of her with the fervor of her embrace.

"Oh, God, Denny," Rachel whispered, burying her face against the brunette's neck.

Denny held her close, feeling her world righted for the first time since the day she'd watched Rachel climb into that plane and fly away from the island, away from what they had shared.

The rest of the world disappeared, only Denny's warmth against her existing, for one solid minute. Finally Rachel pulled away, looking up into Denny's tear-streaked face. She reached up, briefly touching her cheek, dimly aware that Maureen was sending them to a commercial break.

"And, we're clear!" a crew member announced.

Rachel whirled to face the hostess. "I can't believe you did this for me!" she choked out, tears flowing down her face.

Maureen's face was alive with a beaming smile as she held her own emotions back. Bringing in the rest of the Island Six had been a gamble, as they were not entirely certain how Rachel would react, but her response couldn't have been more marketable. Ratings were going to go through the roof!

Rachel found herself surrounded by her family as prop people quickly took away the two armchairs, replacing them with a long couch, five more glasses of water, and microphones standing by.

"Hey, baby girl," Dean said, claiming Rachel in another hug, careful to not smash the roses she held. She hugged Dean back, then looked at each one with a broad grin. Every one of them had been crying, too. It took all of her self control to not bat the make-up girl away as she touched up her artwork.

"I can't believe you guys are all here. God, I'm stunned." Rachel found herself the middle of an Island Six sandwich, the group hug lasting until they were asked to take their places.

Each of them was fitted with a microphone as they sat, Rachel flanked by Dean and Mia. Dean immediately took Rachel's hand and squeezed it, leaning down to whisper in her ear, "You look beautiful." He kissed her cheek then wrapped his other hand around Denny's, who had been very grateful to get the call from him on a lonely May night.

The Island Six stayed for the rest of the show, telling amusing stories about their time on the island as well as sharing details of their current lives. Rachel couldn't remember the last time she'd been so happy. She could feel Denny's presence on the other side of Dean, and had to fight against leaning forward to look at her.

Dean smiled out at Will, who had been planted out in the audience, along with everyone else's family. He was thrilled to be amongst his second family again. He loved every single one of them and, though his life was a happy one, nothing made him feel so completely happy as to have Will and the Island Six all in the same room. He couldn't wait to introduce them all.

Mia felt fresh emotion rising in her throat; she was ready to burst. It felt amazingly right to be sitting there next to Rachel and Michael, the big Texan's arm around her shoulders and Rachel's hand clasping hers. She had been nervous about being on national television, but that no longer seemed to matter.

Michael felt like a proud father with Mia sitting next to him, his protective nature immediately kicking in. He kept glancing down the line; the faces were familiar, yet everyone looked so different. Even so, the camaraderie and bond was still there, as strong as ever.

On the other end of the couch, Pam rested her hand on Denny's shoulder. Pam couldn't keep the smile from her lips. She couldn't wait to introduce Tracy and Luke to everyone, and vice versa.

Denny sighed in contentment for about the third time. Everything she'd been searching for clicked into place the moment they had all come together again in the Green Room. It had been emotional for all of them, not much said, just tight hugs. Denny had been excited yet nervous about seeing Rachel again for the first time since their return. She was afraid she'd feel the same way as she had on the island, and equally afraid that she wouldn't. Not having any clue what to expect from Rachel in reaction, Denny had held onto the rose she'd been given, awaiting her cue. She had actually been slated to go on after Michael, but Dean had insisted she trade places with him and bump Mia up. He said she should make a "dramatic entrance". So, she had.

When she'd felt Rachel against her, their bodies melding together, Denny had wanted to cry from the sheer bliss of it all. It was like no time had passed since she and Rachel had separated that last day on the island.

The show came to an end and the audience members milled about, talking to the Island Six and swarming Rachel. Michael strode over to Dean, who stood with a tall, handsome man with sandy hair. Michael put a large hand on Dean's shoulder.

"Hey, Dean, come with me fer a minute. I want y'all ta meet my kids."

Dean followed his friend to a trio still sitting in their seats — a very pretty teenaged girl, a young boy, and a good-looking, twenty-something male.

"Dean, this here is my eldest boy, Alan, my little angel, Jennifer, and my youngest, Conrad."

"I've heard so much about the three of you," Dean said, giving them his biggest smile.

"Kids, this here is Dean."

"It's so nice to meet you, Dean," Alan said, taking the attorney's outstretched hand. Jennifer smiled and gave him a quick hug, remembering how fondly her father had talked about this man. Conrad shyly nodded his greeting.

Will, who had followed behind, was quickly introduced to the big Texan, then his kids.

"It is an absolute pleasure, Will," Michael said, taking the architect's hand in both of his. "Dean sure loves you an awful lot."

Will smiled. "It's totally mutual. I'm so sorry about your wife."

"Thank you." Michael tipped his hat.

"Hey, we're all talking about getting together for dinner," Mia said, joining the small group. Dean put his arm around the girl's shoulders, pulling her to his side. Her arm automatically went around his waist. "Are you in?"

"Hell, yeah!" Michael whooped.

Denny stood off to the side, watching as the studio began to clear, leaving the Island Six standing in a small group. Rachel was cornered by the producer of Maureen Conifer's show. Nodding at something the man was saying, the blonde glanced up, her gaze meeting Denny's. They shared a smile then Rachel turned her full attention back to the man.

"So, we're talking about dinner, everyone catching up. You coming?"

Denny turned to see Pam standing next to her. The brunette gave Rachel a lingering look then nodded. "Yeah. That would be good."

"It's so good to see you, Denny. I've really missed everyone."

Denny gave Pam her full attention and a tight hug. "I've missed everyone, too. It's been one helluva year." She grinned as the older woman nodded in agreement.

"Amen to that!" Suddenly Pam squeezed Denny's shoulder and then walked away.

At first confused by the abrupt abandonment, Denny realized Rachel was walking toward her. Taking a deep breath, she turned toward her. "Hey."

"Hi." Rachel looked up into the blue eyes that had haunted her for so long. She reached out, briefly touching Denny's arm. She wanted so badly to hug her again, but dozens of eyes were on her and she didn't feel comfortable.

"We're going out for dinner, catching up. You interested?"

"Definitely." Rachel looked into Denny's face. She looked fabulous, her eyes bright and alive, skin smooth and much softer than the deeply tanned, almost leathery appearance the last time she'd seen her. She looked casual in jeans and a capped sleeved t-shirt. "You look good." Denny's smile made her face all the more beautiful.

"Congratulations on your book. I'm so proud of you." Denny gave Rachel a quick hug, knowing they had to be careful. What she really wanted to do was take Rachel in her arms and never let her go again.

"Listen, I've got a suite downtown. Why don't you all come over and we'll order room service."

Denny served up a smile along with her enthusiastic nod. "Sounds great. I'll tell everyone."

The Ambassador Suite on the fourteenth floor at the Regent Beverly Wilshire was more than three of the Island Six could take in one look. Rachel was used to it, as her publisher had put her up there many times over the years. Will and Dean were also used to such luxuries. But Pam and Michael and Denny, eyes open wide, were dumbfounded by the 1800 square foot space, the rich, luxurious appointments, and the huge marble bathroom.

"Good God Almighty," Michael breathed, "and I thought the Blue Room was nice!"

"That's the *Green* Room, there, Red." Dean smirked.

"Well, them walls was painted blue."

Rachel chuckled as she walked over to the phone. "Who's hungry?" Receiving a vociferous round of acclamation, she ordered ten large pizzas to accommodate the six islanders, as well as their families.

"Make yourselves comfortable, guys. Please, enjoy all this opulence, 'cause I know I certainly won't." She saw Denny open the French doors leading to the balcony and followed. "Hey. How are you?"

Denny was surprised by the soft voice, but it put an instant smile on her face. "I'm okay. And you?" she asked, crossing her arms over her chest. She wasn't sure what to do, how to act, what to say. Her doubts about whether she would feel the same way the next time she saw Rachel disappeared in a flash. Not a thing had changed. In fact, if anything, time and distance had made the feelings more acute.

"I'm good." Rachel took her arms and pulled them open, then stepped into the space she'd created.

Denny held Rachel tight, resting her cheek against the soft, blonde hair that reached to just about her shoulders, one side tucked behind an ear.

Rachel could hear Denny's heart beating and wondered if it matched the cadence of her own. "I've missed you," she finally allowed herself to say. Eyes closed, Rachel inhaled the scent she could never forget, now enhanced with clean clothing and the slightest hint of perfume.

"I missed you, too."

"Let's not lose contact again, okay?" Rachel asked, not lifting her head from where it rested on a strong shoulder. She felt Denny's nod and heard a whispered, "Okay."

"Ladies, want to join us?" Will asked, feeling sheepish at interrupting what was obviously a very personal moment. Dean had filled him in on the feelings between Denny and Rachel and his thoughts that the two women belonged together.

Denny looked up. "Sure. What's up?"

"Dean brought some champagne. He wants to celebrate the reunion."

"Sounds wonderful," Rachel said, giving the brunette one final squeeze before letting her go, following Will inside just in time to hear the popping of a cork.

Dean handed out glasses of the bubbly then held his up. "I have to admit, over the last ten months, I've missed all of you more than I ever thought possible. My life, though full and wonderful, just hasn't been the same without my island family." He turned to the author. "Rachel, the best of luck with your newest novel. I've heard it's wonderful and I can't wait to delve into its pages. Denny, good luck on your recent move into the northwest, I know it's been a long road for you. Literally." He winked as Denny chuckled. "Michael, to you and your beautiful children. Pam, I'm so proud of you." He leaned over to the woman who was standing next to him and gave her a kiss on the cheek. "Way to go, Mom," he said softly. "And finally to my sweets, Mia. Here's to a beautiful young girl with her whole life ahead of her."

"Hear, hear!"

Glasses were raised.

Michael sat on the couch, Mia sitting next to him, head on his shoulder. Pam had snagged Rachel to sit next to her on the loveseat, showing her the photo album she'd brought with her. The other four had looked at it in the Green Room at the studio before they'd gone on. She showed her pictures of Luke and Tracy, things they'd done over the past year, her new house, and home state.

Denny lay on the floor, her head on a couch pillow, hands tucked behind her head. She was listening to Dean talk about his work with WorldWin, his voice filled with the pride of shutting down a company that had been illegally logging in Maine. His eyes were lit up, his face flushed. Will, Dean sitting in front of him and talking animatedly, smiled at his partner and ran his fingers up and down his arm in loving support.

"That's wonderful, Dean. I'm so proud of you," Denny said.

She heard Rachel's lilting laughter and blue eyes flickered over to see the blonde pointing at something in the album that Pam was explaining. It didn't matter what was being said, Denny couldn't take her eyes off Rachel, visually caressing her face, the soft skin of her neck, the lush softness of her hair. Even as Rachel asked Pam questions, green eyes met Denny's, holding her gaze. Denny felt her heart pound and breath catch. The attraction that had drawn her to Rachel on the island was still strong. In the hours since she'd first walked out onto the stage on the talk show, until now — in a hotel suite surrounded by the people who mattered most in her life, and half-eaten pizzas scattered around — Denny had been gripped by an overwhelming longing. She knew the people surrounding her would be in her life for the rest of her life, but Rachel would play a starring role.

The thought both comforted and scared her. Though it had been no one's fault, what had happened with Hannah had devastated Denny in its complicated confusion, and she felt responsible for it. Her guilt had slowly melted away, leaving her with a sense of emptiness. The time alone on the road had helped to change that, and she was now filled with a sense of who she was at a core level again. She also was starting a new life in Hermiston, Oregon, where she'd been for just over a month. She liked the area, liked the job she had as the manager of a bookstore, and most importantly, liked herself.

She'd spoken with Hannah a few times since she'd left the East Coast, happy to hear Hannah had moved on with her life for a second time. She wished her nothing but happiness. Denny hoped that perhaps someday they could become friends again.

It had taken her almost a year to find peace within herself, and find out who she was again. Now, once again mostly complete and happier than she'd been since returning from the island, could she possibly allow her heart to feel what it was asking for? There wasn't any reason to believe Rachel had any room in her life for Denny, except for the wonderful feelings they were both obviously experiencing. She could see it in Rachel's eyes every time the blonde looked at her.

Denny shrugged. Maybe she was just being a chickenshit and trying to talk herself out of approaching Rachel. During her journey, she had kept to herself, even in the towns she visited and worked in. She had made few friends, preferring to observe and absorb, wanting no women in her life. It had been so long, she was almost afraid to make room for someone else in what had become a safe, secure life.

As she looked over at Rachel, she was surprised to feel much of the fear fading. In its place, she felt good old fashioned love.

"What's on your mind?" Dean asked, noting the soft, serene smile on his friend's lips. He followed her gaze, not surprised in the least to find he was looking at Rachel. "So, Rach?" he called out.

"Dean," Denny growled, warning in her tone.

Rachel looked up from the snapshot of Pam's new house. "Yes?"

"Are you dating anyone?" he asked, feeling Denny's steely gaze on him.

"Why, you interested?" Rachel asked, an eyebrow quirked.

"Not exactly," he drawled, nodding toward the woman on the floor, who had shot up to a sitting position. "But I know someone who is."

"Do you, now?" Rachel's eyes snapped to Denny. The fury and embarrassment she saw in the blue eyes made Rachel's heart soar.

"Dean, I am warning you," Denny hissed between clenched teeth.

Dean subsided, confident that he'd gotten his point across. He smiled prettily, amused by Denny's bared teeth.

"Well, as fun, and humiliating, as this has been, I have a plane to catch," Denny said, struggling to her feet.

"Oh, no, Denny. You have to leave?" Rachel asked, all humor vanishing, feeling devastated. She jumped up from the couch, and everyone else stood, as well.

"Don't you *dare* be a stranger, Denny," Michael said, walking over to give her a parting hug.

"You, either, big guy." She accepted his tight embrace, returning it with vigor. In the Green Room, the five had exchanged phone numbers and promises to never allow another year to go by without contact.

Mia was next in line, the girl wanting to cry as she knew Denny's leaving was the beginning of the end of the most wonderful day she'd had in a year.

Dean and Will nearly broke Denny's ribs with their enthusiastic hugs, and Pam and Gloria wished her well.

"I'll walk you to the door," Rachel said, taking Denny's hand. In the small alcove at the door to the room, away from the others, Rachel rested her hands on Denny's shoulders and looked up into smoldering blue eyes. "I can't believe you have to leave so soon."

"I know. I'm sorry. I was only able to get today off from work. New job, you know..."

"Yeah, I know." Rachel rested a palm against Denny's cheek. "Please, please stay in touch, Denny."

The brunette nodded. "I will."

"Hang on a sec." Rachel hurried into the bedroom and scribbled her phone number and address down on a piece of hotel stationery. She folded it and tucked it into Denny's hand. Leaning up, she pressed her lips to Denny's in a lingering kiss. Backing away, she tried to smile bravely, feeling as though her heart were breaking all over again, just as it had the day she'd had to leave Denny on the island. "Take care of yourself."

"You, too." Denny's throat tightened with unshed tears, which she knew would catch up to her on the plane. She grabbed Rachel in a tight hug, then quickly turned away and left the suite.

Rachel closed the door behind her, resting her forehead against the cool wood.

"You okay, honey?" Dean asked softly, placing a gentle hand on the blonde's shoulder. Rachel turned and buried her face against his neck.

Chapter 30

Denny enjoyed her job, working with books and being back in a position of management. She was good at it, and it had nothing to do with coffee or food! It was a nice change.

The day had been long, with Denny putting in some overtime to help out when one of the girls was a no call/no show. She didn't mind; it kept her mind busy, not giving her a minute to think about anything or any*one*. But now, the warm, early June night was facing her as she walked out to her vehicle. Digging her keys from her pocket, she walked over to her Dodge Dakota, unlocking the black truck and climbing inside.

Sitting behind the wheel, Denny sighed, her body tired but her mind still whirring. She folded down the sun visor, smiling at the picture of the Island Six, taken behind the studio four days earlier. She plucked the snapshot from the paperclip holding it to the visor and ran a fingertip over each familiar face, her gaze settling on Rachel. Every day she looked at the tantalizing number and address, long ago memorized, wanting so badly to call. She had no idea what stopped her. Maybe it was that she hadn't heard anything from Rachel either, though she didn't even realize she never gave Rachel her number.

Putting the picture back in its place, Denny revved the engine to life and pulled out of the parking lot. Deciding she wasn't ready to go home, she drove around the area, taking in the sights of her new hometown. It was so different from Buffalo. She loved Oregon; the beauty of the state was incredible.

Realizing it had been a long time since lunch, Denny pulled into a fast food restaurant drive-through, then decided to go for a drive. Window down, she loved the feel of the wind in her hair and the freedom of the road before her. She drove for about twenty minutes before she realized she was on I-84 West, and alone on the highway. Denny squeezed the steering wheel, her palms beginning to sweat as she weighed her decision. Glancing at the clock on the dashboard, she saw that it was after ten p.m. Her thoughts were crazy, outright *mad*, but she wasn't going to stop herself this time.

Music blaring, Denny felt her heart pounding with every mile, her need almost overwhelming. It was amazingly peaceful, the weekday traffic easing to a trickle the further she went, passing town after town, only to find herself on another lonely stretch of road. It was very much like the journey she'd just completed, but this time she knew where the drive would end.

Rubbing her eyes, Rachel closed her laptop and set the computer aside, finished for the night. It was time to hit the sheets. Walking around the beachfront cottage in the small town of Seaside, Oregon, she made sure all the doors and windows were locked. The sound of the breaking waves was comforting. Flipping off the lights as she went, she stripped out of her clothes, readying for bed. With a heavy sigh, she slid between the sheets, enjoying the feel of the cool cotton against her naked flesh. The rain was beginning to fall, the sound as beloved and comforting as that of the ocean.

Denny nudged the windshield wipers to a faster speed, amazed at how the heavens had just opened up. Glancing at the dashboard clock, she saw that it was almost two in the morning. In her exhaustion, she wondered again whether she was doing the right thing. She turned up the radio and Pink Floyd's *The Wall* filled the cab. Her head bobbed along with the music, letting it fill her with confidence and assurance.

Denny looked at the directions she'd printed out from the Internet two days earlier, making sure she was in the right neighborhood. Picking out a house number in the dull glow from a porch light, she saw that she was heading in the right direction. Two blocks further on, she pulled to a stop in front of a single story beachfront house, set the brake, and cut the engine.

Rachel started, something rousing her from a deep sleep. Looking around her dark bedroom, she tried to figure out what it had been. Hearing the rain still pelting down around her house, she thought maybe that was it. Maybe the rain had become louder, tugging at her subconscious. Then she heard the slam of a car door.

Looking at her bedside clock, she saw that it was almost a quarter of three. Resting her head back on the pillow, Rachel figured it was the neighbors; they came and went at odd hours. That assumption was dashed when she heard footsteps hurrying up the walk toward her front door. Sitting up, Rachel flicked on the lamp then shoved the covers aside. Tugging on her shorts and tank top, she listened. Sure enough, she heard footfalls on the deck that started at the front door and wrapped around the cottage.

Padding her way toward the front door, Rachel peered out the window, noting a dark-colored vehicle which looked like a truck or SUV. A knock sounded on the door and her heart jumped. Pushing aside the filmy curtains that covered the flanking windows of the front door, Rachel cried out in surprise and concern. With trembling fingers, she unlocked her door and pulled it open. Denny stood on the stoop, her clothing and hair plastered to her body from just the short walk to the door.

Torn between feeling contrite and elated, Denny didn't know what to say. From the looks of it, Rachel had been asleep, and who wouldn't be at such a ridiculous time of morning? "I'm sorry," she said, bringing a hand up to push her bangs out of her eyes. "I had to see you."

Rachel noted Denny's nametag still pinned to her shirt, the khaki pants clinging to her legs, and the polo shirt emblazoned with the name of a popular bookstore almost black with the saturation. "Oh, Denny," Rachel breathed, reaching out and taking her hand, tugging her into the house. She closed and locked the front door behind them before leading Denny back through the house to her bedroom. She got towels and a t-shirt. "Here. You need to get into a hot shower and then put on some dry clothes. I don't want you catching pneumonia when you've just barely arrived."

Feeling foolish, Denny numbly did as she was told. Even so, it felt amazing to be standing in a shower stall in Rachel's house. She smiled, eyes closing as she inhaled the scent of Rachel's shampoo as she lathered it through her own hair, knowing that probably not long before, Rachel had been standing in the very same spot.

Lying on her bed, Rachel's heart was pounding. She'd been taken off guard by the arrival of Denny at her doorstep in the middle of the night. It had been five days since they'd seen each other, since Denny had walked out of the hotel suite in Los Angeles. Rachel had wanted to call so many times, once actually had the phone in hand, Denny's phone number, which Dean had given her, at the tips of her fingers, but she'd chickened out. She hadn't known whether Denny would want to hear from her.

Dean had told Rachel what little he knew about the situation with Hannah, which wasn't a great deal. Essentially, things hadn't worked out for the couple and Denny had left, setting out on her cross country trek. Knowing how much Denny loved Hannah, and how hard she had tried to stay true to her while they were on the island, Rachel could not imagine what could have come between them. Now Denny was here, in her shower, having driven through the night just because she wanted to see Rachel.

The shower water stopped and Rachel's heart lurched. Swallowing nervously, she leaned back against the pillows, trying to act nonchalant. Denny entered the ring of light created by the single bedside lamp. The t-shirt fit her, which was good, since Rachel found it huge. Denny was using Rachel's brush to smooth back her long, dark hair.

At a loss for anything else to say, Rachel asked, "Feel better?"

The brunette nodded. "Yes. Thank you." She gingerly sat on the side of the bed, looking down at her bare legs. She felt strange, sitting on Rachel's bed in panties and a borrowed shirt. "I'm really sorry, Rachel. I shouldn't have—"

"Hush." The voice was soft, soothing, as Rachel pulled back the covers and patted the mattress. "Come here."

Denny set down the brush and slid between the cool sheets, automatically lying on her side with her back to Rachel, as they had on the island.

"Sleep now, Denny. We'll talk later." Rachel placed a soft kiss on the back of Denny's neck then wrapped her arm tightly around Denny's middle, holding her protectively.

Denny opened her eyes. Despite the mild light sifting into the room in slanted bars through the louvers on the windows, she was disoriented. She felt another presence. Turning her head to the side, she saw Rachel sleeping next to her, on her side and facing the brunette. Denny rolled onto her own side, feeling the blonde's gentle, even breathing on her face. She studied the smooth skin and gently arched eyebrows. Dark blonde lashes were traced with morning light. Denny's gaze fell to Rachel's mouth, the lips curled into the slightest smile. She hoped she'd put it there.

Denny lightly traced Rachel's features, fingers running along the side of her face and barely brushing the blonde strands that rested there. Suddenly green eyes were looking into her own, searching. Denny met her gaze, fingers brushing along Rachel's jaw to cup the curve of her cheek.

Rachel was lost in the depths of Denny's eyes, her heart about to pound out of her chest. She needed to be touched, needed so badly for *Denny* to touch her.

Denny wanted to tell Rachel everything she was feeling, everything she'd been feeling since the moment she'd laid eyes on her in First Class on Flight 1049. She wanted to tell Rachel she loved her, needed her, desired her. Her throat was too dry; she was unable to utter a single sound. Staring into the beautiful green eyes, she thought that perhaps she saw everything she wanted to say reflected back at her.

Desperate for contact, Rachel scooted closer, Denny's body heat drawing her like a moth to a flame. She pushed Denny to her back, then settled her body atop Denny's and rested her head on the tee shirt clad upper chest.

Denny's eyes squeezed shut as she wrapped her arms around her fantasy, holding Rachel close. Hot breath burned through the thin material of her shirt, and she could feel the softness of Rachel's breasts against her, the wonder of the bare skin of her arms and legs against her own. She could smell her hair, smell her skin, and smell...her arousal?

Rachel thought a hug was all she wanted, but when she felt Denny against her, her mind began to cloud. The skin of Denny's neck was temptingly close. Placing a soft kiss at the juncture where neck met shoulder elicited a soft sigh. Liking the subtle reaction, she decided to do it again. Again, Denny sighed, her arms tightening around Rachel's neck, fingers stroking the golden strands.

Denny could feel her heart beating faster as Rachel's lips moved up her neck in a slow trail, then the barest hint of a tongue at her earlobe. She guided Rachel to her, needing to feel her mouth.

Rachel whimpered into the kiss, reveling in the softness of Denny's lips, the feel of a warm hand moving down her tank top-clad back and coming dangerously close to the hem. She pushed herself up slightly so their bodies were a better fit, both gasping at the feel of breast against breast, only thin layers of clothing separating them. Denny teased Rachel with her tongue, the blonde sighing as she responded by caressing the skin of Denny's face and neck. Denny slid her hand up under the tank top, feeling the heat radiating from the skin beneath. She luxuriated in the smoothness of the expanse, running her fingers up the length of the spine, feeling the delicate bones and muscles in the shoulder blades as Rachel adjusted herself, pushing herself up to her forearms so she could have better leverage as the kiss deepened.

Denny welcomed Rachel's tongue, her left hand skimming under the shirt to join the right. Rachel sighed into her mouth as the questing hands brushed along the velvet of her breasts. Never in her life had Denny wanted so badly to make love to someone. She felt like her very life depended on being with Rachel, sharing herself, showing Rachel how she felt.

Rachel raised herself slightly, a silent invitation which Denny gladly accepted. The blonde broke the kiss, eyes closed as she rested her forehead against Denny's shoulder. Gentle hands cupped her breasts, fingers pressing, palms rubbing across her erect nipples. The last time, their only time, had started much like this, but this time, nothing would interrupt them.

"Oh, Denny," she gasped, finding the warm mouth again. She willingly cooperated as Denny rolled her to her back and slid on top of her. Wrapping her arms around Denny's neck, Rachel pulled her close, parting her legs when she felt an insistent knee press against them. They both moaned as Denny's thigh made contact with Rachel's saturated panties.

Denny left Rachel's mouth, her lips and tongue exploring Rachel's neck, teeth tugging playfully at the neckline of the tank top. Rachel ran her fingers through the soft, thick hair at the back of Denny's head as she absorbed every sensation. Suddenly a very hot mouth closed over one cotton-covered breast. She cried out softly, arching her back as Denny flicked at her nipple then tugged playfully before leaving it. The sudden loss made her groan, the cool, rain-scented morning air cool against the wet spot on her shirt.

Denny lifted the tank top and ran her hand up Rachel's side, kissing the newly exposed skin. Rachel helped her remove the shirt, baring the breasts Denny remembered so well. "Gorgeous," she whispered before taking the other nipple into her mouth, batting at it with her tongue.

Her body alive and on fire, Rachel couldn't stay still. She thrust her hips up against Denny's thigh still pressing against her. She tried to find purchase, but Denny removed her leg. Concentrating on Rachel's breasts with her mouth, Denny ran her hand down to the satiny material of her panties. Denny's hand reached down to cup her through the wet material.

"Oh, God, Denny. Oh yes, touch me," Rachel panted, crying out when a single finger stroked her engorged clit.

Denny couldn't believe how ready Rachel was. She left the perfect breasts, loath to do so but knowing her attentions were needed further south. Kneeling, she looked down at the woman who had stolen her heart, marveling at how beautiful she was, how perfect she was, and how totally in love with her she still was.

Rachel met her gaze, read the love in her eyes. Sitting up, she cupped Denny's cheek.

Rachel's kiss was so soft, so gentle, so filled with what neither of them had been able to say, it almost made Denny cry. She lifted her arms to allow her tee shirt to be removed and tossed to the floor. She closed her eyes, her head falling back as Rachel settled back, drinking in the body revealed to her.

Rachel had thought she might be shy or embarrassed, never having made love with a woman or touched one as intimately as she longed to touch Denny, but her eyes were hungry for the lithe body, mouth watering to taste her, to touch her. She cupped Denny's breasts, feeling their weight and unbelievable softness. They felt wonderful.

Driven by the need to taste the blonde, Denny's eyes opened, and the look in them made Rachel gasp. Rachel lifted her hips as Denny tugged her panties down over her legs. Freed, she opened her legs again in invitation, not sure what Denny would do. It didn't matter, as long as she touched her.

Denny pushed her own panties down, kicking them off onto the floor. She slid down the bed, nudging Rachel's legs further apart so she fit better between them.

Rachel's head fell back, a long hiss of breath escaping at the realization of what Denny was about to do. Never before had anyone's mouth been on her and at the first touch of Denny's tongue swiping through her wetness, Rachel moaned. Lost in a world of pleasure as Denny feasted, Rachel's trembling hands pressed on the dark head, eyes closed, breathing ragged.

The feel of Rachel responding to her mouth was wonderful, and Denny throbbed with pleasure. She wrapped her arms around the moving hips and entered Rachel with her tongue. When Rachel pleaded for more, Denny replaced her tongue with two fingers, moving her mouth up to Rachel's clit and suckling it.

Feeling Rachel's body tense as she drew close to orgasm, Denny increased the friction until Rachel cried out, pressing down onto her fingers and tongue.

Seemingly endless waves of pleasure crashed over Rachel as her body fell back to the bed, limp, little whimpers escaping her throat.

Denny climbed back up her body, lavishing the flesh with kisses and small licks until she cradled Rachel against her, whispering soft words and caressing her face.

Rachel nestled in Denny's arms, overwhelmed by sensations and emotions she had only ever written about but never experienced for herself with any lover. But Denny had; she was sure of that. Rachel wanted to explore every delicious part of this wonderful woman. She wanted so badly to show Denny what words couldn't express. Determined to try and be whatever Denny needed her to be, she pushed Denny to her back and claimed the brunette's mouth.

Denny was surprised by the sudden aggression, but welcomed it. She felt a tentative hand on her breast and arched up into the touch, her body aching for release. Rachel left her mouth and began to explore her neck and chest, tracing her collarbones with her tongue. "Oh, baby," Denny gasped, as her nipple was tugged between two fingers. "Oh, yes."

The feel of Denny's skin was incredible, softer than Rachel ever fantasized it would be. Her mouth and hands tasted and probed, and Denny shivered when nails scratched gently along the inside of one thigh. The heat pulsing from Denny drew Rachel in, her hand skimming over slick thighs.

Not having expected to feel Rachel's fingers flitting dangerously close to her sex, Denny gasped as her clit twitched in anticipation. "Please touch me, Rachel. Oh, God, I need you to touch me."

Rachel was surprised at the desperation. She deliberately kissed Denny, slowly, sensually, seducing her, even as her fingers trailed through the saturated patch of hair, evidence of Denny's need. Her fingers pushed past the swollen lips and became encased in a liquid inferno. "Ohh," she breathed, her own arousal rising again. "God, you're so wet, Denny. Feels so good."

Denny couldn't respond to the words whispered against her mouth; her legs spread and hips began to move with the rhythm of Rachel's touch. She reached down to guide the blonde deeper inside, both moaning at the sensation. Denny grabbed the back of Rachel's head, holding their mouths together as Rachel thrust into her. Soon Denny was breathing too hard to kiss, but Rachel stayed with her, their panting mingling as Denny neared her release. She cried out with a gasp, thighs tightening around Rachel's hand.

A sense of awe flowed through Rachel as she watched Denny climax — eyes squeezed tightly shut, every muscle in her body taut. She peppered kisses all along Denny's face and neck, brushing damp hair away from her face. "You are so unbelievably beautiful," she whispered, kissing Denny softly.

Denny returned the kiss as best she could, her strength having seeped out along with her pleasure. She had just enough strength left to pull Rachel to her, cradling her head against her shoulder.

Rachel wrapped an arm around Denny's waist, her thigh nestling between Denny's. She needed to be as close as possible. "I love you, Denny. I really wanted to tell you that in LA. I just didn't know..."

"Didn't know what?" the brunette asked, fingers playing with soft, blonde hair.

"How you felt. If what you felt on the island was real enough to outlive our rescue."

"It was real. I felt like the best part of me was torn away when I watched you get into the plane and fly out of my life." Denny met Rachel's gaze as the blonde propped her head up on a hand.

She traced Denny's cheek with a finger. "It tore me apart. I've been so lost." Blonde eyebrows drew together in a frown as she remembered the hurt.

"I love you, Rachel. Always have."

Rachel smiled; her entire world had clicked into place. "We have a lot to talk about, don't we?"

"We sure do." Denny leaned up and placed a soft kiss on waiting lips. "I can't lose you again, Rachel," she said, shaking her head. "I denied my feelings for too long out of some sense of guilt. When I got back to Hannah," she sighed, marveling at how amazingly right it felt to be in Rachel's bed, "it was wrong. From the very start, it was wrong. She tried, and I know I hurt her, but I knew that she wasn't the one for me anymore. I fell in love with you on that island but I tried to deny it. I knew I had to move on with my life. The funny thing is," she chuckled ruefully, "it had moved on without me."

"I'm sorry, Denny," Rachel whispered, seeing the old hurts reflected in the warm blue eyes.

"Don't be. That's over. It's all over. I'm right where I want to be."

"Do you? Want to be here? With me?"

Denny smiled, reaching up to cup Rachel's face, nodding slightly. "Very much. You're the part of me I lost on that island. I finally feel whole again."

Rachel blew out a small cry, grasping Denny in an almost painful hug. "I need you, Denny. God, I need you."

"I'm here, baby. I'm not going anywhere."

Epilogue

The tree was decorated, the lights lit. The rain had finally stopped, and the temperature was still hovering just above freezing. The house smelled of turkey and freshly baked bread. Laughter filled the living room where gifts were being opened near the fireplace.

Rachel leaned against the corner of the couch, Denny tucked between her legs, watching as Rachel's nephews opened their gifts from their aunts, Rachel and Denny. The blonde rested her chin against the top of Denny's head, contentment making her spine tingle. Never had she known such happiness and love as that Christmas, with her two sisters and their families celebrating with her and Denny in Hermiston. Reenie had flown in two days earlier to share in the joyous holiday spirit. Life was good.

Tracy was laughing as her new boyfriend, Taylor, tried to keep up with Luke's sign language lesson. The man's hands waved less than gracefully as he tried to imitate the boy. Pam chuckled from the corner, where she was waiting on the pies to finish baking. Her home was perfectly decorated, and the happiness filling it was making for one of the best Christmases ever.

It had been a crazy year, but she had seldom had such a productive one. She was finally situated in a small animal clinic just outside their small town. She even had her eye on a man whose Great Dane was a patient of hers. It gave her great pleasure to watch her grandson grow every single day, and she often wondered just what had possessed her that she had failed to be a part of his life from the start. And the greatest Christmas gift of all was knowing she had the total acceptance and love of her daughter. Pam would forever be appreciative of the chance she'd gotten, the *second* chance she'd gotten.

The kids had made out like bandits with new clothes and stereos and those crazy little MP3 players that Michael would never understand. Good thing that there had been a helpful saleswoman at the store or he'd still be standing there, trying to figure out just what in hell Conrad had been going on and on about.

He stood back, a smile of pride on his face as he watched his three kids, and Alan's new wife, all showing off the gifts they had received. It was a good thing, a real, real good thing. Michael Dupree was a happy man. There was only one thing missing that kept it from being perfect.

The big man glanced up out the window into the clear, Texas sky. A star winked at him, and he would have sworn he heard the laughter of his Melissa.

Dean could never have imagined he'd see the day that he and Will would leave the city, but they had, and it had been a positive move. Warwick was a wonderful place, and Keller and Garrison had been generously helpful in steering them toward good real estate and providing them with an instant social circle. The women and Dean got along famously; Will had known they would.

Dean sat across from Parker; the seventeen year-old was kicking his butt at a friendly game of chess. She was smart and oozed a charm that made Dean want to lay down his king and call "Check mate" for her. They'd all just come back inside after a brutal snowball fight, and Dean was still trying to thaw. He watched as Will walked toward him, mischief in his eyes.

Holding a small sprig of mistletoe over his head, Will leaned down and placed a soft kiss on Dean's lips. "Merry Christmas, baby," he whispered.

Dean smiled. "Merry Christmas."

Milan was a storybook place, and Mia would always remember the Christmas she spent there, surrounded by every family member she'd ever heard about, plus some! They just seemed to come out of the woodwork to spend the holiday with their American family.

The teen glanced at her mother who was enraptured by something one of the cousins was telling her. Her mother looked twenty years younger, and she was so alive and full of life. Mia had loved watching her mother come back to life since her return. From what her Nonna had said, Gloria had all but died when she thought her daughter had been lost in the crash. Alive and well, that's what both of them were, with the wonders of life ahead of them.

It was a good time, a real good time.

They had started out as six people with six very different lives, filled with love, strife, and all that adds spice to life. For one moment, time stood still, the six colliding as Fate intervened and brought them together. They became a family on the island, and would continue being a family, forever entwined, and forever changed.

They were friends. They were family. They were the 1049 Club.

Kim Pritekel has been writing since she was 9 years old, and is now a full-time writer, working in both the publishing and film industry. She is a native of Colorado, where she still lives.

You can learn more about Kim, as well as contact her, via her website: www.kimpritekel.com.

Breinigsville, PA USA
17 January 2011
253478BV00002B/132/P

9 781933 720722